Stay God, Sweet Angel

A Novel

Stay God, Sweet Angel

A Novel

Nik Korpon

PERFECT EDGE BOOKS

Winchester, UK
Washington, USA

First published by Perfect Edge Books, 2014
Perfect Edge Books is an imprint of John Hunt Publishing Ltd., Laurel House, Station Approach, Alresford, Hants, SO24 9JH, UK
office1@jhpbooks.net
www.johnhuntpublishing.com
www.perfectedgebooks.com

For distributor details and how to order please visit the 'Ordering' section on our website.

ISBN: 978 1 78099 804 6

A CIP catalogue record for this book is available from the British Library.

Design: Stuart Davies
www.stuartdaviesart.com

Printed in the USA by Edwards Brothers Malloy

This novel, as always, is dedicated to the memory of
Elaine Gibson.
Sleep well. You're not the only one.

Acknowledgments

Thank you to Phil Jourdan and Perfect Edge Books for giving this novel another chance to breathe.

Thank you to Pela Via for helping it to make sense.

Thank you to everyone for the support, commiseration, red pens and tough love.

Thank you to Amanda and Donovan for everything else.

Author's Note

When I first wrote this book in a fever dream beneath the ceaseless clouds of a London winter, I never imagined I'd be coming back to it six years later, let alone adding more to the world of the story. But here I am.

There's a saying about the difference between tragedy and noir, that tragedy is falling from the throne to the floor and noir is falling from the sidewalk to the gutter. I think both are applicable to this book, so there are different ways to read it. You can start with either story, but I prefer *Stay God* then *Sweet Angel*. Part of the reason is because that was the order I wrote them and I'm not fond of change. More important, I think, is that you don't realize how great the distance between the throne and the floor is until you've pulled yourself out of the gutter.

Stay Warmed and Bound.

Nik Korpon
Baltimore. September 2013

Stay God

A Novella

Chapter 1

January: Now

Someone stabbed the sun. It's dripping onto Baltimore, seeping through gauze clouds onto the cobblestone street, reflecting off wet tire tracks in pinpoint sparks like the ones that follow a two-by-four across the nose. It's dimming, dying, falling in slow motion, but the city is oblivious. Couples in matching jackets and complementary scarves walk arm-in-arm down Thames and through Fell's Point. They push strollers with babies double-wrapped in winter coats, share hot chocolate and kiss the dot of whipped cream off their noses, window-shop the poster place next-door for the perfect thing for the TV room. Happy lives, happily self-contained in their happy little oblivious universes.

I watch the scene, staring at the reflection on the back window of The Daily Grind. The City Paper I'm not reading lays open across the blond wood table. My right hand quivers. I need a bump, and I don't like that I need a bump. I'm sorry, Mary. I tried.

I pull my stash from my pocket, held in a plastic container shaped and colored like a giant Tylenol, slap it twice in my hand then palm it. Scratch my chin on my right shoulder and scan the room—no one's watching—then bloat my chest like a sneeze is coming and put my hands to my face. Sniff, sniff, hold. Feel it absorb into my blood and tune in the static in my head. Make a fake sneeze with my mouth—so no one suspects anything—and slide it back in my jeans. The synthetic taste of chewed aspirin, snot and white drips down my throat. My hand stops quivering and I can feel the inside of my legs and the blood flowing through every vein in my body.

Steam swirls in tiny tornadoes from my coffee. I scan whatever page of the City Paper is open just to give my brain something to do besides think think think think think. About Mary. About the Twins. Where she is, why she won't call back, what Bruce Campbell is doing right now how hard they can hit a rib before it breaks and punctures a lung whether the Sonny Chiba DVD Christian ordered for me has come in yet whose hand is on my shoulder I bolt to my feet. My coffee spills Rorschach over the table. The chair scrapes across the floor, hands curling as I turn. My eyes are CD size and the light from outside hurts.

'Damon, hi. Jesus, are you okay?' a girl says, her hands palms-out-defensive by her shoulders. She's fake-tanned too much, her skin the color of cantaloupe flesh.

'Oh. Yeah. Hi. What's up—' Kelly? Wren? What the fuck is her name? '—man? Yeah, I'm fine. Just tired. Too much coffee, you know?'

She nods her head tentatively. I steal a glimpse over her shoulder, check the room. Four students sit glued to their laptops, dead to the world; the wrinkled couple in the corner plays cribbage; the girl behind the counter thumbs coins from the tip jar into her palm while her co-worker stares out the window at the harbor.

'Just making sure.' She smiles, her need convincing her brain that I'm not a threat. Her bone fingers, with polished nails the color of old scabs, run over the cuts covering my forearm. She doesn't seem to notice, or doesn't care. I already know what she's about to ask me. 'I wanted to make sure my boy is okay.'

'I'm fine.' I know her name and can't think of it, but she's a leech anyway, so it doesn't matter. 'Just drinking coffee.' I gesture to my wet table. A shark swims mouth-open after a fat man in the French Roast Rorschach.

'Are you going back to your store anytime soon?' she coos. Her tongue traces the edge of her lips, black high-heels sliding over the floor closer to me. 'Or now if you have…you know.' Her fingers on my ribs now, kneading, like a preview of what could come. Yes, I know, you conniving soulless woman. I finger the stash in my pocket, try not to smile.

My lips part to say Sorry the store's closed when the front door opens. Two Twin figures, like bags of garbage stuffed into expensive trench coats, walk into the shop. I pull the girl—Alicia is her name though I don't know why I remember it now—in front of me, bend my knees to sink behind her and push on my eye sockets with my palms. This isn't happening. You've seen this before, you're okay. Then I peel my lids open.

A rainbow of stars floats through the coffee shop and the two are gone. They're gone. Just students and old people and bored, minimum-wage workers. Alicia has pulled her body even closer. She smiles down at me. I can almost see her brain cranking through her irises. She thinks she has me. Straightening my legs, her hand is on my thigh, her fingers in my jean pocket but I could be watching her and someone else and imagining it as me.

The front door is still closed.

Then the Twins are at the counter, ordering orange mocha Frappaccinos. I collapse on the chair, pull Alicia down on my lap and sink my face into her neck. Acrid vanilla paints her skin. She purrs with her head tossed back and I peek up and watch the Twins. I close my eyes and count to three and hope to God that I'm hallucinating again.

The room seeps through the slits in my eyelids, thin slices of light filling in the line drawings in my head with color, depth. Filling in concrete details, and I'm not hallucinating: I'm fucked.

'Get up,' I say to Alicia, throwing my arm around her shoulders and pulling her head close to shield myself. As I grab my jacket, I can feel her hand in my back pocket but try to ignore it. 'Keep walking and don't move your head unless I move it for you.'

'I like this,' she says. 'It's sexy. This whole hostage thing. When we get back to the store, I'm going to—'

'Fuck you. Shut up.' I peer past her profile and check the counter. One of the Twins hits the arm of the other and holds his hand out for money. There's a bulge in his trench coat, shaped like a 'Y' and I'm sure it's the hedge clippers and wonder if they're the same pair. Everything looks Hitchcock: the door slides farther and farther away, the seven steps to the street will take fifteen years.

Alicia's hormones buzz in my ear. 'My god, Damon,' she breathes. 'You are getting me so…'

They turn towards us. Their eyes catch mine and I whisper 'Oh fuck.'

I sweep my foot under Alicia's, knock her to the ground in front of the door—'I'm sorry, Alicia'—then lean my shoulder into the door and barrel onto Thames. I glance behind and there's no one there, but I can still feel their breath.

'Get the fuck out of the way!' My feet smack with dull slaps on the concrete. A pruned Asian woman carrying two bags of blizzard-backup food pauses right in front of me as she tries to figure out what I'm screaming. She figures it out too late and the bags explode into the sky. Cans of peaches and water chestnuts rain down on to the sidewalk. A deluge of dried noodles and dates. They barely miss me, spinning on the ball of my foot. The cartilage in my knee pops and cracks. My palm scrapes the ground and soaks up little pebbles, anything to keep me from kissing the concrete. To keep the distance between the Twins and me as far as possible. A man shaped like a bowling pin screams derogatory epithets about every woman in my family, says I was born in a test tube. I'd stop and argue with him but I don't feel like dying.

The crowd in front of me pricks their ears to all the yelling and turns to gawk. They step back to avoid a collision or my elbow in their neck, and my legs can finally stretch out to a full stride. A few breaths up the sidewalk, two boys with greasy faces and mustaches like crumbled Oreos leave their skateboards at their feet, a mangy dog meanders without a leash, and a suited man finds it a good time to fix his right leg cuff.

I can almost feel Them twisting a corkscrew into my breastplate.

I hop over the skateboards, just missing the dog, and turn back to check the crowd for Them, then step on a lump and I'm looking at the waning January sky, papers floating over me like legal-sized snowflakes.

'You prick!' The Suit scurries to gather his business proposals, vetoed with my size-nine stamp. I scramble to my feet and check behind again, the sidewalk gawkers congealing back together, hiding me. White clouds form in front of my mouth. Christian's whiskey sloshes in my stomach. 'It'll help,' he'd said. 'It's been a rough couple of days.'

Three blocks of sprinting, checking, heaving, choking, swallowing hard and trying not to vomit and I'm at Shakespeare Street. Snagging the light pole, I wing myself around the corner. My foot slides across gravel and a broken bottle. The first alley slumbers desolate, quiet. Perfect. Fences keep it from spilling into the tiny backyards. I slam into the first door in the fence. Locked. Push on the next one. Locked. The mouth of the alley yawns, wide and empty. My ears prickle. Footsteps. They sound monolithic but could be from any of the million people in Fell's today. The next door, locked; I yank on the handle and almost rip it out of the wood. The footsteps are louder. Four steps backwards and I take a breath, about to throw myself into the door to break it down and hide, but if the door is broken down they'll know where I am. Sidestep to the next one, put my weight into it and it swings open. I dip inside and slam the door. It's black, a vacuum, the doorway to another parallel world, hopefully one where I'd never met her. I'm going to evaporate, disappear into nothingness and that might not be such a bad idea. My eyes adjust after a few seconds and it's not a black hole or time portal: it's a storage shed. I stand on the push lawnmower and breathe.

'You're cool. It's okay. They're not there.'

I'm talking to myself. Standing, shaking, breathing hard. Faint Christmas music that's playing too late drips through the door.

There's a metallic scraping, like rusted hedge-clippers. They've snuck up and are poised outside the shed, ready to aerate my chest. Once they've finished the rest of their coffee, they'll kick the door open and drag me face-down across the alley, an Italian-leather loafer on the back of my skull to make sure I'm chewing mouthfuls of concrete.

There's pressure around my neck and my fingertips are cold. The dying sun bleeds through a splinter crack in the middle of the door. I check the walls for something to swing and slice or gouge. Nothing. No trowels. No spades. No tiny scraping-things that look like three-fingered skeleton hands. Not even a bulb planter. The pressure is gone. I look down and realize my fingers were spinning Christian's grandpa's wedding band around on its metal chain. I press it against my lips—'Please'—then tuck it back inside my shirt and peer through the crack. A rat scratches past the splinter of outside. I have to wait.

A minute, two minutes, twenty minutes: Everything seems eternal in a black space in a back alley.

The footsteps slink quiet, bulls with slippers. I squint my eyes to concentrate, hear better. They sound about twenty feet away, trying to be sneaky.

My lungs take every molecule of oxygen from every shallow breath.

The footsteps disappear. I'm just hearing things; it's all imagination. A relieved sigh, and I kiss the ring. Thanks, Grandpa.

Then they're closer.

I perch my hand on my back pocket to steady myself, to keep from slipping and making a noise. There's a lump in my pocket. The lump is my switchblade. It takes 30 or 48 or 132 seconds to open the blade without the lock clicking and giving me away. Shift again, gentle, silent, and scour the sliver of alley between the door and its frame. My eyes narrow, look for a gun, a broken wine bottle. A rusted pair of hedge clippers or flathead screw-driver.

Tinted glass shimmers in the sunlight.

Fuck.

The footsteps are slower, sound a few feet away. Just imagine they're Paul. Imagine Paul's face on their bodies. I'm going to destroy them. A steeling breath, then I kick the door open, my arm cocked at jugular height and ready to slash.

A bum in an army-issued trench coat that used to be black twelve layers of dirt ago drops his wine bottle with a damp shatter. He curls back and slurs, 'Moddlefcker, don' hur me,' through a bird's-nest beard and mechanic-stained hands protecting his face.

Snap my head left and right looking for Them. Alleyway. Trash cans. Recycling bins. Cardboard boxes too big for recycling bins. No Twins. I drop my arm and take a step back, collapsing with relief on the door that's leaning jagged against the shed. The bum looks through his fingers then lowers his hands, stumbling half a step.

'Shit, I'm really sorry, man.' I dig into my jeans and pull out whatever's in the pocket, hand $13 and a Cody to the bum for the inconvenience.

While he examines his take, I creep to the edge of the street and peek around the corner, switchblade still in hand. Just in case.

They're not there.

'Hanks, mifter,' the bum hiccups, then lurches down the alley.

I close the switchblade, look around the corner again to double-check and walk with my head-down along Shakespeare to South Bethel, then veer right towards the corner at Aliceanna and stand for a minute, surveying the faces. A middle-aged woman with cat's-eye glasses and pink Chucks. Two bike messengers resting on their crossbars, smoking. A herd of seven hipsters streaming out of a café.

Gone. The Twins have evaporated.

I turn around and run to 734 South Bethel, pulling out the key before I get to the building, then stab the lock, throw the door open and slam it shut. The deadbolt clicks then I vault up the steps, stab another lock and seal myself inside Christian's apartment. The tattered couch creaks as I let myself collapse. An iceberg of foam floats on the back cushion.

'Jesus Christ.' I grab the pack of Casamirs, shove one in my mouth, light it and check that the cuts on my arms aren't bleeding.

'All right. All right.' I'm talking to myself again. 'All right all right all right.' Talking to an empty room with amber-colored walls. I'm telling Bela Lugosi, Robert Englund and Leatherface that I'm okay. They stay quiet in their poster frames. From the cover of *Changes*, David Bowie gives me a look that says you have it all under control. I nod my head. 'Thanks, Dave.' My voice echoes off the hardwood floor and into the linoleum kitchen.

'All right, I need to rest. I need to think.' I take a drag and feel the smoke fill my chest and nicotine soak into my blood. The giant Tylenol in my pocket. I'd forgotten about that. I think I deserve it. Smack it against my palm—no one's here to see—and take a long snort. Hold my breath, let it drip down my throat, rampage through my veins. Exhale—long, slow and centered.

'I need a pen. And some water.' In the kitchen, I grab a glass from the draining rack and fill it. The cold water feels good on my hands; I want to fill a glass and dump it down the back of my neck then over my face. Over and over.

The hands of the *Beetlejuice* clock on the wall point north and south. Christian won't be home for another two hours. I sit on the couch again, grab a pen from the wooden corner table and a receipt from Dwaine's Dry Cleaners then stub out my cigarette in the glass ashtray I bought Christian for his birthday. It says

"Jesus Hates It When You Smoke" in a banner underneath the stylized face of Christ.

'All right,' I say to the room. 'What do I know?'

I think about everything that's happened, and make a list on the back of the receipt.

Chapter 2

August: Then

'You are out of your mind,' I said.

'I'm telling you, it could happen,' Christian said.

'No way. No. Way.'

'Why?'

'What do you mean, why? Wolverine could never beat Freddy. First off, Freddy controls everyone's perception. Second, yeah, Wolverine has his quick healing…' I focused on the scale sitting on the metal desk in a mess of paraphernalia, squinted my left eye at the notch between .5 and .6 grams then tapped the metal plate against a small tin funnel. The white powder slid down into a plastic bag the size of an infant's eyeball. 'Sorry, what was I saying?'

'Perception.'

'Right, okay. So, Freddy controls perception. Wolverine is stronger no doubt, but even though he can heal himself quickly, Freddy cut off his finger in the first *Nightmare* and it grew back in a second, so he has the obvious advantage.'

'How do self-mutilation and a missing finger make him a better fighter?'

'Because he can do whatever he wants.' I scooped more powder onto the scale. 'If Wolverine gets hurt, he has to wait to heal himself. Yeah, it'll be quicker than a non-mutant, but it still takes time. Freddy's missing finger grew back in an instant.'

'But Freddy's finger was in the dream world. He got killed when Nancy pulled him into the real world, so that means he's vulnerable. Point, Wolverine.' Christian nodded smugly.

'History is malleable,' I said. 'Physics is not. And from what I can recall, I've never seen mutants walking around Baltimore, so that would mean we're still talking hypotheticals. So game, set, match, Krueger.'

Mary leaned against the reinforced-metal doorframe that separated the main area of our store from the back office. Her rosewood-colored hair pulled back from her jaw into a small ponytail. She crossed her arms over the plaid shirt that clung to her curves and made her eyes sparkle like sapphire oceans, standing like she was bored of listening to Christian and me argue. Every thirty seconds or so she peeked her head through the curtain we'd hung over the doorway—so no one could see into the office—and checked the front of the store.

'But that's assuming Wolverine falls asleep.' Christian pinched the tip of a Casamir cigarette between his lips and pulled it out of the pack. Printed in black and white on the side of his Zippo was Ronald Reagan with KISS paint. He scratched the toe of his right Van on his left calf, then the left Van on his right calf. His hair, the same auburn as his Vans.

'You're saying mutants don't sleep? Bullshit. What do you think happens after Scott bangs Jean Grey? Go fight crime? Don't think so.' I dropped the bag into a row labeled 'single' inside a small red toolbox and threw a knot of bags rubber-banded together to Christian. 'Can you separate some more of these for me?'

'What do you think, Mary?' Christian said. He wiped ash off his t-shirt, leaving a grey scrape over the black.

'I think you're both Chatty Cathys, and you should worry about getting this packaged and not who would win in some theoretical fight which, I might add, could never and would never happen because they're owned by different studios.'

Christian tipped his phantom hat in Mary's direction. I ignored her. Scooped and scraped, then squinted, and slid. Lather, rinse, repeat.

'And regardless, Vincent Price was a better villain than either of them. He's the gentleman's villain.' The brass bells over the front door clanked and she stepped through the doorway.

'Whoa! You cannot make a statement like that and just walk

away. Completely different things.'

'Wolverine isn't a villain,' Christian said. Mary poked her head through the curtain.

'There's someone in,' and walked to the counter, muttering, 'All that talent...'

'And Freddy's a tragic anti-hero,' I shouted towards the vacant doorway, ignoring her muttering.

'That's a stretch.' He readjusted his posture like a marionette doll might, pulled on the right leg of his jeans, then left. 'You done yet?'

'This should last for at least a few days, but it's been busier than usual, and I doubt we'll get our full shipment.'

Mary reappeared. 'I've got a guy looking for a CD.'

I checked the yellowed TV monitor sitting on the edge of the desk and brushed away a patch of dust to get a better look at the wet stalk of a man standing at the counter. He brushed off his sweatshirt and drummed his fingers on the plexiglass over the jewelry display.

'Yeah, go ahead.'

Mary turned to the Stalk.

'What band?'

He sputtered. 'Uh, Duran Duran.'

'Which record?'

'*Notorious*.'

I took a bag of white from the full-length row and handed it to Christian, who put it inside an empty CD case and handed it to Mary. I watched her hips sway on the TV as she walked through the door, then took the Stalk's fifty dollars and opened the register, put it in the slot to the far left. The Stalk turned and double-timed it back into the summer rain.

'So,' I called to the front, 'Vincent Price?'

She peeked around the corner, said, 'At least he has all of his fingers,' then disappeared.

'She's right, you know,' Christian said. He dropped a small

pile of bags on the desk.

'What do you mean?' I scooped and scraped.

'Vincent Price is a better villain.'

I smiled, squinted and slid. 'Yeah, I know.'

Christian laughed. 'Crotchety old man.'

'Fuck off. I'm not old.' I touched the back of my head without thinking. 'This isn't a bald spot. It's from the way I slept.'

'And it gave you those greys, too, right?'

'You can't get grey hair when you're twenty-nine. That's a scientific fact.' I tossed a one-gram bag into the full-length row. 'Don't you have your own store where you can bother people?'

'Depends,' he said. 'I told Matt to sit by the door with a shotgun, in case the landlord comes by.'

'That bad?'

'He finally figured out what the place is worth. Gave me six months' notice and an option to buy, though it's almost twice what I'm paying now.'

'Can you swing it?'

'Selling six-dollar records?'

By my foot sat the larger bag of white, now the size of a four-fingered fist. Three toolboxes under the desk: one red box for the white, two blues for the brown. Two grey boxes sat under my chair on the carpet I found behind a real-estate office. Inside of the boxes were rows labeled Cody, Adam and Cameron, piled with handfuls of Vicodin, Adderall and Diazepam.

'Anyway, what's happening tonight?' Christian stubbed out his cigarette in the mouth of an ashtray shaped liked George Lucas' head.

'Get a pint and see who's playing at the bars down here?' I lit a cigarette and tossed the pack onto the desk. It landed on a pile of mail. I noticed a periwinkle-blue envelope sitting second from the top and inspected it. Addressed in calligraphy, it was sent to Mary and me, but to our home address. The return address was Megan's, Mary's recently married former college roommate.

Megan's wedding was about eight months ago, and the envelope was the same size as an invitation—probably to her baby shower—so I slid it into the drawer to open later. More headaches and complications I didn't feel like dealing with.

Part of our problem: we didn't have any backup plans. Hobbs and his Cockroaches were it. The business wouldn't have been that hard to run if everyone followed procedure. Thursday, we called Hobbs with our order. Sunday, one of the Cockroaches should slither in, exchange a suitcase of product for a VHS case of money, then scurry out. His part was pretty hard to fuck up, but they carried the fate of our store inside those suitcases we rarely saw these days.

Once they delivered the shipment, we'd portion, package, and sort. After the product went into its own special box, we went to the safe.

Open the floor safe across from the desk. Remove the rolls of coins, DVDs, the salt-and-pepper composition book and $200 or so inside. Look in the corners for the cutaway notches. Look close, they're hard to see. They're supposed to be.

Take a flathead screwdriver and gently, to avoid making any visible scratches, pry up the false bottom. Slide out the sheet of black metal, again gently, and remove the duct-taped concrete blocks underneath. Stack the blocks at least three feet away from the safe. I wrapped them in tape to keep concrete dust from getting on the carpet where there shouldn't be concrete dust.

Once it's hollow, rub the surrounding carpet eighteen to twenty inches from the footprint of the safe. Push with some pressure; it's supposed to be hard to find. Scrape with the fingernails and it's easier.

After finding the seam, lift the safe. Lift with the legs, the arms, the back: it doesn't matter. It's a prop safe from a movie set—looks real, sounds real, feels real—that we bolted to a wooden floor panel. Wedge the metal bar into the notch in the top left corner to keep the floor panel up.

'Do you know who's playing?' Christian said.

'Brent said The Garnet Hearts are playing at Full Moon Saloon. The Perfects are at that bar up the street from Hollywood Diner, I think.'

'What are they like?'

'The bastard child of Einsturzende Neubauten, Joy Division and,' trying to think of the right band to describe them, 'I don't know, The Stooges? But dance-y.'

'The Stooges?'

'No, not really. But every band should try to sound something like The Stooges.'

Put the stacks of bills in double-layered plastic bags then place them on the left in descending order, front to back: $100, 50, 20. Any ten-dollar bills, staple together and put inside the safe. Check the packaging around the bills for holes. When they built Baltimore, most buildings had dirt basements. As the city grew, they laid concrete over the dirt. No foundations, just concrete on dirt. When rain deluges the city, basements can leak. If basements leak, the $100,000 contained within could soak up said rain, and the stacks of $50 bills could buy luxury termite condos. I covered the sides of our storage pit with concrete and waterproofing, but get paranoid regardless.

Place toolboxes on the right in order of use: red, blue, grey. Each box also has a layer of weather stripping around the lip of the lid to keep it watertight, but as with the bills, put them inside a plastic bag and check that there are no holes. Extra protection.

'Cool,' Christian said. 'I can't go to Full Moon, though.'

'Why not?' I scooped, scraped, squinted, and slid.

'Remember last time? The guy and the window?'

After the stock is organized, remove the metal bar, ease down the floor panel, replace the blocks, lay the black sheet metal, put the extra money and composition book in the safe and smooth the carpet seamless. Do this every night after closing. In case of an emergency, look for the cigarette burn directly under the handle of the desk drawer, pull back the carpet and remove the piece of plywood. Up to four toolboxes will fit in that storage pit. Perfect in case anyone unwanted drops in. Lather, rinse, repeat.

'But you didn't throw him through it.'

'Yeah, he was drunk, I pushed him, he fell through it. Either way, I don't want to go back. They might put something in my drink.' He rubbed his right thumb with his left, then his left with his right.

'Let's go to Laughton's then. The girl with the nose ring that you dig bartends there now.' I scratched the tattoo on my forearm: a K inside a shield, the size of a roll of film, from when I was fifteen. Amazing that it hadn't disintegrated yet.

The other part of the problem: we were almost giving away pills. Med-school kids used to be big business. All of the medical malpractice cases—they shouldn't have been any surprise. End of term time, those kids would chew Adams like they were M&Ms and wash them down with a double tall latte.

Then they discovered white.

It had become a sepia world. Everything was brown and white.

'Yeah, she's cute. Good idea. I'm out, Jet Black is calling my name.' Christian picked up his canary Ben Sherman jacket, the one that barely reached his waist, and walked towards the front. 'While I still have a store to head back to, that is.'

'Call me if you're chained out.' I packaged a Depeche Mode single and three Duran Duran CDs—two "Hungry like the Wolf" singles and a *Notorious* full-length—then leaned back in the chair and watched the TV monitor. Mary pushed the hand sweeper over the carpet, starting by the register. Christian talked to her for a few minutes while she swept before covering himself for the rain. She organized two boxes of records at the end of the display counter, then put the sweeper in the corner and leaned against the front window, looking out at the street.

I wouldn't have been able to run the place without her. She

kept my loose ends knotted.

She propped up all the bikes.

Squared off the vacuum cleaners and Weedwhackers.

Arranged the DVDs inside the plexiglass case into rows by genre, then from A Bronx Tale to Zulu.

Alphabetized the records at the end of the counter. Sometimes, if she was annoying me, I'd slide *The Best of Ray Charles* and *Led Zeppelin IV* in front of *Whitney Houston's Greatest Hits*.

She boxed the jewelry from left to right. The ones on the left—the high-school graduation rings, the sweet-sixteen heart pendants traded for a white night—turned your skin into moss, and the ones on the right—the aborted-wedding and broken-promise rings—turned your finger into a Zircon disco ball.

We were the unassuming alchemists. We'd take a fistful of unwanted sentimentals, spread our fingers, and out dropped a night of being someone important, all in an eyeball-sized bag.

I dropped the bag of white on the desk, snuck up to the window and slid my arms around her waist. She jumped, then smiled and nestled herself into my chest, pulled my arms tighter around her. My stomach squished against her back, fingers nooked in between her bottom ribs. I matched my breathing to hers.

Outside, the sky spat rain onto Broadway. We watched people scuttle towards Broadway Market and its awnings. Wrinkled men held umbrellas for shrunken women. Blondes in business casual grappled a lipstick-smudged coffee cup with one hand, the other holding yesterday's Baltimore Sun paper over their coif. Waist-high neighborhood kids ran through the run-off gutter streams. When it storms during the summer in Baltimore, the air is wet cotton. You can feel every molecule of carbon, oxygen and smog.

Raindrops smacked the front window. Part of the neon in our sign had burned out. Instead of STAY GOLD, it read STAY GO_D. I'd just read The Outsiders for the hundredth time as I was opening the store and thought it sounded like a good name for a junk shop.

Ten minutes later, the spit lightened to a mist and I grabbed my James Dean jacket from the back. Mary had bought it for me three years ago, when we went as the posthumous James Dean and Natalie Wood to Brent's Halloween party.

'Beef or chicken?' I asked. She sat on the wooden stool behind the jewelry counter with *Love in the Time of Cholera* split open.

'Chicken. I'm supposed to be on a diet.'

'Mary.' I frowned. 'Seriously.'

'Chicken, please. I'm supposed to be on a diet.'

I shook my head. 'Whatever you say. I'll be back in a few, beautiful.' I kissed the back of her neck, snuck in a bite that made her laugh, then hurried down to the Taco Truck.

I was about to open the foil of my chicken taco when a pale piece of a Barcode I recognized shuffled through the door. His scuffed combat boots squished waffle-prints across the carpet. Part of my small intestine knotted with guilt. Every job had its disadvantages. Ours was no different.

He had worked at The Daily Grind last summer and every time I went to get coffee for Mary and me, the Barcode and I would talk about horror movies. He tracked down a Beta copy of *The Re-animator* for me once, because someone had stolen mine, so I gave him a bag of green to say thanks. The pudge of his cheeks had creased in a smile. Now, the bags under his eyes were as dark as the greasy, chin-length hair that cut stark lines against his vampiric teenage face.

He gazed glass-eyed at the DVDs for a minute, first standing a few feet from a guy and his kid in matching Orioles jerseys pointing at PlayStation games, then walked to the counter where I was sitting. He mumbled something and slid a stack of records across the counter. The kid bartered with his dad for two games, then just one, then three and he would eat all of his broccoli for a week. I watched them for a moment, then flipped through the Barcode's vinyl, checking for scratches and albums that would sell— Motörhead, Jawbreaker, a Jane's Addiction import. He had good taste, and probably still liked most of these bands.

'Can I trade it for a CD?' fell from his lips. He saw my taco sitting on the counter and shifted his gaze to his boots. His eyes were as bland and soulless as our eggshell-colored walls. I flipped the album sleeve over in my hands, tapped it on the counter, inhaled, exhaled.

'Which one?'

'Depeche Mode,' barely audible through his hand. He spoke into his fingertips like they might be microphones. Through the slivers of his hair, I saw his eyes peek up, then drop back to the floor as they met mine. He mumbled to himself. I could hear his soles rubbing against the carpet.

I held up five albums. 'This will get you a single.' He nodded. I sighed, 'Give me a minute,' then walked into the back and took a "Master and Servant" single from the blue toolbox in the office. Mary reclined in the chair with her feet on the desk, an iced tea next to her fashionable cowboy boots. Printed on the side of the plastic cup was Che Guevera, eating a taco and giving the 'thumbs up' sign. She made a sad I'm sorry face, said, 'It's not your fault, sweetie. It's not our problem,' with a piece of saffron rice stuck to her bottom lip. I asked her to help the guy and his kid, then hid the bag inside an empty CD case. She kissed my cheek as we went through the door.

'Here you go,' I said to the Barcode, handing him the CD cover-down, just so another customer wouldn't realize that *Synchronicity* wasn't a Depeche Mode album. 'There are other CDs, you know.'

He looked at me like he was looking through me.

'You don't always have to listen to Depeche Mode,' glancing up at the Oriole and his kid then adding, 'or Joy Division. Try something less morose.' He probably didn't even know what morose meant.

He nodded, sort of, and turned around. Mary laid two PlayStation games and her book next to my hand and rubbed her fingers on the small of my back. The clink of her pewter skull and heart bracelet tied another hangman's knot in my intestines. Hobbs had bought that bracelet for her; he thought she'd appreciate the juxtaposition of love and death. I rubbed the ring on my necklace to try to calm myself, then rang up the Oriole and over his shoulder, watched the Barcode slink out the front door. Mary took the rubber band from her hair and said she would watch the front for a while.

In the office, I opened the desk drawer looking for some relief, and instead found the periwinkle-blue envelope. I pushed it and all of its connotations—idealized but futile marriages, screaming brats, general malaise—to the back of the drawer and grabbed a pill.

One Cameron, chewed, washed down with some of Mary's iced tea.

The brass bells over the front door clanked and I looked up from my Gameboy to the TV monitor. A Sallie came in from the jaundiced night, pushing a cotton-candy-colored bike half the size of an upright vacuum cleaner. Mary finished reading a paragraph before she lifted her head towards him. His high-tops had been white at one point, around the same time that horror movies were still original and scary, and his cooking-oil-stained shirt was a size too big, even for his swollen frame. The flag of El Salvador flapped across his chest.

'Damon,' she called to the back. 'It's for you.'

The Sallie wheeled the bike to the counter and propped it up on the kickstand. I hit pause on my chess game and set it on the desk, slid the suitcase the Cockroaches had delivered—this afternoon, two days late—in the corner and went to the front. Three moves from checkmate and I stopped playing for this?

'¿Sí?' Why bother telling anyone anything?

'Necesito vender este.' He looked down at the bike. His skin was ruddy and pocked like a potato.

I fanned my fingers, raised my eyebrows. '¿Y?'

'¿Y qué? Necesito vender este. Quiero comprar un collar del oro.' The Sallie bobbed from his right foot to his left.

'You want to buy a gold necklace? ¿De quien bici es ese?' Thieving bastard. That wasn't his bike.

He glanced at the bike, at his shoes, at me. 'Es mio,' sputtered out.

'You are going to tell me that you ride a pink bike?'

He thought, then, 'Sí.'

'That pink bike?' pointing at it.

'Sí.'

'Ride it around the store.' Mary looked at me as I started to breathe deeper and bit the inside of my bottom lip.

'¿Qué?' the Sallie said.

'I said, ride it around the store. If it is your bike. ¿Comprende?'

Sallie stood silent. 'No puedo. My foot hurt.'

'Look, I've told you and all your little friends before.' I paused. 'Nothing. From. Kids. Okay?'

Sallie stared at me like he didn't understand English. His girlfriend was probably American. He looked early 30s, so she was probably 19. His wife was probably late 20s, at home with their kids.

'Nada de niños,' raising my voice. The Sallie faltered back a step.

'¿Por qué?' he squeaked.

'¡Miré! You bring in another bike you stole from some fucking kid and you'll walk out with that rim as un collar.' I stepped forward. Sallie faltered back, tipping the bike to the side. Mary snickered as he dragged the bike over the floor, trying to get it on its wheels while still watching me.

'Lo siento. Lo siento.' He backed into the door, opening it and dragging the bike at the same time.

'Give that bike back to whoever you took it from and tell your girlfriend she needs to find a man with a job.' The door slammed, bells clanked. I walked back to the counter and took a cigarette from the pack sitting by Mary's elbow.

'You're so hot when you're bilingual.' She ran her hand over my chest. 'My little chicano Steve McQueen.'

'Silencio, mujer.' I stifled a smile, lit the cigarette. 'They can try to sell that shit somewhere else.'

'Aww, they're just trying to do something nice for their girlfriends,' Mary cooed with a wicked smile. When she smiled, when she really smiled, her eyes disappeared as her cheeks swelled. It embarrassed her, but I thought it was painfully cute.

'I don't care about their girlfriends.'

She brushed her lips over my cheek, light as a breath. 'You're such a romantic.'

'Hopeless.' We sat quietly, me holding Mary's waist, Mary resting her head on my shoulder. The streetlights glinted in the raindrops on the window, a thousand sodium-yellow bugs splattered on our storefront.

'So, how do you like the book?' I looked around for an ashtray.

'I dig it.'

'Good, thought you would.' I knocked some ash into a soda can. 'I read him in one of my Lit classes a while back.'

'You took Lit?'

'Haven't we talked about this?'

'I can't keep them straight. You did a million things anyway, so fuck off.' Then quieter, as if I wouldn't notice, 'Can do a million things.'

'Lit before film,' I said. 'But after painting, I think. And before dropping out.'

'Of course,' she said with a pained smile. She leaned forward.

'If you liked that book, I've got a couple other things you might want.'

'Oh, do you?' she purred.

'Yeah, sure. They're not exactly like Garcia Marquez, but, maybe, Graham Jones or Cleven…' I peered down at her hand. The corners of her mouth curled up like the sides of her rosewood flapper hair.

'Yes, you do have something I'd like.' She stood. I tried not to laugh.

'Have you been reading porn poetry or something?'

'Something like that.'

She gave me a squeeze then sauntered towards the back of the store with her thumb in the waistband of her midnight jeans and flashed a seashell hip. I locked the store and followed her into the back, closed the door, closed my eyes.

Chapter 3

September: Then

My socks squished inside my Docs with every slow step to the back. The rain had been too lethargic to leave, and lurking clouds made Baltimore a smog-filled greenhouse for the last ten days. Junkies sprouted in alleys, around dumpsters like crabgrass. Prostitutes blossomed from latex tube tops like decaying orchids. Down the glass walls of the city, depression dripped in ribbons the color of corpse cheeks. Maybe that was why the Cockroaches were late. Again. For the fifth week in a row. Maybe they were too sad to get out of bed and deliver our shipment.

But when it rained, everyone stayed inside. When they stayed in the house, they got bored. Then once they were bored, they needed stock. That's where we came in. And depressed or not, Hobbs' Cockroaches—or the lack of them—were seriously fucking up our business.

And all of this to deal with, as I slowly squished into the office with a pistol lodged against the back of my head. The occipital lobe, I think Raymond Chandler called it.

Being held up was part of the business. It didn't happen that often, but was still something we had to deal with. We kept $150-200 cash in the safe for that reason: it was usually enough to get them to leave without shooting Mary or me, but wouldn't set us back much. Just stay cool, let them think they're in control, and get them out.

One of the guys wore a Britney Spears mask, the other had Debbie Gibson. Britney looked like he'd left his face by the radiator. His left cheek sagged like the Phantom of the Opera.

'Now open the fucking safe!' Debbie's voice deep, exaggerated, trying to disguise itself. I kneeled in front of the safe, in measured movements, and spun the dial. 'How are we looking?' Debbie said to Britney.

'We're fine. Hurry the fuck up.' Britney stood lookout in the office then hurried to the front to lock the door. I dipped my head, like I was trying to remember the combination, and stole a look behind me. Debbie tilted to the left, as if an inch had been hacked off his left leg. He wore Docs with a green lace in the right boot. Always check the shoes. If someone robs a bank, they always bring a change of clothes, to blend in afterwards. But usually—according to heist movies, at least—no one remembers to bring another pair of shoes. The same should apply to stores. I didn't recognize his Docs, but if I ever saw them again I would beat him until he looked like chunky tomato soup.

I spun the dial to the second number as Debbie's boots shuffled behind me. Then, for a flash, everything stopped. The safe, his boots, my hands disappeared into whiteness. I drifted around, my eyes spinning circles inside my head, until I felt cold on my cheek. It was smooth, refreshing almost, like ocean water on your feet after running across midsummer sand. Then the swell of feeling curled over and crashed on my head. Every shadow and color sizzled on my eyes. The muted crack of Debbie's gun across the back of my skull sent delayed tsunami waves through my brain.

'The fuck you think you're doing?' His voice screamed through wet tinfoil straight into my ear.

'Opening the safe,' I croaked.

'Then keep your fucking eyes forward!'

I blinked hard, tried to make the three safes come together into one. My hand touched my face, held my head up. Feeling around, I found the dial, turned it and opened the door. Debbie tossed me to the side with his foot.

'Where's the rest?'

Screwdrivers jabbed my temples from the inside. I slumped against the desk, waiting for it to pass. 'That's all we have.'

'Where's the fucking rest of it!' He looked around the back room frantically, wobbling towards me, then the door, then the safe again.

'What's going on?' Britney yelled.

'There's no fucking money,' Debbie said.

'Yeah there is.' They were a Mickey Mouse Club version of the ex-presidents from Point Break. I tried not to smile, because it hurt. Even the laughing inside my head felt like centipedes in stiletto heels tap dancing on my brain. And, they might've shot me by accident.

Debbie pointed his gun at me. 'Give me the rest of the money before I open your head.'

'You have everything.'

Britney rushed beside Debbie and pointed his gun at me. 'You just said there was more. Where the fuck is it?'

I shook my head, and there were four guns. Blinked hard and two of them disappeared.

'He said there was no money. But he has almost two hundred bucks in his hand,' I said. 'So there is money.'

Sometimes I'm too smart for my own good. Debbie's boot in my ribs reinforced that thought. Britney hurried behind the desk, flung papers off the top, ripped open the drawer. It rained cigarettes and Post-it notes and old bills. Pens and packages of staples and halves of Casamir Light filters hailed down on me. Then lightning hit the floor next to my hand: the envelope from Megan. I almost laughed.

'Look at this,' Britney said. Something flew over my head. Debbie caught it, turned it over in his fingers. A bag, full of white powder. The last of our supply. Mary had put away the CDs but forgotten the back stock before she left for lunch.

God damn it.

Debbie looked at Britney. He scratched his chin with the gun in his right hand. 'What the fuck am I going to do with this?'

'Put it back where you found it,' I muttered.

'I said get the money!' He tore the bag in half. The last of our product, all of our income except what was already packaged, drifted over the carpet like powdered sugar on a cake.

'There's no money,' Britney screamed. The sagging part of his face quivered. 'There's nothing fucking here!'

'I'm giving you one last chance,' Debbie said to me. He cocked his gun and made sure I had a good view of the barrel. That was when I got very, very nervous.

It wasn't the bullet hovering four inches from my brain or the amateur holding the gun. It wasn't even the boot that would've pushed my rib through my heart if it kicked me again. It was the missing finger on his right hand. The finger that Freddy had cut off in the first Nightmare. The finger that won the argument I'd had with Christian ten days before.

Someone set us up. They bugged our store. Mary and I had the only keys. The Twins. No, that would be stupid. *Small breaths, Damon.* These two definitely weren't cops. I touched my chest with my fingertips. No actual breaks, just a shit-ton of pain. Cops kick down doors and break windows, not send in undercovers to reference a conversation I'd had a week and a half ago to freak me out. Hobbs would've done that because he had nothing better to do than make things overly elaborate. And because he hated me almost as much as I hated him. A mound on the back of my skull pulsed against the desk. Rhythmically, in Morse code, my subconscious was trying to tell me who these two were. Psychologically torturing me was a fine way for Hobbs to pass a Thursday afternoon, but he didn't know that Mary wasn't here. *Please don't come back yet, Mary. I don't want you here.* Britney and Debbie had stormed in and didn't have time to check that she'd gone out. They had to have been watching because they came in when I was away from the counter and couldn't get my gun. It wouldn't be another one of Hobbs' dealers. They all knew better. If Hobbs found out that one of them had endangered Mary—

Britney threw the drawer onto the carpet. He paced back and forth, between the desk and Debbie, muttering and losing his nerve.

The Stalk. That fucking guy. He was in the store when Christian was here. He could've heard our conversation and he would've known that we held product and would've had money lying around. I didn't recognize him, didn't know if he dealt or was just some gangster. The Stalk had walked without any self-confidence. Debbie was the big-dick, so he was probably the smart one. If the Stalk was smart enough to plan a robbery, he would've acted small and nervous when we first saw him—when he was checking out our operation—so he wouldn't raise any suspicions, then walk tall with a gun through our front door. If I ever see this piece of shit again I'll—

'Do you want to die?' Debbie said, the muzzle cool against my cheekbone. I tried to burn him with my mind, like the girl in Firestarter. The gun pulsed on my clenching jaw. His fingers relaxed, then tightened around the handle grip, the same way he'd drummed them on the counter as I watched him on the TV monitor. There wasn't anything within reach that I could lodge into his temple.

'Come on, let's get the fuck out of here.' Britney grabbed Debbie's arm. The gun hopped on my face, cracked back onto my cheek. It cut the inside of my mouth against my teeth. I swallowed the taste of metal, spoke slow and enunciated every word, made sure he knew exactly what I was saying.

'I will kick out your teeth if I ever see you again.'

His eyes flinched, fingers relaxed and tightened. He was debating whether to pull the trigger, whether $200 was worth trying to find the surveillance tape before the cops got there, whether he wanted someone's dying scream—that scream—echoing in his ears, whether or not I would've come after him.

'Let's get the fuck out, man! Come on!' Britney grabbed his shoulder this time. Debbie pulled the gun away from my face, teetered towards the door.

'You'd better buy a rosary with that money, cocksucker,' I yelled to his back. It was better that there was nothing around me. The scream, that scream. I couldn't handle another one like that poor kid's. The bells on the front door clanked and their footsteps disappeared. Paper scattered on the floor around me. I leaned over to the safe, planted my lips on the door. 'You did great,' I told it.

My ribs throbbed as I stood up. That bastard had an accurate boot. I dropped our salt-and-pepper bible on the desk to update it. When someone suspect came in, or when someone robbed us, we rewound the surveillance tape and took a Polaroid of their face, then taped it in our bible. Every night after closing, we erased the tape, turning everyone in the previous day into ghosts. I winced my way to the front, touching the back of my head. A big lump, but no blood. The neon sign in the window buzzed, the L in GOLD still burned out. My organs slid back into place. Some lady tried to come into the store, but I wedged my foot under the door—'We're closed'—and locked it. I needed a Cody, maybe two, to blot out the fire in my chest, and clean up before Mary got back. I didn't want her to know how bad it went.

A clean store or a numb torso?

Mary could've come back at any time, so I went with clean store. But as I bent over to collect papers from the floor, it felt like a rib made lung shish kebab, so I went to the emergency pit.

Two Codys, chewed, washed down with stagnant coffee.

I put the pieces of the drawer back together, moving as efficiently as possible, and made a mental note to glue it later, then scuffled around on my knees tossing random stationery debris into it, staying away from the dusting of white. A missing finger. Who had we seen with a digit missing? The envelope from Megan still sat by the foot of the desk. Picking it up with a piece of paper like cleaning up after a dog crossed my mind, but it was the pain and endorphins talking. I dropped it into a corner of the drawer and piled bills over it, then caught a glimpse of a leather string beneath a notepad. I cupped it in my palm, ran my thumb over the blue lotus medallion on it for a minute, then shoved it back into the drawer. The image of a deformed hand floated on the side of my brain. I tried to focus without looking at it, like remembering a dream. I checked the clock. Mary had been gone an hour already. Picturing her breezing through the front door, holding our sushi, and me crawling across the floor brought—

The door. A clean backroom wouldn't matter much if she couldn't get in. She'd want to know why the door was locked, and one pointless lie after another that I'd have to keep straight would follow and I didn't have the energy for it. I inched to my feet and when I got to the front door, the phone rang. Wincing my way to the counter, I took a deep breath to sound normal.

'Hey, it's me,' Christian said.

I let my breath out, a hurricane in the phone.

'Hello? Damon? You there?'

I pushed the curtain aside, assessed the back room. 'Yeah, I'm here. I'm busy. Call me later.'

'Wait, real quick. I need advice.'

'Call Miss Cleo.'

He laughed. 'You know she isn't really Jamaican, right?'

'She's probably not a psychic either.' I gasped as I started cleaning.

'I told Matt about the landlord deal.'

'Splendid,' I said. 'I really gotta go, man.'

'He can get a brick.'

Papers fluttered from my hand. 'Matt can get weight?'

'Guy who knows a guy who knows a guy, you know?'

'Does the guy have all of his fingers?'

'Sure, why not,' he said. 'What should I do? Get it? Pass?'

An extra shipment would help our stock. We were a day from running dry. 'Get it and I'll buy it from you.'

'Really?'

'Yeah, really. Get more and I'll keep buying them from you.'

Silence cradled the phone.

'Christian? You there?'

'Yeah,' he said. 'Yeah, we'll see.'

'Get this one, I'll buy it, and keep my proposition in mind.' It could've helped our situation a ton if he did. Especially with losing all of our back stock.

'Okay. Matt's going to set up a meeting next week. I'll let you know how it goes.' He hung up and I continued clearing debris.

The backroom looked somewhat normal by the time the bells clanked again. I scooted papers behind a box with my foot and tried to conjure an excuse that she would buy as to why the floor was so dirty. Peeking through the curtain, I checked that my gun was still under the counter—just in case—and watched a woman float in on cloud-white heels with black straps, box-blonde hair and a scarlet dress that slunk down to the top of her knee. In the front V-cut, I could see the bottom of her sternum. Hands: five and five. Her eyes drifted over me before she turned to a crate of vinyl. She craned over the records, flipped through them. Her calves tensed as she rose.

For a guilty three seconds, I hoped she was like the girls who'd hang out at Julian's house, when I lived in western Massachusetts. He was the supplier for my friend Eric and me, and we covered Amherst, Northampton and most of western Mass, so there was always some at his house. I used to call the cadre China Girls—after the Iggy Pop song—because they'd fuck me whenever they needed to score. Never talked to me around campus or if I was at a coffee shop. I was invisible unless they were fixing. Those were about the only times I had sex before I met Mary.

I ducked around the corner and tried to hurry through cleaning. I turned the TV monitor around so that I could watch her, and make sure there was no one else lurking outside. My legs wobbled like bent pipe cleaners and my stomach had folded into an origami animal; the Codys were starting to work.

Covering up the incident became a little easier. The big pieces were gone, but bits of paper and staples speckled the floor. Something about the hand seemed familiar. Not the actual hand, but the concept of it. Like I had seen it or heard about it, and I hoped I hadn't watched *Nightmare* too many times and thought it into real life. I went to the front—attempting to move normally and test my ribs—to get a vacuum. Her fingers danced over records still, though absently. Nothing with a reflection anywhere near her, but I still felt her eyes caressing me. The only weapon she could've hidden in that dress would've been a plastic spork or dental floss. Except for watching the last of our back stock disappear, vacuuming didn't hurt as much as I'd expected and I finished in a few minutes. I made a final inspection and plopped on the stool behind the register, let go a long sigh and lit a cigarette. The nicotine massaged my body internally and I sighed again.

Now, who the fuck set us up?

The inside of my body was Stay Puft marshmallow, skin a softer velvet than Prince's "Purple Rain" suit. I could turn to watch her without holding my ribs and hoped it wouldn't bruise. The last time someone kicked me like that was the last time someone robbed us. Axel, another of Hobbs' dealers, had been in the store with me. I'd remembered a bit of the idiot's face—he hadn't even worn a mask and deserved what he got—enough that I would've recognized him if I saw him again. A few days later, Axel came around the shop with a bruised cheek and a cut over his eyebrow. He mumbled something about falling down the steps even though I didn't ask, but had forgotten to wipe the blood spots off his shoes. I never mentioned anything to Axel and never saw the guy who robbed us again.

I fished another cigarette from my pack and slotted it between my lips, flipped through a Spiderman comic lying on the counter. Peter hung upside-down from a building ledge, watching Mary Jane walk across a park square. Her mundane moments, magic to him. And agony.

When I started in Amherst, I never had to worry about these kinds of things. Most people got along, except for Paul. No one ever robbed anyone else. I filled in part of a crossword puzzle that Mary had started, figured out how much to tell her. She couldn't know I was hurt because I didn't want her to worry, but she had to know about the Stalk. Knowing what happened in her past, I tried to keep the violence as far away from her as possible, but it would be worse for her to be uninformed.

She'd been pretty depressed around the last time we were robbed and I didn't want to make things worse, so I thought it'd be better not to say anything. Axel said he'd meet her for a drink while I watched the store. He was a funny guy and a good person overall, making him nice to be around when you were feeling bummed. While she was waiting for him, a guy started chatting with her. Two pints later, he'd flashed a wad of bills stapled at one end and, like an asshole, bragged about what a gangster he was. Axel finally got there and recognized the guy. They all had a pint, then Mary said she was tired and was going to leave. Axel offered to buy the guy a drink and told Mary he'd catch up with her. When she got back to the store, she told me about some jerk-off who was trying to hit on her at the pub, and how Axel thankfully showed up and distracted the guy so she could leave without looking like a bitch. Next day, Axel came in with the blood on his shoes. I couldn't ever let her get into a situation like that again. Most likely, nothing would've happened. But if it did… Fuck. I couldn't ever let her get into a situation like that again.

The Scarlet Lady meandered her way to the counter, said, 'Do you have any EPs?' Her voice was sweet and almost made me diabetic.

I raised my head, tilted it to the side. 'You were just looking at them.'

Her arm rose to my face and she made fire with a gold lighter, a baroque floral design engraved on the side. Her eyelashes were delicate, like feminine spider legs. The hand holding the lighter, scented jasmine. Tell Mary: we'd been robbed, someone set us up and ask her to try to remember what the Stalk looked like, height, weight, stature. Mention the finger and the green lace in his Docs. Nothing about my ribs.

'Try Jet Black.' I pointed to the street. 'Out the door and down Broadway. Turn right at the water and stop when you hear the music.'

She paused. Something in her eye unnerved me. Her lips pursed like an air kiss, and she tapped her cheekbone, nodding at me, and said, 'You're red.' Her dress clung to the small of her back and ducked under the bottom of her ass, thighs rippled as she opened the door and disappeared.

I dragged my hand over my face, wiped the streak of blood on my jeans then smoked a cigarette and chained another, shaded in some of the half-filled boxes of the crossword puzzle. I laid my forehead against the top of the register and closed my eyes. Nine fingers. Who set us up?

The door slammed and I almost jumped off the stool. A tight pain spread over my ribs. I grunted and pressed my hand against them.

'Sleeping on the job?' Mary laughed.

I squinted the drowsy fog away and smiled. 'Just resting my eyes.'

She set a bag and two drinks on the counter, kissed my forehead, then looked at me and frowned. 'What's wrong?'

I glanced at my hand, then slid it around to my back and started massaging. 'Nothing. Sore back. I didn't think I would fall asleep for so long.'

She raised an eyebrow, then forgot about it and pulled maki rolls from the bag. I separated the chopsticks and rubbed them against each other to smooth out any splinters. 'You were gone for a while.'

'I know, I'm sorry. It took forever at Ishii's and then I ran into

Dave and Caleb on the way back and talked to them for a bit. Are you starving?' I shook my head, mouth already full with two rolls, patted my hand on the small of her back. 'Just worried about me?' she smiled. A few harder pats for yes. 'You're so sweet.' A few more pats for yes as she giggled.

After I'd eaten a few rolls to keep from passing out, I took her hand in mine.

'Hey,' I said. 'We had a little incident today.'

The salmon roll in her mouth buried her words.

'Well,' I started, never having figured out a good way to go about this. 'We got robbed this afternoon.' Her chopsticks clinked on the counter as she coughed. Pieces of rice shot from her mouth. 'It's okay, don't suffocate yourself.' I smacked my palm on her back.

'What happened?' She wrapped her arm around my waist and pulled me close to her. Face to her neck, I inhaled her scent, like salt water floating in the onshore breeze, let it calm me then explained the situation: Britney, Debbie, the money, our stock, the missing finger, the Docs.

'Here's the catch though,' I said, taking a sip of iced tea to wet my mouth and pulling out a cigarette. 'He knew about the Freddy conversation.'

Mary blinked, looked to the side like she was thinking. 'Freddie Mercury?'

'No, not Freddie Mercury. When did we talk about Freddie Mercury?'

'What Freddy conversation?'

'The one about Freddy Krueger we had last week. Me, you and Christian were in the back talking about Freddy versus Wolverine and Freddy cutting off his finger.'

She thought for a second then nodded her head, waited. 'And?'

'And a week later we get robbed by some guy who's missing the same finger. It had to be that guy who came in to score. The tall guy when Christian was here. Do you remember what he looked like?'

'Not really. But I don't think they have any connection with each other.' A woman wearing a safari hat, her skin like an alligator's, pushed the front door open. Bad enough, but with Prada shoes? If there was supposed to be irony, it was lost on me.

'Of course they do,' I whispered. The woman's outfit was something my mother would've worn trying to look glamorous and exotic, as if she would make my father jealous because of all the men who were supposedly ogling her. He was too busy in the basement to notice, though, with his wine coolers and Trome-ho and Juli-wet or whatever bargain-bin porn he'd bought to further his delusion of being cultured. 'You can't have a conversation about something random then see it manifested a week later and it not be connected. Do we know anyone missing a finger?' Her eyes examined the room as she thought, eyebrows making a puzzled 'V' when she saw the woman's feet.

'I don't think so,' she said, shaking her head. 'There was a guy who used to work for Hobbs who is missing fingers, but I don't actually know him.'

'Wait,' I said. 'You know someone missing a finger and you think it's not connected? A guy who used to work for Hobbs? Are you crazy?' I fought to keep my voice down.

She leaned away from me. 'All right, calm down. Hobbs said the guy had too many fingers in too many pies, so he saved some of the pies and took fingers instead.' I looked at her, exasperated. 'But that doesn't mean it was him, Damon.'

'You're joking, right?'

'No, I'm not joking. That guy got off pretty light and I highly doubt he'd come back around here, especially not to rob one of Hobbs' dealers. They'd torture him if they caught him.' She took another bite of sushi. 'And I think they took more than one finger. Probably be a more effective deterrent that way.'

I shook my head. These two had to be connected. It was too

coincidental not to be. 'Well, let's just make sure we keep an eye out for him, okay?' I flicked my head towards the front. 'Can you take care of Crocodile Dundee? There are still CDs in the box. I need to make some cigarettes.'

For transient orders, I lay out the following: a pair of tweezers, a pair of haircutting scissors, a full pack of cigarettes, and eighteen singles. The number of each bag varies, depending on where I'm going that night and what the clientele is like. I prefer eleven "Girls on Film" and seven "Master and Servant"; it keeps everyone sated.

On the TV monitor, Mary was wiping drips of soy sauce and wasabi off the counter with a paper towel printed with motivational sayings—If you can dream it, you can do it. Don't give into the FEAR—when the phone rang. She picked it up and threw the paper towel into a white trash can with "Truman Drops the Bomb" and other World War II headlines screen-printed around it. 'I thought it was quirky,' she'd said. 'I was hoping they'd have a toilet seat cover, too.'

First, remove the foil from the pack and lay out the cigarettes. With the tweezers, remove the cotton filter from the cigarette, then open the scissors and scrape out some of the tobacco. Cut the filter in half with the scissors.

My eyes knee-jerked back to the TV monitor as I heard her talking. Dragon roll, revival, tennis floated into the office. I felt a moth gnawing on my stomach lining.

Take the bag of product and roll it into a cylinder thinner than the cigarette. Slide it into the cigarette, making sure to leave enough room for the filter. It's like that game Operation—steady hands, slow movements. A twitch of the arm and the cigarette rips. It's not costly, just annoying. But, too much pressure and the bag tears. Insert the filter then press the end to make a flush tip and the cigarette will feel like a normal one.

Mary stepped into the office with the phone clamped between

her ear and right shoulder and a cigarette pinched in the side of her lips. She patted her pockets while awkwardly talking into the phone, like you do with a cigarette in your mouth, then flicked a phantom lighter and held her palm out. I lobbed her mine and she blew me a kiss, then looked at the vacuum plugged into the socket and arched her eyebrows. I fiddled with the cigarette in my hand. 'Testing it. Someone brought it in today.'

After assembling all the cigarettes, arrange them inside the box. If it's a mixed pack, turn the brown cigarettes tobacco-side up and leave them to the right. Leave the white ones filter up on the left and the two normal cigarettes in the front row, middle two slots. With the scissors, make a small notch on the filter.

Who is that? I mouthed to Mary.

'Hold on,' she said into the phone, then looked at me. 'Do you want to see a movie at The Charles?'

'Possibly. The Rotunda has better popcorn butter, though.'

She rolled her eyes. '*The Seventh Seal* is playing for Revival Night.'

'Yeah, sure.'

'It starts around ten-ish.'

She talked into the mouthpiece again.

Who is that? I mouthed again, waving to get her attention. I closed the red toolbox—if we didn't see a Cockroach in the next day or two I was going to be royally pissed, not to mention broke—and set it on the floor.

Organization is important. If someone wants a brown smoke and you give them a white, they'll be pissed. Or, they might die. Neither is good for business. If someone notices smoking from one pack and bumming from another, eyebrows raise. The notch in the front two prevents giving away both product and profit, and more importantly—evidence. It also deters trying to smoke a cigarette with half a gram in it.

It's Hobbs, Mary mouthed back.

I jerked my head side to side. 'No way. I'm not going.' If I'd known it was Cocksucker I would've vacuumed the office again.

Her body drooped with exasperation.

While managing a pleasant expression, I said, 'Why don't you find out where the hell his shipment is while you're talking.' I didn't bother to mouth it, hoping he would hear me. 'Or ask which of his cronies is missing a finger.'

'Okay, we'll see you in a bit.'

'No we fucking won't,' I yelled, but she'd hung up before I could say it. She stood and stared at me. I tapped a cigarette on the desk, matching the tapping of her foot, then slid it into the pack.

'What is your problem?'

I put down the Casamir Lights. 'I want to know who robbed us.'

'Don't be stupid, he didn't rob us.'

'Maybe he heard something. How should I know? Forgive me for being proactive.'

'What are you going to do? Chase them down and bus a cap in they ass?' She made guns with her thumb and forefinger, gave me a look that said *Damon, you're not tough and you're a fucking idiot to boot.* 'That's not what I mean anyway. Why don't you want to go to the movies?'

'I can't go to the movies. And I definitely don't want to go with someone who can't keep up his side of a business agreement. Ask me, we need to find a new supplier, because this isn't working.'

Her breath, an annoyed hurricane as she exhaled. 'We're not finding a new supplier. We're fine.'

'Whatever,' I said. 'I've got stuff to do here.'

'What stuff? You just said a few minutes ago that you wanted to go.'

'That was before I had stuff to do.'

'What stuff? You don't have any stuff to do.' She crossed her arms over her chest and stuck out her right foot, her hip jutting forward.

'You're doing it again.'

She looked down at herself, in the same position that her mother used to stand in when they argued, shook her arms and rearranged her legs. 'Why don't you want to go? I thought you liked Bergman. We can see a different movie.'

'I just can't, all right? He probably won't even show up, anyway. He can't seem to get anything delivered here on time. And I have to—' I yanked open the drawer and scoured it with my eyes, pulled out another pack of Casamirs, '—do another order,' defiantly smacking down the pack.

'We don't have any more stock, remember?'

I shoved the smokes back in the drawer. *Jesus God, Christian, loosen your morals and please get those bricks.*

Mary stood quiet, chewing on the inside of her cheek, staring at me staring at her. We held eyes for almost a full minute, neither of us willing to look away. It had been a shit day already and spending the evening with Fuckface wasn't the way I wanted to end it. We should be at home, in bed, watching a film with Gael Garcia Bernal, sharing a bottle of red. Not hearing his pathetic whisper during the film, her giggle a second later. Not listening to him spew his analysis of the film to her, or telling her little tidbits of interesting information that I knew he'd read in a magazine because I'd read the same one and had already told her. Going on and on about the coming-of-age story in *Menace II Society* and how it parallels Michael Corleone in *The Godfather, Part II,* then commenting, 'Oh really, Damon, I didn't realize you'd noticed that aspect.' I was the one who'd written a paper on it in college and told you in the first place, you ass-hat. Even though he blew his chance with Mary fifteen years ago, he still waved cash or his watch or an expensive handkerchief, just to remind her how much more he had than I did and try to steal the best thing in my life. The passive-aggressive fuck. Julian never did that stuff to me. I was his golden boy. If only Paul hadn't fucked it up, that kid would still be alive and I'd be coasting.

Then again, if I hadn't fled Amherst, I would've never met Mary.

'Is it because Hobbs is going?' she said.

'I don't know. Is it?'

Her face screwed, like she had taken a gulp from a glass of gin, expecting it to be water. 'Stop it, Damon.'

'What?' I tried to look confused.

'You know what. Do you not want to go because Hobbs is going?'

I sat, then took out a cigarette, patted my pockets. 'Can I have my lighter back please?'

'Not until you answer me.'

I jerked the drawer open again and scattered rolling papers, sticky notes, receipt tape and halves of filters looking for a lighter. Tucked in the back—where I'd slid it when I was cleaning up, hoping to forget about it forever—lurked the periwinkle envelope I still hadn't opened.

Mary slammed the phone on the desk. 'You are so childish sometimes. Forget it. Don't go. I'll just go with Hobbs.' She spun on her toes and hurried out of the office. The door rifle-cracked closed behind her.

'Dumb son of a bitch,' under my breath. I winced as I jumped up to follow the trail of her in the air, cigarette still hanging from my lips. A warm and dull ice pick wedged between my ribs. I'd need another pill soon.

'Okay, fine. I'll go. Can I have my lighter now?'

'No, you're not going. Why do you want to go now anyway? Ten minutes ago, we were going. Five minutes ago, you weren't. Now you are.' Her cheeks swelled with pink. The corners of her mouth sunk. She tapped her fingernails on the countertop. I looked at her, at the freckles she got only during summer when she'd been out in the sun, and watched us in her eyes: saw the two of us at a subtitled film; saw us sipping gin and tonics at the Zodiac, in a velvet booth the same color as candle shadows; saw us on our couch with my head sunk in her lap, her moaning and smiling, wrists bound behind her head by her pantyhose; saw her, laughing, happy, glowing. I swallowed hard and breathed deep.

'Mary, I'm sorry, okay?' I covered her hand with mine. 'I'll do the order later.' Her chest rose and sunk and she dropped car keys onto the counter. Her eyes rose to mine, slow and measured. She sucked in her lips, exhaled through her nostrils like a bull.

In my head, I grabbed Hobbs by the back of the hair, smashed his face against the admission booth, swept his feet, lashed him to a chair with his belt and took $20 from his pocket to buy tickets for Mary and me.

I laid my hand on her waist, cupped the slight hill that rose from her jeans.

'I'm going to get some lemonade from the pretzel place,' she said, unenthused. 'Do you want anything?'

'Can I share some of yours?' I wedged five dollars in her pocket, wiggling my fingers against her thigh.

Sighing, she said, 'Fine. I'll get a large,' then dropped my money on the counter with a sour, patronizing smile. She started towards the door, then paused, faced me. Her eyes bored a hole through my forehead. 'While I'm gone, figure out what you want to do, okay? And don't go just because you think I'll be mad if you don't.'

'Okay.' I smiled, hoping to defuse her. 'I'll see you in a few.'

She went out the door and I stood behind the counter with my happy face on, clawing the bottom of the register. I waited until she was out of sight and counted to five, then took a deep breath and stormed into the back and screamed until my lungs caught fire and I started to cough. The burn spread to my ribs, filled in the boot-print of a Doc Martin with green laces. The desk drawer came off its guides as I tore it open. I knocked it straight with my knee, scoured the inside for some pills, and saw the envelope. That fucking envelope. That fucking scream. Everything was inevitable but Megan would have to wait; the drawer was pill-free. I pulled a grey toolbox from the emergency pit under the desk.

One Cody, chewed, washed down with some of Mary's water.

Hobbs. That dumb motherfucker. The stupid son of a bitch. He was fucking up my life before I even met him. Of all the dealers in Baltimore, Mary, why did you have to be his friend?

I sat for a few minutes. Mary's sweater was draped over the chair. I pressed it against my face and breathed her in. Eventually, I nudged open the drawer with my knee. The envelope still sat in the back corner—where I'd hid it a week and a half before and then again this afternoon—all looping Ls and curling Ys. In Megan's perfect Is, I could see the white picket fence around the nine-by-nine lawn that looked imported from the wizard's front yard in Oz. In her Os, the smiling faces of the 2.5 peering from inside the aerodynamic grocery-getting caravan with drips of ice cream on their fingers. A perfect Catholic school dream in perfect Catholic school writing. The dream that dies within a few years, a slow and agonizing disintegration. After the smiles and best wishes we gave them at the wedding they'd taken out a second mortgage to pay for. The wedding Mary roped me into attending, with napkins color-coordinated to the table mints—each bag containing the same amount, so no relative or guest would feel less favored than another—both a complementary shade of lavender to Megan's bouquet and her husband's carnation. The idealized union, strangled blue by the claustrophobia that lurked behind neighborhood potlucks and suburban community organization dues and affairs with bridge-club partners. Like my parents. Like Mary's parents. Like Christian's parents. No thanks, Megan, we were quite all right.

Then I saw the jagged tear-line at the top of the envelope. Tiny white icebergs in the periwinkle Arctic. The envelope was already open. Not only had she brought it in for me to find, but then opened it and put it back where I'd hidden it. God damn, she was sneaky. I had to admire her. A little bundle of terror stared at me from the front of the card. It was chubby, but a cute kid. Then, written underneath: *Mary – I can't wait for you and Damon to experience the same joy we have. Promise me I can throw your baby shower. When is the wedding?* Beneath the card I saw the lotus medallion winking at me but let it lie. With Megan's cursive to my lips, I said, 'What's the point?'

After lighting a cigarette, I shoved the card back into the envelope and opened the toolbox again.

One Cameron, chewed, washed down with the rest of Mary's water. And not for my ribs.

I took a long drag and looked around the office for no reason. A robbery and boot in the ribs, then a movie with Hobbs and visions of sugarplum weddings dancing in Mary's head; it was going to be a long night.

Chapter 4

October: Then

'Of all the superheroes,' Christian said, almost pensive while sipping his bottle of Newcastle, 'Batman is the worst.'

Dave's brother Caleb and I threw our arms in the air. A bite of cheeseburger almost fell out of my mouth. 'What are you talking about?' Caleb yelled.

'He's a normal person, there's nothing special about him,' I said. Smoke from Mary's cigarette curled up into my eyes. 'That's what makes him so great!'

'Exactly. Listen to your boyfriend, Christian,' Caleb seconded. Christian shook his head.

'Batman's just a normal dude who is real messed up. You could do a psych case study on the guy.' I pushed my burger to the side and lit a cigarette.

'Exactly,' Caleb seconded again.

'You just said that,' Christian said.

The door that connected the two rooms of the bar opened. Richard peeked through the doorway, motioned to me. I stretched my hand out, put up three fingers—one per minute. *Some guy is looking for you,* he mouthed back to me.

'Tell them to wait,' I shouted back. 'Okay,' to Christian, 'you have two minutes to make your case.'

He stretched his palms out. 'Then both of you shut up for a second and follow me on this. Batman is the worst, because he is the capitalist of the superhero world.' Our mouths opened to argue and Mary covered them with her hands. Caleb tried to speak through her fingers. 'All the superheroes, they do it for the good of the general population, right?' he continued. We sat quiet. 'You can talk to answer me, just let me finish my points before you interrupt.'

Mary took back her hands. 'Right,' we said.

'But, most villains are of a good standing. Doc Ock is a scientist. Norman Osborn is the C.E.O. of Oscorp. Magneto was a genius.'

'What about Lex Luthor?' Caleb interrupted.

'Batman's the only DC comic I like.'

'Bigot,' I snickered.

'Like I was saying,' Christian said, determined to defend himself no matter how wrong he was, 'the other superheroes protect against supervillains who can defend themselves. Batman, however, is a rich bastard who has nothing better to do than torment the dregs of society. Look at his enemies. Penguin: he's a cripple and lives in the sewer. He finally gathers a supporting group, of flightless birds no less, to revolt and Batman puts them down. Catwoman—'

'Eartha Kitt was hot,' I said.

'So was Halle Berry,' Caleb said.

'Eartha Kitt was hot,' Mary said, pointing her finger at Caleb and me, 'but the Catwoman movie sucked so that negates Halle Berry's hotness.' I smiled and touched her foot with mine under the table.

'Catwoman:' Christian continued, 'an abused woman and petty thief with an overactive libido who Batman cock-teases then throws off a building. Joker: a burglar who likes squirting flowers and dumb jokes. Batman chases him into a vat of acid. Batman preys on the weak. He's the anti-Robin Hood.' He sat smug in his seat, sipped from his bottle.

'You're taking all this out of context,' Caleb said. 'First, Joker was a chemical engineer and I think he fell into acid that he had created. And second, yeah, they're freaks of nature but they're also malicious archrivals. If Batman didn't fight them, they'd take over Gotham.'

'And as I said before,' I began, 'he doesn't have any superpowers. No web-slinging, no flying, no nothing.' The pint glasses and bottles strewn over the Toxic Avenger-green table were all empty. I dropped my cigarette into one of the bottles and stood. 'And on that note, I need another drink. I can't handle you anymore.'

'Because you know I'm right,' Christian said.

'Because I know you're an idiot. Does anyone need anything?' They shook their heads.

'I'll come with you,' Mary said. 'And by the way, Christian—Damon is right. Batman works on the same principle as Michael Myers, which is why he's my personal favorite. There's nothing extraordinary or supernatural about him, other than being a murdering psychopath.'

I threw my arms over my head, 'I love this girl!' and leaned her back, planted my lips on hers like we'd just finished a swing dance number.

Christian groaned.

We wrapped our arms around each other and weaved through drunken bodies whose skeletal support had clocked out early towards the end of the bar. Dwyer slid drinks across the maple top. He finished with the pack of lushes and came down to Mary and me. I ordered two Yuengling and two Jameson.

'Who's in the back bar?' I peeked over the bar top, out of habit. Black high-top Chucks with flames, the same color scheme as the flame tattoo that licked his forearm. I wondered if it was a coincidence or the reason he bought them. Ten fingers as well.

'Richard. Gordon is off but holding up the corner of the bar.'

I scanned the booths, looked for clients and anyone missing a finger. The place hummed quiet, but it was early, just past eleven. 'Is Nik working tonight?'

'Nah. He got fired,' Dwyer said as he set down our drinks.

'What'd he do?'

'Stole steaks from the refrigerator downstairs.'

'Isn't he vegetarian?' I handed a Jameson to Mary.

He laughed and his billy-goat beard bobbed up and down. 'So goes the story,' he said.

Mary and I raised our whiskey. She had on one of my t-shirts, a blue rec-league soccer logo across her chest, and it gave her eyes the shimmer of a sunset ocean. 'To Batman,' she said. We smiled and I kissed her cheek before we downed the shots. She put her glass in mine. 'Okay, now go be important,' and she grabbed my butt with a smirk as she took her Yuengling to a booth with some girls I didn't know. The lamp over the table seemed to shine only on her. One of the girls said something and Mary tossed her head back, currents of hair falling soft to the side, curling around the bottom of her earlobe. She had one of those laughs. Not just one that made you smile, but made your cells warm, made your blood flow a little smoother. Morrissey Mason—this girl who was obsessed with The Smiths that I pined over for a long time when I lived in Amherst—used to laugh like Mary. But there was something different about hers, detached almost, like the laugh wasn't hers but a tape recording of one she'd play at appropriate moments. When I'd try to impress her with how witty I was, she'd laugh and I'd feel like her face would go stone blank at any moment, right before she ripped my heart out through my chest. We hung out before I split during my junior year of college, but by that time she'd become a China Girl and it wasn't flirting as much as a game to see which one of us could be more manipulative. But Mary's laugh, it was pure. It made things okay.

Christian waved his arm to get my attention. *Not now,* I mouthed. Mary had been with me all night and I hadn't been able to find out how the meeting about the brick went. I walked around the pool table, ringed with bottle stains like watching eyes, and dodged the errant cigarettes of emphatic conversations on my way to see Richard.

Gordon's body followed the top curve of the bar, his head held up by a bottle. I nodded towards him. 'Rough night?' I asked Richard, who stood at the edge of the bar, twirling a chrome bottle opener. Ten fingers. He reminded me of Father Karras in that great shot from The Exorcist, enveloped in a fog of cigarette smoke. Blue high-top old school Vans. He'd lined up the legs of his Dickies wrong when he cut them into shorts; the left leg was about half an inch longer than the right.

'Lady troubles.' He pulled off his hat and smoothed back his hair. 'Where's Mary?'

'In the front being chatty.' I sat on a stool, sipped from my beer. Richard came behind the bar and slid a napkin under my glass. A tagline of baseball scores ticked along the bottom of the TV over the liquor cabinets. A guy plopped onto the stool next to me. In the mirror behind the bar, I clocked him with a glance: stalking forty, patchy goatee and greying hair under a Cleveland Indians hat, worn black leather jacket with no zipper. Ten fingers. Besides cheap drinks and knowing everyone at the bar, we came to Frazier's because of its layout. In the long mirrors behind both bars, I could watch most of the room without moving from my stool, no poles to block my view or crannies for anyone to hide.

Sitting next to me, the Goatee gestured towards the highlights playing on the screen. 'Damn Os, man. Can't seem to win a game.' His accent made me want to throw up. He thought I was holding. People treat you different when they think you're holding. They think you won't notice. But whether it's selling shoes or product, psychology is psychology. Al Bundy could've been Al Capone if he'd applied himself. The China Girls—at a party, they'd pull me into a bathroom by my Charles Manson belt buckle with the beer-cap opener in the mouth. In the beginning, when I first started slinging white, I told myself they cared. Made myself believe that they really enjoyed being on their knees in front of me. I don't think I ever really believed it, but it was still physical contact, however it came. It was the same with the boys, when rumor told them I had brown. Neither of us was gay, neither was engaged in what was happening. We were both looking for something, just in different ways. And this guy next to me, he assumed I liked baseball, from the way I was staring at the screen, I guessed, and figured the Orioles have to be our team, even though he's wearing an Indians hat and I couldn't give a shit about a bunch of overpaid guys running in circles. I checked in the mirror on either side of him, looked for anyone watching us. Anyone with an undue interest in a middle-aged plumber sitting next to a guy he dead-obvious has nothing in common with.

'Yeah. Pretty bad, huh.' I leaned down and pretended to cough—tan work boots, speckled with cement and plaster—then turned away from him, towards two pool tables next to the bathrooms. Richard wiped the bar top with a grey rag. I raised my eyebrow at him, motioned with my eyes at the Goatee behind me. His eyes said yes. Neither the boots nor the face of the Goatee looked familiar. Richard had said some guy, not someone, or a friend—nothing to insinuate that I should've known the guy, and I could tell by the way that he wore his pants that he was suspect. I touched the ring around my neck. I could almost hear the gears in his brain chunking and scraping together a better way to approach me. Checked the mirror again. Still nothing unusual.

'Hey, buddy.' He was being cordial, friendly. 'You don't know anyone who, uh—'

'I know a lot of people. You?' Get him thinking. Make him uneasy.

He leaned back in his seat. 'Huh?'

'What do you do for a living?' My calves tingled. The alcohol was starting to catch up. I needed a little white to straighten out.

His face screwed. 'Construction, man. The fuck it look like?' He paused. Metal grinded on metal in his head, cog by cog. 'What're you talking about, man?'

'Just getting-to-know-you talk,' I said. He was agitated, not thinking straight. Too old to be a cadet. Didn't have their composure, either.

'What d'you think I am?' He said it like he was offended.

'Don't know, that's why I'm making small talk. Buddy.' I was supposed to initiate the word, make the effort to make the sale. If I didn't, he would have to draw the transaction out of me, without making any direct reference to it.

'Been doing it for years.' He smacked his palm on the bar, made sure I knew how adamant he was. 'Drywall your house faster than you can cook a burger.' Deep Blue. An informant. He couldn't have denied that he was a cop or he'd be misrepresenting himself and it would've been entrapment. But if he was just some normal guy, he could be a puppet. Either he'd had a bad night once and they picked him up on possession or he bought from the wrong guy. The cops held out two hands: jail in one, NARC-ing in the other. Now, he was sitting next to me.

'I don't eat red meat. I don't know what you're looking for, either.' I pushed my glass towards Richard—'Watch this for a minute?'—and walked through the Exorcist fog to the bathroom. Water-stained prints of Baltimore through the years hung on the wall. The handle of the bathroom door didn't turn, so I looked at one of the prints and tried to find an apartment I used to have on St. Paul Street, checking the reflection to see if the Goatee had moved. He sat in the same stool, watching me. I dropped into the leather waiting-chair and watched meth-heads and hipsters play pool, thinking I should've blown a line right in front of him as a big fuck you. Across the room, Dave, Richard's roommate, sat cross-legged in brown flip-flops on a couch with some people. He waved and scratched his nostril while lighting a cigarette, holding my stare the entire time. I faked an aborted sneeze and scratched mine back. He smiled and exhaled a cloud of smoke, and the bathroom door opened. I was "Hungry Like the Wolf."

When I came out of the bathroom, five minutes later and two lines sober, the Goatee was gone. Part of me—the stupid testosterone part—was disappointed. My head buzzed, thoughts flying around like BBs shot inside a metal box. I took my pint from

Richard, had a mouthful to wash the drip of white down my throat. Dave slid into the stool next to me.

'What's happening?' He clapped his hand on my shoulder.

'Same poop, different scoop.'

'Cool, cool. Can I bum a Cas White?'

I leaned my head towards him. 'Don't look, but check the room and see if you can find a guy with a goatee. Looks like a biker version of Danny DeVito.' He turned in the stool, waved at the girl he was sitting next to on the couch.

'It's a lint brush.'

'Huh?'

'The fuzz is gone,' he said. 'You know, lint brushes take away the fuzz.'

'Oh,' I said, still not quite understanding. 'Right.'

'I was looking for some EPs, too. You got your hands on any?'

'Talk to Christian. He has more than I do.' I drained the rest of my glass and pulled a pack of Casamir Lights from the pocket of my denim jacket. My brain fizzed, crackled with activity. 'Don't hand me the money. Buy me another pint. He's probably still lurking around. I'll buy your next one.'

Dave's brow folded. 'You sure it's okay?'

'Just act normal and go see your brother in the front bar or something,' I said. 'Hey, have you ever seen anyone around who only has nine fingers?'

'Uh uh. Saw a guy without a leg trying to tap dance in Fell's the other day, though. Don't worry about the beer, I owe you one from Red Bottles the other night.' He motioned to Richard and another Yuengling appeared in front of me. I handed Dave a cigarette—left side, filter-end up—that he tucked behind his ear, and pressed one of the normals between my lips. 'Richard, I'll get his drink,' Dave said. He laid a twenty and a ten, one covering the other, in front of my glass then said thanks and headed to the front bar. Lather, rinse, repeat.

'How about you?' I said to Richard. 'Any nine-fingered

customers?'

'All drunks look the same to me. I'll keep an eye out, though.' Richard nodded at the money, smiled. 'You want change?'

A hand fell on my back, heavy and abrupt. The Goatee snuck up behind me when I wasn't watching. He'd radioed the raid-squad sitting next door in King's Pizza. Tall, kind of pudgy, brown hair. Sitting at the back bar wearing a denim jacket, trying too hard to look inconspicuous while drinking a lager. I collected myself, resolving not to run or do anything brash and stupid, turned around.

'Hey, Damon,' Brent said. Only Brent. I fucking love Brent. 'You okay?'

'Splendid. You?'

'Great, man. Great.' He shifted from foot to foot, like a kid who can't wait to see the guy dressed as Santa Claus at the mall. The overhead Christmas lights made canyons of the valleys in his cheeks. His skin looked translucent; lips were pallid, like he'd spent a week under an anemic sun. I glanced behind him. No one had kicked in the doors.

'Aren't you supposed to be at the bar?' No Goatee, no raids, no nothing. I needed a line to gather myself and could almost taste it in the back of my throat but took a drink of my beer then a deep pull from my cigarette instead.

'Poe's watching it. Hey, can I get a Cas White from you? Got a taste for a different smoke tonight.' His left hand made a friendly gesture, quivered despite itself. 'Oh, Dave asked me to ask you if you had any EPs around, too.'

Left side, filter-end up.

'Yeah, he was just sitting here,' I said. 'You know, Christian—as in, our friend Christian—owns a record store.'

'Yeah, I know.'

'Be careful, these things can kill you.' I handed him the white cigarette. Why was everyone crazy for vinyl all of a sudden? 'I'll put it on your tab.'

Brent owned a shoebox bar called 99 Red Bottles on Eden Street, a few blocks from Jet Black. It's the door you'll never find, was how he described it. Just East of Eden. He never explained the name, but I figured it was some combination of the "99 Bottles of Beer" pirate song and the Nena song, "99 Red Balloons." His musical taste stopped with his physical growth in the late 80s, and it amazed us how much a 5′6″ man could drink.

99 Red Bottles was a six-table, poorly-lit, broken-tiled corpse of a bar, but it had a good jukebox and no one to bother you. Our friends and a few toothless locals kept it alive. Brent had organized three art showings featuring a few people we knew, to try to bring in business and turn it into a proper bar, but each night had ended in whiskey-soaked displays of internalized angst tacked to the wall, so he had to settle for a poorly-lit, broken-tiled corpse of a bar.

Since we were in the same sort of business, we helped each other out, ran imaginary tabs. I gave him product when he ran short; he gave me blurry vision at his bar.

'Thanks, man. I'll catch up with you later?'

'Yeah. You doing anything this…' He was gone before I finished. I lit a cigarette, and as I slipped a normal into the Cas Light pack, an alabaster hand caressed my ribs and a velvet tongue traced the bottom of my earlobe. I craned back my arm to slide it around Mary's waist, and realized that Mary wasn't Mary. Mary was Melody.

'Hi, sweetie. Where've you been hiding?' she cooed into my neck. She could've been the star of a Mötley Crüe porn. Her voice had the raspy tone of a Long Island JAP without the over-privileged accent, and pupils threatened to overtake the rest of her eyes.

'Around.' I should've gone when I had the chance. But I'd wanted to make myself available for clients—the ones who paid with bills, not blowjobs—and now I was looking at Melody and her friend, a double-bodied slut hydra with a mess of over-sculpted black hair that didn't move as they shuffled in vinyl boots, trying to look sultry in a BDSM innocent schoolgirl way. An aura of hairspray trailed them like Pepé Le Pew.

'Did he ask for a Cas White?' Melody slurred. The liquor was catching up with the white, and she would get more brazen. They always did. At my worst, up until that last party at Julian's, I'd have little contests between them. See who would offer the most depraved things. Leaving Mass was the second best thing that ever happened to me, and led to the best: meeting Mary. She probably didn't realize what a great thing she was for me. I probably didn't tell her enough, either.

'Light,' I said. 'With an L.'

'Oh.' Her eyelids narrowed, schemed. 'Can I have a Cas Light?' Her velvet tongue ran over the magenta that had crossed the boundary of her lips—lipstick either slathered on quickly in her car's rearview or reapplied drunk in the bathroom after a few lines.

I shrugged. 'Sure.'

Front two. Slight notch on the filter.

She lit it, took a drag and realized it was just a cigarette, then dropped it under her heel. 'Say, Damon,' she said, her face sliding from disappointed back to fuck for white. 'Have you met my friend Alicia?'

Alicia extended a skeletal hand, nails like polished scabs, and I shook her fingertips with a vague smile. Melody sunk her fingers in my pocket, almost to the zipper. Her warm pouches of silicone wrapped around my upper arm. I could smell the chemicals in her perfume, floating amid the smoke and beer. My head buzzed with alcohol and sperm. Her nipple, hard like a clay thimble, rubbed against my bicep, finger ran over a vein. For a second, I wondered how many other biceps she'd had between her tits tonight. Everything's inevitable.

'So we're getting bored of here and are thinking of heading back to my apartment.' Alicia traipsed her bone-fingers over

Melody's stomach and their eyes tried to eat me.

'Either of you ladies fucked anyone with nine fingers recently?'

Melody smiled. 'It's not their fingers we're looking at.'

'What're you doing tonight,' Alicia said, running her hand up Melody's ribs, 'Damon?' Blood rushed to the wrong part of my body, through the vein under Melody's finger. Melody closed her eyes, bit her bottom lip. A hot trickle ran down the side of my face. I scanned the room, checked who was around me, more to pull my attention from them than looking for under-covers. Fingered the ring around my neck. Rubbed it for a few seconds, focused on the metal surface worn smooth by love through years of weathering things worse than this.

'We were thinking about waiting to see the sun rise,' Melody said, her eyes still closed in what I was supposed to think was a pleasure-trance. Alicia lifted a corner of Melody's shirt, showed the scythe curve of her hip, slid her finger into the waist of Melody's jeans. My blood rampaged through the vein. Mary, your Mary, think of your Mary. 'You want to stay up with us? We could use another person.'

I turned and looked into the almond-shaped abysses on either side of Melody's white-rimmed nose, and saw Mary and me watching a Hitchcock revival at The Charles, Mary and me in Kawasaki eating sushi at the table by the window that sits on the floor, Mary snoring on the couch as I rubbed her back.

A cool breeze with salt water in the air loosened my neck. Breath moved in my lungs and blood flowed back to other parts, the right parts, of my body. I stepped back and grabbed the pack of Casamirs in my pocket. As I put one in my mouth, I studied the floor, hoping to find a trapdoor I could fall into, away from the Herpes hydra.

'Actually ladies, I think…' I started. Alicia pulled her hand from Melody's waist, moved back from her—regrouping—and in the space between them, I saw it. A guy with brown hair, a little taller than me, hugged a girl in checkerboard Vans and started towards the door. He walked away, his back to me, in black Docs. Green laces flapped as he stepped.

The Stalk.

The fucking Stalk.

I stepped around the sluts, crept behind a few people so he couldn't see me. The cigarette fell from my lips. A tiny dry feeling in my mouth. The end of a filter. I spit out the slice of cigarette I'd bitten off, heard Alicia say, 'I thought you said he would,' behind me. The Stalk stopped again, shook hands with a burly short man in a leather jacket. His hair was turning grey under an Indians hat. The Stalk was a NARC? I lit another cigarette, looked to my left. Alicia danced by herself to a non-danceable Björk song crackling through the speakers, and Melody leaned over the bar trying to trade her tits for free drinks from Richard. NARCs didn't rob stores. The Stalk had to be another dealer. Then was the Goatee a rival, too? He was shorter and fatter than Britney, so he couldn't have robbed me. Fuck, he was the one who'd stood outside before they hit us. Why didn't I think of that before? He was confident that I was holding.

They shook hands, smacked each other on the back like guys do, then the Stalk's arm snuck around the Goatee's back and dropped something in his pocket. They pulled away, nodded and parted. I turned around, looked inconspicuous. The Goatee bumped into me.

'Hey, brother.' He smiled, showing me a mouthful of gum disease. In my head, I grabbed two bottles and played the xylophone on his teeth then crushed one on the bridge of his nose. I pushed past him. The Stalk opened the glass door and turned right. I shoved a few people to the side, trying to get to the street before I lost him. My hand curled, finding the switchblade in my back pocket, then opened the door onto the sidewalk.

A girl wearing a Ravens jersey tucked into white jeans tucked into white high-top Reeboks walked up 36th Street towards me.

She pushed a baby stroller in front of King's Pizza, arguing with herself. Even from twenty feet away, her face looked like attempted suicide with a Maybelline shotgun. Across the street, four boys in various shades of grey sweatsuits and Nikes yelled something I couldn't understand and pushed each other. Marty, the bar manager, stood by the door to the front bar, whistling and snapping his fingers.

The Stalk was gone. He'd seen me coming behind him and dipped into the alley behind Frazier's. Or he played it cool until he got to the door then ran as soon as he was outside. Picked up by an associate. Threw some kid off their moped and took off. Didn't matter. More time we'd have to spend watching our backs and other people's feet. I spit on the ground and started to clip my knife back in my pocket.

Then a shrill noise made me jump. Assorted yelling, different from the grey-boys. The squeal of tires. The clink of a metal blade on concrete. I covered my face, by instinct, and crouched down, ready to split or start throwing punches. The grey-boys ran in the opposite direction of the noise.

Flashing lights two blocks down, in front of Salamander Books. Two cop cars angled against the curb, the Stalk sprawled on the ground in front of them. One cop stood over him, another leaned through the window with a walkie-talkie at his mouth. He'd moved fast for a guy with duck feet. The Goatee had a wire, then. Called in reinforcements, flashed smoke signals. Don't drop the soap, fucker. He deserved it, for robbing us. Even with the Stalk off the streets, though, we'd still have to watch behind us for the Goatee. He suspected me, was confident that I was holding. It'd only be a matter of time before I'd run into him again. Smalltimore. I sighed and picked up my knife. After almost being nailed and watching the Stalk get picked up, I needed a drink. A double. Maybe a bump or two and—

I watched the Stalk get picked up. He was picked up and not me. He'd sold, but why were they looking for him? The Goatee had his eye on me, chatted me up for product. So why single him out when I was the one being probed? Tall, kind of pudgy, brown hair. Something wasn't right.

I hurried to the bar. Richard was serving a redhead who'd been giving him the eye. I pushed her to the side. 'You said some guy was looking for me.' Richard's face screwed. I turned to the redhead, 'Can you give us a second? I'll buy your drink,' then to Richard, 'Earlier. You came through the door. I was sitting at the table. You said some guy was looking for me.'

'Oh,' he said, eyes drifting towards the girl. I snapped my fingers to get his attention. 'Yeah, it was the guy with the goatee you were talking to earlier. That guy.' He pointed to the Goatee, walking out the front door, whistling.

'But was he looking for me?'

Richard sucked on a cigarette, thinking. 'I don't think he said your name. He asked where he could score and said he'd heard about a guy who comes in here a lot. I just assumed—'

'Don't,' I said. 'Don't ever assume it's me. Not a word about nine fingers either. I need to see the person before anyone uses my name. Unless they ask for me specifically, I don't exist. Remember,' I leaned in close, made sure he heard every syllable of every word, 'I. Don't. Exist.'

His face withdrew into itself. 'But, I didn't say your—' I turned and went back to the front bar. They hadn't been looking for me when I came in, but were they now?

'Just the man we're looking for,' Dave said as I sat down at the table.

'Hi, handsome,' Mary said with a kiss on the cheek. 'Where'd you go off to?'

'Long story,' shaking my head. I wrapped my arm around her, put my face in her neck and smelled her saltwater breeze. 'We can stop looking at hands, but start looking for Danny DeVito. I'll explain on the way home. Why were you looking for me?' Dave scratched the side of his nostril and smiled. 'I just gave you a smoke.'

'Wrong,' he said. 'I bought a smoke from you, then shared it with your lovely girlfriends.' I cocked my eyebrow, then looked at Mary sitting next to me, Christian sitting across from me.

'Fuck you.' Everyone at the table laughed. I raised my white flag, gave up and tossed the pack of Lights on the table. 'Enjoy it, because this is the last of our supply.'

'Don't be a party pooper,' Mary cooed into my neck. 'We love you for more than that.'

'She does, at least.' Christian laughed as he slotted a white cigarette behind his ear, stood to go to the bathroom. Mary threw a wet napkin at him and went to the bar for another round. I poured a bump the size of a pencil eraser on the back of my hand, sniffed between my thumb and index finger, felt the burn in my nose and drip down my throat. I dipped my finger in water, then put it in my nostril and sniffed to clean the pipes.

'Hey,' I said to Dave, calmer now, feeling like someone new. 'What's up with these records you keep asking about?'

'Not vinyl. There's something called EPs.'

'A product called EP?' I paused. Not vinyl? All the customers I'd thought were morons, who thumbed through records then asked for EPs, who I'd sent to Christian, this was what they wanted? Maybe my idiocy had helped his business.

'Never heard of it,' I said. God, and all of the sales we lost because I had no idea what they were talking about. At least three a day for the last few weeks.

'Supposed to be unreal. Thought you might have gotten your hands on some.'

'No, but I need to.'

'Think it's EP for epiphany or something. Like a wet and sloppy one from God in a gelatin capsule.'

Christian materialized from the bathroom. I checked that Mary was at the bar, then leaned over to him.

'How'd the meeting go?'

'Good,' he said. 'It's good stuff and he'll give it to us cheap. Family discount.'

I raised my eyebrows.

'Matt's stepbrother.'

I laughed to myself. 'How many can you get?'

'Dunno.' He lit a cigarette, watched his fingers fidget with the pack.

'I'm not trying to pressure you, but more bricks means more money you'll have to buy your building and keep your store. Just so that you think about all the angles.'

He laid the pack on its end, looked up at me and sighed. A napkin fluttered. 'I had the same thought.'

Mary's voice startled me. 'What are you two doing?'

'Whispering sweet nothings,' Christian said.

She smiled, smacked his arm. 'Hands off my man.'

Mary nudged my ribs and leaned in, her lips against my ear. 'We should probably chill with that. You know, sleeping and—' her irises glinted with innuendo '—stuff.' I nodded. We didn't listen to Duran Duran often and a big night out was rare whenever we did listen.

'Who is that?' Dave nodded towards the bar. A shoulder-high bob-cut brunette with a half-sleeve of tattoos stood at the end waiting to order.

'Don't bother,' I said.

'Is that the girl Seth was talking to,' Christian asked.

'No. That was...what's her name? Gayle? Tall chick. Photographer or psychologist or something.'

'I thought that was Brent's girl,' I said.

'She was,' Dave said. Everyone in Baltimore dated everyone else, so by six-degrees-of-Kevin-Bacon, I'd slept with everyone at our table, though I preferred not to think of it in that way. 'So why "don't bother"?'

'She's Baptist or something,' I said.

Dave ogled her for a minute, then under his breath but louder than he meant, said, 'I'll fuck the Jesus out of her.'

'Yeah,' Christian smiled.

Mary's face dropped to the top of her glass. 'You two are depraved! I can't believe I hang out with you.'

Dave and Christian laughed, then stopped abruptly. 'Sorry, Mary.' They lowered their heads a little, laughing to themselves.

'All right, well on that splendid note…' Our table fell quiet for a minute. Everyone seemed to reach for a cigarette at the same time—something to do to ignore the silence. I leaned back in the booth, my arm around Mary's shoulders, and relaxed. A woman passed us, pausing for half a second by our table. I checked her without Mary noticing. White heels and pants painted on by a brush dipped in shadows. The Scarlet Lady, who'd asked about EPs after looking at them for twenty minutes. I slid the Cas Lights in my pocket. She glided into the haze of the back bar, disappearing like a crimson ghost. As I took a drink, the jukebox seeped into my consciousness. A somber wail. A quick screech of guitar feedback. I strained to pick out the notes of the song, tapping my finger in the air.

'This is "Mayonaise",' I said, almost to myself.

'What are you talking about?' Mary said. 'You hate mayonnaise.'

'Not the condiment. The Smashing Pumpkins song,' I said. 'I haven't heard this in forever.' I remember exactly the last time I heard this song. The lighting, the smells, the context, the atmosphere. The sounds. That scream.

Christian's head started to bob. 'I have first-press vinyl of this at the store if you want it.'

'I bought the cassette tape when I was in high school,' I said. 'I put this song on every mix tape I made for years. We used to sneak out of my friend's house at night and get high, then put his mom's car in neutral and push it halfway down the street before we started it.' Christian sipped his beer to cover his grin. His mom would've killed us if she'd found out. I tried not to look at him, to keep from returning it.

Didn't work. Mary caught us. 'What are you girls giggling about now?'

'We used to make out to this song,' Christian said. Mary gave him a scowl that quickly turned to smile.

'I've been saying that all along,' Dave said.

'It's not gay if your eyes are closed,' I said.

'Don't worry, Mary,' Christian said. 'It was before he met you.'

'Anyway,' I said. 'That whole summer we'd listen to this album and stare out the window and drive around the neighborhoods. God, that was a great summer.' Morrissey Mason's breath on my neck. Smashing Pumpkins over Julian's stereo. Paul's raging, animal eyes, his pupils like black marbles. That kid. That poor fucking kid.

'Is this the video with the junkie couple,' Dave asked.

'Nah, that's Try, Try, Try. Different record, but a great song too,' Christian said.

'Disturbing,' Dave said.

'What is it?' Mary said.

'These two junkies steal stuff from grocery stores and bag-snatch, then the girl has to turn tricks so they can score,' Christian said.

'Lovely.' Mary didn't look amused.

'Then they shoot up in a bathroom,' Christian continued, 'and the girl ends up in the hospital and the guy runs around trying to find her. He eventually finds her in the E.R. and hugs her. Oh, she's pregnant the whole time, too.'

'And how is that a great video?' she said.

'It's beautiful. When you start seeing the lump in the girl's belly, the guy rubs it and talks to it,' Christian said, touching the curve of his bottle like it was a womb. 'Then when the girl's ODing she sees flashes of her and the guy as adults in suits and dresses and a little kid running around.' The chair leg swinging at me. The tingling in my elbow. The twinge of my finger against the trigger as the gun collided with the side of Paul's head.

'I knew someone who wanted to make beautiful things once upon a time,' Mary said, looking at me out of the corner of her eye.

Dave shook his head. 'I thought that was her parents.'

'I took it as them, because the guy was rubbing her belly and all. You have to read between the lines. The actors overplay it a little, but all they really want is a nice house with the two-point-five running around the yard.'

'Hmm,' she said in a slighted tone, squeezing my hand. 'All the two junkies want is a nice little family.' The scream. That scream. That poor nameless, faceless kid. *God, I'm so sorry. It was an accident*. 'Just like Kurt and Courtney, yeah?'

'Who else even listens to this anymore?' Dave said.

I turned to face the jukebox, but no one was standing there.

Chapter 5

January: Now

'Hobbs wouldn't kill her though, would he? Don't they go back a long way?' Christian lights his cigarette, then mine. He came home an hour late. I thought he was dead, too.

'Yeah, she introduced the two of us,' I say, exhaling smoke.

'If they have that much of a history, I'd find it hard to believe that he'd kill her. Especially if you're the one he wants dead.'

'But Hobbs is a crazy motherfucker.' My foot taps staccato on the hardwood floor, the same color as the tobacco in my cigarette.

'You don't know this, though. I mean, what have you seen? Or, you know, just what 'they' told you?'

I reach for the Jesus ashtray, pull my sleeve down to cover the cuts and scabs on my arms. How do you convince an atheist the Devil is real, and wants to steal your girlfriend? 'I've heard from reliable sources, or as reliable as you'll find in this business, that he's a nut. Mary has told me some things, too. I've never seen him do anything personally, but there's also the Twins. Usually I flake out if we have plans with him, so I only see him once every few months.'

'You, a dealer, only see Hobbs, your dealer, three times a year? I think you should have a more stable relationship, Damon. You're not selling Jolly Ranchers to kids on the bus.'

Hobbs. That gutless fucker. That scheming bastard. Even hearing his name drags nails across my eardrums. Does he want to kill me because I fucked him? Or does he want to kill me because he wants to fuck my Mary? Again. 'Mary maintains the relationship. They go way back like I said. He's a prick anyway and I never talk to him unless I have to.'

'All due respect man.' He pauses, bobbing his torso while he shuffles words in his head. 'But is she, you know—'

'No. She's no liability.'

'Are you sure? Don't get me wrong. You know I love her to death and all, but there's always—'

'She's straight okay? She has to be. I'm not worried.'

I'm not just worried. I'm gigantically fucking worried. Actually, I'm tight-roping between terrified and devastated. Worried is the light breeze drying my sweat. Mary wouldn't turn on me, not after all we'd been through, but who knows what Hobbs might do to her. A slighted man is an unpredictable man. If she's even with him now.

I crush my cigarette on Jesus' face in the ashtray sitting in my hand and put it back on the coffee table. 'You have anything to drink that isn't old eggnog?'

'Iced tea, Coke, and Brita are in the fridge. Gin and Jameson are in the cupboard over the fridge.' I walk into the kitchen and take a highball from the draining rack. 'I didn't mean anything by it,' he shouts to me. 'I'm just trying to look at all the options.'

'It's okay. Just drop it, all right?' Ice cubes clink into the glass and crack as I pour three fingers of whiskey over them. 'You want anything?'

'Gin and tonic. And a lime. Thanks.'

Breathe deep, press my palms against my eye sockets—get yourself together—try to wash all of this away with a mouthful from the bottle. Another deep breath, pinch the back of my hand, hard, almost until it bleeds—then walk back to the couch and hand Christian his glass.

'So Mary is straight,' he says, 'but Hobbs might still be nuts.'

I tip a finger and a half into my mouth. Squinted eyes. Whiskey-burn. 'I'd say more than might.' The sound of a watermelon cracking echoes in my ears.

'But the only thing we know is the Bajet incident. And we don't even know how true that is.' He leans back on the couch and sips from his glass, takes a drag of his cigarette.

'There's more than just Bajet.' My voice, just louder than breathing.

'That wasn't Hobbs and that wasn't your situation. It's completely different, so shut your fucking mouth about it.' He takes a long sip of gin. He has the same look that he had sitting on his porch in Amherst, smoking a cigarette next to his dad, the February when we were sixteen and his grandpa had just died of a stroke on their couch. That pained, faraway look, trying to arrange uncomfortable things into their place by ignoring them until they resign themselves to the sidelines.

'That's not what I'm talking about.' I can't even say that out loud. It drags me by the hair to some place darker than watching Mrs. Grady, Christian's mom, sit in the rectangle of carpet where their couch had been before she put it at the end of the driveway with FREE taped to the cushions, and organize the scraps of paper and pieces of popcorn and pretzels that had fallen between the cushions. Watching her walk through the coma she lived in for months. That feeling, but worse in a hundred different bloody ways. 'I heard about another guy.'

'Heard?'

'I take what I'm given,' I shrug. 'And I'd rather not find out firsthand.'

'So what's the word then?'

There was a guy called Freeze who used to work for Hobbs. Apparently, the guy had been messing around on Hobbs, cutting his product and selling it on the side—the usual stuff you get from amateurs in this business—and Hobbs found out.

'You know those compartmentalized showers? Like boat showers?'

'Yeah, sort of.' He pauses. 'Actually, no.'

I shake my head, start again. 'Basically, it's a sealed-off shower. Imagine that light-containment thing they used to hold the bad guys in Superman II, but as a shower and not as cool-looking. Hobbs stripped Freeze and the Twins smacked him around for a while with car radio antennae, then threw him in this shower and pumped in butane, left Freeze there for a while.'

Tiny bumps on my arm as I recount the story, can't even remember who told me.

'And?'

'What do you mean and? You know how bad that smells normally. Imagine being trapped in it for an hour. Good thing he was a huffer. Not to mention all the open wounds. Must've burned like hell.'

'You mean he lived through that?'

I nod. 'I told you, Hobbs is a sadistic fuck. Well, allegedly sadistic. Story goes, after he took him out, he waited for Freeze to become conscious again, then gave him a cigarette to say sorry.' Christian's face screws, wonders where this is going. Wait for him to try to work it out, then, 'Butane's heavier than air. It sinks. To the bottom of your lungs. And stays there.'

Christian half-laughs, shaking his head. 'So Freeze thawed.'

'From the inside out,' I say. I didn't believe it either when I first heard it. 'But, this is just water-cooler stuff. That's my problem. I don't know if any of this actually happened.' I look around the room, shuffle facts and incidents around, slide images over one another, try to concentrate on what's happened, try not to think about what else has happened and the ice in my drink is clinking against my glass again.

I pick at a piece of foam in the couch jutting between the stitches Christian had put through the fabric to keep it looking nice. My mother used to do the same thing, but she had a leather couch—because she could bring it to the house that she was going to buy in Malibu, she'd said—so there were all of these leather patches stuck on the cushions. I used to cut them out sometimes, to piss her off. Then she'd blame my father, accuse him of stealing her patches for the elbows of his tweed jackets. Pobrecita. The poor bastard. I would've felt bad for him, if he would've stood up to his bulldozer wife instead of acting like something torn from a jellyfish. He should've given her his balls as a wedding gift. It would've saved us the drama and her the energy of walking down the hall to my room to tell me what a waste I was, just because divorce was a sin and she'd married the wrong man. Everything's inevitable, and Christian's voice is coming from somewhere down the hall by my old room.

'What?'

'Could it be stories?'

'Could what be stories?'

'Could it be stories? Like a,' gesturing with his hand like he's rolling phantom dice, 'a psychological thing or whatever. Could he put out all these stories to make sure that people are terrified of him, so that no one would act up and he could kick back and relax?'

I bite the inside of my cheek and sway my head, doing psychological calculus. Hobbs is smart. He has to be smart to have made it this long. But is he that smart? Or that dumb?

'Yeah, he could.' What if he's more conniving than that? If God could make a rock so heavy he couldn't lift it, can the Devil outthink himself? 'But couldn't he also put out stories that he puts out stories?'

Christian raises an eyebrow.

I take a slug of my drink. 'Say that he is a real badass, but circulates these rumors that he's just a pussy and has no real pull. So, according to the same rumor, because he's this pussy with no real pull, he allegedly has to make up stories that he's a tough, Joe Pesci gangster-motherfucker so everybody will stay in line.' My glass drains clear. My brain is on fire, hand shakes. I really need a bump.

Christian stares for a minute, thinking. 'Yeah, I see what you're saying, but if he's not this fictitious pussy, then he'd be leading everyone to believe that he is, and that would make people more prone to challenge him, wouldn't it? That doesn't make sense.'

I give a mock smile and set my glass on the coffee table. 'It doesn't have to make sense. All it has to do is keep people in line and guessing. Maybe, because it doesn't make sense, he's even more dangerous. And anyone who would actually take the time to think, "Why would he make himself look like a bitch?" would probably realize there's some kind of psychology behind it. Even if we don't know what that psychology is. Hypothetically, that's what would make him so volatile. Because we don't know what he's thinking. And that's assuming that even part one of all this is true.'

Christian smiles. 'Just like Kaiser Söze.'

'Don't give Cocksucker that much credit. You'll disgrace that film.'

I pull another cigarette out of the pack with my lips and light it. My brain has folded its folds over each other like grey-matter Velcro, switching memories and thoughts from one hemisphere to the other, scrambling any logical train of thought.

'Look,' exhaling, 'we don't know either way, and I wouldn't put it past him to just tell Mary a load of crap to try and impress her. All I know for a fact is that two Leatherfaces in Italian suits chased me through Fell's Point, presumably to turn me into rat food. And I want to find out where my girlfriend is before Hobbs kills her.'

'How are we supposed to do that?'

'I don't…' I sputter, taking a breath and pulling on the tips of my hair. 'I don't know. I didn't come here to recruit you into some epic search and rescue. I just need a place to chill and sort things out for a couple days, and I can't go back to my place without an arsenal. He knows where we live. They know where we live. It's not safe.'

Christian puts his hands up, palms out. 'Chill, you know that you can hide here. At least you asked this time.'

'Fuck you.' In my head, I throw the highball at him, hitting the side of his face, then walk to the kitchen, pour him another drink and clink it onto his coffee table with a "This will dull the pain."

'Sorry. I didn't mean that,' he says. 'I take it you never told her about that kid?'

I don't answer.

'It was an accident, though, wasn't it?'

I shrug. 'Kind of defeat the purpose if I told her.'

The room falls comatose. The only sign that it isn't dead are the veins of smoke branching from the life support clenched between our lips. Christian takes a slug of his drink. The street-light outside flickers through the slits in the blinds. If I stare at it long enough, it might send an answer to me in Morse code. I fish into my pocket and pull out my medicine, snort three times hoping it settles everything in my head, and it occurs to me how much time the two of us have spent on couches—or the space where a couch used to be—sorting through the debris when our lives implode and someone dies or somebody leaves or you wish that one of them would just shut up, and it makes me want to turn Japanese and just sit on floor cushions to head off disaster before it finds my new address.

'Want any?' I hold out my stash to Christian.

He shakes his head. 'I don't think it'll help me any.'

It's quiet again. David Bowie stares at me from the wall. He doesn't have any consolatory words for me. I don't blame you, Dave.

'How much have you told her?' Christian says after a few minutes.

'Some.' I shrug. 'Enough.'

'Holy shit.'

'What?' I rub his grandfather's ring between my fingers.

'You've never told her about Michael, either, have you?'

Chapter 6

October: Then

'I hope you die soon.' Christian rolled on his side and put a pillow over his face. He showed up around eleven the night before with a bottle of Jameson and a soccer game for PlayStation. Half a bottle, a handful of pills, one game and twenty-three rematches later, he was crumpled on our couch, thinking he's dying.

'So you don't want any coffee then?' I stood over him, eating a cherry yogurt.

'Die.' He turned onto his back and pulled the pillow away, still trying to squeeze daylight away with his eyelids. 'I can't feel my face. Let me sleep.' His voice sounded like Louis Armstrong.

'I'm sure you can feel it. Caffeine will help.' I spooned yogurt out of the cup and held it two feet over his face.

'Caffeine killed little people,' he mumbled.

'Are you even conscious?'

'Mmphs,' he said. I tipped the spoon. The glob of yogurt landed with a plop on the side of his nose. I bit my hand so I wouldn't laugh. He lay on the couch like a hungover buffalo. Then my mind ran over the night before: the whiskey, the Codys, the mixing of them. A splash of anxiety broke on my face. I tried to push away the thought he might really be in trouble when I felt a bright white burning in my leg.

I fell on the floor, my spine rubbing over the wooden stripping. Christian was airborne then on top of me, the pillow headed for my face. My skull bounced off the wood and I put my hands up to keep the pillow from suffocating me, then I was on my stomach with my right arm wrenched behind my back.

'Motherfucker! It's gonna break if—' He twisted it further. Electric storms raged in my shoulder and wrist. I swung my other arm behind to try to smack him and turned the storm to a supernova. His mouth was next to my ear, stale whiskey breath coursing over my face.

'Dump yogurt on my face again,' he said. 'I could break your arm with just a little more pressure.' I tried to yell at him but only managed to drip spit from my lips. Yogurt touched the top of my earlobe. 'I'll let you go. Just say "I like little boys."'

'I like little—' He wrenched my arm again. A thousand hot needles jabbed my fingertips.

'Forget that one. Say "I want to have Patrick Swayze's love child" and I'll let go.'

'Fuck you. Break it!'

'Just have a kid with the Swayz and I'll give you your arm.' I could hear him grinning.

'Break it now!' He twisted a little farther, seeing how much he could hurt me before I would give in, then finally let go. I rolled onto my back, cradling my arm. It burned with blood. Mary sat on the bottom step, smiling. 'If I could move, I'd kill you,' I said to Christian.

'Your arm belongs to me now. I want it strong, like my coffee. Black, one sugar. I'm going to have a shower.' He wiped the yogurt from his face with a dishtowel and walked towards the stairs. 'You have any clean towels?'

I sat up. 'The Batman one should be clean.'

'If you don't mind supporting capitalists,' Mary said. Christian was an elephant going up the steps. 'You boys are so cute when you flirt,' she said to me as I pulled myself onto the couch.

'Callate, mujer.' She looked cute sitting there. I considered tackling her.

'So are you two going to become masons?'

'Sure,' I said as I tied my Docs.

'I heard you talking about bricks last night.'

I untied my Doc. Tied it again. Her statement stalked around the room.

'Yeah,' I said, putting on my jacket. 'He needs a second job so he can buy his building. I'm going to get coffee. Want to come?'

'What's that look for?'

'What look?'

'That look.'

'I don't have a look.'

Squinting her eyes, she said, 'What are you scheming?'

'I'm not scheming, I'm fetching. You coming or not?'

She sat on the stairs, fingers kneading her bottom lip. 'No, I'll wait here with Christian.'

I shrugged. 'Black or cream?'

'Doesn't matter,' she said.

'See you soon.' I leaned over and kissed her forehead. 'I love you.'

'Yeah, me too,' she said.

The raw wind bit my neck as I closed the door. Overhead, the sun dug its fingers into the clouds and tried to stop the coming storm.

Two hours later, Mary sat reading Rue Morgue in the office chair behind the DVD counter, eight steps from the stool where I sat. She'd disappeared into the office and emerged dragging the chair behind her, just to prove her point. We were close enough to have a conversation, but she refused to speak to me.

It was her fault, though. I'd told her to drop it.

After Christian had left our house, she'd asked—intentionally off-handed—if I had seen the letter from Megan. I said I had, that she had already shown it to me and pinned it next to the door. Then, wasn't the baby cute? I thought it was very cute, but how could anyone call a baby 'it'? I didn't know if it was a boy or girl, so I used a general pronoun, and I agreed that the name is a boy's name, but I didn't know it was called Nathan, and I felt the numbing in my legs that came before another fight about this.

And, yes, I could have stopped referring to it as 'it', because I knew the sex. And no, I didn't regard babies as things to poke or objects to amuse me. And yes, I thought I would be an all right father, just not yet. And no, I didn't know when yet was, but I knew that theoretically I should be a good husband before I was a good father, and it might've been the theoretically that got her. But most likely, she threw her coffee at me because I'd equated marriage with reduced health insurance premiums.

I followed her stomping upstairs and smoked two cigarettes while trying to coax her into a face-to-face conversation through our bedroom door.

'Mary, seriously. Just open the door.' I loved her more than anything, but was madly in love with my girlfriend. I wasn't trying to be an asshole, we just had different ideas. 'How are you going to argue about getting married when you won't even talk to me? Fuck's sake, it's like we're married already.'

She'd ripped the door open. It startled me and I dropped my cigarette. 'Talking through a door doesn't mean you're married,' she growled, then slammed the door again.

Chasing my cigarette down the hall, I called, 'That's because you didn't grow up in my house!' Something like I wouldn't know seeped from under the door. I blew dust from the filter and slumped against the wall. Beads of coffee dripped down our wall like a minimalist painting. 'Mary, c'mon.'

The door creaked opened. 'Do you really plan on doing this forever?' Her voice, strained, clawing its way up her throat. When she blinked, the corner of her eye leaked a tiny drop.

'¿Que me quieres dicer?' Why would I plan to argue through doors forever when I was the one trying to make peace? I stood, so we could look at each other's eyes.

'Damon, you know I don't understand what the fuck you're saying, so stop it right now. Do you plan on doing this forever? The store. Everything.' She paused, waited for me to respond. 'Do you really plan on doing this forever? Do you really want to raise kids like this? Do you really—'

'Not want to hear you start another question with "Do you really?" No, no quiero.'

'Don't start that—' she'd screamed, then breathed, reined herself in. She pushed words through gritted teeth to try to keep the exchange from exploding. 'Don't do your sarcastic defense-mechanism shit on me. How long do you plan on doing this?'

'I don't know.'

She looked at me, waiting for me to expand on my life plans. Our life plans.

'And?' she'd said.

'And… I'm not sure?'

Her chest jumped and fell. Hot breath coursed from her mouth, tiny bits of spittle at the corner of her lips.

'What? What do you want me to say?' I'd said, forgetting and crushing my cigarette under my foot. In the puddle of coffee. On the hardwood floor of our hallway. 'Yes, Mary, I want to close up shop—a shop that you own half of, by the way—close up shop next week but only after I know I've knocked you up—' words flowing faster to keep her from cutting in, '—then we'll get married fifty-three weeks from now so you can have your female universally sanctioned year of looking through Bride Guide or whatever the fuck the Necronomicon is called now and we'll live happily married ever after forever and ever, despite the fact that your parents, my parents, Christian's parents, and everyone-else-that-we-know's parents are either divorced, miserable, or having affairs. Actually, you know what, Mary? Fuck it. Let's just get each other's names tattooed in baby-daddy cursive on our biceps to give our relationship the pre-emptive kiss of death and save ourselves the trouble and lawyer—'

She'd stolen my train of thought and left me with a right-handed welt on the side of my face. I paused, shocked.

'What was that for?'

'To save your life.'

'What?'

'It was either slap you or stab you.' She swallowed, her subtle Adam's apple protruding like it did only when she was holding in a hurricane of tears. Her voice changed pitch when she spoke, her glass-cold demeanor cracking. 'I'm not getting tattooed,' she'd said. 'And you are the biggest fucking asshole in the world.'

'I'm not an asshole, Mary. I'm a realist. I love you, which is why I don't want to get married.' I tried to breathe, calm down, make my point without yelling. 'Marriage doesn't work. It's antiquated and oppressive.'

'You are a cocksucker,' she spit.

We stood, trembling, staring, our faces fighting each other to see which one would break first. Her breath was tremors, like a record skipping. The edge of her hands, ghost-white and gripping dents into the door handle. I'd started for a cigarette, then stopped. Started again, stopped. Two hundred million synapses in the brain, all firing at the same time, and mine couldn't make a single decision. Legs tingled that tingle, like life was being sucked from the bottom of my feet.

She spoke, quiet, rigid. 'What,' each word and syllable measured, 'do you want, Damon?'

'I want world peace.' What an asshole I can be. 'I want horror movies to not be remade. I want George Lucas—'

Another handprint, right over the first one.

'I'm not fucking kidding, Damon.' She ran her hand down the side of her face, like she had an itch. The edge of her palm glistened, the edge of the tidal wave hiding behind her irises. She didn't want to acknowledge that she was crying. Didn't want to let me know. 'What happened to all the shit you used to talk? Huh?' Her voice had slipped into mocking. 'All the movies now, they're shit. All the books now, they're shit. I could do better, I could do better.'

The jab made me step back. 'Hey, fuck you, all right. I could do better.'

'Then why don't you do better then?' Two more drops leaked from her eye. 'Fucking use some of that energy you waste arguing with Christian and do something! Something more than dealing.' She smacked her palm against the doorframe with each syllable.

'Well what about you?'

'What about me?'

'You run half of the store, remember? You're as big of a part in it as I am. And Fuckface seems pretty goddamned happy to have you in the business.' The rims of my eyes burned, blood bashed against the inside of my face, trying to get out. 'Or are you just trying to bring this self-realization shit on me to cover up something with him?'

Her face melted.

'Fuck. You,' she said. 'You haven't heard a fucking word I've said.'

'What?'

'Cheap shot, Damon. Cheap fucking shot.'

The tips of my hair blew back from how hard she slammed the door.

'All I'm trying to say is, we live together already, and you know that I love you, so what's the big deal? Look at Peter Parker and Mary Jane. They love each other and they're not married.'

She said something not English, didn't look up from the page.

'What'd you say?' I tried to sound defusing.

'I said, "Then go fuck Mary Jane."' If only she knew.

And then the store fell quiet.

I could hear the static electricity on the soles of shoes as customers walked in. The scrape of grains of sand as they slid Desperado: Special Edition, Donkey Kong Country, PlayStation consoles and gold charm bracelets across the counter for me to exchange. The rustle of each club flyer and napkin as they slid a Depeche Mode or Duran Duran CD in their back pocket. The hurried scuffle of rubber on real-estate-office carpet as they left.

She eventually went into the office, probably so she wouldn't have to look at me anymore. In between customers, I read the same five pages of a guide to contortionism for three hours. The words didn't make sense. Letters changed identities, reformed as phrases.

What do you want? I could do better. Forever. Marriage doesn't work. Kids are fine. All that talent. Forever.

People came and went. Exchanged necklaces for CDs. Sold vacuum cleaners and blenders.

What do you want? Forever. You haven't heard a word I've said.

If she was talking to me, meant it for me, in my opinion, we were okay. But if she was angry because of some unfulfilled desire on her part, I had nothing for her.

You haven't heard a word I've said.

Maybe I was being hard on her. I couldn't do anything about Fuckface's feelings towards her. If she said there was nothing then I'd have to trust her. But, what if I wasn't enough for her? Two regulars came back into the store because I'd forgotten to put the bag inside their CD case. Thankfully, I hadn't switched cases and given some little kid a gram of brown. I needed to get myself together.

What do you want?

Night bled into the sky and subdued the sun. The streetlights flickered on like old movie projectors and cast the city in a sodium-yellow pall. Jackets went on as day shift went home, some of them stopping by to grab product for the evening. One of the guys who bartended at Laughton's, the English pub by the water, didn't want the rest of his shrimp salad sandwich and left it for me. In the chaos of the morning, I'd forgotten to bring in something for dinner, and Mary wouldn't speak to me, much less watch the front while I got food.

A few teenagers came in while I ate, looking for props for their Halloween costumes. Brent slunk behind them, hunched like he regretted eating three burritos. He tried to straighten, to seem casual, as he dragged himself to the counter, wearing the same clothes—red Asics—as the last time I saw him. I wondered if he'd even changed them in the weeks since. The day was grating like sandpaper on metal down the rings of Hell. I nodded my head at him.

'Hey, Damon. How're things?' The skin under his eyes looked like two rotten orange slices.

'All right. You?'

'Oh, fine, you know, the same I guess.' His eyes, black pinpoints surrounded by a subway map of blood vessels.

I sat silent, watched the kids pick up random objects, and nodded my head. Waited for the inevitable.

'Hey man, um, I'm sorry to come in here like this...' He cringed in pain when he glanced over his shoulder, scanned the store. 'But, uh, I'm running a little late on payments and...you know how he gets. See, the bar's been a ghost town the last two weeks. I mean, I've really got tumbleweeds inside, and I tried to charge them but they just rolled out on me.' He laughed like it hurt. I missed his old laugh.

I sat, quiet. Smoked. My friend, the vinyl record, only working when there's a needle in him.

'Do you need money?' I spoke slowly, drawing out every letter, for lack of a better response.

'No, I should have enough in a day or two for, um,' he looked around again, lowered his voice, 'to pay Hobbs. But I was kind of looking for a little tide-over. You know I'm good for it. You know, tabs and all. Actually I wiped out your tab.' He spoke like Willy Loman, his defeated voice pathetically hopeful.

'I never had a tab, Brent,' I said.

'Oh, yeah, right.' His face dipped and inspected the carpet. The tallest one of the teenagers bought three old VCRs and an armful of blenders. He was going to be a killer robot from outer space. I didn't really get it.

The moths gnawed a hole in my stomach. I sucked in my lips, exhaled through my nostrils and muttered. He bobbed from foot to foot and managed to smile at the robot kids. I walked into the back—blue toolbox, "Master and Servant"—and dropped it into a CD case. On my way back, the cover of a Hubert Selby, Jr. book I'd brought in for Mary caught my eye. I took the bag out of the CD case and slid it between the pages, then crushed my half-smoked cigarette in an ashtray when I got to the counter.

'This will get you through the next forty-eight hours if you ration it, okay?' I felt like the dodgy uncle that smuggled him booze when his parents weren't looking.

'Okay. Yeah, totally. That's great, that'll be fine.' When he said it, his jaw moved but the skin of his face dripped towards the carpet.

'You need to start chilling out.' I held out the novel in front of him with my left hand.

'Oh yeah, definitely man, I know it, I know it.' He was too eager to grab the book. I caught his hand, clamped it in my fist and twisted. The bones in his ring and middle fingers rubbed against each other. I locked his eyes and wouldn't let go.

His irises flickered like projectors starting a reel. I watched us playing PlayStation at four in the morning, beer bottles scattered around his old apartment like dead soldiers. I watched us in booths at Sip&Bite, drinking metallic diner coffee and eating French fries, smoking cigarettes. I watched us staring out over the city as we drove his car without any real direction, just wanting to not be alone. I watched his body dissolve in a spoon with a lighter under it and disappear into a syringe as if it never existed.

I let go of his fingers, but held his eyes. Then, so no one else could hear, 'You should read this book. You might learn something, or at least—'

A hacking wheeze outside the front door. I looked over Brent's shoulder and saw a Cockroach butting out its cigarette on our front window.

'Fuck.' I grabbed Brent's wrist and yanked him around the counter, pointing to a spot behind the counter. 'Get over there.' He stumbled as I pushed him. The front door opened.

His eyes were hurt and I tried to tell him I'm sorry with a look.

The Cockroach slunk through the door, pulling a Samsonite-knockoff exoskeleton behind him. The wheels squeaked as they rolled. He looked as if someone had tried to drown him in a deep fat fryer.

'I wanna exchange this.' His voice sounded like a meth-head with laryngitis pinching their nose closed.

Brent coughed. I coughed loud a few times to cover him.

'It's a fantastic suitcase,' I said in a car-salesman-TV-commercial voice. 'You sure? You could probably get more money if you put an ad out for it.'

'I just want to exchange it, okay?'

'I have no problems with taking it from you. I'm just trying to give you all the relevant information.'

'I don't want information. I want you to exchange the suitcase and shut the fuck up.' His eyelids slid over the eight-balls in his sockets.

'There are a lot of people who don't know their rights as a seller. I aim to give the highest level of customer service and support.' In the corner of my eye, I could see Brent's legs curl against the counter, staying out of sight. Thank Christ.

His thorax heaved. The robot kids looked at each other, nervous. 'I'm losing my patience with you.'

'Don't get upset, my good man. This life is the only one we have and if we spend it upset, well that's no life at all, now is it?' I dipped my head for emphasis, like a preacher calling the Holy Spirit, and saw the paper towels on the shelf under the counter. 'Quoth the late Henry James: "It doesn't so much matter what you do in particular,"' I straightened the towel with my knee to read the rest, '"so long as you have your life." Great words from a great man that, I believe, if we take to our heart of hearts, can finally unify—'

'Take your fucking suitcase, Damon!'

I sighed as if he'd stolen the wind of God from the sails of my soul, and took the VHS copy of The Great Rock n' Roll Swindle next to my gun—holding my finger up to Brent, just a little longer—dropped it on the counter and slid it to the Cockroach. The robot kids hurried out of the store.

'Please, kind soul, heed the words I have giveth unto you and in the spirit of—'

He grabbed the case and checked for money under the tape, then coughed twice and spit half his lung on the floor, muttered, 'Every goddamned time.' As he crept out, I threw a calendar from Yummy Palace Chinese at his back.

'Learn how to fucking use it!'

He spun around, hissed at me, 'That's the last time. You're done. Say hi to Trevor, cocksucker,' then slammed the door so hard I thought it'd shatter.

'Fuck you!' I snatched a remote off the counter and hurled it at him, though there was no way it would hit him. It hit the glass with a gratifying explosion, plastic shards raining down on the carpet. As soon as he turned the corner, I went back around to the counter.

'God damn it.' I helped Brent up. 'I'm sorry, man. I didn't—'

He nodded and clapped his hand on my shoulder. I barely felt it. A meek smile and he shuffled like a Parkinson's patient after listening to "The Reflex", clutching the book like a Bible. He checked both ways before leaving the store.

I dropped a wad of paper towels to soak up the Cockroach by-product. You're done. Where was Christian's package? Behind me, Mary's belabored breathing. I squinted my eyes hard to compose myself, then turned around.

'I think that was completely uncalled for,' I said, sounding innocent. 'I was just informing the buyer of his rights.'

'What was that all about, Damon?'

'What are you talking about?'

'That.'

'What? He's a prick. Forget that guy.' Was she defending him, or Hobbs?

'I could hear you in the back. What did he do to you?'

'It's what he didn't do. He should've been here three days ago—'

'And assaulting him is going to encourage him to help us?'

'He's just a bitch, he won't do anything. And Hobbs is fucking up if you ask me. I'm so over all of this. He doesn't have enough supply. He's never on time. I know he's your friend, Mary, but forget it. We can do better somewhere else.'

'No, Damon, we can't. We've talked about this. We can't kill Frank and start calling ourselves Scarface.'

'Why?' I yelled, louder than I meant.

'Don't fucking yell at me like that!' Her voice cracked. 'You know how it makes me feel!'

'I'm sorry, but I don't have to give a shit about him just because you do.'

'For someone who says that right now is all that matters, you have a hard time letting go of my past. Do I give you shit for who you've been with? No, because it's not important.' She took a deep breath. 'Damon, it was more than ten years ago. I am with you now.'

'Well at least you two kept in touch.'

'Fuck you. You do realize that if it wasn't for him, we wouldn't have jobs.'

My lungs shriveled into raisins. Breath, evaporated.

'You mean I wouldn't have a job,' I choked out.

'I didn't say that. I said we.' She grabbed my hand, harder than I think she meant to, and tried to look at me without spitting. 'We're in this together, for better or for worse and all that other bullshit. We need him. This store doesn't sell enough and we can't keep the doors open without his supply.'

I imagined Hobbs in a leather recliner chair, wearing a suit from a designer he couldn't pronounce and smoking French cigarettes in an Art Nouveau holder. He sipped Scotch from a crystal snifter, a candid snapshot of Mary looking beautiful inside an ebony and gold-filigree picture frame on the polished rosewood table next to him.

In my head, I dropped my face on his and gnawed until it was hamburger.

'If all we need is supply, we find someone else—'

'Damon.'

'—then give me one good reason that we can't say, "Fuck you, very much. Thanks for coming out." Just one.' I felt something squish in my hand and looked down at the roll of paper towels creased in half.

'The only way anyone leaves Hobbs is in a dumpster, except for us. Since we're special, we can quit the business. Because he likes us.'

'Fine. Tell him we're out of business, then.'

She opened her mouth, a shout caught halfway up her throat. 'What are you saying?'

'Tell him we're done.' Even if Christian wouldn't go for it, I'd find something.

Her fingers knitted the air like she was holding mine. 'You want to get out?'

'No, but we'll tell him that and find someone else,' I said.

Her face imploded. 'You fucking prick. It's final. We're not leaving. We can't. Because it's Hobbs.'

'Fuck that. You can't because it's Hobbs, and you're choosing him over us.' Those words were the car in Thelma and Louise. As soon as I stepped on the gas, I knew it was stupid and I was going to die but I couldn't turn back. That car drove right into Mary's heart.

Her bottom lip quivered. She placed her magazine on the

counter and started for the office. To stay out of grabbing distance, far enough away that I couldn't wrap my arms around her and tell her I was sorry. That I didn't mean it, I was just angry.

'Mary.' Words and phrases and consolations flew around my head, but nothing found its way down to my lips. Open-jawed, mouth full of dead air. She paused, turned towards me. She was coming back, knew I was just angry. I took two steps forward, then stumbled against the counter as her fist connected with the side of my head. The office door slammed. A hot wet trickle from where she hit me. My fingers touched it. Sweat, not blood. She should've gotten a better hit.

I left the store without saying anything. My brain ran too fast to form any coherent sentences, and even if I could have, Mary wouldn't have listened to a second conversation through a door in one day.

Down Broadway towards the water, I headed to a pub where I wouldn't be bothered. Two Indians played thick bamboo flutes into microphones, huddled in the abandoned doorway next to the Brick Oven Pizza shop. The generator powering their speakers droned underneath sedated techno-remix beats. Their songs were probably updated versions of old spirituals. Songs they'd play before going to war. Melodic pleas for good health or prolific crops. One of their friends hurried around the group of tourists, hocking CDs for fifteen a pop.

Across the circle of people surrounding them, I saw Melody.

Everywhere you went in Smalltimore, you were bound to know someone. It was like that in Amherst, but it's expected in a small town. Going back had crossed my mind, but the thought was as fleeting as it was appealing. Mary wouldn't be there. No one would believe my name was Damon, either. And even though Julian was the top guy—pretty much the only guy—and I wouldn't have to worry about anything, from other dealers or the law, the place was too small to avoid people I didn't want to see. Eric and I had speculated that Julian had something on the cops. He didn't throw it around, though. It was more in the cool way he sauntered, the way he left a pound-and-a-half pyramid of white sitting on his desk. No one in our group used straws or bills then. Just dropped our heads and inhaled until we were someone new.

After listening for ten minutes, I needed a drink more than a spiritual epiphany and snuck away before Melody tried to rape me.

99 Red Bottles was a cave: dark, quiet, and exactly what I needed. A vaguely familiar guy called Poe stood behind the bar. Brent had told Poe he was sick and asked him to cover. Tea candles in red glasses lit the few tables, and a recessed light shone down on Poe, picking at his nails with a butcher knife. Two of the five people inside were already comatose on their tabletops, streaks of still-wet disinfectant under their palms. Billie Holiday bared her soul in the Wurlitzer jukebox between the doors to the men's and women's bathrooms, and in that space I could see a painting hanging, a mechanized goldfish with a pneumatic ridge running down its spine. I shook away the image, sipped Jameson and smoked, watched the hypnotizing flame flicker.

Back when she was in high school, Mary dated a guy called Trevor for a while, after she'd ended things with Hobbs. If I'd known her then, I would've told her he was a douche just from his name, that anyone slapped with that label can't be held liable for the douchiness that results. I gathered that Hobbs had told her something similar, but Mary persisted. At some point, the relationship went wrong. Mary's never spoken about it explicitly, but from snippets of conversation and inference, I cobbled together the picture that he either beat her or got her pregnant or got her pregnant then beat her. Whatever actually happened, I know that Hobbs did in fact confront him, and Trevor ended up in the ICU with a decimated ocular cavity and the end of his arm bone jutting through his skin. I would've thought that relationship would throw a blanket on Mary's family fire, but maybe I was underestimating the fuel those flames fed on.

Or maybe I was approaching the whole thing the wrong way. Maybe it wasn't a problem with Mary, but with Hobbs. Hobbs, who bought her bracelets and necklaces. Who called to ask her to go to the movies. Who flashed a fist of bills to insinuate that he was John Holmes. If I could stomach him long enough to conduct business, I could take away opportunities for him to flirt with her. And if he disliked me anywhere near as much as I couldn't stand him, talking to me would piss him off, which was an added bonus.

Then again, maybe I was the dickhead:

Not yet, Mary.

Some point in the future, Mary.

What's the point, Mary?

What's your name? I'm Damon. It's very nice to meet you.

Of course I love you, Mary.

Christian, you shouldn't call me Michael anymore.

Maybe she was right. She didn't even know my real name. What was my problem?

Everything's inevitable; I ordered another round.

My third pint was half clear, head down in a candle-flicker trance and my face Irish-flushed, when a chair at my table moved. I didn't care, didn't bother to move my head when someone sat. I smelled jasmine.

'Hello, Damon.' I knew it was the Scarlet Lady before I looked up. She wore a deep blue version of her scarlet dress. Maybe it was black, I couldn't tell in the light. Her voice sung when she spoke, but the underlying rasp said she liked handcuffs, biting and role-playing.

I tilted my head up. She had three freckles in the shape of a triangle at the corner of her right eye.

'Hi.'

'Where's your friend?'

'Store. Working late.' The cherry glass made her blonde hair flame. I blew smoke from my nose like a cartoon bull.

She drew a slender cigarette from a gold case, engraved with a baroque floral design to match her lighter. Flicking fire, her hair became blonde for a flash, the top of her eyelids swathed in the blue of an electric shock. Her lips left pale prints on her cigarette. Teeth, tinted by wine. In my head, I watched Mary and her for a few seconds. Then got jealous and told her to leave.

Echo and the Bunnymen came on the Wurlitzer. 'I've always loved this song,' she said. She spoke in a hushed voice, as if any of the other four people now in the bar gave a shit about sugar kisses or what we were saying.

'Yeah, it's good.' I tipped my pint and watched her distort through the bottom of the glass.

We listened to the song, though I barely heard it. My brain ran equations trying to understand why she was at my table. She wasn't trying to take me home. I didn't think.

After a few minutes: 'I'm sorry, how rude,' she said. 'My name is Isabela. You can call me Bela.'

'Like Lugosi.'

Her lips stretched into a smile.

'How about Izzy?'

'I'll slice off your testicles.' She sipped her wine, casual.

'Like, Izzy Stradlin' from Guns 'n' Roses.'

'I hate Guns 'n' Roses.'

My face went mock-astonished. 'You have no soul.'

'You have no idea.'

In my head, I ripped her dress and threw her taut, pallid frame on top of the bar, spilling drinks that dripped down her thighs and pooled at the back of her knee.

I set a cigarette between my lips. In her palm, a black and gold matchbook emblazoned with the shop's logo materialized from nothing. Or maybe the whiskey was catching up.

'Come in and pawn when the welfare is gone.' She tapped the tagline with a painted nail. 'A bit cynical, no?'

'Just good marketing.' I shrugged. 'It's catchy.'

'So how is your store, Damon?'

'Fine.'

'Why don't you sell EPs?' She slid the filter of her cigarette along her bottom lip, locking my eyes.

'We do,' I said, though I had a feeling she wasn't looking for vinyl. 'You saw them. For five minutes.'

'There's a lot of money in EPs, you know.'

'I run a secondhand store, not a record store.' A drunk at the next table sat up, hiccupped, knocked over his glass then dropped his head back to the table.

'I know. It was just an observation.' She swirled the wine in her glass and took a small sip. 'I took your suggestion.'

'Which suggestion was that?'

'I visited Jet Black.'

'Did they have what you wanted?'

'Mostly.'

I took a long drag of my cigarette, nodding my head as equations started to balance then teeter again.

She motioned to my forearm. 'Get that in jail?'

'Never been. It was a great idea when I was fifteen.'

'What is it?'

'Remember that song "Lounge Act" by Nirvana?' I said. She shook her head. 'Basically, Kurt Cobain got a tattoo of the K Records shield on his forearm to impress a girl.'

'And you got it to impress him?'

I smiled. 'Something like that.'

'Too bad he's dead.'

'So it goes,' I said.

'I like that book, too.'

My eyebrow rose. She smiled. This girl was quicker than I

thought. The drunk next to us snored a slow rhythm. I tried to think of a Slaughterhouse Five joke.

'Your friend, Christian, right?' she said.

'Huh?' I drew a blank on Billy Pilgrim.

'The tall man. Wears a black shirt, jeans and Vans every day. He owns the store?'

'Oh, yeah. That's him.' Her quick—and odd—change of subject short-circuited my hormones.

'He's very helpful. Very knowledgeable.'

'I'll make sure I pass on the nice comments.' I motioned to Poe and ordered a pint of Yuengling and a glass of wine. She lit another cigarette, sipped her wine. I sat and chewed on the inside of my cheek. 'So,' I started, 'without being rude, can I ask what is it that you want?'

She feigned surprise. 'What do you mean?'

'Why are you talking to me?'

'Am I not allowed to start a conversation with a man I find attractive? I can't imagine you've never been approached by a woman at a bar.'

Melody and her dead eyes. The queue of China Girls, trading BJs for CDs.

'I have a girlfriend, you know.'

'I do. Such a shame. We could have been lovely partners.'

'Yeah, bummer.' I leaned back in my chair and tried to look comfortable. She wasn't trying to take me home. She didn't seem like she was trying to score. No mention of horror movies or superheroes. Ask Mary, there weren't any other reasons to talk to me.

She tasted her wine again. 'Though, maybe we still can be.' She slid her hand over the table to mine, picked it up and drew it to her mouth. Swollen crimson lips, aching to be bitten. Her eyes rose to mine. She spoke into my fingertips. 'How much do you know about EPs?'

'Do you remember,' she said, 'how you felt the first time you heard your favorite song? You've had the worst day. Your dog was run over, you failed a test, one of your grandparents died, your high school girlfriend broke up with you and your best friend stole your stash. You pull the razor away from your desperate wrist, get out of the bathtub and collapse in your bed. Your arm flops to your side and turns on your radio, and you hear the song that was pre-destined to be on the station's playlist right at that moment, because God or whoever knew your life depended on it. That artist had had the inspiration to arrange the melody, the words, the accompaniments, in that specific way. That song grabs you and makes you feel complete. Complete in a way you can't bear to describe to anyone because words would taint the very concept of completeness.

'Imagine hearing that song five years later, lying in bed again. You're next to a beautiful girl and you're falling in love to that song. The planets are aligned, the woodland animals are dancing, and Victor Lazlo doesn't mind you taking that ticket to get out of Morocco.'

I nodded, barely. My fingertips tingled.

'Now, dry that feeling into powder and scrape it into a gelatin capsule,' she said. I drew my hand back from her lips, her breath seeping into my pores, and pulled a cigarette from my pack. Her lighter was at my face again, and I smoked with my finger pointing up towards my nose, smelling her jasmine.

'I've heard of it,' I said, trying to be Bogart-cool.

'That's what Mr. Ashe and I are offering, and with the possibility of a two hundred percent mark-up. Along with the usual requisite products at market value, of course.'

'That's a very nice offer. I can't make the decision on my own, though.' The carbonation in the beer popped on my tongue. In my head, my grin overtook my face as I smashed in the side of Hobbs' head with his whiskey decanter.

'I know. Consider our offer. The Black Gardenia, a week from tonight. Half past nine.' She dropped her cigarette case into her purse, like a chic 1920s house-call-doctor's bag, and stood to leave. 'You won't even have to close early.' I looked up at her, silhouetted against the backlighting.

'Why EP?'

She smiled. 'Because it all started with a song.'

She picked up a napkin from our table and pressed it to her lips, then set it in front of me. A goodnight kiss, guilt-free.

'Until then.' When she walked, she glided. Her skirt slid over her body but her legs didn't appear to move. She walked through the door, towards a man in a shadow across the street, derby hat tipped over his face.

I lit another cigarette then downed half of my pint in one gulp, set the glass next to her lip prints. She'd crinkled the napkin when she kissed it, and as I flattened it, two slices of her lipstick disappeared. It looked like she had fangs.

Chapter 7

October: Then

The sandman had stolen in during the night with chains and a pipe wrench. He found me on the couch, then went Jason Voorhees on my ass. Despite walking around hunched like an old man, sleeping in the car would've been worse.

At the store, 'Help him please,' 'I'm not thirsty,' and 'Thanks, you too' were the only things Mary said to me all morning, and I wasn't sure if the last was to the guy who said 'Have a nice day' or to me when I told her that the shirt she was wearing looked nice on her. I alternated between chipper—hoping to make her smile—and staying clear of her until she wasn't angry anymore. Part of me was tempted to start saying crazy things or orgasmically eat a candy bar, just to get some type of reaction out of her.

Every time the front door opened, I hoped and feared that it was Isabela. My brain was already running like a hamster chasing a hundred crumbs through the Labyrinth, and with Mary acting like a mime, it wouldn't have been a good time to bring up the possibility of switching suppliers. Besides, what did she mean "something more than dealing"?

All of this shit about Hobbs, it never happened with Julian. I was his golden goose, his cash cow or whatever other gilded farm animal you value, and he took care of me. The white cigarettes—my idea. My intellectual property that I brought to Julian's operation. At Fast Feet, the shoe store where Eric and I worked, I figured out a way to distribute green. People asked me for green Nike Air Force Ones, a color we never carried, and I told them we were out of stock. They'd say, 'That's okay, I need to get some shoelaces anyway,' and give me twelve, twenty-seven or fifty-two dollars and walk away with some laces and a bag of green. A two-dollar service charge and three pounds of shoestrings sitting in their dorm room was fine with them, because they knew that if they came to me, I could always supply them. I even convinced the slug who owned Fast Feet that we sold so many laces because they were gang signs. Both of those, the white cigarettes and the green laces, they tripled sales and cut the risk in half. Fuck's sake, the first time I met Julian, he put a hundred-dollar bill in my pocket, just like a retainer. And I didn't even work for him yet. All of that stuff I brought to Hobbs. And what did I get? Snarky comments, late shipments and an annoyed girlfriend.

My stomach spoke up around two in the afternoon.

'I need to eat before I die,' I said to Mary. 'I'm feeling a burrito. Can I get you something?'

Dermaphoria, Charactered Pieces, City of Glass, and *Transubstantiate*—all books I'd brought in for her—sat underneath three celebrity magazines next to her feet on the desk. A fourth had stolen her attention, or so it would seem from the way she'd posed herself. Her eyes weren't moving, though; she wasn't reading. She didn't even like those kinds of magazines, only knew that I hated them.

'Okay. Well,' drawing out the word, trying to figure out what to say next, 'the store is slow. Did you want to watch the front or should I lock the door?'

More silence. I wanted to put a mirror under her nose, to see if she was breathing or just a statue of my girlfriend.

'Right, then,' I said. 'I'll be back in a few.'

Twenty minutes later, she was in the same position, but there was a tack stuck in the bottom of her right boot. Setting down the bag, I tried to conceal my smile. She'd been bored of staring at the magazine and walked around while I was gone.

'Anything interesting happening in Hollywood?' I pulled two burritos from the bag, set one where she could reach it without moving, started to unwrap mine. 'I got you chicken, with salsa, no sour cream or cheese and low-fat guacamole. In case you got hungry at some point.'

Her eyes flicked up to me, then to the burrito, then back to her magazine. 'Thank you,' dribbled from her lips.

Three minutes of silence. Her stomach growled. Still, she wouldn't move. I wiped my mouth with a napkin, set my burrito down.

'Can I ask you something?'

No response.

'Okay, I'll ask it anyway and if you want to answer you can.' She looked at me. I was making progress. 'What did you mean when you said "Do something more than dealing"? When we were…talking yesterday.'

Her nostrils flared when she exhaled, weighing the benefits of staying silent and making her point that much further. She started to speak, then coughed, clearing out the cobwebs and getting things in her throat to move again.

'What did it sound like I meant?'

'That I should do something more than deal.'

She dropped her eyes back to the magazine. This seemed like it was going to be a rhetorical conversation.

'What did you mean, though?' I was a pupil talking to my Zen sensei: ask a question, get a nonsense answer, then answer it myself.

She sighed. 'What did it sound like I meant?'

'Could you be a little more explicit? Look, I'm sorry we fought, but I'm trying to see what your point is and help. You know, meeting halfway and all that.'

Her eyes narrowed, the animal sense that could anticipate an attack before it happened. 'I meant that you used to do a lot of things, and talk a lot of shit, and now you just talk shit,' she said. 'And the difference between those two is huge.' She fell back into her magazine. The oracle had closed.

'Okay.' I stood. 'Thanks for the talk,' and I went to the front.

What was I supposed to do? Go back to college, get a hold of some paintbrushes, buy a Porsche. Sell all of our stuff to finance a film. I wasn't the only one who was accustomed to our lifestyle. Dealing wasn't the best gig—and definitely not the safest—but it was a job. And, if we switched to Isabela and Mr. Ashe, we'd have EPs, which would mean more money, which would mean more time that we could take off. There'd be no worrying about shipments or dealing with Fuckface. This was the way to cut all of our problems off at the knees, kick them down the street and into the Inner Harbor. EPs were the answer.

Halfway through my burrito, I heard foil crinkle in the back as she tried to eat without letting me know. It wasn't much, but it was a start.

In bed that night, after she fell asleep, she rolled over to my side and curled into me. I hoped it meant that I was forgiven.

I brought her coffee and orange juice, scrambled eggs, baked beans, sliced tomatoes and toast in the morning, to apologize for fighting. We'd had that for breakfast at Laughton's a few months before, after a whiskey night. Maybe I was being a dickhead. If Cocksucker could get EPs, we'd have the product to get the money to have the free time to help our relationship. Granted, I'd still have to deal with him, but I wouldn't have to bring up a bad subject with Mary and risk another—possibly lethal—fight.

After we ate, we got dressed, brushed our teeth, and then got undressed again. We lay in bed and opened Stay Gold two hours late. Even with her draped naked over me and snoring softly into my neck, though, EPs kept spinning in my head.

The front of the store was a drainage pond for the sludge of Baltimore. Junkies, grifters, club kids and hipsters swirled around, waiting for the door to open and funnel them inside. Across the street, three kids sat on the charred stoop of a building that had burned from the inside. Within the first fifteen minutes, we made almost twenty exchanges and sold ten or twelve CDs straight out.

My mind still floated somewhere between the inside of Mary's thighs and Isabela's proposition and I was totally unprepared for the onslaught. Two NARCs browsed through video games. One picked up Tomb Raider for PlayStation, asked go now? The other signaled not yet, wait for backup with Mortal Kombat for Sega. A guy with blue Chucks, ripped jeans and a denim jacket wandered aimlessly, with a sense of purpose. Like he could become anonymous before he made his move. A tall guy picked up a toaster, coughed into the inside of his elbow. The elbow pointed out, arm at ninety degrees, so his people were around the corner. What was his signal? Looking at a toaster…bread goes in, toast comes out… Watch for a white guy with a Sallie. Maybe an Italian. I said 'red, buckles, Vans, blue, black, Nikes, Docs, laces' to myself so many times that I couldn't remember which shoes went to which person. Identities changed hands as quickly as the product. A kid with a pompadour ordered a "Master and Servant" and by the time I came back to the front he'd aged fifty years and was buying a new vacuum.

'We need to get everyone out of here now,' I said to Mary.

'It's fine, chill out,' she shrugged. 'What are you so worried about?'

'That guy,' pointing to a kid about twenty-four with black Vans, spiky black hair. 'I've never seen him before. He's got something going with her.' A blonde girl with red babydoll shoes flipped through the records, occasionally showing one to her friend in white Keds.

'They're not even talking to each other. Or looking at each other.'

'Of course they're not. If they spoke, the gig would be up.' I lit a cigarette. 'Watch her. She'll show something to her friend, then the friend'll signal to the guy. Look at the name of the album. It has to be the code.'

Mary shook her head, trying not to smile. 'Okay, I'll watch out.' The guy with blue Chucks stood in line behind a woman with video games. A Cocksparrer pin flashed on his lapel.

'Don't patronize me, Mary. I'm serious.'

The white cap of his shoes gleamed under the lights. There weren't threads at the heel of his jeans, as if he'd never walked on them. The edges of the holes on his knees were two-washes frayed, only five or six white threads dangling. His hair piled unkempt, but in an intentional way. He made me uneasy.

'Anything I can help you with?' I said to blue Chucks.

'Yeah, I think so.' He glanced to the side at a Weedwhacker he'd never use. 'Nice store you've got.'

'Thanks.' He was either a cop or a poseur.

His eyes wandered around the store, still canvassing things he already had at home. His hands were steady, fingernails clean and trimmed.

Cop.

Shit.

'So, what can I help you with?' I gave the most reassuring smile I could muster, shoved my hands in my pockets so he couldn't see them twitch. We'd only had one CD transaction since I noticed him, and the client wasn't very notable. Hopefully, Poseur Cop hadn't noticed.

'I was looking for a CD,' he said, tipping his eyes over my head and to the corners of the room, mentally cataloguing everything he could about our store. Mary demonstrated how to use a cassette tape player to some little kids.

'And which CD would that be?' I checked the reflection on the register screen. Thankfully, Mary had closed the door to the office. As long as she'd put everything in the emergency pit this time, we'd be golden.

'I don't know. I was hoping you could help.' He smiled a showroom smile. 'Something that could chill me out.'

'Ah, something chill.' I nodded my head as if I knew just the thing, suddenly feeling a bit cocky, wanting to show off to the line growing behind him. 'Yeah, I might have something for you.'

The showroom smile turned smug.

'Cool, man. How much?' His hand went to his back pocket, for his wallet. Or cuffs. Or gun. Or just to put his hand in his back pocket and strike a rock-n-roll pose.

I shrugged, breathed deep without looking like I was breathing deep. Mary looked over to me, cocked her head and nodded as if to say, "If you're so worried, shut the fuck up and get these people out."

'Depends,' I said.

'On?' He leaned forward—I could confide in him, give him the real deal. Speak loud and articulate so the mic behind Cocksparrer would pick it up.

'Whether it's new or used. A double CD. An import.'

'Ah.' He looked disappointed, like he wouldn't have to work so hard. 'Actually,' he checked over his shoulder, smiling at the woman glaring at him, 'I was looking for some real ace CDs. Know what I mean?' Then he winked.

First, jack-off, nobody said ace around here and second, unless you were James Dean or Paul Newman—Cool Hand Luke-era Paul Newman—you don't wink.

'Oh, right,' I said, nodding my head. 'I'm sorry then. I have no idea what you're talking about.'

He tried to smile. 'Okay, cool. I'll try back later.' After he regrouped, reported everything he'd seen to his superiors.

'Right on. Have a nice day.' Mary set the tape player on the counter, shook her head and laughed.

A Goth girl in thigh-high vinyl boots paid for three records, asked for EPs. I grabbed Mary by the armpit as I ducked through the curtain into the back.

'Hey! I was doing something,' she said.

'We're going to get hit soon. That guy was deep blue.' Over her shoulder, I watched the TV monitor while I talked. 'Everyone needs to go outside and line up single file. It isn't safe like this.'

'You're worried about avoiding attention and you want to line people up when you think an undercover cop was just scoping us?' She laughed. 'It'll be an addict welfare line. I know you're just being cautious, but chill the fuck out. You're too paranoid.' She reached around and grabbed my butt, tried to make me laugh. My eyes were on the monitor.

'Hey!' she said, snapping her fingers. 'I'm trying to seduce you here. You could at least pay attention.'

'He was a cop, Mary. I know it.' I lit a cigarette. 'At least, I'm pretty sure.'

'Look, it'll be fine. Wait for a bit and everything will settle. I promise.' She brought my hand to her lips. 'And if you're still freaked in twenty minutes, we'll close and have a siesta or something. Okay?'

I swallowed, watched the kids flip knobs on the tape player. Poseur Cop's men hadn't come around the corner. The video game NARCs hadn't crashed our party either. And we'd sold a lot of CDs already.

'All right,' I said. 'Twenty minutes. And we need to get our sign fixed. One of the letters burned out.' If Mary hadn't been there, I would've gone through seven rolls of film for our bible.

By the afternoon, the degenerates had found somewhere else to slowly kill themselves, and the store finally calmed. Red and yellow leaves blew past our window. Gusts of wind flipped up the collars of coats. Fall had killed summer and was lulling the world into sedation for winter to take us without a fight. I asked Mary to watch the front while I made a phone call.

'Who are you calling?' Her cheeks were still flushed from the morning's glow.

'Cocksucker,' I said. Her face drooped, the glow evaporated. 'Sorry, force of habit. I'll be nice. I promise.' She pleaded with her eyes. 'Hey,' I slid in next to her, stuck my hand under the back of her argyle sweater. 'I said, "I promise." Okay?'

Her lips bent into a tiny smile and mouthed *okay.* I leaned in and kissed her, then again harder, and slid my hand up her back to unhook her bra. She snorted when she laughed and tried to pull away, smacked my chest and bent her arm behind her back to grab my hand. 'Stop it, you pervert.' She laughed and dismissed me with a wave, said, 'Go gossip, Cathy,' then kissed me, slid her hand down past my waist and squeezed. 'And remember we need costumes by tomorrow. Brent's Halloween party is only two days away!'

I plopped in the office chair and laid the cordless on the desk. Deep breath, exhale, deep breath, exhale. I felt too cheery to call Hobbs, so I reached down to a red toolbox and cracked it open, pulled out a "Hungry like the Wolf" single then glanced at the TV monitor. Mary was rearranging the jewelry. She picked out a ring and tried it on, splayed her fingers wide like she was Holly Golightly. Put her stretched hand in the middle of her argyle, oh thank you, it is a lovely ring isn't it. Then she yanked the ring off and looked around as if she'd been caught. I mumbled 'I am the dickhead, I am the dickhead, but I am the dickhead with EPs' so she would think I was talking on the phone.

The single went back in the box. I dialed his number, felt like I should've been dialing 976-EVIL. It rang five times before he picked up.

'Hello?' I hoped he was in the bathroom and had to pinch it off and rush to pick up the phone.

'It's Ponyboy,' I said. Every store had their codename. No one was ever who they were, and you weren't supposed to know who anyone else was.

'Ah, my boy.' His voice drilled like teeth into the back of my skull. 'How is everything?'

'Fine. Busy.'

'How is your stock level?'

'All right. For the moment. The truck finally came yesterday.' And every action wasn't what it was. A truck only delivered one suitcase and returned with a VHS case holding thousands of dollars.

'Did everything arrive? Nothing was broken?' But the worst part of the code-talk was the banal comments he threw in. He'd taken all my ideas from Amherst and expanded them to ridiculous proportions.

'No. Everything is intact. We liked the delivery so much we'd love one every week.'

'Patience, my boy. Things at the home office are busy. We're busy ironing out the kinks in our forecasting.'

'Right. See what you can do for us.' Mary had indirectly told Cocksucker—after one of our alpha-male skirmishes—that if anything ever happened to me and she found out that he was even remotely involved, she would claw his eyes out and never speak to him again. Even though I had some liberty after that, I still had to watch what I said because he was a sneaky fuck. If I said me instead of us, I'd see the Twins as likely as I'd see a Cockroach. After my 'accident,' Mary would need someone to hold her up during my funeral and he'd slither right into place.

'Of course. You're one of the best stores. I look out for all of my employees.' I thought hamburger and breathed, the urge to strangle him with a phone cord subsiding.

'I'm calling to see about a new product. See if you have it in the sales catalogue.'

'What product is that?'

'Electronic Programming Servers. Supposed to be the hot new gadget this winter.' He stayed silent. The breath coursing in and out of his nostrils made me pull the phone two inches away from my ear.

'I don't know if it's in the catalogue. What are the specs?'

'It's like being God. You can create your own universe with the server. Like the SIMS games, but they're cavemen compared to this new one.'

'Do you know who manufactures these servers?' he said. I paused, thinking, trying to remember what manufacture meant. We didn't get new products very often so I was a bit out of practice. 'Hello?'

'The same company that makes the Adams products.'

'Do they come from the same production line?' Production line? The bells over the front door clanked from far away.

Right, production line. 'No. They're servers. Servers that make you God.'

'Hmmm,' he muttered to himself. There was a man at the counter talking to Mary. I wiped away dust on the monitor with a pencil eraser to make a beard on him while Hobbs fucked off on the other end of the phone.

'Well? Do you have it?'

'It's showing up in our catalogue, but—' He wasn't going to get them for us. Because I asked him. I knew I should've told Mary to ask. I tried to appease her by dealing with him and I get bent over for the effort, '—I'm not sure that it's a sound business move.'

'Why?' I exhaled hard. 'It's going to be big this season. I…we frequently have customers asking for them.'

'I'm not convinced that it's not a fad.' I tried to remember my promise to Mary.

I pushed 'it's not' through my teeth. It's not a fad. It's not a phase. It's an opportunity to make a lot of money off a lot of dumb people. 'Trust us.'

'I'm sorry. I'm just not convinced. I'd hate to order 5,000 units and the demand turns out less than what was projected. We can't return 3,000 units unused on account of not having the demand we had forecasted.'

I pressed the ring into my breastplate, hard, to make it hurt and divert my brain from screaming at him or saying anything that could be possibly incriminating. Breath rushed through my nose. I dug my hand in my pocket.

One Cody. One Cameron. Chewed and washed down with some Merlot Christian had left in the office last week.

'Well then,' I said, slow and measured. 'Thanks for looking.

Deliveries are on Sunday. Send out a memo if you have to remind your people,' then clicked the phone dead and rocked on the chair; back and forth, back and forth, back and I hurled the phone across the office. An explosion of plastic shards and batteries. My head dropped and hands went to my temples and squeezed, grabbed handfuls of my hair and pulled, almost ripped it out. Mary rushed into the office.

'What was that? Are you all right?' Her hand, cool on the back of my neck. I blinked my eyes like camera shutters, so angry I was almost crying; I didn't know what else to do. I'd tried, but I was fucked.

'No EPs,' I whispered.

'What? Sweetie, what's wrong?'

Turned my head, tilted it up to her. 'There are no EPs,' I said. 'Nothing.'

'Babe, we have records up front. Christian has more if we need any.'

'No…Mary…I,' I sputtered, then sighed and patted my palm on my left knee. She lowered herself onto my thigh. 'Can you give me a cigarette, please?' She pulled a pack of Casamirs from the desk drawer and lit two, handed one to me. 'How many times has someone come in and asked for EPs? In the last few weeks.'

'I tell them the records are in the milk crate at the front.'

'No, Mary. EPs. Not records.'

'Aren't they the same thing?'

'Not anymore.'

She giggled. 'Why do you sound like a Steven Seagal movie?'

I didn't smile back. 'Mary,' I said. 'Close your eyes for a minute.'

I told her to imagine her favorite song, falling in love, and God's kiss.

I told her about the aligned planets, the woodland animals, and Rick and Ilsa's new apartment.

I told her that EPs weren't just on vinyl anymore.

I explained what all of those people really wanted.

She readjusted herself on my thigh, her back against the wall. 'Fucking hell,' she exhaled.

'We're in it,' I said. We sat and smoked until the cigarettes burned our knuckles. I patted her back. 'My leg's asleep.'

'Sorry.' She stretched her arms out. 'So what do we do?'

The words "fuck him" almost slipped out but I closed my lips and swallowed them to my gut for later. 'I don't know. It could be a lot of money.'

'Money isn't always everything.'

'Thank you, Hallmark Movie of the Week.' I looked at her face, said, 'Sorry, I didn't mean that. We'll figure it out.' I hung my arm over her shoulder and we walked to the front of the store where she pulled out the stool and opened another book I'd brought in for her. *Kiss Me, Judas*. Fitting. The fallen leaves blew down Broadway while I stood by the front door. Different scenarios of how to tell Mary about Bela ran through my head like news headlines. I watched them, looked for one that wouldn't get me killed.

I waited until we'd cleared the dinner dishes from the table to bring it up. No potential projectiles.

'Didn't we just discuss this?'

'Sort of. But situations have changed.' Her eyes said that she was trying to remain calm, to have a civil discussion. Hopefully, the sentiment would last.

'No, Damon,' she said. 'Nothing's changed.'

'Okay, this is what I don't understand.' I paused, shuffled through words for something logical, feasible, and, 'Why?' was all I could conjure.

'Why what?'

'Why are we still with Hobbs, keeping in mind that there is another viable option available to us, and that option fulfills all of our needs.'

'Please don't start talking like him. I hate that business jargon shit.'

'I just don't understand why we can't switch. We can get all the usual stuff at the same price. We can sell the EPs for at least twice as much as we pay for them. And we won't have to worry about Cockroaches not showing. It's perfect, Mary. Even I couldn't screw it up.'

'Damon, I'm tired of talking about this.' She breathed deep to try to remain calm. 'We are committed to Hobbs.'

'It's not like we signed anything. ¿Que hace él? Sue us for breach of contract?'

'Speak English.' She took a sip of wine. 'I'm trying not to kill you for bringing this up again. Don't antagonize me.'

'Sorry, but really, what's he going to do?'

Mary slunk in her chair, palms massaging her face. She let go a long breath, spread her fingers around her eyes and stared at some point behind me. 'Do you remember Joe Bajet?'

'The Hoser who OD'd?' She nodded her head. 'What about him?'

Hesitant, she said, 'He didn't OD.'

I stayed silent.

'Hobbs got word that Bajet was going to defect. He confronted Bajet about it and Bajet denied it. So he followed him. Watched who Bajet dealt with, where he went, what he did.' She took a mouthful of wine, squinted as she swallowed, then continued. 'He put two and two together and figured out that Bajet was going to defect to this other guy. Simon, I think his name was. Small-time guy. British accent.'

I lit two cigarettes, gave one to Mary. Tried to hold her hand, but she pulled it back.

'So Hobbs set the Twins on Simon. He went to see Bajet personally, brought him back to his basement and duct-taped him to a mattress.' From somewhere between bemusement and horror, an almost-smile started to surface. 'Hobbs thought he would be kind. Since Bajet had a habit, Hobbs didn't want him to go through withdrawal.' The cherry crackled as she pulled hard on her cigarette. 'So he would get Bajet real high, then give him nothing for four days. But each day between those shots, Hobbs injected him with diluted antifreeze. It wasn't enough to kill him, just make him really sick. Then he'd force-feed Bajet Ipecac, to purge some of the antifreeze. Didn't want him to die, you know? After two weeks, he started feeding Bajet normally and giving him stuff to make him better.'

'But Ipecac wouldn't get rid of the stuff in his veins.'

'Biology has never been Hobbs' strong suit.'

'Why did he do all that then take care of him?' After I asked, I wasn't sure I really wanted to know the answer.

'Because once he was strong enough to stand, they shot him up till he couldn't move, put a White Power shirt on him and stranded him in Whitelock. Let the locals take care of him.'

Somehow, I knew she was going to say something along those lines. I sipped my wine. 'At least he didn't feel it,' I finally said.

The phone on the counter rang. She turned and looked at it, then ignored it. I didn't move, just said, 'How do you know all this?'

She shrugged, seemingly cleansed after getting the story out. 'It came up in a conversation.'

'How does that come up in a conversation?' I said. 'A conversation about us?'

'No.' Her tone said "you dumbass". 'There was speculation that another guy, Freeze, was going to defect.'

The answering machine picked up. Christian's voice. 'Dude. Call me. Now.' Shit.

I spoke before Mary could say anything. 'But you never actually saw Bajet or any of it?'

'I'd be scarred if I saw that.'

'Then how do you know it really happened?'

'What do you mean?'

'If you didn't see it happen, then how do you know it really happened?'

Her face screwed up. 'Who the fuck would lie about that? Jesus, who would want to be known for doing that to someone?'

I shrugged my shoulders. 'Hobbs,' I said. 'And if it's so horrible, then why are you still friends with him?'

'Because we are.' She shook her head and exhaled a long breath. 'I'm done talking about this.'

'Mary, just be reasonable.'

She killed the rest of the wine, straight from the bottle. 'I said I'm done.' Then she walked out of the room.

I ran numbers on her explanation. Even if Hobbs wasn't a homicidal maniac, I could probably spark those types of tendencies in him, but he'd never touch Mary. And I thought Brent had said he'd seen Bajet after he OD'd. Bajet had a habit, so most likely he'd OD'd more than once.

'Hey,' I called to her. 'I'm going to visit the Virgin. Do you want to come?'

'Are you going to continue to bother me?'

'No.' I meant it as a statement but it came out more as a question.

She gave a noncommittal grunt.

Sitting on the wooden bookshelves in the couch room was a statue of Our Lady of Guadalupe Mary covered in 80s pink felt. I closed the curtains, dotted with Pop Art prints of Andy Warhol, and fished a pack of rolling papers from the drawer of the wooden coffee table, set them on a stack of DVDs. Mary sat next to me with a fresh glass of wine in her hand that would likely leave her with a stunning headache in the morning. I stuck my fingers up the Virgin's dress and pulled out a bag of green. We rolled a joint, then made fire from the barrel of my pistol lighter. She sat next to me, but leaned against the side of the couch. I laid my arm around her. She didn't move. We sat—together, separated—passing the joint, and spaced out to *Goodfellas.*

Mary was snoring against a pillow on the armrest by the time Tommy shot Spider. I spun the lighter around my fingertip like I was a cowboy gunslinger, my other hand laid on her hip. Thumbing through a copy of GQ—the mailman had delivered it to someone who used to live at our address—splayed open on my lap, I imagined what John Wayne would've been like in *Goodfellas* instead of Paul Sorvino. Would Hobbs really do any of that stuff? My eyes traced the contour of Mary's breasts. There had to be a way to win her over.

If Mr. Ashe had a security team, they could watch Mary and me. I could find Hobbs' address and give it to Mr. Ashe. He could send his people to visit Hobbs. Mr. Ashe would get additional stock while eliminating competition, and I would take care of two problems.

I could be an extra big dickhead to Hobbs and hope he fired me. Hang up every time he called. Burp in the middle of whatever he said. But he wouldn't fire me because of Mary. Even if I was in the way, he knew that Mary was with me and he had to slither his way around that.

I could kill Hobbs. Him and his Twins. He wouldn't expect it from me. Arrange a meeting, say I wanted to smooth things out between the two of us for the sake of business. Just like *The Godfather*. The Twins would have no reason to search me. I would state my case to Hobbs, offer solutions and concessions, express remorse at how bad things had become, then give him a .357-inch third eye. Pop the Twins before they knew what happened. We'd have access to the home office and could set up our own distribution company. It would play out perfectly. But I couldn't murder anyone.

There had to be a logical way to get around it. Mary had to see that Hobbs was puffing his chest and/or trying to impress her like a barbarian so that he could lovingly drag her around by her hair. She had to see how much better our lives would be with Mr.

Ashe. No more stressing about late deliveries, no more snide comments about Cocksucker. No more worrying about anyone trying to fuck my girlfriend.

I ripped a subscription card from the magazine and grabbed a pen to make a list.

-Call Brent tomorrow. Find details of the Bajet incident.

-Find out anything Brent knows about Hobbs being a psycho.

-Go see Christian. He's smarter. He'll have an idea.

-CONVINCE MARY I'M RIGHT WITHIN 5 DAYS!!!!

Chapter 8

November: Then

I should've been an architect. Or a stockbroker. Or a detective or a plumber or a librarian or even the fucking Muffin Man. Anything but this.

Standing behind a scratched-up counter in a shitty neighborhood. Slinging product to ungrateful lowlifes who rushed to our store faster than bums to a bologna sandwich. Having guns pointed at my head by halfwits who almost used their real names by accident because they were caught up in the excitement. Bargaining with whatever deity was popular at the moment so that our pre-scheduled shipment would actually get delivered when it was supposed to. And lapsing into Sam Spade moments just to reinforce my girlfriend's faith in my judgment.

'Brent, it's Damon. Again. I need you to call me as soon as you get this message. I have to ask you a couple things. Please call me, Brent. It's important.' Seven messages in three days and no answer. Two days until meeting Isabela and I had no answers. I dug my hand into my pocket.

One Cody, one Cameron, chewed. There was nothing to wash it down.

I coughed and tried to make spit in my mouth, swallow the unchewed bits before I vomited them up. My watch said it was almost one. We'd probably stay busy for another few hours, then I could go and get Christian's take on everything. On the TV monitor, six or seven people were in the store; a few of them were genuinely interested in purchasing something, the others milled around until they felt comfortable buying or exchanging. Two men in Ravens jackets leaned against the counter and talked, a stack of DVDs sitting by the register. The one with the mustache like an obese caterpillar stared at Mary's chest while she checked the discs for scratches. He'd turn his head back, as if he hadn't been staring, and continue talking, then stare again. I jammed the phone in my back pocket and walked to the counter, wrapped my arms around Mary's waist and glared over her shoulder at him. She jabbed me in the ribs with her elbow.

'I'm trying to do something.' She'd been irritable since the EP conversation. We hadn't even gone to the Halloween party. Our Michael Myers and Jamie Lee Curtis costumes sat at the bottom of the closet. The Mustache smirked and muttered something to his friend.

'Make sure they're not blank discs. Can't trust these people,' I said, scraping to save some form of masculinity.

She put down a disc and exhaled a short, annoyed breath, smiled like she was biting the inside of her mouth. 'Thanks, dear. I'd forgotten after these last four years.'

The two guffawed and my crotch sucked itself into my lower intestine.

I really should've been an architect.

I exchanged fifteen CDs and sold thirty more before the sun abandoned us. It was only Wednesday and we were already scraping the inside of bags for extra. We'd be dry before the weekend. Mary muttered 'whatever' when I told her I was going to meet Christian for a few minutes.

Tiny clouds of condensation grew from my mouth as I walked to Jet Black. A random cold front had attacked the east coast during the night. It wasn't deadly cold, just not November weather. Within three days, it would probably be sunny and 72 degrees. Viva Maryland weather. I pulled the collar of my peacoat closer to my neck and blew steam into my hands.

A voice that had swallowed a can of nails sung "Hound Dog" in the brick square by the water, where Broadway collided with Thames. A crowd of tourists, jaundiced by the sodium street-lamps, clapped and whistled. At the center of the tourist circle, a bum in a grey suit styled by Freddy Krueger's fingers tried to dance on his toes like the King and slurred 'hound dog' with some other random syllables. He stopped a minute later and the crowd clapped louder. When he smiled, his lips split like a stale baguette, crumbs of skin sticking to the gangrenous shards wedged randomly in his dark gums.

'Hanks y'all. I'm Blelvis, the Black Elvis. Come back tomor an I'll have Blibberachi.'

Kids in winter jackets dropped coins from their parents' pockets into the accordioned tophat by Blelvis' feet. He tried to teach a sandy-haired boy in Teenage Mutant Ninja Turtle Velcro shoes how to dance on his toes.

I left Blelvis before he started Blelton John and turned down Thames towards Jet Black.

'Hey, Mister.' A kid in a FUBU warm-up suit who looked like he was still in single digits stood in front of me. Black, white and red Air Jordans. He pointed at his friend leaning against a wall, trying to look tough.

'Buy us some Black Hand?'

'Sorry, I'm broke,' I sputtered, trying to avoid saying something vile to a pre-pubescent hood rat.

'We gots money.' He rifled his cavernous hoodie and exhumed a crumpled and stained ten-dollar bill. 'Only nine dollars. Keep the rest.' I imagined myself doing a favor for some random kid and walking out of a liquor store in handcuffs.

'Don't think I can.'

'C'mon, man. Thought you was down.'

Who the fuck was he? 'Sorry, kid,' and walked off.

'You faggot,' he yelled behind me. 'That faggot tried to grab my dick!' I sighed, dropped my head and watched the cobblestones pass under me.

When there is no more room in hell, the dead will walk Fell's Point.

Eventually, I made it to Jet Black. Christian had already left for dinner. Matt sat behind the stickered counter concentrating on the computer, camouflage hat resting on his lap.

'Is he eating out or coming back,' I asked Matt.

Matt shrugged.

'Do you know where he went to get food?'

Matt shrugged.

'Do you know how long ago he left?'

Matt looked at his wrist, shrugged.

'Do you fucking know anything?'

Matt shrugged.

I lit a cigarette and paced in front of the counter, stared at the ochre walls.

'What the fuck are you looking at anyway?'

Matt shrugged.

'Are you watching porn?'

Matt stayed still.

'You're watching porn, aren't you? That's why your hat's in your lap.'

Matt spoke. 'No.'

'What are you looking at then?'

'Nothing.'

'If you're not looking at anything then why aren't you speaking?'

'Nietzsche.'

'Nietzsche?'

Matt nodded. 'Vow of silence.'

'When did you start reading Nietzsche?'

Matt shrugged.

'You don't even read instructions,' I said. 'You saw that in a movie didn't you?'

Matt stayed still.

'Enough of this bullshit.' I clenched my cigarette in my teeth and vaulted over the counter. Matt stared at me mid-air, then jerked the mouse, the button clicking like a nervous heartbeat. I stuck my head next to his before he could close the last window.

'You're an online dater?' I laughed directly in his ear.

'Shut the fuck up, man!' He closed the last window and pushed his stool at me. 'You don't even know what you're talking about.'

'Bullshit! I saw that.' I put my hand on his shoulder.

'Dude, you don't even know. There's some hot girls on there.' He walked to the other side of the counter, took two of my cigarettes. I sat down on his stool.

'You really think that they're girls?' I exhaled a little laugh and leaned against the poster behind the counter. I'd never seen it before. Morrissey loomed large over me, his tongue curled out like a frog and I was the fly in front of him.

Morrissey Mason. "Mayonaise". That poor kid.

'Just wait, man. One of them is going to come in here one time. You'll try to hit on her and she'll say, "Sorry old man, I'm with him." Just wait.'

'Who's going to say she's with you?' Christian had walked through the door during Matt's defense plea.

'And fuck you,' I said to Matt. 'I'm only three years older than you are.'

'Who's this fictitious woman, Matt?' Christian set his food bag on the counter.

'Her name is Anastasia.'

Christian and I shook our heads. He looked at me. 'What are you doing here? Don't you have a store to run?'

'Mary's watching it. I had to get out.'

'Ah, so.' He dug two napkins from his bag and tossed them to Matt. 'Tell Anastasia we said hello. And don't get anything on the keyboard.' Miles Davis, Turbonegro and The Stone Roses watched us from the walls as we opened the door between Blues and Rock n' Roll.

Album covers from The Clash, Rancid, Johnny Cash, and At the Gates hung on the mahogany-colored walls, posters from

Evil Dead, Vertigo, Straw Dogs, and *The Cabinet of Doctor Caligari* interspersed between them. Each frame, perfectly level, the space between them equal. I used to tilt the album covers when he was stocking records, to see if he'd notice. Until he threatened to decapitate me if I did it again.

'So what's happening?' He pulled a foil bowl from the bag, let out a mushroom cloud of steam as he took the lid off. 'I've been trying to call you.'

'Sorry, I've been busy. I need to talk.'

'So,' setting a carton of steamed rice next to his Kung Pao chicken, 'talk.'

'What do you know about Hobbs?'

'Nothing really. Why?'

I rehashed the Cockroach problem, the lack of infestation. I told him about his favorite song, God's kiss, and Isabela. I speculated on Hobbs, Mary and the Bajet incident. He chewed his chicken, listening.

'So what do you think?'

He picked up the carton of steamed rice, speared chunks with his chopsticks. His eyes drifted around the room while he chewed, looking for an answer or analogy hanging on the walls.

'That's shit.'

'Could you be more explicit?'

'That's really shit.' He smiled. 'Do you believe Mary about the Bajet thing? Or rather, do you believe Hobbs about it? Does anyone else know anything?'

'Brent mentioned something once, but I can't get in touch with him,' I said. 'They used to, uh,' smacking the vein in the ditch of my elbow, 'hang out.'

Christian nodded, pointed behind him with his chopsticks. 'Go to his bar.'

'I'm headed there. He was sick a couple nights ago when I went in.'

'Sick sick, or just sick?' he said. I shrugged my shoulders, not wanting to get into it. 'I guess my vote,' through a mouthful of rice, 'is to see if Hobbs is lying and make a choice. Either stay, or go.' He swallowed his rice, washed it down with iced tea.

'That's not very helpful.'

He shrugged. 'Call the Ed Norris Show then. Write Dear Abby. I just sell records. But if you do switch, don't forget about our little deal.'

I laughed. 'What deal?'

He tapped the chopsticks on the desk, squinted one eye. 'I vouched for three bricks.'

Reaching for his tea, I coughed, paused. The oscillating fan, quiet in the front of the store. 'Are you sure?'

He looked around the room, chewed on his lip.

'Well—' hesitating, my feet tingling like fighting with Mary '—you need any money to front?'

'We're all right. It's family business. Just make sure you plan for your weekly brick.'

'One a week?' I said. 'I thought it was a one-time thing.'

'You said keep getting them and you'll keep buying them.' He dropped the rice on his desk, leaned forward. 'And I wasn't sure about it but you kept telling me I'd be able to buy my store with the money. Sound familiar?'

'I'm not backing out on you. Just thought you didn't want to get into the business.'

Lighting a cigarette, he tossed me his pack. 'I don't, but I did anyway. I didn't have much choice.'

'Yeah,' I said. The molecules of air tripled in size and I could feel the weight of each on my skin as we went quiet. To change the subject, I said, 'How's your mom doing?'

'Fine. Talked to her a few days ago. She sends her love,' he said. 'And asked if you quit smoking yet.'

'Did I ever tell you she used to smell my breath when I'd come over for dinner? After you moved down here.'

He laughed, shrugged. 'You can't hide anything from that

woman. She knows everything you do, even before you do it. Freaks me out sometimes.'

'Tell her I'm trying to quit.' Once, before I came to Baltimore, she was walking across the parking lot and Eric and I had a carton of cigarettes in our hands—to package white—and like an idiot I waved at her. She told me how stupid it was and threatened to take back the ring if I didn't quit. Eric had snickered, and she lectured him, too, even though she didn't know him.

I grabbed a chunk of rice with my fingers, shoved it in my mouth. He yanked the carton away, face turning upside down. 'You know how many germs are on your fingers?'

'Sorry.' I licked my finger and stuck it into his rice again, then opened the door. 'I'll call you later.'

'Fucking barbarian,' he shouted from the office.

I passed Matt, back on the computer. 'Good luck with Athena.'

He groaned. 'Anastasia, dude. Anastasia.'

I pulled my collar around my neck again and headed to 99 Red Bottles.

Someone had dragged Brent out of *Night of the Living Dead* and through a field of burning tires, then dropped him into designer jeans and a striped black shirt behind the bar. He slouched on his forearms against the blond bar top, head hanging between his biceps. It rose like from the grave when I called his name.

He looked at me, vacant. The rotten orange slices under his eyes had grown into putrid grapefruit. 'Holy shit,' I said, louder than I meant. 'You look like death.'

'Working for Poe,' he said, making an effort even just to speak.

'What's wrong with you?'

'Sick.' Veins breached on his forearms. A blind man could have read the scabs cascading from the crook of his elbow like Burroughs in Braille.

'Obviously.'

'What are you drinking?'

'Seriously, are you going to die?'

He breathed like there was a railroad stake wedged between his ribs. 'I'll be better soon,' with a meek smile.

'Kicking?'

'It is.' He laughed and sounded like a bagpipe with a shotgun hole in the bellows. 'And I'm trying to.' At least the sickness was positive.

'Should I come back later?'

He shook his head. 'Pull up a squat.'

I draped my peacoat over the stool then sat on it. Brent and I were the only souls in the place. He lifted a glass of tomato juice to his lips. 'The closest I could get to soup,' he said.

'Renton would be proud.' I lit a cigarette and pulled an ashtray next to my wrists. 'Tell me again about Joe Bajet.'

His face tried to screw up, but only his eyebrows managed to move. 'Canadian. Junkie. OD'd. Dead.'

I smiled. 'Now, that's my problem. I heard a slightly different story.' I rested my cigarette in the nook of the ashtray then walked around the bar to pour myself a soda. 'I heard that Hobbs OD'd him. With antifreeze. Then gave him an all-inclusive to Whitelock.'

Brent wheezed a laugh. 'That's pretty different from what I heard.'

'And therein lies the problem. You said you saw him before he died. When was that?'

He stared at the sagging ceiling. The red light inside the smoke detector blinked like it was on the nod. 'Few days, I think.'

'Are you sure?' I sipped my drink.

'That it was a few days? I guess. I don't really remember.' His voice evaporated into my smoke.

'Right, right. But it wasn't, say, a month, two weeks?' I leaned forward and knitted my fingers together, like a lawyer trying to nail a witness. 'You saw him pretty soon before he died?'

'I don't think it was that long. But, I sort of lose time, sometimes.'

I couldn't count on Brent's brain to pull up exactly what Bajet had worn or what he smelled like, but the gap between a few days and two and a half weeks seemed big enough even for him to be able to tell the difference. 'How do you know Hobbs? Are you a way station or just a client?'

'Both. Well,' he paused to sip the blood-colored pulp from his glass, 'distributed a little, but mostly client. And,' crossing his charcoal-pencil fingers, 'nothing after this. Pay him back then tell him to fuck off.' His fingers cracked as they untwisted. I smoked and ran my eyes over the remains of my friend.

A man works in a liquor store, hocks bottles of rotgut to every walking case of cirrhosis. Another man works in a quickie mart, doles out packs of menthol 100s to wheezing old grammas. A third man works in a junk shop, slings product to a never-ending line of the afflicted with pincushion arms. Who was the bad man, and did any feel the guilt I did?

'Do you know anything else about him? Does the antifreeze thing seem right?'

He shrugged. 'Same water cooler bits as you.'

'Like?' I leaned forward.

'Strung a guy up and painted a dart board on him.' My eyebrow rose. I didn't like where this was going. 'Had Manhattans while they played. Twins used lawn darts, Hobbs had regulars. He'd had more practice.'

'Did you see it?'

He shook his head. 'Jesse told me. The one who's obsessed with Fulci. Works corners by Washington Ave.'

'Yeah, I know him. I think he's killed about all his brain cells.'

'You don't mistake something like that. He said Hobbs did it, he did it.'

'So you think the antifreeze is possible?' Which would mean

all the other stories are possible.

'Mary told you about this?'

I nodded.

'Then I'd say it's probable.'

I sipped the rest of my drink. Brent looked like shit. The years of slamming needles hadn't treated him well, and I wondered what the inside of his head looked like, if it was as bad as his skin. Human bodies are terribly resilient, and despite our best efforts to destroy ourselves, they keep regenerating. I doubted his cognitive processes were quite so reliable.

He tipped his head to the side, inquisitive. 'What's with all the questions, Damon?'

'Independent research.' I walked behind the bar and dumped my drink into the sink, then washed the glass and put it back on the shelf.

'For?'

'An independent party,' I said. 'Heard anything else?'

He frowned, thought, shook his head. 'The usual. Drive-bys. Hot-shots and stuff. Doesn't strike me as the drive-by type, though. Too hood-ish.'

I pursed my lips. 'All right. Thanks for the info. Good luck with the kick.'

'Yeah.' He let his head fall back between his biceps.

Brent said self-induced. Hobbs told Mary antifreeze. Jesse said dartboard. I called bullshit on all of it. Two weeks was too big of a gap for Brent to mistake, even considering the external influences. Mary didn't say anything about Hobbs letting Bajet out of the basement until they took him on a tour of Whitelock, and if Bajet had managed to get out of Hobbs' lair, there was no possible way he would have stayed in Smalltimore, lest someone see him and he wake up dead.

A bum materialized from the night at my side. His face looked like someone had molded it from grey clay, then punched his cheeks and didn't bother to fix it. 'Look, man, I ain't gonna lie. I need a drink.' The swish of his iridescent polyester tracksuit quickened as he tried to keep up with me. 'Can you help me, brother?'

I pulled three dollars and two Codys from my pocket, stuffed the pills back in, and handed him the money.

'Actually,' I said, digging in my pocket. 'Get something to eat, too. You look like you're going to die.' I handed him five more and a cigarette. 'For after your meal.'

His clay face stretched upwards and he started to junkie-hop away when I grabbed his wrist. 'Hey man, what the hell?' His eyes darted for an exit.

'If I see you in ten minutes and you're high, I'm going to beat your ass,' I said.

'You ain't one them gays, is you?'

I shook my head, almost laughing, then walked away as he took tentative steps in the opposite direction.

Stay Gold was full of ghosts. Standing between two cars, I watched Mary dust the empty store. Though she cleaned a lot, she only dusted when something was wrong. I looked at my watch. Twenty minutes to figure out how to approach her, defuse her. My brain strained itself throwing scenario over scenario, picking them apart and recombining them. Mary and me. Mary and Hobbs. Isabela and Hobbs. Hobbs and me. Isabela and me. Mary and Isabela. The sum total of our equation was Damon equals fucked. Something nudged my back.

'You want a flyer, man?' A mass of jacket shoved a shiny rectangle at me. 'It's at the Patterson Theatre tomorrow night. Five bucks and they serve beer.'

I took it and watched Mary again. She leaned against the jewelry counter, her head down and hands on the back of her neck. Tiny splats hit the sidewalk, like Christmas lights thrown from the roof. A wet drop on my cheek. I scraped it with the flyer.

The drop slid onto the flyer and soaked into the paper, a tiny crater bulging from it. 'AD' distorted with the water. I held it up into the neon glow of STAY GO_D.

Dawn of the Dead. Nice.

Not only the original, but my favorite of Romero's also. Mary and I could've gone out to eat before catching the movie, if she was through hating me by then. Under the title sat the yellow zombie head from the poster, the tagline underneath:

When there is no more room in Hell, the dead will walk the Earth.

Hey Mister.

When there is no more room in Hell, the dead will walk the Earth.

Nine dollars. Keep the rest.

When there is no more room in Hell, the dead will walk Fell's Point.

That faggot tried to grab my dick!

I could've kissed that little piece of shit.

Two cars screeched to a stop as I bounded half-blind across the street, tasting heartbeat in my throat. The door almost shattered, I burst through it so hard. Mary startled upright.

'Jesus Christ! You asshole! I thought someone was robbing us!' I ran behind the counter to try and grab her. 'Get the fuck away from me!' She stutter-stepped back against the wall.

'No, babe, everything's cool. We're going to make it!' I spoke so fast I wasn't sure if she could even understand me between gasps.

'What are you talking about?'

'Here. Sit.' I pulled the stool to her and ripped off my peacoat, tossed it into the corner.

'What is wrong with you? Are you high?'

'Sort of. Not really. Sit. Listen.'

'Complete sentences, please.' I ignored her sarcasm.

'I fixed our problem.' I was almost bouncing. '*Dawn of the Dead*. Hey Mister. We're set!' She didn't say anything, just stared like I was the Invisible Man unraveling myself. 'Okay. We buy the EPs for, say, two dollars—'

'Damon,' she sighed.

'No please. Just listen. Say we buy the EPs for two dollars or whatever. Apparently kids are going so crazy for them that we can sell for two or three times what we buy for. So we buy them for two, we can sell them for six or seven.' She started to open her mouth, but twisted her fingers around her chin instead. 'I don't know how much they cost but it doesn't matter. We can figure it out later. So if we made four dollars off each EP, we can set aside a dollar or two for Hobbs. Like a severance package. He'll still be getting his money and we won't have to worry about all the other crap. Christian has some bricks, but we can give him some of the EP money. Or we'll buy one and he can sell the others. It's not important. We'll be better off. You and I, I mean.' I stood in front of her like a puppy waiting for a treat because I'd pissed outside.

She was silent.

'So,' I said. 'What do you think? It's perfect. Everything will be okay. We won't have the stress. Hobbs will get his money. They probably sell for ten or fifteen anyway, so he can get four dollars for every EP.'

Her right eye leaked.

'I thought you'd be excited. Think of it as money for the future.'

'I said I'm done talking.'

'But this will work.' The shrillness in my voice made me want to hit myself in the teeth with a bottle. 'Babe, I figured it all out.'

'Damon, don't make me choose.' She went into the back room and I followed.

'Choose what?'

She grabbed her jacket from the desk and walked past me toward the front door.

'Mary,' I called out. 'Choose what?'

She paused by the door and stared at me for seconds that stretched into years. I counted heartbeats and crashing waves of blood.

'Just don't,' she said, then she left.

I stood paralyzed against the wall. The hemispheres of my brain fused with a tiny twist of smoke. Stared at…the wall? the floor? the bikes?

Fifteen minutes passed before I realized that we had ridden to the store together. I grabbed my jacket, pulled a green and white striped scarf someone had left in the shop tight around my neck, locked the door and started walking into the night.

Chapter 9

January: Now

The overhead light glints off the blade of the knife. I press my back against the wall, an arm's length from the middle of the door. With one swing, the knife should go into the heart, or close enough to stop whomever knocked from coming closer. The circle of light on metal quivers with my breath. A few minutes, Damon, and you can have a bump. If you can just stay calm.

Another two knocks. A drop trickles down my forehead, along the edge of my eye. The back of my head is tight, like a rubber band is stretched around my skull.

'Come on. I know you're inside. Just open the door.' It's garbled, the voice. Unnatural.

Squeezing the handle of the knife, forearm muscles still lined with scabs and scars contracted, I'm ready to explode, to slash and destroy anything that comes near me. I'll imagine Hobbs' face. Bash my forehead on his and sweep out his legs then pummel and slash until I need a really big mop to clean Christian's floor then carve my name into his cheek so he remembers I was there.

My watch says Christian called thirty-three minutes ago. The Twins are holding his slumped, red body between theirs and trying to disguise their voices, to get me to open the door. I can smell the rust on their hedge clippers, the metal of blood on their breath. They tracked him down, brought him back to me.

I smell the beach. Fuck. It's Mary. They shaved Mary's head and stapled her soft hair to her chin like a beard. Two brown circles on her shirt where they sliced off her breasts. Flakes of rust, dappled around her eyes like eye shadow. Hobbs' spit still damp on her lips, his last kiss. He wants me to kiss her, to taste him, to have him in me.

'Open the door.'

Don't move, be quiet, listen for more breathing, moaning. The gurgling of an aerated throat. The slosh of bloody footsteps. I can't hear anything and I slide inch by deadly inch towards the door, rubbing the ring like a genie's bottle. If I put my ear on the door I can hear more, see if the Twins brought any friends to play. But if I put my ear on the door, one shot can turn Christian's place into their own private party room, sprinkled with wet bits of brain confetti. Hobbs will put on Duke Ellington and dance the Lindy Hop with Mary's mutilated body while the Twins pour dry martinis and wait for Christian to come home.

'Open. The. Door. Damon.' They know I'm in here. 'It's Christian.'

Sneaky fucks. They're not lying because Christian really is there, only he's blue and brown and lumped between them.

A thump, wet and metallic. My heartbeat pushes my eardrums out of my head.

'Do I have to do that stupid knock just so you'll let me in?' It's Christian's voice. Can they do that? Do they have one of those voice modulators that you can buy in the back of tech maga—

Five thumps, slow and dulled, rhythmic: shave and a haircut.

So, maybe I overreacted.

I rub the ring, slide the seventy pounds of metal weights away from the door and stand on the scratches they left, so he won't notice and get mad, then open the door. Christian stands with three bags in each arm and something yellow at his feet, shooting mind-bullets at me.

He shoves an armful of bags at me. 'Next time, you pick up the food.'

'I can't go outside. They'll find me. I'll pay because you got it,' I say.

'You're paying next time, too, because you decided to be such a dick.' He looks at the yellow by his feet. 'That's part of our dinner. Clean it up. I don't want ants in here,' and he steps past me.

I set the bags down and scoop the saffron rice into the paper bag to throw away, checking both ways down the hallway. *You're okay*. Look around the corner, down the stairwell. *You're straight*. A few deep breaths, kiss the ring, then peek through the blinds on the way to the kitchen—just to make sure—and scan the streets for anyone unusual. Nada.

'Thanks,' I say, feeling more secure. 'How much do I owe you?'

He shrugs, his back towards me, emptying the plastic bags of groceries and putting them in the cupboard, organized according to size and food group. 'The receipt is in the bag. I borrowed two video games from Matt so you'd have something to do during the day besides blow lines and get paranoid, although you could always clean a bit.'

'Thanks,' I mutter, feeling even more like a jackass. 'Sorry about that thing. I thought you were someone else.' I take two bowls from the cupboard and put them on the counter next to the bag with our Indian food.

'Don't you think you're overreacting a little?' He pulls two bottles of beer from the refrigerator.

'Well,' I start, thinking of course I don't think I'm overreacting otherwise I wouldn't be doing it, would I? 'maybe a little. But you're supposed to call half-an-hour before you get home. I thought you were dead.'

'I called and said I was leaving in a minute and that I had to pick up food and some groceries on the way. It takes fifteen minutes to walk home. And I stopped to buy a pack of cigarettes. That doesn't really constitute being late.'

'Oh.' But he could've been dead.

'And how am I supposed to do some secret knock if my hands are full? I'm taking my share of the rice first, then you can have what's left over,' he says, half smiling.

'I'm just being careful. If anyone came to find me, they wouldn't know that they had to knock to get into the apartment.'

'But that knock?'

'Who would know that our secret knock is from *Who Framed Roger Rabbit*?' I'm more crafty than he gives me credit.

'Yeah, no one will know that my mom took us to see it when we were little and no one will know the inside joke and'—his voice getting louder, words quicker, to keep me from interrupting— 'no one will realize that was our secret knock when we were eight. But it's shave and a haircut, man. It's like a,' he gesticulates with his hands, 'a default knock. You need something a little more original.' He takes two spoons from a drawer, then pauses, like an afterthought. 'And don't you think a secret knock is just kind of Hardy Boys?' I don't know if he's laughing at me or at the idea of two twenty-nine-year-olds arguing over secret knocks from an 80s cartoon movie, so I watch my hands spoon most of the rice and Punjab eggplant into his bowl, dump the leftovers in mine.

'All right,' I concede. 'We don't have to do the knock. But keep calling me before you leave work so I know when to expect you.'

We sit on the couch and he holds the food while I clear the mirror and razor blades and DVDs from his coffee table.

'So how long do you plan on being a refugee?' Christian says later, lighting a cigarette with his President Ronald Frehley lighter and nudging his half-full bowl to the side with his foot.

I shrug. 'Until.'

'Until…'

I purse my lips. 'Until.'

'You can't hide forever. I'm not kicking you out or anything, but for your sake, you have to make a move at some point.'

'Yeah, I know,' I mutter.

'You need to do something.'

'Yes, Christian,' I say in the same tone Mary would get when I was pestering her. 'I know.'

I look at my untouched bowl. My stomach has shrunken into

a kidney over the last few weeks. 'You want any of this?' I slide the bowl towards Christian. He shakes his head, says he hasn't been feeling so well. I pick up a piece of naan bread and run it through the sauce.

'Is there anything I can do?'

'Honestly, I don't know what I can do. I've left a million and seven messages for Mary. I can't go to the store. I can't go to our house. Fuck, I can't even change my clothes.' He smirks and nods at my chest, at his favorite Morrissey shirt that I'm wearing. 'Can I borrow this?'

'What are you going to do then? Sit? Wait? Hide behind corners for the next six months? Attack me with a knife when I try to get into my own apartment?'

'I apologized for that already.' I pick up a joint lying on the table, flick fire with his lighter and inhale, pass it to him. 'I'm sorry, but I don't really want to think right now.'

He sighs, stamps out his cigarette and sinks into the couch, mutters whatever.

A blue silence floats from the burning cherry and fills the space between our sentences. If I smoke enough, maybe I'll go comatose, just stay in this position on the couch for a couple weeks, a few months. Let the world pass me by, small bits filtering in through my unconscious ears, constructing scenes out of context from random information and create a whole new world inside my head. One that I can control, build and destroy with the crack of a synapse firing. A beach materializes over the horizon of my eyelids. Mary walks down it with two coconuts held over her breasts, the grass skirt around her waist floating in the breeze. She's a pinup girl from the magazines Christian and I used to steal from his asshole dad when we were little. All she needs is a ukulele and Sailor Jerry's signature under her feet. Just our footprints in the sand, and the palm trees you see in cruise commercials. A little thatched hut to sleep in. Fish made of primary colors on a wooden spear, rotating over the fire we built with driftwood. A hammock where she can read. The wind is light and warm and smells of salt water, of her. It blows her hat off her head, makes it samba down the beach. She laughs, chases it over the sand, not caring that she dropped the coconuts. I sit and watch her bounce back to me, feel the water run over my legs like we're in a Cary Grant movie. My face is wet, stomach clenching and I taste bile and metal in my mouth. Swallow it back into my gut and try to sink back under the water but it's drying up, flowing away from me. Mary stands up to her calves in the shorebreak, waving to me. I don't know if it's water or tears on her cheeks.

The mirror's on the floor. I pick it up, dip my head to it and inhale until my hands stop shaking. 'I need some fresh air,' I say to Christian. In the bathroom, I duck under the window so no one can see me then pull it open. I sit on the toilet with my legs crossed, feel the dry winter air fill the room and watch the fog flow from my mouth.

Fire spreads through my nose. Two dots of blood on the mirror, in the middle of my reflection's forehead, like he's been shot. I sprung a leak.

Christian sits stoic on the couch as I hurry to the kitchen for paper towels, hand cupping a pool under my nose. He's in the same position, has the same expression when I come back. The air is empty, has been for over an hour. Whether he's angry or just doesn't have anything to say, it's a crapshoot.

When the silence gets too heavy, I say, 'How's your mom doing?'

'Fine,' he says. Takes a drag on his cigarette.

Silence.

'I haven't talked to her in a few months,' I say, just to make some noise.

He shrugs. 'You can see her if you want. I've already asked you to come visit with me.'

More silence.

'You want anything?' I stretch the blood back through my legs on the way to the kitchen.

'I'm fine.'

Ice cubes crack against the bottom of the glass and I pour Coke until it almost fizzes over the top, gradually adding more over the grey carbonation. 'I'll figure something out,' I say, uncomfortably, as I sit next to him.

'When?' he says.

'I don't know. Soon. I'll get in touch with someone. See how we can sort everything out.'

'It's always call someone, get with someone, think of something,' he says. 'Just do it.'

'What am I supposed to do, then? Go ahead, enlighten me.' I crush a cigarette in the ashtray. 'I'm not asking for your help so don't play the martyr.'

'You got me involved when you came here. And you're no saint, either,' he says. 'I'm not saying I know everything. All I'm saying is that it sucks to see you like this.'

I light another cigarette. He opens his mouth, about to speak, but cuts himself off.

'What?' I say.

'Nothing.' He turns back to watch Bart and Homer on TV.

At the commercial break, he stands and stretches, gets a drink from the kitchen.

'You know what we should do?' he says as he sits.

I sip my Coke. It doesn't taste right.

'We should make a movie,' he says. 'A zombie movie.'

'Okay,' I laugh. There's something on his mind he's not ready to bring it up, so he's making small talk, just like his mom. At least he's lightened up. 'But weren't you the one who said there are too many zombie movies out now?'

'There are. But this one would be different.'

'I'm game.' There's no whiskey in my Coke. That's why it

tastes strange.

He lights another cigarette. 'See, people always look at zombies as the enemy of humans, but what if humans were the enemy of zombies?'

'They are, kind of. Humans destroy their brains.'

'Yes, but, when you take the whole smart-zombie thing to its fullest, you have anti-humans. Like an anti-hero,' he says. 'The zombies have remembered actions from when they were human, so says the Reverend Romero. And gradually these remembered actions start forming into some kind of consciousness, I guess the word is. Like a human, but not a human, you know? The cavemen of zombies, you could say. So what do humans remember, at their most base level?'

I shrug. 'Fucking?'

'I don't want to make zombie porn.' He shakes his head. 'No, at their deepest level they have, first, self-preservation, and second, a sense of community, like hunter-gatherers. Their evolution has brought them to a point where they start congregating and eventually form a zombie colony. You following me?'

'Sure.' I sip my Coke and take a drag.

'So once the zombie colonies are established, they have their own little world. And it's idyllic. Warfare and all that didn't come around for thousands of years with humans, so it should follow that the zombies won't figure out how to bomb each other for a while.'

'What about the zombie economy,' I ask.

He pauses, looking to the side. 'I haven't thought that far. Anyway, what's the biggest problem that they'll face?'

'Zombie taxes.'

'Humans, man. Humans.' He leans forward with his elbows on his knees, starting to gesticulate with his hands. 'Zombies are the biggest adversary to humans, so it should figure that humans are the biggest adversary to zombies.'

'I'm sorry. I'm getting lost. What are we talking about now?'

He sighs and I cut him off. 'I understand the zombie colony and all that. But what's the point?'

'Instead of the normal zombie deluge onto human communities, we're going to make a movie from the zombies' point of view. What happens in a zombic utopia when humans invade? How do they react?' The words race each other out of his mouth as he gets more excited about the movie. 'Humans have all their weapons and shit, in normal movies, but they can never kill all of the zombies. The zombies are always taking over the place. So, we'll show how zombies defeat the humans who try to settle in their land,' he says in a rush of breath. A slight smile forms around the cigarette perched between his lips. He nods his head, proud of his idea. I admit, I'm a bit pissed I didn't think of it myself.

'That is one of the most well-thought zombie arguments I've ever heard. Well played, my friend.'

'Thank you.' He takes a mock bow.

'But,' I say, seeing an aspect he hadn't thought about, 'even though that is a great idea, what's the point? Like all the social commentary Romero puts in.'

The smile spreads across his mouth from one ear to the other. 'The point is that you have something fine—such as human civilization—and then it goes to shit—zombie infestation among humans. But you have to look at it in a different way, the undead way, in this case. When the zombie colonies form, something productive spawns out of all the chaos. Maybe the zombies are even happier because in their colonies, their lives are better than if they stayed in the human cities. They created something beautiful out of all the bad shit that happened. And they need to fight to protect what's important to them.'

'Okay,' I say.

'Even zombie infestation can be a good thing if you look at it from the right perspective,' he says, raising his eyebrow. 'Know what I'm saying?'

My eyes narrow, lips pull on the cigarette. In the most round-about way he could, he lectured me. And I didn't even see it coming. 'Yeah,' I say. 'I understand.' Sneaky fucker.

Chapter 10

November: Then

I dreamt I'd been in an accident. I was ten years old. A woman leaned over me. She had the same fuzzy outline as the babysitter Christian's mom used to hire to watch us. Her collar of medic uniform hung loosely from her neck and I pretended that I was comatose. I had a crush on the babysitter and Christian said he was going to marry her. The medic asked me questions. Christian would scream as if he'd hurt his foot so the babysitter would pick him up, even though he was eight. What's my name? Can you feel this? Is it tight? As the babysitter walked around with Christian in her arms, he would flick me the bird behind her back and smile. The medic yanked at my pants. She said my name and it echoed down a wet stone corridor to my ears. Damon, Damon. Then she threw me from a building and I was falling, falling, the wind warm and damp on my stomach and I opened my eyes before I splattered over the street and Mary was grinding her hips into mine, screaming paramedic questions at me.

My peacoat, scarf, and shoes were still in a pile by the couch. I'd spent the night in the couch room. I remembered laying down on the couch to think about the Hobbs situation, then the medic was asking questions, then Mary was raping me.

She went to shower before we went to work. Two cups of coffee from Patterson Perk—mine with a shot of espresso—and banana chocolate chip muffins—my favorite kind—sat on the kitchen table.

The store was only silent for twenty minutes of the first five hours. CDs, video games, brown, jewelry, white, in every combination possible. Before I could say anything though, Mary was kissing the back of my neck and telling me that the customers were just customers and buying a toaster only meant that they wanted a different kind of bread. Maybe she'd become psychic overnight.

After it slowed down, I stood at the register organizing the bills, running mental catalogues of the stock before I called in our order. The Cockroaches had started delivering half of what I ordered and there'd been a complication with the bricks, so I figured if I ordered more than we really needed, they might deliver somewhere around the amount we wanted.

I'd counted 138 ten-dollar bills when Mary pushed the curtain aside. Pausing, I looked up. She emerged from the office with a smile. Her shirt ebbed, seashell hip poking past the waterline of her low-cut jeans. I smiled back, then counted. A tug at my belt almost made me lose count. 'What are you doing?'

'I need some paper towels,' she said, unzipping my jeans.

'I'm going to lose count, you know,' and her mouth was around me. I dropped the bills on the open register and closed my eyes, didn't care if anyone saw.

An hour later, Christian came in while I was finishing the order with Hobbs. Mary stood behind the counter, smiling, looking around. Not reading, not organizing or straightening—just looking. On the TV monitor, they stared at each other like contented iguanas on rocks. Mary didn't even give him shit about the bricks.

'Yeah, that's the full order.'

'That's a large order,' Hobbs said. 'Are you sure there won't be any returns?'

'Yeah, I'm sure. The store's been really busy. Don't worry about the product I was looking for earlier.'

'No?' He sounded surprised. You're not as smart as you think, you dumb bastard.

I smiled, but kept the same business tone. 'No. I think the home office was right.'

He was silent for a few breaths. 'Well,' he half-laughed, 'we get lucky once in a while.'

'Yup.' What a pompous asshole. Short me this week. You might as well get all you can out of it.

'We'll review this order and have it shipped to you by Sunday.'

'Sure. Sounds good.' I hung up before he could say anything else and leaned the chair back, put my hands behind my head and feet on the desk. Then: red toolbox, "Girls on Film" single. Listened twice, quick and short, just to celebrate. I dropped the single in the desk drawer then dipped the tip of my index finger and thumb into a glass of water on the desk, put them in my nostrils and sniffed hard to clean everything away.

Christian walked off the edge of the TV and into the office. He sat down on the edge of the desk nearest to me. 'Okay. What the hell?'

'What?'

'Did you kill Hobbs? Are you Tony Montana now? Why is Mary so happy?'

A wry smile. Shoulder shrug.

'This isn't post-coital. This is different.'

'That's because you've never had sex with me.' I scratched my cheek. 'That came out wrong.'

He shook his head and stuck a cigarette between his lips. 'What happened?'

'We talked last night. I explained things. She explained things. She thought it over in bed. Everything was gravy this morning.'

He stared at me, lighter held inches in front of his mouth. 'So she's going to go to the other guy?'

I shrugged, half surprised myself. 'I guess so. Right now, I'm just enjoying her being in a good mood. She knows I'm supposed to meet Isabela tomorrow night, so I'll wait for her to bring it up.'

'Wow.' Christian whistled. 'Congratulations, I guess. We're still good on our end, right?'

'Yeah, don't worry.' I'd have to tell Isabela about that later.

'Because I'm really depending on it, Damon.'

'I know. I said don't worry.' I pulled the single from the drawer and held it up to Christian. 'Want a quick listen?'

Two bumps off the back of his hand, like he was in Studio 54.

'So are we going to go out tonight?' He wiped his nose and sniffed.

I nodded my head towards the front. 'Think we're going to lay low. Wait until everything is finalized, then we'll have us a solid gold celebration.'

Another listen, a little slower and a little longer.

I cooked Pad Thai that night while Mary went to the liquor store to get wine. Adam Ant shook from the rockbox on the counter and I danced in place on the tile as the chicken sizzled and oil popped in the wok. Ginger and sesame floated in the air. Her laugh cut through tribal Ant drums and I spun around.

'And I thought George Michael had some moves,' she said, setting the bottles on the counter by the music.

'That video is gay.' I turned back to the stove, embarrassed. She slid her hands into my pockets and wriggled her slender popsicle fingers. 'No no no,' I said. 'I'm cooking. I'll burn the house down.' She rubbed the frozen nub of her nose on my ear and bit the side of my neck. My hair stood up, arms turned to Braille.

'Mary, seriously.' I faked exasperation. 'It'll be done in ten minutes. Go take a cold shower or something.'

'Are you coming too?' she purred.

'If you'd like charcoal and noodles for dinner, then yes, I'll come.' I smiled.

She smacked me lightly on the back. 'You're no fun.'

After we ate, we crawled under the blankets on our bed and passed a second bottle back and forth while reruns of *Black Belt Theatre* played on the arts channel. My arms felt like they had cotton wrapped around them and a train of ants crawled around the bottom of my earlobes. As the wine crept further up our heads, we made up our own dialogue for the movie, like *Mystery Science Theatre 3000*.

'There's no woman on the spaceship, though,' I said. 'So you have to be the robot.'

'I wonder what that's called.'

'Huh?'

'Robophelia, maybe?'

When the kung fu ended, she excused herself to the bathroom. I clicked through reality shows, hot-dog eating contests, infomercials for superfluous items that I hadn't realized my life was incomplete without, and celebrity profiles of Texas Hold 'Em poker players.

I held the bottle in the light from the screen and looked at the dark portion of wine left. 'You're not going to be enough if this is what I have to watch,' I said to the bottle.

After more televised slush, I settled on a science program explaining nature's mysteries. The segment was about the Bermuda Triangle.

According to the show, the ocean floor in that area is really unstable and there are a ton of underwater avalanches. When there's an avalanche, bubbles of methane seep out and float to the surface. Since the weather is usually nice, ocean cruisers run with their windows open. The methane gets into the cabins and floats to the back, I guessed—I'd gone downstairs and missed a few minutes—and because methane is lighter than air, it lifts the tail of the boat, sinks the nose. The engines are still running full-bore, because the sailing weather is fine, and the propellers push the cruiser into the ocean—screaming sunbathers, bratty kids, geriatrics and all. The same thing happens to planes. They hit a pocket of methane, their altimeter goes wonky, and they think they're too high up so they end up nosediving into the ocean. Interesting segment, but sort of disappointing: one of the greatest mysteries of our time, the notorious Bermuda Triangle, is caused by the ocean's farts.

A triangle of soft light fell over our blanket.

'I thought you fell in.' I pointed at the screen with the remote. 'Dude, check out this show. It's crazy.'

'Dude, check out this show.' Her voice, throaty and sultry.

'What show?' I turned my head towards her voice. She'd put on a black wig with bangs that cut a stark line half an inch over her eyebrows. The black vinyl of her bra and underwear glinted blue and red from the television. Her heels clicked as she sauntered in thigh high boots to our bed, a braided whip trailing behind her.

'Holy Bettie Page, Batman,' I exhaled.

'I thought you would like it.' She clicked off the screen. The ceiling was a light show, shards of light from the bathroom reflecting off her swelling and thrashing pinup outfit.

Two hours yawned between Isabela and me. The pistol lighter twirled around my finger. Mary hadn't mentioned anything about the new deal. Different ways of subtly bringing it up swirled through my head then blew away like newspapers in a windstorm. I analyzed the last six days, scrutinized the details and events. Fishhooks dug into my brain and pulled in four different directions. I searched the desk drawer for a pen and grabbed an envelope, listed what I thought I knew:

-Mr. Ashe has a good deal for us.

-Mary was pissed about it. Now she seems fine. Happy, even.

-Hobbs might be a psycho. New evidence says he's probably a liar with a good imagination.

-'Future' hints have stopped.

-Mary is horny as a Catholic school girl. Mention that later tonight.

-I think everything will work out?

Mary sat at the register, looking again. I lit a cigarette and took a few deep breaths before I went to the front. She wrapped her right arm around my waist, drummed her fingers on my hip. I looped my left arm over her shoulders and pulled her against my ribs.

'Can I take you on a date tonight?' she asked. 'I was thinking eat at the tapas place next to The Charles, catch a movie, then get a drink at Zodiac. I think there's a Kurosawa double feature tonight. It'll go along with *Black Belt* from last night.' I hmmmed and chewed on my bottom lip. My stomach spasmed with nervous convulsions. She looked up at me and smiled, then nuzzled her head into me. A purr vibrated in her throat like a train creeping through a tunnel. 'This could all be so nice, I think. So secure, so nice.'

I took a procrastinating drag from my cigarette, muttered, 'I think I'm supposed to meet a friend for a drink.'

Her fingers stopped drumming. The buzz of the neon STAY GO_D swept away our breathing. Her arm loosened. Billions of particles of oxygen, carbon and hydrogen smashed against the glass, against the counter. Synapses fired with tiny chemical snaps inside my rapidly aching skull. My fingers involuntarily tapped on my thigh.

'So you've decided then,' she stated, tilted her head up. Her eyes, glass water, the way the ocean lies just before a hurricane. I shifted on my feet.

'It seemed like you had, too.' We spoke in voices fragile as hummingbird necks. 'I mean, I thought we had the same decision.' The neon sign was a jet engine.

'I need something to eat.' She slid from under my arm, ducked her way around me and disappeared into the office.

'Mary,' I called, holding the curtain aside. 'Mary, everything's going to be fine.'

She awkwardly pushed her arms into her zip up sweater, maneuvered past me.

'Babe, remember? We figured everything out.'

She shuffled across the carpet. I jabbed a low shot, something to keep her from leaving, even if it meant that she was angry. My jaw clenched as I said it.

'Mary, you're being dumb. This is what you wanted. It'll give us something else.' My eyes half-closed, expecting another right hook. She stopped at the front door and turned on her toes. A thin smear of black, from the corner of her right eye down her cheekbone.

'Be safe,' choked from her epileptic lips. 'It's dangerous outside.'

'Mary,' I pleaded. My head fell in exasperation as I started to speak. Then the exploding sound of shattering glass dropped me to the floor. The bells clanked. A cloud of dust. I jumped up as the door swung closed and sprinted past the hand-held vacuum cleaner she'd thrown at me that jutted from the jewelry display and out to the street yelling her name. My voice echoed down Broadway. Three kids out past their bedtime mocked 'Mary, Mary, Mary' and laughed to themselves on the sidewalk. A bum stumbling in front of the shop asked me for change. I spun and crushed my fist across his face, then yanked open the door as he rolled on the ground.

'Double Jameson, please.' Five dollars on the bar. Behind the piano, an orange circle bobbed beneath a fedora. A gramophone voice licked the lacerations in my chest with an acid tongue. Soothed. The Black Gardenia buzzed annoyingly with pleasant conversations. Strangers on blind dates, suits telling anecdotes about profit sharing and TPS reports, couples grabbing a drink before their movie or play. I wanted to claw out eyeballs and let them bob in celebratory pints. After a few minutes, my eyes adjusted to the lighting and the piano player's charcoal face became distinct. He set his cigar in an ashtray and doffed his hat at a woman who was probably a call girl, then leaned back and began to serenade her.

My second pint glass sat half brown. The metal ashtray, three cigarette butts from overflowing. I stared across the tables, saw crosshairs over every smile in the room, felt the Patti Smith tune soak into my wounds. Of course, she'd be playing. The two Codys had dissolved into my bloodstream and my bones floated in liquefied muscle. The clock over the bar said it was 9:10. Twenty minutes meant at least another drink, then however many once Isabela came. The bartender flicked his chin at me to ask what I wanted. I ordered two more whiskeys, dropped my jacket on my table and went to the bathroom with Notorious in my pocket.

A line for every year we'd been together.

'Let's celebrate, Mary!' A two-inch snort. 'To us, babe!' Another two-inch snort. Hornets flew inside my skull, hit the sides and sounded like raindrops on the sidewalk. 'To better times!' Snort, cough, hands shaking. 'To our health!' Only an inch snort, pinch the bridge of my nose. I smelled the metal, tipped back my head, felt blood and white flow down my nasal cavities into my throat. Then one more for good luck.

Fuck.

'We keep meeting like this,' I said to Isabela as I sat down at the table again.

'I have impeccable timing,' she said. Her hips and ass were covered by shadows of a midnight forest, shirt the red of rabid wolf eyes, but white heels, always walking on clouds. 'How is Christian?'

I tipped back one of the whiskeys, coughed out, 'Fine.'

'And your store?'

'Fine.' Tipped the other back, shook the burn from my head and the room went Tilt-o-Whirl for a second.

'And Mary?'

The image of an airborne vacuum cleaner flashed in my head.

'Do we really need to play twenty questions?'

She smiled wryly. I drank the rest of my pint in two mouthfuls. 'I take it then, that you have considered the offer from Mr. Ashe.'

'Yeah.' The alcohol would sedate the hornets.

'And?'

'Yeah.' I saw Mary's face, webbed with splinter-cracks, begin to fall apart. Part of her ear. An eye. The left side of her nose.

'Well.' Her lips curved into a smile like a tanto blade. 'I guess we should celebrate.' She waved to the bartender, called out, 'Jimmy.'

'I'd like to talk about terms and arrangements while I can still focus if that's okay.'

'That's fine with me.'

I pulled a cigarette from the pack with my teeth, brought the pistol lighter to the tip then scratched the underside of my jaw with the muzzle. 'When do we get deliveries? When do we place orders? How do I contact you? How do we exchange?' I splayed my fingers as I asked each question. 'Who is Mr. Ashe?'

She nodded, smiled. 'You're thorough. We can keep all arrangements as you have them now if you'd like. Just write down your schedule. Mr. Ashe will be excited to see you.'

Jimmy set a glass of wine, a Yuengling, and two Jameson on our table. A bruise in the crook of his arm, black dots swarming to his vein like opiate insects. We raised our shots. 'To new partners,' she said. Glass clinked and I poured fire down my throat. Drank half my pint, felt my stomach clench with whiskey, beer, anxiety.

'Excuse me for a minute.' Back in the bathroom, I listened to Duran Duran a few more times.

There was another round on our table. Then another, and another. She'd scooted her chair closer to mine. Her jasmine surrounded me. Everything slid and shifted like I was looking through a greased lens. I tried to concentrate on what Isabela said, but her words floated through blue cigarette smoke and evaporated as I tried to catch them. My watch flashed 11:21 or 1:38. The white was supposed to sober me up, but it made the scenes shift faster. Isabela was next to me then singing on the piano. My glass was at my lips then tipped over on the other side of the table. 'It's for the best, Mary,' I said. 'Trust me. Honestly.' A cigarette was in my mouth then a woman was smoking it, telling me she charged by the hour.

I leaned in towards Isabela to say something, fell into her by accident. She tipped me upright, her ear brushing my lips.

'I think I need to go home,' I thought I remembered whispering.

Chapter 11

November: Then

Mary engulfed me. She raised my arms over my head and licked the bottom of my earlobe, kissed the divot of my neck. Her forehead was a moon rising over the horizon of my chin as her tongue ran up my throat, her eyes taking mine, looking through mine and biting my Adam's apple. I wanted to press pause and stare at the creases in her forehead, run my fingers from left to right with different pressures and sensations. Her red bra strap slid from her pale shoulder and I held it with my hand, pulled it towards me. I put my fingers over her eyelids, touched her eyelashes. My skin was damp with sweat where our bodies met, warm and sticky, pressing together, pulling apart. Epidermal Velcro. Her toes pushed into the tops of my feet, felt every bit of my foot, my toes, my ankles and calves. Took my big toes between hers and stroked. Salty air tickled my nose and I locked my teeth on my tongue to focus. I breathed deep, took in her jasmine. Let it fill my lungs and slowly absorb into my bloodstream. Thighs soft like jersey cotton sheets over mine, the inside of her knee from mine to my hip. I was aqueous and she splashed in me, swirled me around and drank me in. A lit candle, the sun rising over the sea of us and I was on fire, hairs standing and skin puckered. Through my eyelids, I saw her tongue traipse over my ribs, tiny red islands of wax forming from my belly button to my sternum. I moved my hands to run my fingers through her hair, see if she was water like me and send a wake over her, splashing us down her spine and watch it drip over her sides but my wrists were the sandy floor under us and my head lolled to the side. She sat upright and the warm shadow of her smelled of summer nights and eucalyptus and sand. Blood rushed from my head and my toes flexed, fingers spasmed and I tasted the bitter metal from my tongue. My calf twitched and the red waxy sun burned her in my brain. Head back, chin to the ceiling, throat striped like a xylophone, grabbing handfuls of my stomach, smooth seashells floating on stomach sides and white where skin barely covered bone. Her head fell to my neck, our bodies splashed into each other and lips parted, still, breathing, twitching and I was warm and could feel every limb, every finger, every hair, cell, particle and atom of her settle into me and I never wanted to feel anything else.

Chapter 12

November: Then

White-hot blades of light sliced through my eyelids. I squeezed them tighter, to block out the world, and it aggravated the pulsing welts the hornets left on the inside of my head. I relaxed my eyes and the welts deflated but the blades cut again. I dry-mouthed Jesus Christ and felt the Dremel that had replaced my tongue grate against my teeth. My eyes pried open and the sunlight fractured my skull. Tanks chasing a stampede of water buffalo in the bathroom split my eardrums in half.

My body erected itself. I reached for my water on the table next to our bed, but there wasn't any water. Or a table. The stampede faded into a running shower. I scanned the room as fast as I could turn my head without getting dizzy.

This wasn't my bed, or my house. I'd never seen this room before. Panic burned bright through my hangover. Every other step I stumbled, held myself up, tried not to vomit on the carpet. The shower fell quiet and I heard soft singing and the shower curtain sliding back. I scratched my leg and felt skin, looked down at my naked body, retched. I yanked on my jeans and t-shirt and stuffed my socks and boxers into my back pocket, then crept to the other room and stole my shoes from the middle of the floor. The scrape of tooth brushing in the bathroom. Fuck, the ring. Back into the bedroom, rifling through the sheets, ignoring the pounding head. Checked under the bed. Gargling in the bathroom. Ignore the throbbing under my foot. Mouthwash splattered into the sink. My foot? I lifted it, saw my ring, picked it up and kissed it, then realized what I had just done and swallowed my puke until I could get outside.

The concrete burned cold on my bare feet but I couldn't put on my shoes because I couldn't stop throwing up in the alleyway. My fingers, frozen claws around the edge of a dumpster. Arms prickled in short sleeves. My jacket was inside, and I threw up again.

After ten minutes of gagging, I brushed the glass and rocks from my feet and tried to dress myself, using the brick wall behind me to stay upright. I crouched down against the wall, patted my pockets for cigarettes. They were inside, probably in my jacket. I could've gone back inside, but she'd probably be out of the shower and standing in her room, looking around for me. Or maybe she was smiling and thinking I thought I'd have to stay in the shower for two hours until he left, like all the mornings with all the China Girls. I could've left and gone home. But Mary would be at home, probably still pissed. I'd have to say I stayed at Christian's and I didn't want to lie to her but I couldn't tell her what happened. What a fucking idiot. I didn't even remember what she looked like naked. What neighborhood was this anyway?

I checked my pockets and found four dollars, then swerved to a quickie-mart for cigarettes and a soda, and started walking. An hour of smoking and puking later, I stumbled across Patterson Park.

The house was silent as a stolen breath. I crept in, took off my shoes. The front room was empty. The kitchen too. I tucked my boxers between the couch cushions, slunk up the stairs like a thief in my own house. Halfway up, I paused to listen. No television, no radio. No stereo, shower, or crying.

'Mary?' I called. 'Hello?'

Silence.

Our bed was made. Folded clothes sat in the same place. Back in the kitchen, no food was out. No glasses used. No bottles broken. No knives missing. Thinking of where she might've slept made my stomach clench, then my feet burned and I realized I was in the shower so I threw up again.

I sat naked and wet on our bed, looked around the room. At

the picture of her and me at Megan's wedding. At her clothes folded and stacked next to mine on the dresser. The mess I had made of our lives in our clean room.

Eventually I dragged clothes over my body and shoved my feet in some shoes, grabbed a bagel from the kitchen and went to work.

The store lurked cavernous, empty and cold. STAY GO_D buzzed in the window; I'd forgotten to turn it off before running to the bar. The vacuum still sat in the jewelry display, glass confetti shimmering as I turned on the lights. We should've opened two hours before. The fluorescent hum made me sweat, so I kept the office dark and stared at the TV monitor. When people began to filter in, I forced my body up and to the front. I sold and exchanged CDs, waited for the inevitable Isabela, and hoped for Mary.

Four hours caterpillared by and I didn't see either of them, but I'd left my mind at the bar the night before and couldn't handle being in the store.

A tall girl with streaks of blue and pink in her blonde hair leaned on the counter of Jet Black. Shiny black boots touched the bottom of her knee, and the black sleeveless shirt and black pants could've been shimmering skin. Her face was delicately beautiful and flashed when light caught her piercings.

'Hey dude,' Matt said, sitting smug. 'This is Anastasia.'

It figured. I nodded at her. 'Christian here?' to Matt. He pointed to the back and I shuffled my way into the Blues.

The stench of beans and salsa made me retch. 'Hello, sunshine,' Christian said, holding a tinfoil-wrapped burrito.

'It's done.' I dropped into a chair.

'The deal?' He put down his burrito and wiped his mouth with a napkin, then put out his hand. 'Congratulations.'

I sat still and he took back his hand. 'Mary's gone,' I whispered. His face sank. He tapped his thumbs on the armrest of his chair, started to speak then stopped himself. I reached for his cigarettes, took a sip of his iced tea instead.

'I'm sorry,' he said eventually. Then after another silent minute, 'You know where she went?'

I shook my head. 'Not at the store. Not at home. I left a message with Megan and both of her parents.' She's with Hobbs almost slipped out of my mouth, but thinking it was bad enough.

'She's probably just pissed. I mean, after all the shit about getting married and all, I'm sure she'll be back.'

I shrugged. 'Hope so.'

Silence buzzed like electricity, hurt my head. His burrito sat on the desk, feet shuffled on the tile. *Why did you sleep with her, you idiot?*

'Just chill for a while. She'll come back. And you've got a better deal now, so you'll stay busy and it'll pass like it was nothing and...' I watched his lips form words but couldn't concentrate through the fog of Mary and Hobbs and whiskey in my head. I bit my cheek until I tasted metal, tried to focus my mind on the business and keep it from wandering into areas that would make me throw up on Christian's floor. I hoped that everything with Isabela had been decided and I'd just killed the brain cells that remembered the conversation. Christian's lips stopped moving.

'Huh?' I said.

'I said you haven't been listening to anything I've said, have you?' he smiled.

'Not really.' My head dipped. 'I'm sorry.'

'It's okay. Maybe this will cheer you up.' He bent under the desk, came up and dropped a brick on the desk. 'Got it yesterday.'

I blinked, tried to fall into the black flesh vortex behind my eyelids. 'Money's at the store.'

'No worries. Why don't you hang out here for a bit and then we can go do something.'

I hauled my body up. 'I need some air.'

'Then let's make a visit to the Virgin and watch a movie.' Christian liked my Virgin so much that I'd bought him one of his own.

'I'll bring your money with me.'

The cold air helped slow the carousel inside my head, and my stomach started to growl. I slunk along Thames, keeping my head down to avoid anyone I knew, to the pretzel place in the square that we liked. Maybe if I stayed on autopilot, did the same things I did with her, ate the same food and said the same movie quotes, I could trick the universe. Convince it that there'd been a glitch and she would reappear next to me like a *Star Trek* teleportation. Cigarette butts and dropped pennies and plastic bags the size of an eyeball decorated the cobblestones. People ran into my shoulders, seemed to move faster than they should.

I looked at the other side of the street to see if there were fewer people to ram me, and in the stream of window shoppers and tourists and families, I saw the back of a couple holding arms. She wore a black cocktail dress too thin for the cold and he had a grey overcoat and derby. Her hair was a bright blonde against her dress, and she glided over the sidewalk as if the breeze moved her.

Isabela and Mr. Ashe. Was that his real name or just a description? My brain was too far gone to talk with them so I started to step into Bernhard's Books to hide, and landed on Melody's feet.

'Fucking hell,' I groaned.

'Nice to see you too, Damon.'

'No, sorry,' I said, 'not you, it's…shit. I have to go.' I stared at the sidewalk and hurried down Thames to an alleyway, ducked in and slumped against the wall, cigarette clamped in my mouth and head resting on my palm. Took the ring in my fingers and massaged it.

I reached into my pocket for a Cody, a Cameron: anything I

could chew.

Two dollars and a gum wrapper. My stock was at the store. 'Just one break, huh? Just fucking one,' I said to the alley.

Another cigarette and two deep breaths in front of Stay Gold, like a man in tin-can armor standing in front of a dragon's cave. *Make it quick and get to Christian's so you can chill and tune out.* Tiny glass eyes winked at me from the floor.

Unlocked the door.

Ran through the front.

Grabbed a handful of pills from the office.

Stuffed a knot of bills in my back pocket.

Ran back through the front and right into Isabela.

'Don't let me interrupt you,' she said.

Seeing her was inevitable. I shouldn't have been surprised. 'I forgot something. I had to come back for it.'

'Why are you closed so early?'

'I can't really work today,' I muttered.

'Mr. Ashe wouldn't be excited to hear that. You still work for someone, remember?' She looked at the shattered display case, the vacuum jutting from it, shook her head. 'It'll be our secret. Consider it a gift for last night.' She gave me a wry smile.

My stomach wrung itself out. The waves of nausea splashed over me again.

'Yeah, about last night—'

'Don't worry. I said it's our secret.'

'Okay, but it really shouldn't have happened. I mean,' I trailed off, looking for words around the store. A piece of glass crunched under my Doc.

'I know,' she said. 'For Mary's sake, I hope you're normally better.'

'Yeah.' I paused, then sputtered, 'Wait, what?'

'Do you remember anything?'

Islands of wax. Jasmine in my bloodstream. Warm shadows.

I shook my head. She laughed.

'You're as big as a baby's arm and just as useless,' she said. 'A bottle of whiskey and two grams aren't aphrodisiacs.' My palms sweated. I stifled a laugh. Warm air swelled in my lungs. She motioned around the store. 'Mr. Ashe will not be happy if this happens again. Go home and sleep. I'll be in tomorrow with your first delivery. I'll bring your jacket with me, too.' She turned around, said, 'And you need to get your sign fixed. The L is burned out,' then floated out the door.

It was all I could do to not skip to Christian's apartment. I was a chump—and a limp-dicked chump at that—but I didn't sleep with Isabela and once Mary came back, I wouldn't have to lie about anything. We'd be able to work through our issues and sort out whatever was wrong and live like all this had never happened.

Then, mid-happy-stride, in my head, I saw Hobbs and Mary, wrapped into one body on his floor. I grabbed Hobbs' ankle and ripped him off her and dug my fingers into his calves until I heard a squish and felt wet bread dough. I sunk my teeth into his ear and bit until my teeth clacked together then chewed and spit it in his face, swung my heel at his temple over and over. Mary coughed and I froze, fell prostrate in front of her, my cheeks and chin dripping. I ran my hand over my face: shiny and clear.

The armchair was a guillotine. My neck bent over the side, paralyzed, waiting for my head to roll over the floor and survey the damage. Christian's jacket lay crooked over me. He was snoring on the couch, shirt off and curled under his chest. Theme music from the *Evil Dead* DVD looped.

It felt like our visit with the Virgin had lasted too long. The posters were a little too vibrant. Styrofoam packing-peanuts shuffled around inside my head. I watched my body move but wasn't sure I was the one controlling it.

One of his mugs slipped out of my hand as I tried to make

coffee and shattered in the ceramic sink. Christian's feet stomped on the floor, followed by the crash of glass bottles hitting the wood floor and crinkling of potato chip bags, then a muffled groan. I turned as he lifted himself off the ground. We stared at each other, mouths starting to curl into lethargic smiles. He put one foot in front of the other until he could grab a chair, then lowered his head onto his kitchen table.

'Thanks for making coffee,' he said, his words eroded by the sandpaper in his throat.

'You have bagels or anything?' I rooted through his cabinet.

'There are some in the freezer, I think. Cereal should be in there,' pointing with only a finger. 'No, the next one over.' I pulled two boxes of generic Cheerios off the shelf, shook them, put them back. 'Make me a bagel, will you?'

'Cream cheese or peanut butter?'

'Cream cheese, please. There's milk for coffee in the fridge, too.'

The world started to look normal as hot coffee ran down my throat. Under the buzz of the toaster, the question stalked us. We looked at each other like antelope at a watering hole, neither wanting to acknowledge its presence. Christian cleared his throat. My fingernails clinked on the coffee mug. *Evil Dead* looped in the living room.

'So,' he said.

The toaster bell dinged.

'Bagels.' I took out two plates and laid the bagels on them, opened the container. I picked up half of the bagel and spread the cream cheese, sliding the knife again and again until there were no marks and the tops were as seamless as a drawing of a polar bear in a blizzard. Then I moved to the next half. After both of the bagels were covered, I washed the knife, scraping my thumbnail against the metal to take off the piece of dried food that wasn't there. I checked the counter for any other silverware, stains, crumbs, dead bugs, bowls, cups, mugs, or severed hands:

anything I could clean. He was too OCD to accommodate me. Eventually, I sat down at the table with the plates. He patronized me with a smile.

'You're going to have to deal with it sometime, you know,' he said.

I shoved half the bagel in my mouth, tried to chew it without choking myself.

'And now my bagel is cold,' he said.

I looked at my plate, chewed.

'So now what?'

I pointed at my mouth, chewed.

'Damon. Stop being an idiot.'

I sipped my coffee, chewed.

'What are you going to do now?'

Stay Gold was approximately twenty normal strides long, fifteen wide. On one side, it housed about five strides worth of DVDs, another five of video games and video gaming systems, and another five of jewelry and assorted knives. On the other, there were between four and seven strides of bikes and six or so of random household accessories—vacuums, leaf blowers, Weedwhackers. Behind the sales floor extended an additional ten strides of office and stacked boxes. If the wind was right, I could've thrown a cat the length of the store.

And without Mary there, I might as well have been in Antarctica with fucking penguins waddling around me.

Idiots and junkies flowed through the store. I darted from one half-finished task to the next, to the next, to the next. Organized stock. Exchanged CDs. Checked for messages from Mary. Took orders. Found more CD cases. Left messages for Mary. Called a Chinese delivery place and ordered two meals because I wouldn't be able to leave the store for dinner either. Answered questions. Left messages for Mary. Restocked. Repackaged. Modeled chainsaws. Left messages for Mary. Demonstrated how to use a blender. Told people to fuck off. She was barely gone, and already my knots were fast unraveling.

It was quiet for fifteen minutes as the sun started to set and I stepped into the office.

Two Codys, chewed, washed down with green tea.

Isabela wafted onto the TV monitor and I went back to my stool. She wore the same scarlet dress as the first time I met her, laid a black purse the size of a human heart in front of me on the counter. It was screen-printed with a Japanese drawing of a white crane with a fish in its mouth.

'Rough day?' she said.

'I've had better.' I lit the cigarette hanging from my mouth. The first drag was an orgasm in my lungs. I'd actually forgotten to smoke all day, I'd been so busy.

'Where's your help?'

I exhaled until there was no trace of smoke in my chest. 'She's sick.'

'Ah, so.' She looked at me, tilted her head.

'Is this the delivery?' I nodded at her purse.

'That it is.'

Silence.

'Well,' I said, 'I don't really know how to do this. Do I take it and give it back to you later or exchange it for another purse?'

'Let's go back to your office,' she said. I cocked my eyebrow and bit my bottom lip. 'Damon, it's only business.' She smiled. 'I won't even lock the front door.'

She unzipped her purse and emptied it onto the desktop. Three bags fell out. Two had smaller bags inside them. The other held a rainbow of tiny ovals, a cross between Skittles and Camerons. I picked up the rainbow bag, held it close to my face.

'So you're what all the noise is about, huh?' Pills slipped over each other.

'Those are the ones.'

I pulled one out, rolled it between my thumb and index finger.

Hard and shiny and just like every other product; a lot of clamor for something that didn't look that special. 'What are the different colors? Body, mind, soul-type thing?'

'It's like Special Edition DVDs. You buy something you've already had because you think it'll be different.'

'Nice marketing gimmick.'

'I took the liberty of packaging the other products for you. I thought we could save you the trouble.'

'Very courteous.'

'One half and one whole, I assume,' she said.

'We call it single and full-length,' I said. 'I'll weigh it later.'

Her eyebrow rose. 'Thorough. We're going to get along famously.'

I shrugged. 'That's why I sold my soul to you, right?'

She smiled. 'Don't be so melodramatic.'

The house lay comatose as I walked up the sidewalk. I imagined Mary curled under the covers watching *Black Belt Theatre* and holding a bowl of popcorn with Old Bay on it, a bottle of red on the night table, her clothes in a pile by the bed. I smelled her saltwater breeze, heard her laugh-snort.

My footsteps echoed through the kitchen. I shoved my leftover Chinese in the refrigerator and grabbed a beer, pausing on the bottom step to listen for any noise from upstairs. The television was off because she was already asleep. I crept up the stairs—to not wake her up—and cracked the bedroom door, slipped inside.

No light except for the red numbers on our alarm clock. Breathing. I heard her breathing, like the ocean rolling, and smiled bigger than I remembered smiling in a while. Silent as a shadow, I slid off my shoes, jeans and shirt. 'Mary, Sweetie, I'm so sorry. I really missed you,' rolled to the front of my tongue. I flicked fire with my pistol lighter to see where she was in bed, so I wouldn't accidentally jab my knee into her stomach or roll on her hair.

There was no shadow over the covers. I stepped closer, listened to myself breathe. The bed was flat. Empty, vacant, full of phantom Marys. I turned on the light, checked under the covers, in the bathroom. The house was Mary-less. Back to the kitchen, returning with a bottle of Jameson.

Black Belt Theatre was on the arts channel. I played a drinking game. Every time the overdubbing didn't match the actor's lips, take a sip. Lather. Rinse. Repeat.

God damn me.

Chapter 13

December: Then

Word that the record store was open had spread like gonorrhea in a whorehouse, but I was the one covered in warts. I went to the back every seventeen seconds to restock. I called Isabela to order more EPs. I watched my reflection passing in store windows to see if anyone was behind me every time I went outside. Stopped in the middle of the crowded sidewalk to mess around with my shoe and check behind me. Pen marks covered my arms, tattooed shoe descriptions because I couldn't keep them straight anymore. Every fifth person was the poseur cop, the Goatee trailing behind. The Santa on the corner of Eastern and Broadway watched me every time I walked by. I started carrying Casamir Lights on me, as a personal supply. I floated above the register, watched myself move by rote, without any expression, a pill-slinging zombie.

During the two minutes of quiet I had every few hours, I checked my voicemail and left messages for Mary. Her parents wouldn't answer my calls and Megan threatened with the police. Then I would listen to Duran Duran a few times.

When I dragged my body home after work, I shoved my leftover Chinese containers in the refrigerator next to the others, grabbed a bottle of Jameson. A box of empty bottles waited by the front door. I'd watch the arts channel and play the Bruce Lee game until I passed out. I started having two white cigarettes a day.

The store had become such an epidemic that I had to start turning people away. Without Mary, I was worthless. There was no one to help with orders. No one to watch the front or get lunch. No one to talk to or try out stupid jokes on. No one to reassure me that customers were just customers and people actually came in just to buy a toaster. She'd opened the choke on my brain when she left, and it roared full throttle until I was slumped behind the counter with my head between my knees, pulling my hair. I said aloud that buying a DVD and VHS at the same time wasn't a signal, Ninja Gaiden was just a video game and not an attack strategy. Yeah, I had everything sorted. Something had to change. And fucking quick.

I started to draw up the new Ten Commandments, but got distracted halfway. Told everyone to spread the word and no, I wasn't fucking around.

-No less than fifteen EPs per order.

-The same unit price as before.

-Before purchasing, the phrase I am not affiliated with any law-enforcement agency in any way, shape, or form must be said.

-Anyone attempting to buy an order without something to sell will be shot.

-Stay Gold retains all rights of refusal.

My new rules cut down some of the foot traffic in the store and I could give proper attention to inspect every person who stepped through the door. For a few days, I debated making customers wait at the front so I could pat them down before they shopped, but thought that might be too conspicuous.

Things became more manageable with fewer people coming through. And it gave me more time to check for messages.

Hours dripped into minutes. Seconds exploded and shot their particles into days. Time became visceral and a week was nothing more than an arbitrary way to measure misery.

Christian knocked on the front window one night after I'd closed. I'd been sitting in the chair in the office with a straw between my fingers, staring at the nothing that was happening on the TV monitor. I unlocked the door then dropped myself back into the chair. He tossed a sandwich at me.

'You need to eat more than just Chinese delivery.'

'I'm not hungry.'

'You look like death.'

'I'm hearing that a lot lately.'

'Maybe you should listen then.'

'Fuck off.' The calendar on the wall next to me said that it'd been years since I'd seen Mary.

'Your sign is burned out. The T is missing now.'

'Wonderful. Mary was supposed to remind me to get it fixed before she left me.'

'Are you ever going to fix that display case?' He laid a backpack on the desk.

'I swept up the glass, didn't I?' I nodded at the backpack. 'That time again?' He bit his lip. Reaching into the drawer, I pulled out a fist of bills and tossed it to him. 'That better be the best goddamn sandwich on the face of the earth.'

'Better than a five-dollar shake.' He smiled, lodging the bills in a pocket inside his jacket. 'I know it's not much in the current situation, but I owe you a ton.'

'How so?' I put the straw to my nose, leaned down to the desktop and snorted.

'Without this, I would've lost my store.'

'Fuck it.' I opened the drawer again, threw him another fist.

He stared at it like I'd thrown a DVD of amputee porn. 'What's this?'

'Money.' I shoved the backpack under the desk.

'For what?'

'The store.'

'Damon, I can't take this. This isn't what we agreed on.'

'Just take it.'

'This has to be at least five grand.'

I shrugged. 'What am I going to do with it?'

He sighed, lit two cigarettes and passed me one. When the ash was an inch long, he said, 'The only reason I'm taking this is because I love you.'

'Same.' I nodded, smiled. A rip spread down my throat. 'Mary would've had a field day right now.'

He laughed. 'How are you doing?'

I shrugged my shoulders, watched the TV monitor. 'You just said I looked like death.'

'That's not what I meant.'

I shrugged again. A tear touched my cheek. I faked a sneeze so I could wipe it off without him seeing.

'Remember in *Better Off Dead,*' I said, 'right after Beth breaks up with Lane, and everywhere he goes, he hears breakup songs?'

'That happening to you?'

'No.' I checked the front room on the television. 'I heard that Cinderella song on 98Rock yesterday. It's always on those Monster Ballad CDs you see advertised late at night.'

'Yeah,' he smiled. 'I thought you liked those. You have one, don't you?'

Mary had bought one of those for a Bret Michaels party we'd had once. We'd argued that her clothes looked more Stevie Nicks than Bret Michaels. Either way, she was still hot, in a strange way I hadn't wanted to admit. 'On some level, I wish that it was happening to me.'

'Is this a masochistic awakening?'

I shook my head, glanced at the monitor again. 'If it was happening, I could convince myself that I was in a movie, because things like that happen in movies. Then I would know that I was at the end of Act Two, and everything would be fine soon and I'd see Mary, and we'd laugh about how funny all of this bullshit was at the end of the movie.' Fast forward and give Mary a kiss, rewind and break my hand so I couldn't have moved my fingers at Julian's party that night and just taken an ass-beating from Paul.

'You should be careful. If we're in a movie you just broke the fourth wall.'

'Fuck it. Worked for Ferris Bueller.'

'Well, Ferris Bueller was the shit. You're just a miserable

bastard.'

I bit my bottom lip hard, took another long drag and rubbed the ring between my fingers. Tiny spiders crawled in my throat and I tried to swallow them down to the acid and whiskey in my stomach.

'I don't think I'm in a movie,' I whispered.

'I don't think so either,' just as quiet.

Inhale, exhale, drag, exhale. My ribs were hollow and heart was ready to burst through them. I saw splinters of bone spear into flesh, fountains of life spurting at every beat, a mass of mauve tissue that would make a street dog thumb its nose. Christian chewed on his thumbnail. The spiders sprinted up and down my throat in stiletto heels. My lungs burned and the words lacerated as they rolled over my tongue.

'And I don't know if she's coming back.'

A bomb had gone off in the storage pit under the safe. Bills of different denominations grouped together, with nothing in bags. There had never been this much money to take care of, and I didn't care about organizing it. After the store closed, I'd lift the safe to try to sort things, then stare at the pit, listen to my fingernails scratch against my face. I'd grab a handful of bills, probably a few thousand dollars, and laugh. The dead president's face would slide into Mary's and I'd drop the handful and take two lines.

I sat in the chair and opened the red toolbox. The entire bag from Bela was inside. The multicolored EPs and the brown and the white. A post-apocalyptic rainbow. Nothing separated. My head lowered to the desk, nose snorted. I leaned back and covered my eyes, pressed them back into their sockets with my palms until I saw bright dots and felt the fluid form an uncomfortable shape. Three amoebas floated across my cornea and I watched them disappear, watched the bright dots make shapes and I tried to connect them. Connect dots like days and understand what was happening and what had happened and what was going to happen. I dried my cheeks, so I wouldn't cry into another line, and bent my head to the desk again.

A second box of empty bottles in the kitchen was almost full before it occurred to me to take out the garbage. I opened the refrigerator, snaked my hand to the back and slid all of the bottom-heavy Chinese containers into a garbage bag. One missed the bag and spilled over the tile. It looked like chow mein, made with flesh from a body pulled out of a swamp bog. I threw up twice in the sink, then washed my mouth and collapsed against the cabinets, my forehead on my palms. I grabbed my hair and pulled, just to feel some pressure.

I was in Christian's kitchen obliterating the past, pouring drinks. The television was turned low in the living room. We'd decided to have a Romerathon: start with *Night of the Living Dead*, and work our way up. Halfway through *Day of the Dead*, we lost interest. The brain can only take so much socio-political commentary from purple-faced zombies.

'Holy shit,' he called from the couch. 'Come here. You'll want to see this.'

Christian hunched over a mirror, framed by Buddhas in tie-dyed shirts holding up peace signs. A few white lines and a razor blade covered part of his reflection. I stood with a gin and tonic for him and the bottle for me.

'…report a recent rise in the use of so-called club drugs. The rise is reportedly due to a new type of drug that was previously unknown to authorities. Some users report opiate-like sensations while others experience severe hallucinations. Detectives are investigating the source as we speak.'

Next to the newsman's head, the video changed from a rave to a rainbow of pills on a pharmacist's table. I pulled one from my pocket, put it up to the screen, laughed despite myself.

'Stop bogarting the goods.' I took the straw from Christian, bent over the mirror, snorted hard, wiped my nose.

Eyes on the screen, he said, 'Germs, dude. Get another straw when you're done.'

'Police are urging anyone who has any information regarding this dangerous drug to contact them immediately. Any information will remain anonymous. In other news, three men were shot today in unrelated—'

Christian clicked off the television, turned to look at me. I smoked a cigarette.

'How's it feel to be famous?'

I saw Danny DeVito from Frazier's, Hobbs, the Stalk, Alicia, two dozen people from Stay Gold, Isabela, the Barcode, Melody, Dave, Brent, Christian, Mary. I stared at the end of my shaking cigarette and swallowed.

I needed to think. I took an envelope from his floor and made a list.

-Mary probably isn't

Crumpled the paper, got a new sheet.

-Get pinched= Getting raped by Nasty Nate.

-Cops are investigating.

-The store is crazy.

-EPs are more trouble than they're worth.

-About a week until serious heat.

-Things are going to get ugly.

One week. Seven days. One hundred…a lot of hours. Numbers and I never got along. We had the same relationship I had with the law. Sharks and Jets. Greasers and Socs. Sammy and David Lee. Me and my parents.

The air outside was sharp as the first line of the day as I walked to get cigarettes. Even for a weekday, the streets sat quiet, only the dinging of Salvation Army bells. Christmas wasn't far away. Maybe Blevis would be Bling Crosby soon. It would've been a nice day to sit on a bench and eat lunch.

As I opened the door to Tess' Place, a fist of cigar smoke, fried chicken and pine tree aerosol spray hit me in the face. The cuts inside my nose from too much white burned when I inhaled, but I tasted the air if I opened my mouth. Only one man stood in front of me in line, and he was pushing his second century playing scratch-offs. The Korean woman who worked the counter was a sweet lady, but had an odd concept of respect—rare for this neighborhood—and wouldn't serve anyone out of turn. Her son nattered away on the phone off to the side. The old man won five dollars on one of his tickets and bought five more. I checked my watch, and our store had only been closed twenty minutes. Another shop was a few minutes down the street, but by the time I walked there and back this guy would be done and despite all the white flowing through me, I was feeling kind of lazy. Luck was on the guy's side. He won another five dollars, bought another five tickets.

The door opened as I turned to leave. My mouth opened to say thank you, stayed open. On-the-floor open. Standing in the door were Docs with green laces and the face that had been taunting me since that night at Frazier's.

The fucking Stalk.

He looked at me, completely devoid of reaction. 'You leaving?'

The gall of this piece of shit. Crack my ribs. Rob my store. Almost get me nicked in a bar full of my friends. And now holding the door for me with a gloved hand, being courteous. Gloves were a good idea for him; they covered up the hallmark of his decision to cross Hobbs. His neck was bare and he hadn't even taken my advice to buy a rosary. All the better, as I wouldn't have to rip it off him before I sunk my teeth into his face and sent him to Hell.

'No,' I said. 'Just looking for someone.'

He stood behind me in line. The old man at the counter was

almost out of luck. Two tickets sat on the counter. Stall. No one can see us together. He can't see me. Last scratch-off, last chance. The streets weren't busy, but ours needed to be a private meeting. Stay Gold was too far away to stay inconspicuous.

The old man coughed out a woo-hoo, putting his withered arms above his head. 'You're on a roll, Herschel,' the Korean woman said. Another five dollars, another five tickets, another few minutes to figure—

'Can I help you?' the son said to me. Shit.

'Pack of Casamirs, please.'

'Three-fifty.' He grabbed a box from behind him, set it on the counter with a pack of matches. The old man still had two next to him as he carefully scratched all of the covering off his ticket with a nickel. The Stalk stood behind us, waiting for one of us to leave. Wonder if he was planning to hit this place, too. Come in nice and pleasant, nothing threatening or memorable about him so that when he storms in and scares the shit out of this poor woman she wouldn't give any fight. 'Three-fifty, please,' the son said again.

'Right.' I dug in my pocket. Two Camerons—maybe they were Codys—and an EP shuffled between the coins. Old Man still had another two tickets and looked like all the scratching had worn him out. Two tickets. Scratching with a nickel. 'Sorry. Can I get a couple scratch-offs, too?'

The Stalk muttered, 'Jesus Christ.'

Fuck you, buddy. You'll wait as goddamned long as I want you to. I leaned over the counter to scratch a ticket, felt the switchblade in my back pocket push against my skin, smiled to myself.

'Guess the luck's run out,' the old man said as he crumbled his ticket in his palm. 'See y'all tomorrow.'

The Stalk stepped forward, told them to give him a pack of smokes and a fifth of Jack. Head down, I watched him from the corner of my eye, imagined his cheeks flaking away from the rest of his face, lit cigarettes sizzling on his crow's feet, his eyelids blinking away rivulets of blood.

He dropped a fist of change on the counter, coin edges tinkling like spent shells in an alleyway, put the fifth in his back pocket. Three Natty Boh faces lined up on my ticket. In the grid on the side: Three Boh Boys-$50. Right on! Dinner for me and—I peeked up, and the Stalk was an old woman. The swish of a door closing.

I shoved the ticket in my pocket and hurried out. He was two stores up, moving quick for a guy with a messed-up foot. A foot that wasn't pointing to the outside, like a duck. He was thorough when he planned for a job. From one criminal to another asshole, my respect was with him. With quick steps and my head down to avoid attention, I trailed a few feet behind him until the store-fronts stopped for five feet. Quick check—no one was watching—and I wrapped my arm around his neck, dragged him into the alley.

'What the fuck?' choked from his throat. I slammed him against the wall, blade already drawn and on his cheek, resting an inch from his wide eyes.

'Remember me, motherfucker?' My smile felt like A Clockwork Orange. 'Glad to see your foot is feeling better.'

Panic rushed from his nose in short, hot breaths. His body tried to escape without moving his face under my blade. 'What the fuck are you talking about! What are you doing?' His voice cracked.

'Save it.' I put the dull side of the blade on his lips like a cool finger. *Hush, honey*. 'I'll give it to you. You're really good.'

'Seriously, man, I—' he sputtered, terror dripping from the inside corner of his eyes.

'Rob my store. Fuck me up. Try to get me picked up by the cops,' I said, pressing my forearm against his collarbone. 'Then hold the door open for me. I'd almost admire you, if I hadn't already promised to open your throat. I think I'll take another one of your fingers.' The blade rose and fell with his Adam's apple.

'I promise you, I didn't rob your store.'

'I remember your shoes, dickhead. I saw them in Frazier's when you set that Danny DeVito motherfucker on me.' I put my cheek beside his. 'Who sent you in to hit us? Who are you with?'

'I didn't rob your store. That guy busted me. He was an informant, Damon.'

'I know he was—' My knife loosened against the tunnel of his throat. Head cramped. 'How do you know my name?'

'I've seen you around. I bought from your store a few times. Your girlfriend works there, and some guy from the record store.'

Mary. God, where are you?

'So there is a pie-guy.' I choked him back against the bricks. 'I'll tell you, I wasn't sure that Hobbs had it in him.'

'What pie-guy? I didn't rob your store. Hobbs would kill me if I did.' Red veins exploded through the whites of his eyes.

'You're lucky he didn't kill you for stealing from him.' I laughed through my teeth, stroked his hair like *Silence of the Lambs*.

I flicked the tip of the knife against his cheek. His head jumped back, smacked against the brick. Something plastic hit the alley. Shaped and colored liked an oversized Tylenol. 'I fucking said I didn't rob your store, Damon. I didn't steal anything from Hobbs. I never worked for him.'

'Then how the fuck do you know about him!'

'Everyone knows about him. He's fucking crazy. I've heard the stories.'

'Good, because you are one of his stories,' I said, grabbing him by the wrist of his leather glove, tightening my hand around the knife. 'Now listen to me. Are you listening to me?'

'I said I never—'

'You're not listening. You're whining.' He sniffled, then nodded. 'Good. I want you to go back to Hobbs and show him what I think of his stories, all right? Tell him I wrote this story, and I wrote it better than him. He took one finger, I'm going to take two.'

His eyes peeled back, horror spreading at the rate of comprehension. He thrashed under me, cut his face on my blade.

'Don't think I'm unsympathetic. I remember how bad my ribs hurt,' I said, rubbing his gloved hand against his cheek. 'This is going to fucking kill.'

I listened to Duran Duran twice and paced the store. Checked the corners and ran my hands under the edge of the counters. Someone set me up. Again. They set up the setup. Hobbs cuts the fingers off a dealer. Christian and I have a conversation about missing fingers while someone is in the store. Then the store gets robbed by a guy with a missing finger and a limp. A few weeks later, said guy almost gets me picked up. I finally see the guy again. He doesn't have his limp, because he was faking it. And he has all of his fingers. How the fuck do you fake a missing finger? Cops, Hobbs, other dealers, Mary. Someone is toying with me. They're listening.

I looked in the cone of a speaker.

Sifted through records and opened DVD cases, starting at *A Bronx Tale* and working my way down until someone came into the store.

Took the backs off the vacuum cleaners. It occurred to me that that might be a little excessive; emptied them in the alley anyway.

In front of the bikes, I took them apart in my head. The only practical place to hide a microphone would be in the tire. Otherwise, they'd have to drill through the metal, make a bracket, then weld and paint. Even at a quick ten minutes each, taking apart both tires on each bike would waste almost two hours. I let the air out of the tires, bashed the rims with a hammer, all the way around.

The overhead lights hummed. I killed the sound and stood in

the middle of the room, holding my breath. My heartbeat smacked dull in my ears. I strained to hear something, anything. The whir of a camera. The hiss of a tiny microphone. Just the ocean. I grabbed a karaoke machine and walked around the store, holding the microphone up to every item in the store. VCRs, nothing. DVD players, crickets. Toasters, nada. In the front window, S_AY GO_D buzzed. Short-circuiting a sign to hide a bug seemed excessive. Too much signal interference, as well.

Ten minutes later, the microphone squealed in front of a blender. I plugged the blender into a socket and turned it on liquefy, hoped to hear metal scraping against metal, the tiny bug blended into a silicone-chip milkshake.

Nothing.

I ripped the blender out of the wall and walked to the back, climbed on the desk and hurled the blender at the floor. Plastic shrapnel scattered over the carpet. Dropping to my hands and knees, I ran my fingers and eyes over the ground, scoured for the bug. Five minutes, ten. Shards of plastic in my palms and knees.

Nothing.

Flipped the karaoke machine back on, put the microphone to the floor. Squeal City. I stood for a minute, ran my hand over my beard, then looked at the microphone. Slowly, I put my palm closer and closer to it. As soon as my hand cupped the area around the microphone—shriek and shriek. I did it again. Same thing.

Opened the door to the alleyway, checked for cars, and dropkicked the karaoke machine into the cinderblock wall.

Maybe I was overreacting a little.

Lowering myself into the chair, I dipped my hand into my pocket for a Cameron, Cody, "Master and Servant" single: whatever would sedate the roaring ocean in my ears to a rain puddle still enough for me to look at my reflection and see what was happening to me and check to make sure there was no one creeping. Tap my fingertip to the surface and watch concentric circles ripple from my right eye, tap again in the middle of my forehead, like a .357-inch eye. I pulled out two pills.

One Cody, chewed, washed down with more of Christian's soda.

The other pill was yellow. Like the sun, like jaundice, like piss, like flaxen hair. I rolled it around my palm and watched it tumble end over end, contemplated another Cody with an EP chaser. Held between my thumb and index finger, I stared at it, whispered, 'What is the big deal with you?'

Some report opiate-like sensations. Pull the desperate razor from your wrists. The woodland animals and a sloppy one from God's own lips. Mary was gone. I went to bed with John Jameson and Sons every night. I'd been chubby and hated beards, and now I was somewhere around *The Machinist* and ZZ Top.

'Some report heavy hallucinations,' I said to the yellow dot in my hand. My other hand held the last bit of Christian's old soda, ready to dump a swallow of flat sugar water down my throat. In my head, I saw Mary and Hobbs entwined, saw Hobbs and Bajet laughing, saw Christian on the phone with someone. I saw Eric and Paul, his smile like someone tried to clean the street using his face as a sponge. I saw Mary cooking dinner in the kitchen, saw myself dangling from a rope in the basement. I saw a girl holding a body in Julian's living room.

I took a deep breath, then tossed the pill on the desk.

'I'm sorry,' I told it. 'I think I have enough problems figuring out what's real.' It seemed to frown, turn a sadder yellow.

That was probably the smartest decision I'd made in months.

Chapter 14

January: Now

The walls are creeping towards me, but only when I'm not watching.

I stand with a broomstick touching the ceiling, mark the level of my head on the handle—to make sure the ceiling is the same height it was twenty minutes ago—when a flicker in the corner of my eye, the sound of nails scratching, snares my attention. The broom lands on the floor with the sharp crack of wood on wood while I grab the tape measure, check the distance between the north and south walls, then the east and west. A light dust falls on my hair, in front of my eyes and I look up and the ceiling is lower. I drop the tape measure on the floor and grab the broom and check again. This goes on for hours. Sometimes, the walls are clever, and only the south wall moves. Then, while I'm watching the south wall, the east wall will shift forward. I inspect that one. And while I'm at the east wall, the north wall shifts farther back—to make the room look bigger—and once they start to creep forward again, I'm inside a shoebox. They do this to me until I give up and take three or four long snorts off the mirror and curl my arms around my head on my knees in the corner, whispering her name.

I thought about telling Christian, thinking he could call the rental agency and they could get a structural engineer to have a look, but as soon as he comes home, he's straight to bed. The noises from his room hit the bottom of my spine with a nail gun. Guttural coughs that break loose parts of his spleen, and wheezing like an accordion made of spare body parts and tin foil. I made him a bowl of chicken soup and hot tea, but as soon as I opened the door, he was Regan in *The Exorcist*. I asked if he wanted me to call a priest and he threw up in my direction.

'I was just trying to get your mind off it,' I said.

'I'm dying.' Mauve chunks stuck to his lips. 'Leave me alone.' The door slammed in my face.

When I'm not curled fetal in the corner, I play video games and visit the Virgin. If I could focus, I'd beat the games quicker, but there are two or three screens swirling so I do the best I can.

The TV is just atrocious remakes of classic slashers, family programming versions of Lolita, publicity vehicles for nubile-singers-turned-movie stars. If popular culture is any barometer of how aliens will judge us, we might as well put on foil hats and break out the Vaseline because we're in for it. And if I see *Black Belt Theatre,* a samurai movie, fuck even *The Karate Kid* makes me tear up. I'm slipping, Mary. Did you want to see Kurosawa that bad? I'll go out and buy the box set. I'll buy every samurai film I can find. I'll learn how to cook the tapas we were supposed to get and make them every night, I don't care.

Just come back.

I sit on the couch and stare. At the television I don't want to watch but can't help it because there's nothing else to do. At the mirror I don't want to lean over but do because my hands start shaking after an hour if I don't. At the Smashing Pumpkins poster that keeps dragging me through the memory sewage pipeline back to Amherst.

And all I can hear is that scream, and watch how much of that poor kid's blood soaks into hair and feel how Paul's face starts to feel like bread dough with flexible metal rods inside after I've hit it so many times. And it all puts a face on that poor kid's body and it's too much to handle because he's a real person then.

All I want to do is sit in armchairs in Christian's mom's living room—she'd never buy another couch after her dad passed—like we used to do on Sundays after Christian had left for college and pretend Christian and his dad were there. But the good version of his dad, not the one that told us he was leaving by writing a note on the back of a utilities bill. I wanted our odd little family to be its odd little self: a mom who was also my best friend's mom, a creepy uncle who was also my best friend's dad, and my father, who put a hundred-dollar bill in my pocket when I met him and kept me in supply of brown and white.

Not being able to make any noise in the living room or leave the house without fear of dying is bad enough, and watching that poor kid die over and over like using a fifty-dollar coin in a nickelodeon is just the diarrhea icing on my shitty cake of life.

I've visited the Virgin three times since Christian got home and I think she's feeling lonely. If I visit her enough, she'll wipe out the four white cigarettes I've had.

My eyes split in half and my neck is frozen. I've developed a habit of passing out in this chair. The couch is empty and I don't know why I didn't sleep on it like the night before. Maybe sleep isn't the right word. Don't know why I didn't twitch and toss and scratch the cuts and scars on my forearms all night while constantly replaying every stupid fucking thing I've ever done in my stupid fucking life all night like the night before.

I creep to Christian's door, nudge my head in to see if he's still alive. His bed lays empty. My watch is lying. It says it's one in the afternoon. Cotton and thumbtacks fill my head.

As I swerve to the kitchen, my feet get caught on the broomstick lying in the middle of the floor, black marks up and down the handle. I shove it in the back closet. If I can't see it, the walls will behave and stand still. Hopefully. This is bullshit. I need some fresh air, go for a walk. It might clear my head. Then again, if I go outside, a bullet might clear my head, too. Maybe that's…

Christian left coffee in the pot, I'm assuming for me, but it's cold and bitter now. I dump it out in the sink, turn on the water and watch the clear swirls mix with the coffee, bits of granules sticking to the bottom then washing away.

My eyes ache from watching TV all day yesterday and the day

before. And before. There are books I've never read on the bookshelf, but I don't know if I have the energy. I have the attention span of a ferret. I'll pick up a magazine, read half an article then put it down. I'll put on a DVD, get bored after the first twenty minutes and push stop. Everything I look at kills me. The moan of a zombie is Mary making fun of me—¿Donde estas, mi corazon? ¿Por que no vuelvas a mi?—gnawing on my head and groaning braaaaains and ignoring the fact that I keep telling her zombies don't say brains. The chorus of a song from The Clash has the same structure as "Mayonaise" and I look at my fingernails and see bits of Paul's face. Then I look down and I'm staring at my reflection in the mirror with a straw in my hand and a synthetic taste dripping down my throat and how the fuck did this happen?

Something's taken hold of my body. I'd get up to look out the window but as soon as I'd open the blinds, there'd be pinpoint fireflies flitting around my vital regions and some guy I probably sold to four months ago sitting on a rooftop with mirrored sunglasses and a dickhead mustache waiting to pull the trigger. The world goes dark as I slink down into the crevice of the couch and pull a pillow over my face, catch a fingernail in one of the cuts on my forearms. Nails scratch in the other room, but I can't let the walls know I hear them. I peek from under the pillow, catch fireflies dancing on my thighs.

'Why won't you pull the fucking trigger, you asshole!' I'm leaning out the window screaming and the streetlights have made shadows that he's hiding in and I look at my watch to see how quickly he's making me move and it's nine-thirty already and when the fuck did eight-and-a-half hours pass?

The door slams and I spin around, wielding the mirror as a weapon. A fine white mist around me. Thumps and wheezing.

'Thank God you're home,' I say to Christian. He grunts back.

'How was the shop?' He grunts, fills a glass with water.

'I saw a good documentary today,' I lie. He swallows a

handful of pills, retches with his palm over his mouth.

'Can I get you something?'

'Medical insurance.'

I shrug. 'I can find pills to make you feel better.'

'Not the kind that I need.' His jacket falls to the floor. 'Goodnight.'

I kick magazines and shreds of cigarette paper to the ground. 'Chill on the couch. We can watch a movie.'

'I need to sleep. Maybe tomorrow.'

'You know what you need? You need to get your mind off it.' I set the mirror on the table.

'No, Damon, I need sleep. Goodnight.' He walks towards his door, rubbing his hands over his face.

'Can't you hang out for a little? I haven't seen anyone in days. You can still relax on the couch.' My voice sounds needy.

The muscles of his jaw tighten. Red and blue lights flash through the window, a siren chasing them down the street.

'Sorry, man. I'll sleep tonight and we can talk tomorrow.'

'Or hang out tonight and sleep tomorrow. I need someone's help, figure out what to do.'

He sighs, steps into his doorway. 'You've already been hiding for a week. One more day won't kill you.'

'I'm not hiding, asshole. I'm planning.'

'You're cowering, and I'm dying. Goodnight.' His door starts to close.

'What did you just say?' I wedge my foot in his door. 'I'm not fucking cowering.'

'Whatever your problem is, it's going to have to wait.'

'My problem? What the fuck is your problem?'

He steps from his room, coughs into his shoulder. 'Your problems are my problems. You make them my problems. I just want to sleep.'

My fingers twitch, fists tighten. Life drains from my feet like before a marriage fight with Mary, but I've never had this with

Christian. 'What the fuck are you trying to say?'

'I'm saying that I'm tired of fixing your problems. You're parents are fuckups, you stay with me. My mom gets you through it.'

'Hey, fuck you, man. Who took care of you when your Grandpa died, huh?'

Veins explode in his eyes. 'Shut up.'

'And when your dad left, who fucking cooked for both of you?'

'I said shut your mouth.' Flecks of spit fly from the corner of his mouth.

'Who did the laundry and brought home your assignments from school? Don't fucking talk to me like I'm some asshole.'

'Yeah, you're a real fucking saint for doing what families do to help each other. You've got an EZPass to God, and for being such a noble person, I'm sure he'll overlook that you killed some innocent kid and fled to my apartment until someone else took care of it. Take some fucking responsibility for your life!'

'Fuck off.'

He coughs, spits something brown on his floor, grinds his teeth so hard I can hear them over mine. 'It's your fucking fault Mary left.' His finger jabs my chest. 'You drove her away and you're going to do it to everyone who loves you.'

And he falls backward. Blood spurts from his nose like oil, spreads in a dark triangle over the front of the Morrissey shirt I borrowed a few days ago. His favorite shirt.

My eyes are wide. Fist throbs. Then I look down, at the red on my knuckles. My fingers extend, curl again. Dark lines where his blood collects in the creases of my skin.

He hefts himself up, holding onto the doorknob. He wipes the blood from his top lip, gives a laugh like wind blowing through sand and rusted sheet metal. Raising his bloodied hand to eye-level, he shakes his head.

'So fucking typical.' He slams the door in my face.

I sink into the couch, light a joint then bend over the mirror. Joint in my left hand, I wipe my cheeks dry with my right. Take a drag until my lungs can't expand anymore and hold it, hold it, hold it as my cells scream for air.

Hold it.

Chapter 15

December: Then

Bing Crosby crooned from the bottom of a scotch decanter on the radio. "White Christmas."

I had to laugh.

My nose waited, the height of a dollar bill over the desk, exhaled and ready to snort. The product measured: four equal-length white slashes on the wood-printed veneer, two for each nostril so both would burn equally. Christian would've been proud. My cells lined up in their capillaries with paper party hats and kazoos, aching for their first blast of the day; their breakfast of champions. Remember to buy that for something new to read. And then the phone rang. Without moving my head, I looked to the side, watched the handset to make sure I wasn't hearing things. My cells screamed and swirled, ready to riot like a Guns n' Roses audience. The red light flickered, the ring rang. I stared at the white lines like a lost love from across a train station, sighed, and sat up.

'Stay Gold.'

'Hey, it's Brent.' At least I hadn't stopped for a telemarketer. 'How are you?'

'I am.'

'Yeah.'

Brent breathed. My fingers tapped on the phone. Something in his breathing, his voice; it sounded like the kicking had kicked him. I laid the phone down, picked up the bill and got into position then heard Brent's voice.

I picked up the phone again. 'Sorry, I didn't hear what you said.'

'I said if you need to talk or anything, you can come and talk to me. You know, if you want to or whatever. But it's no big deal if you don't. Just if you do, I'm at the bar. But if not…' I could see

Brent at the bar, Braille arms, eyes a tangled mess of veins, staring at his body trying to will it into doing what he wanted it to do. We'd look made for each other.

'Thanks, man. I appreciate it.'

'Hey, the beer delivery guys are here,' he said, his mouth away from the phone.

'All right. I have a few things to take care of, then I'll be over,' but the dial tone was already in my ear. The brass bells clanked. Caleb walked through the quilt of dust on the TV monitor. He'd have to wait. I cracked my knuckles and smiled, then bent over the desk, snorted four times. My hand spasmed and knocked the alarm-clock radio to the floor. Bing's voice disappeared. I dipped my fingers in a glass of water and cleaned the pipes, then went to the front.

'What's up?' I shoved my hand in my pocket so he couldn't see my finger tapping.

'Not much.' He wore a black shirt that had Bart Simpson in a Rasta hat and dreadlocks, with "Eat my Shorts, mon!" in a speech bubble. Brown sandals with chewed edges, even though it was December.

'What can I do for you?'

The bells clanked again. In walked a tall guy in his mid-twenties who I recognized, but couldn't remember from where. He wore a black leather jacket and ripped jeans, the holes conveniently positioned just over the knee. They looked like he'd used scissors to cut a line, then washed them a few times. His Docs were scuffed at the toe, dusted with a light grey film, but directly under his ankle, smooth. He looked around the store aimlessly. The back of my head, in between my ears, tensed.

'Nothing,' Caleb said. 'Just came in to get a CD, say hi.'

'Sounds good,' I said, trying to sound casual. I'd definitely seen this guy before. 'How's Dave?'

'Fine. He got some girl's number but she was asking him to go to a church group or something. But she's got a killer body and I heard that she…' Caleb's voice faded out while his lips moved. I watched the Scissor Man over Caleb's shoulder, ran his face through the catalogue of people in my brain and tried to figure out why I recognized him. If Mary'd been here, she would've remembered. Or could look in our bible, wherever it was. I hadn't even seen it, much less used it, in weeks. I looked where his arms brushed his hips for a gun-shaped bump, watched the way his shirt moved over his chest for a bug like an oversized pimple, just below his knee for an ankle holster. He looked clean, but put-together, like Joan Jett was his mom and she dressed him.

'Let me get that CD for you. Depeche Mode?' I guessed, then whispered, 'Come back later,' but wasn't sure if he'd heard me.

'Yeah. Thanks.'

I walked into the back, picked up a CD case with an actual CD in it, and watched the TV monitor. The Scissor Man waited behind Caleb. Fuck, the cop who came in and said something about ace. The douche bag. When he said he'd be back later, I thought it was just for fear-of-God, I didn't think he'd actually be back. No one was peeking in the front windows, but the streets could've been swarming with backup waiting for his word to crash in and wreck my shop. I grabbed the straw, the bags, the EPs off the desk and put it all in the emergency pit, took a paper towel and wiped off the desktop, kissed the ring for good luck and went to the front, willing my nose not to bleed.

'Here you go.' He gave me money and I put it in the register, sent him a telepathic S.O.S. as I fought to keep my breathing normal.

'Later, man,' Caleb said. Hopefully he wouldn't be pissed that there wasn't any product. Or, at least when he came back, he'd understand why.

The Poseur Cop stepped forward.

'Hey, I was looking for a CD?' A question, not a statement. He was trying a different approach.

'Which one?' The something on my thigh, I realized, was my

hand, squeezing.

'Iggy Pop or the Ramones.'

I looked to the side, as if I was thinking. Last time he'd been cocky, confident. It got him fuck-all, so he'd waited until he thought I'd forgotten about him, then come in as a new person. But he should be asking for EPs, not CDs; he's trying to distract me. 'Nah, don't think I have any.'

'What do you have?'

'Not much. Some Depeche Mode. Some Joy Division. Billie Holiday and Elliott Smith, maybe. I think.' I thought I'd seen those somewhere and I'd give him the album Elliott Smith himself sold me at Amherst if it got him out of here. I should've had a list for situations like this. Mary, you thought of these things. You knew I wasn't as smart.

'That's it?'

I shrugged. 'Might have a few others, not much though.'

'Why do you only carry a few CDs?'

'Misery markets itself well. I only sell what people buy.' I willed the sweat on my forehead back into my skin, fought to keep my fingers from rubbing the ring and looking nervous. 'If you want a better selection, you can try Jet Black on Thames.'

'Yeah, I've been there a few times.' He smirked. 'Haven't found what I'm looking for yet.'

'Ah. Bummer.' A quick glance and he had all ten fingers. 'Well, sorry, man.'

'Yeah, that's too bad. Word was, you could help me.'

No one stood outside, peeked around the corners. A gun could easily fit in his waistband under his jacket but I got the feeling this guy wasn't going to need one. He definitely wasn't a dealer, didn't have that animal glint in his eye.

'You know what they say.'

'No.' He leaned on the counter. 'What do they say?'

'Nothing. Just that they talk a lot. The fictional they, I mean.'

He straightened, smirked as if I'd said something incriminating. 'Well if you do get anything good, let me know.'

'Yeah, sure,' I hesitated, then felt something on my fingertips. I looked down.

Detective J.M. McNally
Baltimore Police Department
Narcotics Division

Oh my fuck.

'Maybe we can help each other,' he said. 'I'll see you around, Damon.'

And he was gone like a breath.

I turned his card over in my fingers, made myself count to ten. Forwards, backwards, in Spanish and what I could remember of French. Uno, dos, tres. Wait for the cop to get far away from the store. Cuatre, cinq, sept. Call Christian. See if he's heard anything. Siete, ocho, nueve. Take a few lines to calm down, covert. Diez. Oh my fuck.

Shoving McNally's card in my back pocket, I ran into the back and slammed the door, dialed Jet Black as I rummaged in the pit for white.

'Jet Bla—'

'Matt, put Christian on.'

'Huh?'

'Put Christian on the phone.' No one on the TV monitor.

'Oh. Hey, man,' he said. 'Dude, I told you my girl was hot.'

'Shut the fuck up and put Christian on the goddamn phone.' Two shaky lines, poured on the desktop.

'Sorry, dude. He's not here.'

'Where is he?' I said into the desk, straw to my nose. Hands shook, scattered the white.

'Went to get cigarettes. Some Bamma came in talking to him and he got freaked. Went to get smokes after the Bamma left.'

I dropped the straw, ground my palms into my forehead.

McNally'd seen Christian in here, and thought Jet Black was an outlet for EPs? McNally had a line on the bricks? He hadn't even mentioned them. Maybe it was scare tactics, something to get me thinking so I'd give something away, the same as I did to people who were suspect. Fuck, Hobbs might've tipped them, just to get back at me.

'Tell him to call me as soon as he gets back.' I had to get the fuck out of there. 'Actually, tell him to come to the bar. I need a drink.'

'Will do, dude. Will do.'

I poured two more lines, though they were probably the last thing I needed, snorted all four anyway, wiped the place down and headed east of Eden to 99 Red Bottles.

The bar was empty as usual, but my watch said it wasn't supposed to open for another two hours.

'Brent?' I called. 'Hello?'

I walked around the bar, poured myself a whiskey, then another. Red glass candleholders lined the edge of the bar counter. My twitching fingers needed something to do, so I laid a candle in the center of each table, took the chairs down and pushed them underneath the tables. A pack of cigarettes sat on a grey jacket at the table by the jukebox. Delivery men. Brent was downstairs in the keg refrigerator, then. I passed through the kitchen that was never used—because Brent never served food—to the top of the stairs, and their voices echoed from the hallway below.

The wooden stairs were worn and slippery from millions of feet running down them, thousands of kegs dragging over them. The stone walls, supposedly over a hundred years old, glistened with condensation. The building had been a house until thirty years ago when some guy renovated it into a crappy restaurant, then lost interest and sold the building to Brent. You would've thought they'd put a cellar door to connect the street and the basement, make it easier to get kegs downstairs and reduce the risk of a Budweiser avalanche if you slipped. At least it wasn't a dirt floor like our shop. Was it still ours, Mary? What was the statute of limitations? How long did I have to wait to see you?

At the bottom of the steps, the keg refrigerator was closed, door locked. I looked around and didn't see anyone; listened, but only heard blood in my ears. Something wasn't right. No way McNally was here. The connections would be too far, too contrived. The ring around my neck spun through my fingers.

A noise, like a tomato smacking against a wet cement wall. A few quick footsteps. Tiny needles poked my cheeks. My palms went slick.

A moan came from the supply room, low voices arguing over the moan. I crept towards the voices. Water dripped from a metal pipe on the back of my hand. Leaning against the wall, I craned my head to try and catch what they were saying.

'I didn't,' said a voice that used gravel for throat lozenges. Another moan.

'Then who did?' the other voice lisped.

'I don't know. Ask him,' Gravel-Voice said.

'Hey.' A thump, followed by a sharp cry, then more moaning. 'Who shot you?'

A grunt, a moan. *Oh, fuck me, Brent. What the hell did you do?*

'See. He said I didn't shoot him.' Gravel-Voice sounded happy with himself.

'He didn't say you didn't shoot him,' the Lisp said.

'But he didn't say I did shoot him.'

'That's because he's gushing like a fucking lawn sprinkler.'

My eyes scoured the hallway. Cardboard boxes and glasses and plastic bags of bar towels and packages of napkins. No weapons. The voices argued more. No mirrors, either. In noiseless slow motion, I peeled back the lid of a cardboard box, found stacks of plates. More moaning put a lump in my throat. I checked another box. *Come on, come on, give me something. Please*

Brent, tell me you hid a gun or a knife. A reset switch—anything. The overhead pipe dripped onto my arm. The second box, old pots and pans. I inched out a lid, prayed nothing shifted inside, breathed on it and wiped off the dust with my shirt. At the edge of the supply room, I angled the lid to see inside, only catching a glimpse of the room near the rim of the lid, so that the voices wouldn't get a light show from where I was hiding. Two dark hulks stood over something on the ground. It was blurred but I knew it before I knew it.

The Twins. The fucking Twins.

My other hand steadied the twitching lid.

'You understand this was just business, right?' the gravel-voiced Twin said.

God damn you, Brent. I pressed my eyelids together until they hurt. *Why the fuck didn't you just take the money instead of a fucking tide-over? You stupid motherfucker.* I wiped the tears off my cheek with my shoulder.

The moaning was quieter.

'All right,' the gravel-voiced Twin said. 'Let's do this.' *Oh fuck oh fuck oh fuck do something Damon. Now!* Fuzzy reflected outlines. *Frisbee the lid at one of them then burst in and steal their guns. Throw plates at their eyes.* Something shaped like a 'Y.' The rustle of a plastic bag. *Gouge a fork in their necks. Something!* The sound of metal grating against metal, pieces of rust. Why hadn't I brought my fucking gun? The 'Y' was a pair hedge clippers. *Brent!*

A sharp cry.

'What'd you want for lunch?'

The sound of a watermelon breaking.

'It's a little late for lunch, don't you think?'

Soft gurgles.

'I'm hungry now, though. I'll still be hungry for dinner.'

The squish of watermelon juice, the crack of the rind splitting.

I bit my fist until I tasted bile and metal—to not scream, to not think, to not feel anything other than the nerves shrieking in the back of my hand. The lid shook like a cymbal. One of them said, 'But these are brand new shoes!' I watched my body move, my feet trip up the steps, my hands brace against the wall, then the counter, the jukebox, the street, my head wrench forward as I threw up stomach acid on a man standing right outside the bar.

Chapter 16

January: Now

Blood caked my hands. I stayed up all night and tried to apologize to Christian before he left for work but I was phantom to him. Twice his jaw tensed, ready to say—scream—something but he only swallowed and dumped the rest of his coffee in the sink. He made a point of leaving the lunch I'd made for him—chicken soup, oranges, three Codys and a white cigarette—on the table where I'd see it.

I can be such an asshole.

Things need to change.

I need to change.

Six days since I've seen natural sunlight. Eight days. Fuck, three years are four months for all it matters. I lean over the mirror and snort six times to steel myself, compose my nerves, then borrow some clothes from Christian. Nothing too nice, nothing too plain, somewhere in the middle where you're no one. Nothing he'll be upset about if I borrow. I peek out the window and it's a Christmas miracle: it's snowing, which means it's romantic anyway, and I can wear more of a disguise without looking like the Invisible Man.

Pair of jeans, blue: one

Pair of Vans, black and red: one

Tee shirt, black, Turbonegro: one

Sweatshirt, hooded, navy blue: one

Jacket, army-issued, olive green: one

Hat, woolen, black: one

Scarf, green and white striped: one

Gloves, woolen, black: two

In the bathroom, I shave, as if I'm molting, then fill the sink with club soda and Woolite. Mary used to swear by it, used it a few times when we got too rough and blood flecked her lingerie. I dunk his Morrissey shirt, rinse it until the water turns milky pink, leave it to soak for an hour or two then check in the mirror that my nose is clean. Golden. I creep down the steps to the front door of his building like a leper traipsing the sandy edge of its colony, then crack the door, scan outside, touch the back of my pocket for my switchblade and I wish I had my gun.

Bethel Street hibernates. No junkies, no bums, no cops, no psychopaths in matching Italian overcoats waiting for me. I walk like I'm a normal person, like I do this every day. Deep breaths, feel the cold air prickle inside my lungs and what's the point of snorting if just breathing feels this good. The street is foreign. I'm in Paris. In Budapest. I've never seen these streets that I live on. Tiny freezing patches hit my face. I stick out my tongue, let it go numb catching the snow then pull it back in and feel blood warm it.

So many shops line Thames Street. Civilizations have risen and fallen and built themselves back up since I last breathed this air. My chest swells, taking in cold and snow and exhaust fumes. The follicles inside my nose jump from scents other than my unwashed body and stale food. People hurry up and down the sidewalk holding bags and hands. The sky hangs like wet grey wool, wringing itself out on the city.

Blelvis is back again, dancing in the square, still singing Christmas songs even though Christmas was a while ago. I think. The ornaments are down, so it must've passed. I walk by him a few times, wanting to watch him, to hear something other than the drone of a TV or rattling of my thoughts but standing in one place for longer than a couple of minutes could mean I'll be gurgling through a second smile across my jugular. I keep my head down and check behind me.

A tremor spreads through my stomach. A fix-cramp. I need to get back soon before I start getting irritable, but it's nice being outside and it makes a noise again and I think that it's growling.

I stroll along the square, checking the lines inside each food place. I have an irrational craving for a burrito and michelada from Mama Iguana's back in Amherst. A tall thin man walks out of Brick Oven Pizza with half a piece in his mouth. I stop for a second, stare but try not to look like I'm staring. He lowers the slice. High cheekbones. Pencil mustache. It's fucking John Waters. Seven years I've lived here and this is the first time I've ever seen him. Christian will freak. We should watch *Pecker* tonight to commemorate it. If he'll sit in the same room with me.

It's not right. This. Everything. I can't do this anymore. Shaking hands and bruised knuckles. My best friend's face with the imprint of my fist. Killing everyone I love. Ruining anything I've worked to get. And that losing my love, my friends, probably my store, is what it takes to make things clear should be only a testament to what a fucking waste I am. Cleaning his shirt is a nice gesture but doesn't excuse dirtying it. My stomach roars, collapses on itself.

Johnny's Deli is empty. I walk inside. A woman rolls her head back and up at me. It's a struggle for her to breathe. Her forehead congeals with her cheeks and covers her eyes, then spreads again. A crab-cake sandwich sounds incredible, but I don't know that I trust it from here. Play it safe, then take Mary out for crab cakes once all of this blows over.

'Turkey sandwich on wheat bread, please.'

She looks at me.

'Lettuce, tomato, onion, please. And Old Bay, too. Thanks.'

The Fat Sea parts over her eyes twice before she hefts herself off the stool that creaks with relief, then she slaps a few pieces of meat and vegetables between the heel ends of a loaf of bread. No onion, but I'm shocked she actually put on gloves. I hand her money and walk out into the cold again, along the water down Thames, looking the other way as I walk past Eden Street and 99 Red Bottles, then stop, force my body to turn. I walk over cobblestones like they're mines, and up to the bar. The sandwich trembles, but it's not the shakes. I swallow bile, and light a cigarette, press my forehead against the window. A cloud of breath forms on the glass. The chairs, tables, jukebox, it's all gone. Seized as evidence by the state or auctioned away. An empty shell, a cold corpse of a bar. A pocket of bile rises in my throat and I turn away before leaving DNA evidence down the side of Brent's bar.

Two blocks farther and there's a pier with benches on it. I check behind me again, then head towards the bench at the end. The snow floats down over the harbor, like rain in slow motion, dances over the water then melts. As I take a bite of my sandwich, I half expect to see the ass-end of a beetle in my bite mark. Two chews and it tastes like pureed gall bladder with Old Bay. I let it fall from my mouth.

Something about standing here makes me feel like Brando. Maybe it's just the title. *On the Waterfront.* There should be a cameraman behind me, or director of photography. Someone in the background, moving around and catching the moment. Maybe you were on to something, Mary. I don't need cues. I've got the scene. I know the actions. A tugboat called *Miss Agnes* slips through the harbor, trailing a white cloud from its smoke-stack. Christian told me once that his ex, Libby or Gibby, lost her virginity on that boat. The lights on the Domino Sugar factory across the harbor blink. I hope they're not Morse and I spin around but there's no one there and it actually makes me smile.

If I can stand here now, I can do anything. Fuck getting more. Fuck getting better. I want my life back. Fuck Hobbs and Isabela and McNally and all my stupid insecurities. I should make a movie. Like *Swingers.* Mary didn't appreciate how great *Swingers* was, and thinking about her in the past tense makes my eyes burn. Just two guys and a little bit of money, bullshitting our bullshit. No licenses, no permits, no help. I'd heard that they filmed part of the Vegas section blind because there was a cop harassing them, so they hit record and just started talking. Once he gets over—once I apologize to Christian and make things better, we can get a couple friends and just make a movie. Sell some stuff to raise a bit of money. Buy an old camera like David Lynch and start filming. If it got really involved and started to go somewhere, sell our house to finance it or something. Or sell the store and create a normal life for us with no Hobbs and no McNally and—

Sell our house to finance the movie.

Sell Mary's house to finance the movie.

The house I slept in had Mary's name signed across the dotted line.

'Oh, fuck.' A damp plop and my fingertips are cold, rubbing the ring. The sandwich slumps on wet boards, soaking up melted snow and dirt.

Mary hadn't shown her face in weeks.

Mary couldn't leave town because of the house.

Mary's name is on the deed.

The Twins. The crack of a watermelon splitting open.

Hobbs gave orders to the Twins.

Everything I'd thought, everything I'd found out from Brent and Christian, it's wrong. All my information is wrong.

'Oh, fuck.' My face is wet.

Hobbs is going to kill my Mary.

Mary is going to die and it's all my fault.

Sprinting back to Christian's apartment, I knock over three or four people on the sidewalk. They were staring at the sky and the stores, so fuck them, they shouldn't have been in the way. Stabbing the lock in the door with my key, I vault up the steps—déjà vu makes me nauseated—and into the apartment, put weights in front of the door. Pace back and forth, step step step, fuck Damon, just think. Think think think think.

I bend over the mirror, snort four times, try to clear my head. Focus. Mr. Ashe might be able to help. If I can get in touch with

Isabela, I can get protection. But how am I supposed to get Mary? I don't even know where she is. If she's with Hobbs, that would be a start. But what am I supposed to do, storm the gates like a Viking? Get a crew and go represent, son, cuz he's dissin my bitch?

The ceiling starts creeping towards me again and I swing the broom at it, 'I've got no fucking time for you!' then a sharp pain, like a knife in the sole of my foot. I look down and I'm barefoot and I don't remember taking off my shoes. A blue circle in my heel. I pull it out with a wince. A thumbtack. I chuck it, but that wasn't such a good idea. Don't go on that side of the room.

Where would Mary go? She hasn't answered any of my messages. She could be dead already. But that couldn't happen. Sadistic fuck or not, you couldn't kill someone you've loved for fifteen years. And I'm the one he wants dead. He has no reason to hurt her, unless it was to hurt me. If he got me out of the picture, he could feasibly have Mary, but Mary wouldn't be with him. Even to spite me, to totally fucking destroy me, I still don't think she would be with him. But what if she in fact wouldn't be with him. He's already pissed because of all this shit with me, then on top of it, I'm finally out of the picture like he's always wanted and he still can't have her. He'd try to kill her out of anger, but when he put the gun to her forehead and stared into the aqueous sunset in her eyes and when she blinked he'd see that everything brightens when she—

A quiet ring.

Sirens?

A quiet ring again.

The phone. Where did I put the phone?

I throw take-away containers and cans of beer around the room, small plastic bags and shredded Casamir Lights. This room needs to be cleaned. The phone rings inside a brown bag.

'Hello?' My voice probes the phone like the head of a frightened turtle.

'Hey. I'll be home in fifteen,' Christian croaks. He still calls, even after last night. I'm such a bastard.

'Can we talk when—'

'Don't leave the apartment. They picked up Matt's stepbrother today. They can trace the bricks.'

'Wha—'

'We need to clean house,' then dial tone. They were never after EPs. I'd gotten us marked a long time ago.

Two plastic trash bags from under the sink. Beer cans and pretzel bags and cigarette papers. A separate pile for the small plastic bags. Chinese containers and paper soda cups and foil curry bowls and plastic silverware and paper napkins stained with pasta-sauce lips. The first bag fills in a few minutes. Then a few bowls and glasses and silverware and mugs from the living room, two mugs and some tea bags from Christian's room, all into the dishwasher.

The pile of small plastic bags. I slit the sides with a razor, peel them open, empty all the white powder, scrape the sides with the blade down onto the mirror.

What am I going to do about Mary?

Lick the sides of the bags. Afterburn. My gums and tongue go numb. I drop the handful of plastic and a few burnt roaches into the toilet and flush, then check his closet, under his bed, under the sink, behind the cereal. It's heavy. I open it, find a brick inside the cereal box and put it in his backpack to take out later.

Five minutes before he gets home. The place looks pretty good. Good enough. I bend over the mirror, snort the rest of the evidence, then lean back on the couch, try to relax. Deep breaths, remember the beach, Frisbee with the starfish, Mary and her coconuts. My fingers tap my thigh. I can't stop my brain from spinning in crazy circles and I need to calm down, be coherent and rational and I probably shouldn't have had those last snorts. Close my eyes, watch the dots and amoebas. Relax. Inhale. Exhale.

A wet thump, like a sack of potatoes dropped in a puddle of pudding.

I grab the butcher knife from the kitchen and creep to the door. Control your breathing, Damon. Just fucking stay quiet. It's Christian. It has to be. It's only Christian.

Everything's okay. Remember, you almost stabbed him last time. Deep breaths.

My ear on the door. An ocean roars inside the wood. Listen close. I hold my breath, to hear better.

Nothing.

He's getting his breath back. If he went to the market, he has bags. He's sick, too, so it's more exertion for him to do normal things. Carrying groceries up the steps can make him tired.

A slight jingle.

He's looking for his keys. Wait for the knock, Damon. Shit, are we supposed to do the knock? I think he didn't want to do it because it was dumb and we never thought of a new knock. Listen close. Hold your breath. My toes are cold. Stop your hand from shaking. Grip the knife tighter. Don't put the other hand on the door because it will start tapping and make noise.

Light breathing.

He's caught his breath. He'll open the door in five seconds. Lean forward, get closer to the door. Four seconds. The apartment is clean. We'll figure out the brick situation and the Mary situation. He's the smarter one, anyway. Three seconds. We'll make a plan and in a week, the three of us will be sitting on the couch, drinking a beer, and laughing about this whole funny mix-up. Two seconds.

My feet are really cold. One second. I rub my big toe on the one next to it.

It slides.

It's slick.

My fingers stop tapping. My heart stops beating. Don't forget to breathe. My hand relaxes and the knife slides out, bottom jaw goes epileptic and I lean my head down slow slow slowly. Brace against the door. I don't have any toes. I don't have feet anymore. My brain sends an electro-chemical reminder to my heart. It smacks against my chest, dents my lungs. I can't breathe. I'm dying. Spiders in stiletto heels sprint up and down my throat and beetles chew on my brain lining, drink the fluid and deposit their eggs. I look down at the floor. At my feet. My feet, islands of skin in a bloody sea seeping from under the crack of the front door.

Chapter 17

December: Then

I woke in the middle of our kitchen floor to the sound of apocalyptic horse hooves trampling clouds. I breathed into my hand, didn't smell alcohol for once. Ashen light bled through the kitchen window. The house, cathedral quiet. My heart had stopped. I was dead. Or it was a fucked up dream. *I shouldn't watch so many horror movies, they're messing with my head.* The thumping started again. I put my hand over my sternum, realized it wasn't my heart, then listened. It wasn't coming from inside the house.

A dull thump. The front door.

The Twins. McNally. Mrs. Grady asking why I never call her back.

I grabbed a butcher knife from the drawer by the sink, then paused and grabbed another. Kneeling down, I crept along the wall to the couch room, nudged back an inch of curtain with the tip of the knife. Christian paced on the steps. Up the steps, thump thump thump, down the steps, drag on his cigarette, up the steps, 'Damon, open the fucking door.' I cracked the window open.

'Pssst.' He whipped his head around, looked for the noise. 'In the window,' I whispered.

He shouted towards the roof. 'What the fuck are you doing? Open the door!'

'I'm downstairs. Did anyone follow you?'

'No one followed me. Now open the door.'

'You sure?'

'Open the god damn fucking door!'

I laid the knives on the window ledge and hauled the couch back from the front door. Christian's arm snaked through the crack and his body slid in behind it. As soon as he was inside, I jammed the couch back against the door. Blood bulged through a vein in his neck. Beads of sweat glinted on his forehead. Even his eyes seemed to pulse.

'Hey,' I said, then spun around as his fist kissed my face.

'The fuck is wrong with you, Damon?' He loomed over me. I hunched myself up on my elbow, rubbed my jaw. 'What the hell is going on?'

'I'm trying to stay alive and you just fucking throttled me, that's what's going on,' I said, a bone-click with every word I spoke. 'You have your own key, anyway.'

'A key doesn't work when there's a fucking couch in front of the door.' He extended his hand, pulled me to my feet. 'What happened? All I understood was Brent and watermelon and you screaming.' The vein pulsed slower.

'The Twins,' I said. Christian's faced eroded from brick to white marble. He stutter-slumped back onto the arm of the couch, stared at me.

'The Twins what?'

I sat, blinked my eyes. Blinked back the thin layer coating them.

'How do you know?' His voice was barely a whisper, afraid to hear it in actual words instead of concepts, because then it's real, it actually happened, and if I didn't have to say it then he didn't have to hear it, and with a few visits to the Virgin we might be able to think it into not being true and we can just go for a pint.

I took a breath. 'I watched it.'

God hit pause on His big VCR. The sparrows' chirp clipped mid-song, breeze-dried laundry froze in sideways ripples, leaves bonded to molecules of oxygen in the air, our house stopped settling in its foundation. There was only breathing. Inhale, exhale, inhale, cough, exhale. The gurgle and choke as we tried to swallow down everything we couldn't bear to admit.

Which was more dangerous: all of the blinds in the house closed—which meant I was inside and hiding—or all of them open, and someone could see inside but didn't know if I was home or not?

Christian spent the days with the living and drank away the darkness with me at the house. While he was at work, I watched parts of movies, played bits of video games, listened to Duran Duran and stared at the ceiling. I shuffled through my life like a film on the back of my eyelids, tried to figure out what I did to fuck myself and when I did it.

If I'd never worked at Fast Feet, I would've never met Eric. If I would've never met Eric, I would've never met Julian and would have never started dealing. Then I would've never met Paul and he wouldn't have fucked up the situation and I wouldn't have had to turn him into a pile of slush with Vanilla Ice lines in his hair because he was trying to kill me. I would've never heard that scream, and that kid would still be alive.

I would've never had to run to Baltimore. I wouldn't have needed to check my reflection in store windows to make sure there wasn't an axe swinging at my head. I wouldn't have heard the sound of a watermelon cracking open. Wouldn't have seen the hedge clippers. I wouldn't have ever had the name Hobbs roll across my tongue. I wouldn't have needed to duck under the windows of my house when I walked by them. I wouldn't have been taking too many white cigarettes a day and my hands wouldn't be shaking like maracas.

But then I would've never met Mary. I would've never curved my body against hers in bed. Wouldn't have ever swam in the ocean of her scent while she slept. Would've never felt how soft her rosewood hair was. I wouldn't have sat in The Charles and watched Hitchcock or eaten sushi and drank sake then made out as soon as we left the restaurant. I would've never made her breakfast in bed and opened Stay Gold two hours late because we just couldn't manage to get our clothes back on.

Everything was shit. I lived in constant paranoia because of the stupid things I'd done. It could've ended at any time, and I was trying to come to terms with that concept. Everything's inevitable. But if I met the fifteen-year-old me, I'd make him watch Donnie Darko, and as Donnie says that when the world comes to an end he'll have so much to look forward to, tell fifteen-year-old me to remember that. And that was Mary. She was worth it.

There was a crash, then gritted teeth sending me through various layers of Hell.

'Can we please turn on a light?' he said.

'Why don't I just take out an ad in the paper to tell them I'm hiding inside the house?'

In the blue glow of the television, Christian rubbed his shin and sat down in a beanbag chair shaped like Mae West's lips. When you fluffed up the chair, her lips were soft and luscious, but once you used it, she was a plastic surgery disaster. 'Can we at least sit in a room, then?'

I shook my head, realized he probably couldn't see me. 'There are windows in the rooms. Someone could see the light from the TV. The hallway's the only place without windows.' I snorted twice.

'Then put a blanket over the window,' he said.

'I might as well turn on a light then.' I handed him the mirror and dollar bill. He tossed the dollar bill back to me and picked up his straw. I'd left the Tylenol at the store, but at least I managed to not ruin perfectly good lines with tears. *God damn you, Brent.*

'He already knows where you guys live. If Hobbs was going to have them do anything, he would've done it already,' he said, then snorted twice. The mirror sat on top of a pizza box, next to two bottles of Blood of Christ wine and the whiskey he'd bought the day before. He made a good point. I switched on the PlayStation, handed him the controller with the tongue logo from The Rolling Stones on it.

'I think you need to go back to work,' Christian said.

'Eh.'

'He knows where you live. He knows where you work. You left him a month ago and he hasn't done anything yet. I mean,' he sipped from the bottle then lowered his voice, 'maybe Mary talked to him.'

Or maybe Hobbs was so busy with her, he hadn't had a chance to try and kill me. I picked up the mirror and snorted twice while the game screen loaded.

'It's arctic in here,' he said.

'December tends to do that.'

From inside the closet, he said, 'You can't really sit in your house all day killing brain cells and playing video games.'

'Thanks, Mom.' My hands twitched. 'I read too, you know.'

'Jesus Christ, Damon.' He pointed at the floor. 'All of the shit you've gone through, and this is what you do?'

I leaned over, looked inside. A few stacks of Mary's shoes, a jar filled halfway with coins, some old VHS tapes, and a knee-high stack of bricks.

'I forgot about them.'

He sat down and took the mirror from me before I could spasm our supply all over the carpet, nodded at my hands, handed me the whiskey.

I tipped the bottle back and poured six seconds of whiskey down my throat. 'I can talk to Bela about protection. That is, if McNally and his buddies haven't bagged my store as evidence.'

'He hasn't been by Jet Black since the day…that day. And he could easily find you if he wanted.'

'That's what worries me.'

'Why don't you come up to Amherst for Christmas? Mom would love to see you. You could drop by your folks, too, if you wanted.'

'Is it evading police or anything if I went?'

'I think they'd have to tell you you're under investigation first.

They always do on *Law and Order*, at least.'

'Maybe,' I said.

'Maybe? What else are you going to do?' he laughed. I shrugged, muttered something unintelligible. 'Then come up. She'd love to see you.'

I took another slug of whiskey, contemplated Amherst and all its comforts and all its ghosts. 'I don't want her to see me like this.'

I'd killed the phone, drawn the curtains, wedged the couch in front of the door. On the TV, a camera trained its lens on a fireplace, burning bright and warm with flickers and flashes that caught the relief of the wooden mantel. 'LOG TV' in the bottom corner. I leaned back against the wall. Cuddled in one palm was Mr. Jameson and Sons, there to join me for dinner. In the other, cupped like a tiny bird with a fractured wing, sat two pills: one red, one green. It being Christmas Day and all.

Two EPs, unchewed, washed down with five seconds of Jameson.

Next door, I could hear laughs covering the voice-over track of *A Christmas Story*. Mary and I had tried to watch that for the whole marathon once—every Christmas Day, a cable channel played it for twenty-four hours straight—but we got tired halfway through the fourth showing and instead went outside and made the snowman version of Rick and Ilsa from the last scene in *Casablanca*. I tipped back more of Christian's whiskey, heard his voice. 'It'll help. It's been a rough couple of days.' I fought to keep myself from saying "Here's looking at you, kid" aloud because it seemed too cliché then I heard a noise in the kitchen. Turning my head, I caught a glimpse of the TV fireplace in the corner of my eye and it shone down like the tropical sun on the water that was ebbing through the kitchen. The palm tree behind the sink bent low with the wind and covered the counter. I dipped my finger in the water, flicked it towards the tree and the giant leaf trembled, flitted to the side and I heard Mary's laugh. I stood unsteady on my feet, watched them slosh through the shorebreak but trying to be quiet, over to the leaf to sneak up on Mary, pull the leaf back and surprise her but when I did it was just her laugh, empty air where her rosewood hair should've been flowing in the breeze, the reason why she'd wanted to grow it longer. She'd said that it was classy, and I creep around the counter, follow her laugh. There's another leaf, her laugh hanging heavy behind it and I know she's there, I can see the shadow of her hand. I reach out, grab onto her hand and slide it in my mouth, what are you doing, Damon? You're so strange sometimes, and I can't help but laugh, laugh that this is all over and finally, finally she's back with me. Her finger bends, says come here, follow me, and I do, but can't let go of her hand. It leads me down the hallway and there's always music in the air, at first trailing under her saltwater breeze then getting louder and strangling it to still air, choking it to the ground as her hand opens the door and waves goodbye and smoke billows through, cigarettes and beer and Smashing Pumpkins covering the scene. I'm walking through the back door of Julian's, from his porch into his kitchen. He's sitting behind me, sprawled on a Barcalounger like some combination of Jay Gatsby and Pablo Escobar. I can hear him say, 'That kid, I'll tell you. Him and Eric, without them, none of this that you see would be possible.' He always says that. Said that.

This isn't happening. I'm not there. I was here. This happened. What's happening?

Eric sits in a chair to the side of the kitchen, a girl with long black hair on his lap. I have two drinks in my hand. Gin and tonics, looks like. Mary's hand has disappeared. She left, again. It's better. She shouldn't be here for this. 'I thought you forgot about me,' Eric smiles. I hand him a drink and he motions to the girl. 'Michael, this is Eliza. Eliza, Michael.' I smile at her, feel Paul's eyes on me, crawling over me and probing every inch of my head for soft tissue, something that caves without much force. A smooth hand on my elbow. Mary's back. No, please sweetie, you can't be here. I turn and Morrissey Mason puts her hands on my forearms, kisses me once on each cheek, like the Europeans, like the Smiths. She guides me to the couch and I crawl on my hands and knees, dodge Paul's eyes.

A bottle of gin between us, and we're leaning closer and the bottle's empty. Two guys try to do a handstand on one of Julian's chairs and it breaks, shatters into pieces that float in the air then flutter to the ground and they're all laughing. My hands tremble but it's not white, it's nerves and I've been waiting for this for three years, walking behind her and trying to be witty and making astute observations and bribing course registration officials with packs of white cigarettes for semesters of painting with Mason and it's here.

I wasn't here. I'm there.

Someone hits play and "Mayonaise" starts again, the third time I've heard it tonight but it's such a good song that it's okay, and Paul's staring at my back, he's in the kitchen I can feel him, and Mason leans over, puts her lips to my ear and my heart flutters and she says, 'I love this song.' I agree, and smile, and we're such a good match, don't you think, Mason, in a small-town college way? But you're no Mary, you'll never be Mary and I know you're going to crush me, Mason, you've ripped out my heart and left it on too many floors. I can feel it even though it has, hasn't, happened but you can't bring me near the edge and make me feel the depths of what Mary will do, did, to me and Mason leans over again, my heart flutters again, despite itself, and she whispers, 'You have some, right? I want to fuck to this song for hours.' I try not to seem too eager even though I've been waiting, watching, dying for this moment for years and maybe we can start over Mason, tonight, maybe we can pretend that you care and that you really want me, me, in you, with you and I'm not just a warm body with a white nose and as I get up to get our drinks to take them upstairs to lay her down on Julian's bed, Paul blocks me, snarling, 'What the fuck do you think you're doing?' I tell him I'm getting a drink and he asks what the fuck I'm doing with her and I mutter then he grabs my arm, digs his fingers between my muscle and bone, eyes raging and hands twitching so hard he's going to dislocate my shoulder. 'What the fuck did you say?' *I said if she's your fucking girl, why don't you go fucking talk to her and leave me the fuck alone.* And I turn my head to Eric's voice, him and the girl with black hair he's trying to sleep with, his arms up saying what's all the noise? and feel Paul's knuckles against my temple.

I spin around and shake my head, and when I look up Paul is charging with a piece of broken chair. His first swing misses but second connects with my elbow and there are white stars in my eyes and his face I've only seen in Albrecht Durer paintings of the Inferno and I do the only thing I can because this is how I have, will, always deal with things. I pull out my gun and put a bullet in the ceiling. With one shot, I killed the party. It's dead silent and all two hundred people listen to the splitting crack the cartilage in Paul's nose makes as I lay my fist against it. He stumbles back, throws his arms over his head and starts to bring the chair leg down towards my face, and from all the adrenaline and endorphins and pain I don't realize my finger is still on the trigger as I try to cave in the side of Paul's head with my gun. A bullet sprouts wings and flits across the room. Paul rolls on the floor holding the lump on the side of his head then I'm on him and the thrashing of blood in my ears has dulled. I only hear acute sounds: the snap of a bone, the squish of flesh caving, the smack of bloody knuckles on a bloody face, the plop of his blood dripping from my face back to his. I watch my fists sink farther and farther into his cheeks, still writhing and cursing me, and from far down an abandoned frigid corridor, covered in rusted shackles and dulled spikes and dripping water, the scream roars into my ears.

That scream.

The scream that I'll hear forever, forever soaked into my brain and a part of me.

Hands on my shoulders and Eric and Julian rip me away, yank me across the room. A bit of Paul drips onto Eric as he locks me into a hold. Julian is shouting and Eric is dragging me, but there's only the girl who Eric was trying to sleep with. She's on her knees, kneeling like in a pew at church, holding someone in her lap. Her hair covers most of them, a privacy curtain in a funeral parlor. Her head falls back, screaming, wailing, begging and pleading over the pale and blood-splattered boy in her arms.

It was an accident, Mary.

Then I'm in my car, Eric asking if I know who Paul is and the look on his face tells me it's not good, the mouth on his face tells me the pile of meat I left behind was Julian's partner. I tell him I'll call him, the words floating in a steam cloud in front of my eyes, and the interstate yawns wide and empty before me and my shaking hands. I'm going to New York, to be Jack Kerouac and Neal Cassady because Christian and I always wanted to but his mom would never let us, and then I see a sign for Baltimore posted on the side of the highway and Christian goes to art school in Baltimore, and I look up and the sun breaks the skyline in pops and cracks like a fire on Christmas Day and I looked sideways, my head on the wooden floor, at my arms, and I heard the echo of a Patti Smith song and started to shiver. My arms, covered in cuts and gashes, and there wasn't a knife anywhere in sight. A small puddle sat next to my chest, run-off from my arms, and I thought I should get a towel before it stains her floor. Where did you go, Mary?

Every person who walked by me on the sidewalk was a cop. I pulled my hand inside my sleeve, cupped my switchblade in my palm, my thumb ready to flick out the blade in case I ran into anyone I didn't want to see. I constantly rubbed my chin on my shoulder to catch a glance behind me. Burped and tasted Christian's whiskey. My forearms burned, even with aloe on them. I parked ten minutes from the store and took a winding path through Fell's Point to make sure no one was following me.

I finally opened the door to Stay Gold a few days or weeks after I had last closed it, on my way to see Brent. The lock clicking was the crack of a watermelon. My dirty hands were Paul's face under my fingernails. Everything was the same as I remembered it. From what I could remember. The same and stalker-free.

Three quick snorts from the Tylenol to calm my nerves. The vacation had slowed business; my eyes fixated on the empty TV monitor for a lonely hour, cigarette smoke filling the cracks between minutes, swirling around me as I paced the office. Under the desk, in the emergency pit, everything was normal. McNally wouldn't raid me yet. If he could catch me in the act, my sentence and his bonus would be bigger.

Then in the front window, two hulking shapes, dark silhouettes with red eyes burning and glistening white fangs. My hand shot to my switchblade, my throat closed, eyes blinked and nothing was there.

The chair behind the desk, collapsed into it. Breathed deep. Tried to steady my hands. Snorted twice. Rubbed my eyes hard until dots floated in front of me, watched the rainbow amoebas floating in the saltwater I wouldn't let leak from my eyes.

I startled in the chair, looked at the clock. Two hours had evaporated like ragged breaths. Sledgehammers smacked the sides of my head. My muscles were liquid floating around bone. I leaned my head down to the desk and snorted twice, long and deep, and when I looked up Bela was tapping her foot on the TV monitor. I set the mirror back in the emergency pit and went to the front.

'Long time, no see,' she said in a dead monotone.

'Yeah, sorry. I've been feeling a bit under the weather.' I forced a cough, pretended it was a struggle for me to be standing.

'I can tell.' She reached into her house-call-doctor purse, massively unamused, and exhumed out a wad of tissues. 'Clean yourself up.'

Dots on my shirt. My upper lip and chin, sticky and damp.

Blood. From my nose.

'Why has the store been closed? This is the second time I've had to tell you this, Damon.'

'I wasn't feeling well,' I said, still wiping my face.

She crossed her arms. 'I never told him about the first time.'

'Thanks,' I said, dropped the mess of tissue into Truman's trashcan behind the counter. A forearm gash caught on the liner of my jacket.

'Are we clear on this?'

I nodded.

'Good,' she said, pulling a smaller bag out of her larger one. 'Not that you'll need it since you haven't been open to actually sell anything, but here is your shipment. Remember that we've been making good on our side of the commitment.' She handed the purse to me. I slung it over my shoulder by the strap, then realized what I looked like and dropped it on the counter. It made her smile, finally.

'We might have some problems,' I said.

She cocked her head, pulled more tissues from her purse. 'You definitely have problems.' My upper lip was wet again. 'But what might these other problems be?'

McNally's card landed on the counter. 'Hobbs and the Twins, too. I think they're going to kill me.'

She breathed a small laugh.

'That might not be more than a business issue to you but it'd be a big fucking inconvenience to me.' I wiped my lip hard. 'And I won't be able run the store in the clink or with my brain splattered over an alleyway.'

Her face went serious. 'Why do you think that?'

The blurred outlines. The hedge clippers. The squish of watermelon juice.

'I have my suspicions. I need some protection. They could help me with the store, too. And,' in a mocking tone, 'you'd have someone to watch me to make sure the store's open.'

She didn't laugh.

'This guy's bad juju, as well.' I flicked McNally's card at her. 'He's been asking around.'

'Damon.' She took my hand in hers. It was smooth and cold as an oyster shell. 'You work for Mr. Ashe. That's all the protection you need.'

I wore a jacket Christian had left in the office and peeked out the front door, checked the sidewalks for Them or Isabela or McNally. The street looked clear so I locked the store, patted my jeans and jacket pocket. Switchblade, Tylenol and Cas Whites.

Deep breathing and I tried to calm myself, repeated 'no one's following you' over and over. When I muttered, people looked at me like I was a schizo-bum and stayed a few feet away from me. It made me smile, so I repeated random things louder to give myself more space, which made me more conspicuous. And as I looked up to cross the street, two hulking masses stood on the opposite side. My head dropped, so maybe they hadn't seen me. I peeked up to see who I could throw in front of me for protection and it was two fat old men. Popped a cigarette in my mouth and crossed without waiting for the light to turn.

There wasn't anywhere in particular I had to go, but I couldn't stay in the store. Too many memories and subconscious hunches gave me too many heart attacks. Every crinkle of a dollar bill was the shearing of hedge clippers. Every tick of the clock was a gunshot and the scream. Every piece of dirt was a flake of Paul's face. And every last fucking thing I smelled was Mary.

Palming the Tylenol, I faked a sneeze and snorted twice. My hands steadied, then heart fluttered when I heard Mary.

This isn't good, Damon.

'What isn't good, sweetie?'

This.

I nodded my head. 'I know, Mary. I'm sorry. I didn't mean to fuck things up like this. I'm so sorry.'

No, babe. I mean you.

'Me? What do you mean?'

I can't see you like this.

I sniffed, wiped my nose. The Tylenol was still in my pocket but I couldn't do it in front of her.

'I'm sorry, Mary. I'm sorry.'

Please try to get better. It hurts too much to watch you do this.

'I'll try sweetie, I'll really try. It's so hard. It's just…I mean…'

Her finger on my lips: *shhhh.*

It'll be okay.

A faint hiss. Metal clinked at my feet. My hands rose, covered my face from the blade. Two flashes caught my eye. Two quarters on the brick sidewalk. A man with a visor and an I BELIEVE in Baltimore sweatshirt said 'God Bless' and smiled at me. Looking around, I figured out that I was standing in front of Daily Grind, shivering. I felt something shake in my hand, looked down at the City Paper, couldn't remember picking it up. I wanted a bump, but I promised Mary I'd try. *I really will, sweetie.*

I opened the door and went inside to get a cup of coffee.

Chapter 18

January: Now

A piece of paper.

It used to be white.

The paper. The note.

Two holes in the top of it.

A piece of wire.

A piece of wire attached the note.

A piece of wire attached the note to Christian's cheek. Through Christian's cheek.

My fingerprints on the note, inked with his blood.

His blood in the hallway. On the floor. On my feet, my hands, my shirt, cheeks, hair, mouth, teeth, and eyelids.

So much blood.

His chest rises slowly, and the gashes spread open. Falls slowly, gashes close. Lips flutter in exhales.

I bite my lips, to not throw up, think about something else. He looks like Paul. But worse. Slashed. Cut. Skewered. Battered. Jesus Christ.

The note in my hand.

Hobbs-n-Mary

4-ever

He drew a heart around it, like you'd carve into a tree if you lived in the 50s.

Then under the heart: *Go have another walk. Stay Gold in the morning with $400K.*

He's dying. Christian. My blood brother whose blood covers me. He can't. I can't let him. I grab the mirror, trying not to let the powder shake onto the floor, lean over and take two snorts—a goodbye kiss—to steady myself. Just a little. Flipping on the kitchen sink, I dunk the mirror under it, turn the powder into a paste and wash it down the drain. Quicker, quicker, come on, he won't die here. Won't. I wipe out the sink and wash the mirror again, then grab the Virgin and put her in Christian's backpack with the brick—nothing incriminating. 'Hang on, man. It'll be okay. You'll be okay.' Don't forget to breathe. Make sure Christian's still breathing. His hand, cold and slick in mine. Eyelids flutter like butterfly wings. He's dreaming, breathing and dreaming.

'You're going to be okay, Christian. Just another few minutes.' Tears shatter my voice as I reassure him. Splash water on my face, my hands in the kitchen sink. Pull on a sweatshirt and shoes. Wipe my bloody footprints off the floor. He'd be smiling at me right now.

The apartment is clean. No traces of anything. Christian's still breathing. Everything will be okay. I grab his backpack and the phone from its holder, close the door and lock it, then dial 911. Lay the phone in his palm.

I kneel beside him, sniffing. Holding his hand. Staring at him. I'm so fucking sorry, Christian.

'911 what is your emergency? Hello? Hello, are you all right? Hello?' They're coming, be here in a minute and he's still breathing.

Leaning my head down, quiet as a chapel, I put my lips on his cheek. The ring around my neck brushes his cheek, his grandfather coming and giving him a kiss, staying with him. I mouth *Love you, dude. You'll be okay. Everything's going to be okay. I'll see you soon.* I hope I'm not lying. I squeeze his hand and hurry down the steps, peek out the door.

The street's empty. Thank fuck.

I hurry down the Bethel, watching the asphalt, shifting my eyes up briefly to check for no one. Turn the corner at Fleet Street and get to Stay Gold as quick as I can without collapsing.

In front of the store, I don't bother to look for anyone. No one saw me leave Christian's. An ambulance flies up Broadway and screams left at Aliceanna. His chariot has arrived. No one will come for me here, not now. As long as McNally takes his time raiding me, I'm golden. All of this bullshit for those stupid little rainbow pills. Christian on his way to the E.R., Mary bound and gagged with a gun indenting her eyebrow, me emaciated and insane.

I lock the front door then go to the safe. My hand quivers. Bills scattered all over the storage pit, filled almost to the top. My mouth cracks into the closest thing to a smile I can manage. The sun is setting, which means I have between ten and fourteen hours, depending on their definition of morning.

Piles of money surround me. Different denominations. No order. I pull out a handful and see the corner of the red toolbox. My hand twitches, shaking bills out of my grip. A drip of drool in the corner of my mouth. 'Control yourself, Damon,' and my hand stings hard across my cheek. I start to sort the money around me, try not to look at the toolbox, to imagine the burn inside my nose and synthetic drip down my throat, the chemical orgasm bursting through my blood. Mary needs me.

I pile bills in stacks by value: $50, 20, 10, and 5. A few $100s to the side. I count to five thousand by fifties once, twice, lose count again and my hand goes epileptic and I can't concentrate. The lid of the red toolbox yawns, lets a mist of white out to catch in my nose, remind me what I'm missing and I really fucking need a bump. Christian should be at the hospital already. He's got an IV drip of morphine and a nurse dressed like Elle Driver taking care of him. A deep breath, center my head on Mary. If I can't count this out, she's dead and it's all my fault. Again.

'A line would sort out your head, help you think.'

'A line will make you worse in fifteen minutes and you'll fuck up again and Mary will be dead. Shut up and count.'

Most of this money is Mr. Ashe's, yet another person we'll have to hide from. Maybe Isabela could help. She's a woman, she'll understand the stupid things we do for love. We'll pay him back. It's just a very large loan, a mortgage I took out on Mary. Or maybe only I will pay him back. Even when I give the money to Hobbs, I doubt Mary will stay with me. At least she'll be alive.

My hands turn cold suddenly and I look down at the open toolbox in my lap. The bags are still closed and my nose isn't burning but I can't do this. I imagine throwing the box and watching it explode like a dirty bomb and sprinkle a fine snow inside the office, a light dusting of evidence. I drop the box in the emergency pit and check for any extra money inside, grab a few hundred dollars.

Eventually, I can make it to five thousand, fifty by fifty and counting aloud to myself. I make more piles, rubber bands holding them together, the value written on the top bill. Each stack buys back another part of her body. I just saved her foot, her calf, her thigh, her other foot, ten toes. Now I have two legs, then her butt, now up to her belly button. Money pours through a Mary-shaped hourglass. She's coming back to life, pulled from the sand and beach of my dreams and funneled into the backroom.

The pit drains fast, faster than her body materializes. I have enough to buy back half of her body, from her toes up to her hips, but the bills are getting smaller. I'm counting by tens now and groups of cells are sliding into the hourglass instead of full limbs and digits. A drip from my forehead puckers the bill in my hand and I have to concentrate on each bill, each number. I knock over a pile when my hand spasms and have to start it over again.

Her foot taps, waiting for me to hurry up and finish, make her whole. She rubs her right foot with her left toes, like she does in bed when we're watching a movie.

Up on my feet. Pacing. Breathing. Try to regroup, to fixate on her and not a bump. I have enough for the bottom half of her body, toes to bottom of the ribs. No arms. No hands or fingers. No face, cheeks, lips, shoulders or heart.

And the pit is empty.

$251,034. And sixty-eight cents in my pocket.

My feet move me from the desk to the pit to the desk to the pit. Fingers twitch and lungs spasm; blood screams for a bump, screeching in my ears, splitting my eardrums.

So close. So much money and so close and it can't happen. There has to be a way. There's more money somewhere. I've already checked under and inside the safe four times. The emergency…no, I already counted the eight hundred twelve from there. Check again, and nothing. There has to be more somewhere…

The emergency pit. The toolboxes. The bricks.

I stack the bricks from Christian. I tear open the lids and dump the boxes on the floor, make a pile of the singles and full-lengths, and Mary has arms up to her shoulders. I count the bags of pills again. I found an extra finger. Gather all the small bags, the rainbow of God's kiss in gelatin capsules. Quick math and Mary has a ribcage, a heart and a few fingers. Count again, hopefully find more of her body, but I counted wrong the first time and she's lost one of her elbows. Then there's nothing else. Everything's counted. I snake my hand around inside the box, turn it upside down and smack the bottom. Count again as I put everything back.

This can't be happening. This isn't right. We're so close. Fucking hell, Mary. All of those DVDs and the useless crap we bought, things we don't need. The posters and take-away Chinese and records. My goddamn stupid fucking special edition things I bought because I had to have it and I've killed her. We sold your arms to buy a new couch. So many PlayStation games piled next to—

PlayStation games.

The couch.

All of the shit in the house. There has to be enough to buy the rest of Mary's body. Throw everything into a garbage bag and sell it. Empty the house.

The house!

'Mary, we can buy two of you with the one house!'

But her name is on the dotted line. Her hand has to sign over the house. The hand that I haven't bought back yet and is probably tied to the other behind a chair in the basement of Hobbs' lair right now.

Her name.

The car is in my name. It's worth at least an arm and a shoulder. I could sell the car and be that much closer. I can sell the car. In two days. My mouth sloshes with metal, a splatter of blood when I spit. It sounds like rain as it hits the floor. There has to be something. Something something something something. Enough to buy Mary her body back. I could put everything we own in a moving van and park it in Hobbs' driveway. Drop the van key in an envelope, have Mary leave a lip mark on the seal and ride off into the sunset on Zed's chopper. But it's not money. He'd have to sell it and that bastard couldn't be bothered.

Walk in with a suitcase full of paper on the bottom, bills on the top, and a knife in my waistband. But he'd expect me to try to kill him.

Cyanide in his martini. All three of their martinis. Do the gene pool a favor. Pose as a bartender and drop in the death pills while they're not looking.

This is getting ridiculous. I need to think realistically and I'll pace until I figure something out and my hands will not stop twitching. I watch as my fingers wrap around the handle of a vacuum, in slow motion. The veins surface like breaching whales on the back of my hands. Muscles flex, differentiate themselves and manipulate the scars on my forearms. Swing it in a graceful arc, and it collides with the ground in a shower of sharp plastic pieces and metal springs and rods, dust floating down like springtime pollen storms.

A film of dirt on my lips. I spit it out and look at the back room. I'm out of options and Mary's ghost is going to haunt me in the store for as long as I live. At least she'll be with me, in some form.

She'll haunt the store.

The store that Mary and I run.

But my name is the only one on the dotted line.

I can cross out my name and Hobbs can sign his next to it.

$362,254.68 and a store, traded for Mary.

Hobbs can clean the store all by himself. It's not actual cash but he doesn't have to do anything with it. He'll have all the cash from the pit then put an ad in the paper and with real estate being so valuable in Fell's Point, it'll sell within a week and he'll have three times what he originally wanted.

I plop down in the chair behind the desk and light a cigarette, inhale, then smile, exhale. Everything is going to be okay. I think. My watch says I still have about eight hours until…shit, I don't know what until. They'll come here, I assume. My eyes run over the red toolbox. I pick it up, trembling, sit back in the chair, staring at it. My cells have traded cone party hats and kazoos for machetes and two-by-fours speckled with nails, threatening to kill if I don't give them more white. Their chants echo inside my ear canals. That feeling, someone new, just one snort away. I wipe my hand across my forehead. It's been more than four hours since my last hit. Fuck it. There's no chemical embrace as soothing as Mary's. With my foot, I flick open the emergency pit, drop the box in and close the pit.

I shove thirty thousand dollars into a double-layered plastic bag and hide it under a cabinet—half for Christian and his medical bills and half for Mary and me. Hopefully. Finally, I sit down in the chair and light another cigarette, turn on the television monitor for something to look at, and slap my feet on top of the desk, fingers woven together behind my head.

And I wait.

Details. It's the details I'm usually good with. I forgot about them this time.

A few hours yawn into millenniums, the apocalypse condensed into half a day. The time it takes to drive from Baltimore to Florida, or Amherst and back. An earthquake of muscle spasms ravages my body. Rivers of bile cascade from my mouth into the basin filled with a half-digested turkey sandwich. The droughts of sleep and my eyes brushfire burn as long as they're open but the world spins like a washing machine when they're closed.

I try to disassociate myself with it. Let the trade winds blow me from a convulsing pile to the warm beach with Mary. Stretched out under the sun. The coconuts and the wind and the starfish, feel the breeze cool us and the sand grate between our toes, smell salt and driftwood and palm trees.

It's warm for a while, until I'm too comfortable on a beach towel and my stomach turns itself inside out and wrenches itself up my throat. A few minutes or years later, the trade winds are back and it's warm.

Lather. Rinse. And fucking repeat.

The front of the store sleeps motionless on the television monitor. Nothing has happened for as long as I've been crumpled here. I contemplate sitting up for interminable minutes, afraid it might push my fragile bile-covered equilibrium the other way, then see a flicker on the monitor.

Two dark shadows at the front window.

Them. The Twins.

I pull myself to my feet and don't throw up. The worst is probably over, and I think my shaking hands are unrelated now. I drag my feet over the carpet, the tiny crack of static lightning bolts between my soles and the carpet. I am the person in the movie I yell at: Don't go there in there, you idiot. Don't you know what's going to happen?

The tumbler inside the lock turns, and I might as well recite some ancient phrase that opens the window and calls in all the demons for dinner. The Twins walk in and my hair stands up. I don't lock the door. Just in case. They walk around me, smiling, sharks circling their prey with a cup of coffee in their Italian-leather gloved hands, to match their shoes.

'I take it you got our note,' the Lisp says.

I nod my head.

'And?' he says.

I swallow, try not to seem like I'm swallowing. 'There's a bit of a complication,' I say, then rush, 'but everything's okay.' Their lips curl into smiles, their whole faces rising, cheeks high and absurd like The Joker. The gravel-voiced one licks his bottom lip. It sounds like sandpaper on polished metal.

'Of course it is,' he says.

'Please,' the other says. 'Enlighten us.'

They hoist themselves on the counter. The Lisp pulls two cigarettes from the inside pocket of his jacket, lights them and hands one to Gravel-Voice. He smiles and extends the pack to me. I light it and feel a bit better.

'I don't have all four. I can get it, but I don't know anyone who can pull that much in less than a day. Not around here, anyway,' I start.

'That's the complication,' Gravel-Voice says. 'How is everything okay?'

I purse my lips and take a drag, blow it out my nose. 'Well,' holding my arms out. 'I was hoping this would make it okay.'

They look at me, heads cocked towards one another.

'You want to show Mr. Hobbs the love his parents never gave? I think he's already been shown enough love by your little friend.'

The walls collapse on me, on my head. Mary. Hobbs. Love. The note. They are lying. Hobbs has her strung up, waiting for the money. Mary wouldn't touch him again. She never loved him.

'I meant the store,' I say.

'Why would Mr. Hobbs want this?'

'To sell it. I have two,' quickly subtracting the thirty thousand stash, 'twenty and change in cash. Another hundred-plus in stock. He can get rid of this place within a week and make at least eight hundred, maybe over a million. I'll even place the ad for him.' I pull hard on my cigarette, hope they buy it. Hope I can get Hobbs to buy it.

'That's generous,' the Lisp says.

'Why would you want to offer all of that?' the other one says.

I shrug. 'Insurance.'

They cackle, look at each other.

'Insurance for what?'

'Mary. Health insurance for her. And to make sure Christian doesn't get another visit.'

They laugh again.

'How is he?'

My feet and toes, slick and slippery. Gashes over his chest. The taste of his blood. 'I think he'll come through.'

The Lisp smiles, baring his teeth. 'When you see him, tell him it was nothing personal. We just wanted to give you some incentive. Now your friend Brent, he was business.'

The cold-hearted fucking bastards. If I hadn't been throwing up for the last nine hours, I'd do it right now.

'But you,' he says, 'you're business and personal for Mr. Hobbs. And what makes you think that Mary will want to see you again?'

I shake my head. 'Probably won't.'

'But since you love her so much, you just want her to be happy, right?'

I pause, not sure how to answer. 'Pretty much.'

Gravel-Voice hops off the counter and adjusts his slacks. 'I never thought a ruthless little cunt like you could express something so lovely.'

'I'm on the verge of tears, myself,' the Lisp says, then stands on the carpet. The sole of his left shoe is thicker than his right.

'Thanks,' I breathe.

'Personally, I could never be so eloquent,' Gravel-Voice says. 'And,' spreading his fingers over his chest, 'from one ruthless cunt to another, I admire that.'

'Okay,' I mumble, eye darting from side to side, stomach clenching.

'We still don't give a fuck,' the Lisp says, dull, cold, and this is bad. They duck their hands inside their overcoats, reach behind their backs and pull out their guns.

'But,' I sputter, 'I have the money! I have more than Hobbs wants!'

They smile, cock their guns, then shrug.

My temples pound, legs fall numb. I can't feel my hands and the Twins stand between me and my gun. Eyes glance around the room and there's nothing in it for me. No golf clubs or chair legs or fire irons. Nothing I could swing and leave a dent in their heads.

'But,' I stammer, words careening through my head faster than I can catch them and none landing on my tongue. 'You said…and I have…all of this…'

They smile sickly, bare their teeth, and I can't believe the last thing I'll ever see is these two spineless fucks.

I close my eyes and pull Mary into me on the beach, crush my lips on hers and hope this kiss will last for eternity.

'Open your eyes.'

I squeeze her into me, try to combine all of our cells, be one person so some part of her will float away with me.

'Damon,' the Lisp says, like a mother trying to coerce her

stubborn toddler. His feet shuffle across the carpet towards me. 'Take your medicine like a man.'

My arms squeeze my ribs and all I can feel is emptiness. My cells are my own and she's gone. The beach is barren. The palm trees have been deforested and the waves drowned. My shadow is gone. Abré sus ojos.

'That's better,' he says.

I whisper her name as they pull the trigger.

A blue flag, with red cartoon explosions and BANG! written on it pops out of the muzzle of each gun. The Twins are bent over in laughter, smacking each other on the back. The store spins and my body burns. I don't know if I'm alive or in Hell already.

'You should have seen your face!' the Lisp says between breaths.

'Mr. Hobbs thought you would appreciate this.' Gravel-Voice shakes his gun, smacks his thigh again.

I stumble backwards a step, brace myself on my knee to stay standing. A rush of bile surges up my throat and I swallow it back down. They stand straight, still smiling, then take a deep breath and their faces fall blank. Cold. Murderous.

'No, but really,' Gravel-Voice says.

The butt of two guns, swung in a sideways arc.

I'm too shocked to say her name.

Chapter 19

January: Now

Razor thumbtacks push into my fingertips, probe my bones and scrape the underside of my fingernails. Knives left in a fire for an hour slice the bottom of my neck, stab my shoulders. A metal vice built like an iron maiden screws tighter around my forearms and wrists.

I strain against the knives and lean my head up, hope they won't sever my spinal cord. My eyes crack open and slide up, towards Heaven. Wooden-beamed ceiling. A length of rope cinching my hands to one of the beams. My temples beat like tribal drums at a sacrificial ceremony. Cuts and scabs burn underneath my jacket. Stacks of cardboard boxes, glints of metal from the shadows and random debris surround me. A musty stink, like spoiled food, mud and decay stings my nose. And stale cigarette smoke. Only the balls of my feet can reach the floor.

'Morning, sunshine,' a voice says. 'I was lonely without you.' I recognize the voice; it's the same feeling as teeth smashing into the back of my skull.

My mouth is desert dry and I can't get a full breath with my arms like this. When the authorities would crucify a person, the victim died from slow suffocation. Their lungs couldn't expand properly in the crucifixion position. Hobbs said that after the three of us saw *The Ten Commandments* with Charlton Heston at The Charles. I never expected it to apply to me.

'Where the fuck is she, you cocksucker?'

He smacks me across the face. 'You kiss Mary with that mouth?'

'If you hurt her, I swear to Christ I will slit your throat and spit on your corpse.'

He steps towards me, close enough to piss on.

'Let's get a few things straight, son. One, you're in no position to make threats. Especially ones that you wouldn't follow through with anyway.' He pulls my butterfly knife from his pocket. 'If I'm dead, how will you know where Mary is? Or if she's even still alive. Second,' pointing the knife into my cheek, 'you are the one that got her into this in the first place. If you wouldn't have gone against me, you could be sitting in some pub having a drink now.' A bright white streak of heat runs across my cheek. I yank my head back, feel my face warm. 'So don't go getting all John Wayne on me, okay?' he says as he wipes blood from the knife on my shirt.

I try to calm my breathing, collect myself. 'All right,' I finally concede.

He nods. 'Better.'

'What do you want then? I told the Twins I could give you more than you asked.'

'Oh, right. The store and whatever.'

'Yeah,' I say, my stomach boiling at the way he casually dismisses all that I have to my name. He lights a cigarette. The lighter flashes gold in the flame. 'The store and whatever.'

'And?'

'And, what? You'll have three times as much as you wanted. Let Mary go.'

He sits, smoking, silent. The scurry of nails on concrete moves behind me. I don't think I have any more options. Either he goes with my idea or he doesn't. If he does, I'm free and poor and alone, but Mary lives. If he doesn't… I'm hoping he does. Actually, I'm banking on it.

'Mary told me once that you live in films, Damon,' he says.

'Recently? Where is she?'

'Have you seen *The Godfather*?' he continues.

'Where. Is. She?'

'I prefer the second film to the first. I mean, DeNiro and Pacino, a brilliant screenplay. Incredible cinematography. Just a beautiful film. But both are at the top of my list.' Even if I keep asking, he's not going to answer me until he's ready.

'You don't like Part Three?' I try to joke.

His eyes narrow. 'I'll gut you where you stand.'

'The reels should be burned,' I say.

'You might learn something from the Corleones.'

My lips purse. I don't like where this is going. 'What would that be?'

His face cracks into a smile. 'Respect and loyalty.'

Moths and barracudas gnaw on my stomach. My hands are numb and I don't know if it's from being tied up.

'I'm sure you know that Mary is a very dear friend. I'm sure you also know, or have at least inferred, that I still carry,' he pauses, gesticulating for words, 'personal feelings towards her. After she ended it, she broke my heart a little more every time I saw her. I knew that we would never again be what we were. But I came to terms with that. It wasn't easy, but I managed.'

He pulls another cigarette from the case in his pocket, lights it, then offers me one. I try to move my numb hands, infer that it would be kind of hard for me to smoke right now. He shrugs and sits on a box, then continues.

'The best and worst day of my life was the day Mary told me she had met a man. An incredible man she thought she could grow old with. I can only imagine she meant you.' He takes a long drag of his cigarette, for effect it seems. 'She loved you, Damon. She really did.'

My body is non-existent. The world has stopped spinning. Oceans flood through my ears and ice picks stab my temples. I swallow the urge to throw up on him. He's lying. He's lying he's lying he's lying. He didn't kill Mary. Please God say he didn't kill Mary. He loved her too much and she was too perfect and beautiful and caring and there was no way he could have killed Mary—fuck please no say he didn't.

'You never deserved her. You were always looking for a distraction. Never gave her half the thought she gave to you.'

He adjusts himself on the box, takes a long drag of his cigarette, stares at me until I become uncomfortable.

'Do you think Clemenza would ever turn against Don Vito? Even when Clemenza was old and his life was threatened and he was completely opposed to what Michael was ordering, he was still loyal to the family. Damon,' he pauses, looking for words again. 'I assume you know of Trevor? At least peripherally?'

I nod.

'No one ever asks for that. Especially not someone like Mary.' He takes a drag that lasts for hours. 'He hurt her, so I hurt him. My only regret is that he died of complications and not by my hand.'

I nod, for some reason. I didn't know Trevor was no longer with us. That shouldn't change things but it does. Oh God, it does.

'I would've killed him then,' he says, 'if Mary hadn't stopped me. She still hasn't forgiven me, I'm sure, but I'd kill him a hundred times more for what he did.' He steps so close I can see the burst blood vessel beneath his right cheek, the healing scrape where he nicked himself shaving. 'That, Damon, is loyalty. That is love. And I'd do it to anyone who hurt her.'

The scrape of his nails on stubble is audible in here.

'And you hurt her, Damon. Not like Trevor.' He shakes his head. 'No. You hurt her worse, cut her deeper. That kind of wound will never stop bleeding.'

I nod again because I don't know what else to do.

'This was never about money.' He blows smoke in my face. 'It was just about being there.'

'I wasn't—'

He flicks his cigarette in my face. 'Don't interrupt when I'm speaking. Respect, remember? We had a good thing going. Why did you have to fuck it up?'

I start to speak, but choke back words when I realize I don't know what I'm saying. He steps right in front of me. I can feel his breath on my face, smell the nicotine. My bones ache for a cigarette and her kiss.

'Damon, my boy,' he grabs my cheeks and chin with one hand and kisses me hard on the forehead, 'you broke my heart,' then throws my face to the side. His saliva is cold on my forehead and beads of terror drip down my face. My legs tingle and feet start to tap.

'I've always wanted to say that.' He smiles. 'Like I said, you can learn a lot of things from the Corleones.'

He takes a step back and reaches into his suit jacket pocket, pulling out a black pistol and holding it eight inches from my right eye.

I thrash, yank my arms until they feel like they're going to rip from my body. Try to pull the beam from the ceiling and if it doesn't get me free at least it will kill me before he has the chance. I kick my leg out to knock the gun from his hand but he already stepped to the side. He moves quicker than I realize and stands on my feet so I can't squirm.

'Honey, sit still and it'll be over in a minute.'

I try to jerk my numb legs from under his feet and can't tell if they're moving or not, but can't look at the gun. Probably the same one that killed Mary. I wish now that I'd gone to church with my mother—Mom, Dad, I'm sorry, I wish I would've called—and I believed in God and Heaven so that, rather than just hoping for the best—because despite everything I've done, I never meant to hurt anyone—I'd be sure beyond all doubt that in five seconds I'd be sent to Mary instead of rotting in Hell with the rest of the people I've spent my life around.

Hobbs looks through me, licks his lips. 'I've been waiting for this for a long time.' He pulls the trigger and I gasp.

A blue flag, with red cartoon explosions and BANG! printed on it pops out of his gun.

He throws his head back and stutter-steps twice, doubled-over laughing.

The room sways like a seesaw and my lungs have collapsed. Sledgehammers smash into my head, nails drive themselves into my chest.

'What the fuck is wrong with you people!' Spit flies out of my mouth. 'Fucking Christ!'

He can barely get words out of his mouth. 'Jesus, you should see the look on your face.' He laughs and laughs and laughs, taking a minute to wind down, then goes blank, his concrete eyes fixed on mine.

'Seriously though,' he says, deadpan, and pulls a pistol from his waistband, presses the gleaming, oiled muzzle against my forehead. My eyes curl closed like clenched fists, and this time I remember to say her name before I die.

At least maybe now, we'll be together. I love you, Mary.

The room is comatose, catatonic. The blood ocean in my ears ebbs low tide, docile. My heart gives a valiant last pump, resigning itself to the inactivity it's about to find.

A voice slices through the silence.

'Hello, lover,' Mary says to me.

Chapter 20

January: Now

I open my eyes, bite my lips to make sure I'm awake. Mary stands in front of me, dressed in shadows and my body tingles just knowing she's alive and she's so gorgeous I might collapse under the weight of it all.

'Mary,' I breathe. Mother Mary, my Mary, my Blessed Mary.

My brain is vacant but for her name. The snap of a single synapse firing echoes inside my skull. I try to absorb her with my eyes, smell the salt water and sand of our beach. My cells scream for her, more than nicotine and white combined.

She smiles at me despite herself.

'I thought you were dead,' I whisper.

'Looks like I'm not.' She raises her arms to the side.

'Mary, what's going on?'

She smiles. 'Do you remember the time we put that record on and listened to it three times? When we made love the entire time?' She got me at my own reference game. Hobbs coughs and spits on the ground.

'That was a good night, wasn't it,' I say. 'Sweetie, I'm so sorry. I never meant—'

'Shut up.' Her smile evaporates. 'You talk too much.'

'I never meant to end up like this,' I whisper. 'I just wanted things to be better for us.'

'Better than what?' she yells. 'You wanted things better for you. Was I not what you wanted me to be? Did you want me to change?'

'I love you exactly how you are. I thought with the switch, maybe, we could get rid of the problems we had. The late deliveries and all.' I look over at Hobbs.

'This is between you two,' he says. 'I'm just a bystander.'

'He's right. If there were problems, you never told me. This isn't about money or drugs—that's right, drugs,' pointing at Hobbs and me with her gun, 'not product like you two try to euphemize it, drugs—and it's not about bigger houses or more power. You and me, that's all I cared about. I wanted to be with you for the rest of my life. And make jokes about how wrinkled we'd become and argue over whether we should watch *Matlock* or *Nightmare on Elm Street*. Those are the arguments we were supposed to have, Damon.'

Hobbs lights a cigarette and hands the case to Mary. She pulls one out and places it between her lips, then lights it. A cloud of smoke from her mouth.

'You hurt me, Damon. Really fucking bad.'

I swallow hard. 'Is that why you went to him?'

'I didn't go to him, asshole,' she says. 'I didn't have anywhere to go.' To the side of us Hobbs picks at his fingernails, bored. 'I didn't see Hobbs until three or four days later, after I was tired of sleeping in the car.'

'You always seem to be there to save her, don't you?' I say to Hobbs. 'That's convenient.'

'That's what friends do,' he says.

She takes a long drag of her cigarette. It crackles as she inhales. She sniffs, wipes her eyes. 'And if I would've stayed with you and the other guy, he would've killed us both.'

I look at Hobbs. He purses his lips, shrugs, like he's saying "yeah, and?"

'Mary,' I start. I want to apologize, say I'm sorry until my vocal cords are shredded like paper under a lawnmower, but none of it will help. No amount of reconciliation will make up for any of this. Hobbs was right. I don't deserve her.

'What, babe?' She steps closer to me.

I shake my head. 'Nothing.'

'Nothing?' Her voice cracks again. 'You have nothing to say?'

I look up at her, at her face, her decorum rapidly shattering, her lips trembling. Behind her, Hobbs walks towards us.

'Mary,' he whispers. 'It's time.'

'There's nothing I can say,' I whisper. 'Nothing will turn it back to the way it was.'

She shakes her head, sniffles and wipes her cheeks, then turns around. Sitting in the palm of her hand, cradled like a butterfly that might flap its wings and rearrange our destinies with its tiny wind, a black revolver. She grips it, holds her fate, mine, tight until her knuckles turn white. Despite everything, I bite my lip to not smile. I'd told her years ago that she should learn how to use a gun, just in case. She'd always thought they were disgusting.

'Tell me you love me before you shoot.'

Hobbs hands her the handkerchief from his breast pocket. She takes it without looking, blows her nose and wipes her eyes, all with the hand that's not holding the gun.

'You know that I loved you. I still do. I always have.'

'Always?'

Hobbs sits on the boxes and lights another cigarette. In the flash of flame, there's the outline of a rat in the corner and a derby on the boxes.

'Always and ever, Damon, despite everything. You should know that.'

My face tries to smile, but can't. I am such a piece of shit. I never deserved her. I hope she finds someone who shows her the love she deserves. Actually shows it, not just feels it, makes her feel every bit as special and wonderful as she is. She puts her cigarette to my lips. I inhale and nicotine shoots through my body, perks up my cells. My brain starts to light up. I exhale and mouth, 'Thank you.' She smiles, nods.

Our eyes lock, drift in and out of each other. Over canal maps of veins, around pupils, through irises, into the real part of us. Past all the cells and molecules that make up our bodies and into the beach and palm trees that make us who we are, who we want to be, what we wish we could be. Her eyes shimmer as she stares, shatter when she blinks. I can see my wavy reflection in her. See myself in her. I wonder if she can see the same.

'So now what do we do?' I whisper.

Her lips purse, then curve up slightly. 'I was just thinking the same thing.' She looks down. 'Where did you get that shirt?'

I try to laugh and it hurts. 'Christian's. It's a long story. I'll tell you later,' and I didn't mean it the way it came out because as soon as I say it, her face falls apart piece by piece. Breathe deep, Damon, be strong for her because this is the last time she'll be able to lean on you.

'Shhh, don't cry. It's okay. It's either you or him.' I flick my head towards Hobbs, sitting on the boxes like he's waiting for a boring movie to end. I lean into her, touch our foreheads together. 'And he's a fuck.'

She coughs and laughs, blinks and sprays a tear on me. 'You were right, by the way.'

'What do you mean?'

'That Smashing Pumpkins video you and Christian were talking about?' she says. 'I watched it. It is beautiful.' She presses her face against mine, wraps her lips around mine. I want to absorb her into me, like the beach. Wrap my arms around her while she puts the gun into my gut and pulls the trigger. Watch her face as I fall down the black hole. Follow her eyes through the darkness. I bite her bottom lip gently, hope I can hold on so she can't move. Feel her pressed against me and remember her soft and wet mouth for as long as I can.

Her lips pull back, then kiss me again, quickly. She has the look in her eyes, like the husband who tells himself he's only going to the strip club because the guys are, but changed his boxers and trimmed his pubes anyway. She steps back, her gun jumping and I don't know if she'll actually be able to get a decent shot off in this state. Hobbs sighs, like he's relieved the movie is over and he can get food now.

'One question first,' I say. 'Fuckface, are all of those stories true?' Mary hides her smile, sniffs again.

Hobbs shrugs. 'Does it really matter?'

'Maybe.'

And the fucker just smiles.

'So, then, yes.'

He puts his palms up in the air and shrugs, that shit-eating grin etched on his face and as Mary's trembling hand raises the gun up to my face, my one other dying regret might be that I won't get a chance to break his fucking teeth.

She breathes deep, tries to steady her hand, stares straight in my eyes. I want to say I love you but don't want to upset her more, so I just smile and nod, placid.

My eyes flick to Hobbs, focusing on something behind me. In my periphery, I see Mary raise the gun over my head. I try to twist and look but I'm too numb.

'Who the fuck are you?' Mary says, her eyes darting.

I hear light footsteps, like high-heels that barely touch the concrete. Mary's hands spasm, the gun pointing everywhere.

'Who the fuck is this?' she screams at Hobbs.

Jasmine wafts through the air. The heels stop behind me.

'I'm the ghost of Daniel Gibson,' the heels say.

I drop my head, exhausted. This day is too much to deal with. First the Twins and their Batman gun, then Hobbs and his Batman gun, then resigning myself to be killed by the love of my life.

'Who the fuck is Daniel Gibson?' Mary screams.

And now Isabela.

I need to get the fuck out of Smalltimore.

Hobbs stands, flips the derby in his hands and places it on his head. A hand rustles through my hair. I don't even know what to say to Mary. My mouth and brain have clocked out, and I have no idea what is happening.

'He's an old friend,' Isabela says, patting my head.

Isabela came to kill me, or Mary, or Hobbs, or all of us, or some combination of us. Running through scenarios is too much work so I hang, quiet and still, and wait to see what she has to say.

'I'd ask why the store has been closed, but that would probably be redundant,' Isabela says.

'Is this your fucking dealer?' Mary screams.

'It's nice to finally meet you, Mary. I've heard so many stories,' she says. 'Really, he won't shut up about you.'

Mary's face has shattered. The gun droops at the floor. I want to grab her and sprint as fast as I can, not stop until we're in India or someplace where no one can find us. I want to hold her, make her stop crying.

'Our friend is so rude. Really,' Isabela says, smacking me in the back of the head, 'you must do a better job of introducing your friends, Michael.'

I can't breathe. My heart has stopped. My brain short-circuits and smokes. Christian is the only one. No one else knew. I forgot most of the time. Christian set me up. To get back at me. For staying at his apartment. For getting him involved with bricks and detectives. For coming to him in the first place. But he couldn't. Wouldn't. And who the fuck is Daniel Gibson?

'Damon,' Mary cries. 'Who the fuck is Michael?'

Chapter 21

January: Now

'Daniel Gibson, as Mary asked, was an angel.' Isabela steps in front of me and holds out her hand. Hobbs lays my butterfly knife in her palm. She opens it and starts sawing at my ropes.

'Daniel was a lovely human being and an aspiring painter.' She pauses and looks at me. 'You remember what that was like, right?' For a long minute she stares at me, then resumes sawing. 'However, after you made his acquaintance, Michael, he became a saint.'

'Damon,' Mary says in sobs. 'What is she talking about?'

Isabela pauses, stops cutting with the knife. 'You should know this, Michael. You were raised Catholic. Someone can only become a saint after they die.' She takes one final hack and I fall to the ground. Blood is molten lava inside my arms. The knives in my shoulders stab and twist. The damp concrete is cool on the side of my face. My knife clatters on the floor.

'What are you talking about?' I say. 'I don't even know anyone called Daniel Gibson.'

Isabela smiles. 'Sure you do. Close your eyes. Think hard. Don't worry, I won't shoot you. Not yet.'

As if I had any other choice, I close my eyes and watch the back of my eyelids, the blank screen before a movie starts.

'Now picture my face, my hair, my neck, my arms.' Mary cries in the darkness. 'Imagine me with long hair, so red that it's black.'

I can see Isabela. I recognize her—not her from Stay Gold, but her with dark red hair. Scenes flash over my eyelid movie screen but I can't focus on any of them. Her face is clear but the background keeps spinning.

'Damon,' Mary says. 'What is your name?'

Isabela evaporates as I open my eyes, turn my head towards Mary. 'Michael,' I whisper.

'Our friend here isn't so good at introductions,' Isabela says, stepping towards Mary. 'But he was probably only trying to protect you. You and I can sort out the details later.'

Mary chokes, raises her gun at Isabela.

'Put it down, Mary,' Hobbs says, walking over to her and draping his arm over her.

'Get the fuck away from me,' she says through gritted teeth, points the gun at him.

'Mary,' he says, like a parent reprimanding their child. 'That's dangerous. Put it down.'

'Shut the fuck up.' She cocks the gun.

'Play nice, kids,' Isabela says. 'You'll shoot your eye out.'

I try to hoist myself up, then make a show of not being able to do it, fall over top of the butterfly knife on the floor. As Isabela faces Hobbs and Mary, I slide the knife into my back pocket and manage to stand. Hot needles stick into the bottom of my feet.

'I don't know who you're talking about,' I say to Isabela. Mary still has her shaking gun pointed at Hobbs.

'In all fairness, you were probably never introduced to him. Whether that makes you more cold-blooded or not, I don't know. My hair was soaking up his blood the last time you two saw each other.'

Her hair soaked up his blood. Amherst. Michael. She was leaning over him. So red it's black. The girl at the party. Paul's face. Morrissey Mason. Two shots. The second shot. Daniel Gibson. The scream.

That scream.

Her scream.

The scream that comes from somewhere inside you, someplace you never knew existed until you see a boy kill your brother right in front of you. The scream of watching your brother beg breathlessly for help while he dies in your lap and you're paralyzed to do anything but watch his eyes cloud, watch his chest rise then fall then rise then fall and stay fallen, watch his life pour out of him and absorb into your shirt, your hair. Your two lives merge and you'll always have a part of him with you.

She smiles. 'You remember him now.'

My head nods by itself. 'I'm sorry, Eliza,' slips out of my mouth. 'I didn't mean to—when Paul swung—his head and an accident—' Every scene in the last seven years of my life flashes through my head. I've always known it happened, but it was always so anonymous, like it never happened.

'I never said that you intentionally killed him. I never said that you trained a gun to his chest and pulled the trigger, but you murdered my brother,' she says, her voice rising. 'You could have stopped and you didn't.'

'I didn't…I'm so sorry,' I say, stumble two steps backwards. Mary reaches her hand out to grab my arm, then pulls it back, then starts to again.

The scenes in my head start to slow down and focus. I killed Daniel Gibson. 'How did you know I was in Baltimore?'

Isabela smiles. 'You're a hard person to find. Especially given that I only knew you through Eric. Apparently, the money you gave Julian didn't cover cleaning his carpet. Or his partner's medical bills. He wasn't too pleased with you when I spoke to him.'

'Julian?' I say, astonished. The father who wasn't my father? 'Julian dimed me out?'

'You seem to have that effect on people, Michael,' she says. 'Actually, "partners" was a bit of a double entendre, so he might have loved you equally in different ways.'

I can't believe Julian betrayed me. Or that he could love a shit bag like Paul. Paul, who would've been cheating on Julian with Mason then, unless 'my girl' was some extension of self-loathing or pathetic sentimentality. I can't believe he betrayed me.

'A local guide helps, too.'

Mary spins towards him, her eyes stretched open so far they might break. 'You?'

"Mayonaise" playing at Frasier's and no one was there.

The grey derby and overcoat.

The late deliveries and shortages in stock.

The fights between Mary and me because of no stock.

EPs were a bad business decision.

He'd planned the whole thing. I was set up from the beginning. How could Isabela, in a small place like Baltimore, have lived here and followed us for more than six months and we never knew?

'You're Mr. Ashe,' I say to Hobbs.

He grins, shrugs, tips his derby to me.

'Technically,' Isabela says, 'there never was a Mr. Ashe. While we're on the subjects of names, Mary, mine's Eliza, for your own edification.'

'You,' Mary spits at Hobbs. 'You fucking lied to me. Not one thing you promised was true.'

'Whoa,' I say. 'What did he promise?'

'Mary, sweetie,' he says. 'That asshole kept so much from you. I swore I'd never let you get hurt again.' He tries to comfort her with a hand on her shoulder.

'Touch me and I'll shoot your fucking fingers off,' she growls. 'Step back. Away from me.' She points her gun at Isabela. 'I'll shoot you, too.'

Mary turns to me. The gun in my face isn't shaking anymore.

'Damon,' she says, measuring her words. 'Tell me the truth. If you say anything even remotely not true, I will fucking kill you. Start talking.'

'I'm sorry, Mary. For everything. I wanted to bury everything and try to start over. If I would've known any of this would catch up, I would've never brought you into it.' I try to laugh. 'You should've killed me when you had the chance.'

'There's still opportunity,' Isabela says, now brandishing a pistol at me.

'Put that fucking thing down,' Mary says, pointing hers at

Isabela.

'Mary, calm down,' Hobbs says, his gun aimed at her. 'Don't do anything dumb.'

'Fuck you, liar. I will never forgive you.'

'Sweetheart, please. Don't say that,' he says.

I whip the butterfly knife out of my pocket. 'Don't you call her sweetheart.'

Hobbs laughs. 'What, you going to rumble against the Puerto Ricans with your Jet friends?'

'What do you want?' I say to Isabela. 'Why not just find me and kill me?' Everything is blurred, surreal, a dream.

'Where's the fun in that, Michael?' she says, then shrugs. 'The thrill of the chase, maybe.'

'Why not just chase me then? I was the one who killed Daniel. Mary had nothing to do with it.'

Her smile flatlines.

'Because I wanted to ruin your life, Michael. Like you ruined Daniel's. Like you ruined mine.'

I am a horrible person.

'Though all I had to do was show up,' she says. 'You were well on your way already.'

I didn't mean to be a horrible person.

'Look at you, Michael.'

I had a beautiful girlfriend.

'Ten years and you're still dealing drugs.'

I fucked it up.

'A store that should be condemned.'

I had an amazing best friend.

'A drug habit.'

I put him in the ICU.

'No future.'

I am a horrible person.

'Your mother was right.' She spits, cocks her gun. 'You are a waste of life.'

Fuck you.

The light glints off my knife. Her mouth smiles back to her earlobe as she screams and covers her opened cheek. Gunshots reverberate off the damp concrete, split my eardrums. My left shoulder is bright white with pain, my arm wet down to my elbow. I turn my head and see Hobbs pointing a gun at me then the ceiling as he falls. A fountain bursts between the fingers over his neck. Mary's hand holding a gun, facing Hobbs, shaking. Her face like a mime's.

I look at the floor under me. Isabela's face squirts blood on my feet. Her gun points up and my right thigh is wet on fire. I clench my leg, grit my teeth until they're about to break. Mary screams, holds her stomach, stumbles backwards into the boxes. Her shirt is so black it's blue. Isabela points at her.

Someone is screaming. It sounds like my voice and comes from my mouth but it's not mine. Concrete is cool on my knees and I'm over Isabela, my knife out and arm up.

One slash.

Hobbs. Isabela. Paul. The Twins. Desiree. Alicia. Julian. They all gurgle for mercy through an aerated windpipe. A hollow noise, like blowing over the lip of a milk jug. My face is covered in Isabela, Daniel Gibson, Paul. "Mayonaise" seeps from somewhere. Everyone who has fucked me over streams down my cheeks. My forearms burn, shoulder and thigh spurt. My knuckles, white around the handle of the knife through the blood. Streams of Isabela cover my lips. Paul is liquid in my hair. Julian soaks my chest.

I wipe them off with the bottom of Isabela's dress. Holy shit. I look at my gleaming hands. What did I just do? Thunderclaps roll down the hallway. Mary, my Mary, she's cursing, holding her stomach. Isabela's gun lies in a puddle next to my knee. I grab it and pray there are still bullets.

The door explodes with the Twins, the cracks of their guns. I squeeze the trigger. One of them twists around and grabs his shoulder. I hit the other in the knee. He stumbles to the concrete, his gun skittering away from him and he looks up at me. I feel like I'm in House of the Dead as I put a half-inch black hole in his forehead.

I drag my leg up and stand, slide over to Mary.

'Everything's okay, sweetie. You're going to be okay.'

Hobbs gasps next to my feet. Blood froths on his neck. 'You fucked it all up, you fucking bastard. She was mine.'

The first Twin pulls himself up onto his elbow and grabs the dead Twin's gun. I plant on my bad leg and swing my other at his arm. He tumbles again, arm flails onto the ground and fingers spread, drops the gun. Nine fingers spread.

'You,' I scream at him. 'You fucking robbed me!'

'You owe me. I could've killed you.'

'You stole from Hobbs! He took your finger.'

'Shop class,' he laughs sadistically, rolling over and grabbing the dropped gun.

That son of a bitch. Hobbs robbed his own people and this gimp-footed bastard went along with it. I swing my good leg as hard as I can at his head. A white tooth arcs out in a splash of red, clinks on the concrete as he lands facedown with a wet thump.

I bend down and drape Mary's left arm over my shoulder, haul her up to her feet.

'Come on, Mary, you have to help me walk. You can do it, babe.'

We limp our way out of the room, my arm and leg wet and the room shifting back and forth.

Out the first door and into another room. The tables, chairs—everything looks familiar. We leave a smear behind us like a gigantic bleeding slug. Metal ashtrays, an old piano. The Black fucking Gardenia. Where Isabela told me to meet her. The fork in the time-river where my life crashed downhill.

I'm back where I started. Baptized in blood. My sins washed away with whiskey and beer. A second chance.

I spit blood on the floor and drag us towards the door. A deep breath to get some strength then shoulder the heavy door open into blinding white light. We've died, gone to Heaven. Everything is clean and pristine and colorless and God, damn me. I'm sorry I couldn't get us out alive, Mary. A cacophony of angels scream around us and my head spins and I feel weak and we're already dead so fuck it.

I collapse and Heaven is freezing, cold burning my back and arms. The back of my head is wet. My thigh throbs and I think my shoulder fell off somewhere inside. My eyes adjust to Heaven's grey sky and I turn my head and see a layer of snow, seeping red farther and farther from us. Outside. The street. Baltimore. Bums and cars and junkies and shops and restaurants and pubs.

Mary and I lie on the sidewalk, painting the snow red. My arm under her has no circulation. I slip when I try to lift myself with my left arm and fall back onto her, my head on her chest, her chest rising and falling. The faraway screams of tourists and window shoppers make me smile. I wait for the oscillating siren of an ambulance, the warm wool blanket of a hospital room, our hospital bed. Blood flows from her stomach and runs down her ribs, onto her chest, onto my face. My right thigh streams, draped over her leg. We're bleeding into one another, absorbing each other cell by cell. We're on the beach. We are the beach. We're becoming the same person.

A quiet noise. My head shakes. Something in my hair.

I look up. Mary's trying to smile at me. She's a pair of eyes and a mouth against the snow. Her mouth moves, but nothing comes out. I lean towards her. She coughs. Wet flecks on my cheek. Her hand smoothes the back of my hair as the sirens get louder and I kiss the bloody hand lying across her stomach, wrap my fingers through hers. She squeezes my hand and we hold tight. Everything's inevitable.

Sweet Angel

A Novella

Chapter One

I'm chasing Mason through a hallway lined by billowing cloths, like the black and white carnivals in old movies. She wears a blond wig, a silver overcoat and no shoes. Electricity snaps from her fingertips. She disappears around the corner and when I find her it's in the reflection of twenty mirrors tipped at horrific angles. Her calls to me echo against cold glass as the mirrors shatter, falling piece-by-jagged-piece, great swathes of her evaporating into silver dust and the drill of a ringing bell cuts through the clouds.

I sat upright so quick the stool tipped backwards, my foot snagging the underside of the counter and keeping me from cracking my head on the cement floor of Fast Feet. I looked around but no one was there to see anything. Splayed open on the counter, my sketchbook now sported a pseudo-gauche drool mark over the robotic goldfish I'd been figuring out before I drifted off.

The Slug stood on the edge of the storeroom, pretending to count our shoe backstock with a pen bobbing in the air. His body hadn't consumed itself yet, collapsing like a neutron star at critical mass and spreading chunks of Oreo Chunk cookie, Herrel's fudge and rare hamburger all over the store. I had to say that this surprised me.

Leaning on the counter, I pressed my thumb into the drool spot and fanned it out, softening the skin beneath the pneumatic ridge of the fish's back so the metal would look harder by contrast. I picked at a bead of the varnish he laid two months ago because I couldn't figure out which crosshatch pattern looked better on the fins. A blind man could've read the screenplay to *Office Space* with all the blobs and seams he left. I'd told the fat fucker to just calm down and let me do it when I had a chance but he thought that with all the new clientele coming in, he'd better get it tip-top lest they be scared away to the other shoe store where they could secretly buy green. Which would be none.

'Sup, bro.'

I tilted my eyes up and clocked the douchenozzle standing before me. Baseball hat tipped to the side, fur-trimmed hooded down jacket, Timberlands, two gold fronts that were likely 24-karat. Of course someone like him would have to come in. Ignore the forty g's his parents shelled out to send him to Hampshire every year, he was straight from the streets. He got the real. I erased the crosshatching in the fish's fins and mimicked the sheen off his teeth with overlaying starburst patterns then checked my watch. Twenty minutes until she was off.

'Welcome to Fast Feet. How can I help you?'

He made the sucking sound they all do, trying to RZA-out all the upper-middle-class in him. 'Looking for some purple Air Force Ones.'

'We don't carry purple.' I didn't mean to sigh but couldn't help myself.

'How bout some green laces, son. Fat green laces.'

'How long might these laces be?'

'Fitty inches, B. I'm packing lots of shoe.' He nodded and showed his teeth, as if I should be impressed or maybe ask to come along.

'One minute.'

I stepped back and checked the Slug, who stood in a different spot but seemed to be counting the same stack of shoeboxes, then ducked into the closet with mailbox letters stuck to the door warning EMPLOYYES ONLY. After another glance at the Slug, I pulled down my backpack, split open my US History book and palmed a fifty-bag from the hollow inside. I'd seen it in a movie once, though it was a gun shape cut out of a Bible. Same principle.

Back at the desk, the douche bobbed his head hard to the Belle and Sebastian album coming from the rockbox in the corner. I grabbed a pair of laces from the wall behind the register, dropped them and the green in a bag and said, '$53.18, including tax.'

He handed me a credit card.

'Really?'

'Y'all don't take American Express?'

I took a long breath. 'No. Fast Feet does not take AmEx. And I'm cash only.'

He made that stupid sucking noise again while reaching for his wallet. I took another deep breath and waited for him to count out his money then put the fifty in the slot on the left side. How sweet of him to have exact change.

'Thank you for your business. Get your feet back fast.' It was trying to be clever but came off as vague. The Slug insisted I say it every time.

'Yeah, bon bon, B.' He turned around and left and I wasn't even sure what bon bon meant.

I returned to sculpting the lines of my fish until I heard Eric's voice.

'Hey, Al Bundy, they pay you to draw or sell shoes?'

I smiled. 'They pay me to keep assholes like you out of here.'

'Don't worry. I'd never shop here.' He sipped the last bit of espresso from his cup and tossed it in the grey trashcan meant for recycling, popped a mint into his mouth then hoisted himself onto the counter and stuck a toothpick between his lips. He shaped the pointed collar of his plaid Fred Perry shirt, smoothed out the front. 'Slow day?'

I opened the register and he let out a low whistle.

'That's just from today?'

'Yep.' Rolling the pencil between my fingers, I tried to tally it in my head but lost count. 'About seven or so.'

'It's a wonder this town can even get out of bed.'

'It's a wonder they haven't let go of their granola schtick and brought in a Cheetos factory.'

Eric conceded the point with a head nod then watched a girl

walk past the store and into the fair-trade coffee shop next door. I thought I'd had Advanced Sculpture with her a couple semesters ago. I also thought she fucked the teacher because her work looked more like frozen cat vomit on the sidewalk than art. But hey, art was art, I guessed.

'Julian notices what you do here,' he said.

'I know.'

'I know you know, but he wanted you to know he knows.'

I roughed out the outer edge of the fish's bowl, put in a crack then erased it.

'He's giving you the nod. Says you can do better than here.'

I squinted and examined the lip of the bowl. 'What about Paul? He should be next.'

'He is next in line.' Eric examined his shirt again, picking off a piece of lint and flicking it on the floor. 'But Julian tapped you to be prince.'

'Oh,' I said, checking my watch. Five minutes. 'I don't know.'

'We could use you out in the field, helping facilitate and all that. You got this up and running quick. He wants to utilize all your talents, more than here at least.' Eric chewed the toothpick. 'And we trust you.'

'You don't trust Paul?'

'Not that we don't trust him. More that we can't rely on him.'

'But Christmas is in, like, two days. I can't just roll out on the fat fuck.'

'Actually, it's closer to ten.' He tilted his head and looked at me. 'And you complain about him on a daily basis.'

'Doesn't mean I want to leave him in the lurch.'

Hopping down from the counter, he shook his leg to adjust his jeans. 'Just think about it, okay?'

'I like working here.'

'No you don't.'

Fanning through the seventy-some sketches in the book, I said, 'I can do this all day. Figure out stuff so I don't have to do it when I'm home and I can just paint, you know?'

'You can do that whenever you want. You don't need to work at a shoe store to draw.'

'I'm saying, I don't want to waste time at home when I can do it here, and get paid. I keep J flush and make better use of my own time.'

'Mike, you're my friend,' he said, 'but you're also a minimally employed college dropout with no girlfriend. Time is all you have.'

I looked at my watch. Two minutes.

He cleared his throat. 'I'm sorry. Am I keeping you?'

'It's almost my weekend.'

Ah, he nodded, the cocky prick. 'He's having people over tonight, so you two can talk then. I'll see you over there.'

I pushed my shoulder back a bit, straightening up. 'I don't know if I'm going over.'

He laughed and rested his hand on my shoulder. 'What else are you going to do?'

My watch beeped.

Time.

Chapter Two

Despite his massive DVD collection, the barista at Haymarket knew fuck-all about horror, though he just wouldn't admit it. Jason Vorhees was the last one alive in *Black Christmas* and his mother was Michael Myers' sister. Freddy Krueger was the lead from *April Fool's Day* and Curtis James was the final Last Girl and all-time Scream Queen. Really, how could you ever watch a horror movie and fuck up Jamie Lee Curtis? Curtis isn't even a woman's name. At points it got so bad that I tuned him out completely instead of pouring my coffee over my face. But the lights in Vital Vinyl were still on, and so I listened to him.

'I just think that, really, *Gremlins* could be the *Jaws* of our generation. You have the unassuming menace that stalks our otherwise safe streets—'

'Gizmo didn't stalk anyone.' I sipped my coffee and it burnt my tongue.

'—and I mean, they're both puppets, so there's that.'

I sipped again, glanced across the street and saw the lights go down. Turning back to him, I said, 'That's it?'

'Well, yeah.' He poured milk into the silver container for a cappuccino. 'Pretty smart, huh?'

'*Gremlins* will be one of the hallmark horror films of our generation—which isn't even our generation because it came out, what, sixteen years ago? In '84—because they both have puppets?'

He shrugged then nestled the cup beneath the steaming wand and started talking but it was all lost under the shriek. I looked across the street and saw Mason standing under the red awning of the store, chatting while her boss locked the doors.

The silence startled me. 'So it's a pretty good analogy, right?' He looked at me like a puppy waiting for a treat. Behind his head hung a triptych of postcard-sized paintings I'd bribed him to hang by trading two *Re-Animator* VHS tapes.

'Yeah, I totally get what you're saying. I'm going to go watch them now, actually.'

He stood holding the silver container to the side. I started to say something about the lurking unseen being scarier than any possible visual because it was the phantom manifestation of all our psychoses and fears and its physical borders were as liquid as our shifting anxieties, but instead just slid a dollar in the tip jar and asked if anyone had tried to buy my painting.

'People think it's cool but no one's bought it. I mean,' he shrugged, 'obviously.'

I raised my cup to say bye.

Out on the sidewalk, my breath formed clouds before my mouth, slipping over my cheeks as I headed up Main Street. The winter sky hugged its grey cloud sweater tight to the mountains around Northampton. I dug one hand into my pocket and hunched my shoulders forward, nestling into my jacket while approaching the crosswalk. Mason watched miniature trains go round their tracks in the window of the CVS across the street. The cackle of some drunken woman rang out in the air. I sipped my coffee and wagered a glance in the direction of the mad hen.

The mad hen, who happened to be my mom. My mom, with her arm hanging in the crook of some man's arm, while my father was at work. He whispered something in her ear and she smiled, bit her lip and slapped his shoulder. His arm constricted, pulling her closer to his body. Her smile was radiant, which made me feel glad in a way I wasn't comfortable with, because I couldn't remember the last time I'd seen her smile like that. I sunk further into my jacket and walked blindly across the street so I wouldn't have to make an actual decision. It being the Happy Valley and all, the cars stopped for me.

Only thin black tights covered Mason's legs and her rumpled boots came nowhere near touching her black miniskirt, but still she didn't shiver. I cleared my throat and loosened my step, humming a Smiths song and trying my best to look vaguely distracted. She didn't hear.

'Cool trains, huh? You know the rails are that distance apart because of Roman war horses?'

She looked up at me. I could barely see her eyes through the squint. 'What?'

'The railroads in America were designed by ex-pat Brits, who learned by studying European rails, which were built by people who used to build wagons, which used that spacing because if they had a different width they would break on all the old rutted roads, which were rutted like that because of old Roman Empire chariots, who built their chariots that width because it was the space between two horses. Pretty cool, huh?'

Her eyelids dropped and rose like day falling to night, back to day. She licked her bottom lip. 'Why do you know that?'

I shrugged. 'History Channel. My landlord spliced the line from the building next door.'

She turned back to the trains and slotted a cigarette between her lips. I flicked my lighter and held it before her lips but she already had a match lit, shaking it dead with a small twist then dropping it to the sidewalk.

'You're full of all kinds of interesting things, aren't you?'

Her tone fell into some smoky register that kept me from understanding what she was really saying, so I kept the flame lit and thumbed out a cigarette for myself.

'I just think, you know, the present is that much more interesting if you understand the past, like—'

'Like how we never really understood our historic national black music until it was prepackaged and sold to us by nice British lads with good haircuts and lips that make girls wet?' The whole time she spoke, she never took her eyes off the trains but I could see her watching me in the reflection.

'Yeah, the way the—' I said, drawing it out because I thought the Beatles covered mostly rock and roll but they didn't have lips—

'The way the Rolling Stones taught us our own blues.'

'That's what I'm saying.' I took a long drag and made abstract gestures with my hands while exhaling, insinuating that she'd cut me off from that exact point.

'I know. We talked about that before, didn't we?' She tilted her head and gave her sad little half-smile. The streetlights' reflection made her teeth sparkle.

Shoppers ambled past us, sheathed in alpaca wool hats, Incan patterned jackets and Tibetan prayer flags sewn into scarves, the mélange of continents making sure that no charge of insensitivity could ever be leveled against them. On one corner of Gothic Street stood two Krishna chanting and banging their tambourines; on the other sat two beatific Buddhist monks, the pamphlets for their new temple fluttering in the wake of passing traffic. Both of them could splash holy water on the church that loomed above them. Still, the trains circled and circled, never getting bored of their scenery.

'You doing anything tonight?' I didn't expect anything but wanted to hear some kind of noise.

'Not sure yet.' She leaned against the window, slinging her bag across her other shoulder so that the strap fell between her breasts and made them even more pronounced. As if I hadn't stared at them for seven semesters. 'You?'

'Julian's having some people over, so I guess I'll go later. I've got some stuff to do at home, work on some paintings, listen to the new Radiohead and try to figure it out.'

'*Kid A*?'

'Yeah. What do you think of it?' I heard a click inside my head, the mental microphone turning on to record, synthesize and regurgitate everything she said, because she said novel things in an off-handedly cool way and I wanted everyone to think I was as interesting.

She dropped her smoke beneath her boot heel. 'I think the guy who wrote that *Rolling Stone* article about them killing rock and roll to save it is a fucking asshole.'

'Succinct.' I nodded. 'It's not a rock album.'

'Exactly. You know what I'm saying.' She touched my forearm in affirmation and my head buzzed. 'If you want rock, get Stiff Little Fingers or the Stones. Fuck, Foo Fighters just put out a good record. But don't create some stupid mythology of slaying the rock godhead in the name of rock and roll. It's just a good record and you don't need to go all Freud to enjoy well-written music.'

To this day, I've never understood why Alex, the king of vinyl to her queen, left her for that other chick. Other than him being a fucktard of epic proportions.

She laughed. 'Sorry, what was your question again?'

'I don't even know.'

'Oh. Julian. Yeah, I don't know.' She set another cigarette between her lips and looked at me, took a step forward. Her nostrils flared and I wondered if it was some involuntary movement, the idea of white sending her cells into instinctive spasm. 'Could be a good time. You're going?'

'Yeah, I will.' My lighter somehow materialized in my hand, like I'd agitated the molecules in the air enough with my shaking hands for them to reform into a lighter shape that I held out for her. 'You should come by, you know, if you want to. Or not, no big deal.'

'Sounds fun.' She leaned forward to light her cigarette and I memorized the arrangement of pale freckles near the corner of her eye. She watched me the whole time. 'Then, I'll see you over there.'

I chewed on the corner of my thumb, looking at the trains, the Krishna, the church, everywhere but her for some reason, like she'd catch on to my little plan even though it was dead obvious anyway. I just sucked in my lips a couple times, said, 'Cool, guess I'll see you around then.'

'Guess you will.' She made an O with her lips and I felt my

cock twitch then she blew a smoke ring at me. It framed her face, as if she was floating away to Heaven or the ground beneath her was on fire.

Chapter Three

Cars sat scattered across the lawn at obtuse angles, some with their wheels edging onto the streets, others with the doors hanging ajar and the dome light burning like buoys in the night. Faint thumping inside Julian's house, something upbeat, and I hoped he wasn't on one of his rave kicks again. Last time he did that, he kept shoving E in my face. I took one and ended up in the parking lot behind the Calvin Theatre with no pants, even though the Calvin is a fifteen-minute drive from Julian's house in Amherst.

I crossed the lawn with a stone Buddha statue in my hand and gave a short wave to the two lugs smoking menthols on the porch, Julian's version of security, then reached through the gap in the fence and undid the lock.

Julian had the idea to turn his backyard into a tropical paradise. We watched a documentary where they said western Ireland had palm trees because of the jet-stream pattern, so he figured, fuck it, Ireland isn't too different from western Mass. I tried to tell him that Ireland didn't have six feet of snow every winter and there were the Berkshire Mountains to block the jet stream flow, but he'd fallen too deep into his Jay Gatsby via Copa Cabana persona, so it was of no use. The way it looked now, though, was more like a US propaganda film about Cuba than tropical Cuba itself. Palm ferns stuck out of the frozen ground like great demons clawing their way out of the earth. The hibiscus trees folded in against themselves, trying to protect their buds from ever-present frost. Sitting along the edge of the pond were various miniature stone temples and incarnations of the Buddha, laughing and fat or emaciated and enlightened. I rocked the cracked one from the frozen ground and set the new one I'd bought in its spot, placing the other one against the side of the house because throwing away a holy statue might be some kind of Buddhist sin. The pond acted as the locus of tropical delight, but it was currently filled with about four inches of ice and probably beyond saving. The sides had likely split, too, the same way they did last year and the year before and the year before that. All in all, I figured it was good that he was the only one carrying weight within a fifty-mile radius, so he had enough money to maintain the dream of Eden.

Inside, the music turned out to be some Japanese electro band covering AC/DC songs. Not as bad as rave, nor AC/DC proper. I passed through the living room, taking my time nodding and shaking hands with two dozen people so I could survey the room and look important, as opposed to desperate, but didn't see Mason anywhere. A backlit couple sat in front of the fireplace on the velvet cushions Julian bought in a Moroccan hash house. The guy held a lighter beneath a piece of aluminum foil, letting the powder bubble and boil before he offered it to the girl with a glass pipe held between her lips. She took a long inhale, held it as she closed her eyes and tipped back her head, then leaned forward, touched her lips to his and exhaled. Tendrils of smoke leaked from their mouths. When they parted, the fire threw light on his face and I was pretty damn sure I had him for Sociology a couple semesters ago. Half of me expected to see the barista sitting on the couch, blowing lines and patting the cushion beside him so he could yammer on at a snowblind pace with his horror-film misinformation. I gave my last handshake then skirted up the spiral stairs before anyone else could grab me.

The thick carpet in the hallway suffocated the music from downstairs, which had a hard time making it up the winding stairs anyway. Julian's office sat at the end of the hallway with the door closed. Four chairs with scrolled hardwood armrests and leather accents flanked either side of the space before his office. I wondered if Julian actively courted the idea of a sovereign state or if he just had an odd sense of grandiose design. To pass the time I examined the fake Picasso on his wall, tracing the wavering lines and trying to figure out some way to rip it off in one of my own paintings.

After a few minutes the door opened. Some fiend I recognized from Smith College limped out of the office—Lila, I thought her name was—her palm wrapped in a torn t-shirt and pressing against her hip. She nodded at me as she passed.

'What happened to you?' I said.

She looked over her shoulder, checking for Julian. 'Undercover caught me handing off in a bar.'

'You kept quiet?'

She shrugged. 'Doesn't really matter, does it?'

'Michael!' Julian's voice rang out. He stood in the doorway with his arms held out, a silk robe flanking his flannel shirt and the only pair of jeans I'd ever seen him wear in the last three years. 'Come in, man. It's been too long.'

I went to shake his hand but he pulled me close for a hug. 'I saw you last week.'

'That was business, though.' He laid his arm over my shoulders and ushered me in, Eric closing the door behind us. A George Harrison record played on the phonograph in the corner and even in the dim office I could see a small streak of blood on Julian's robe. 'We didn't get to really talk. We don't talk much anymore, not like we used to.'

'Both busy, you know. Working and such.' I shrugged but couldn't figure out why I'd shrugged. 'We could catch a movie next week. Pleasant Street's doing the original *Blade Runner*, if you want to go.'

'That'd be great.' He pulled back his chair as he said it, then sat at his desk and handed me a pile of white on it. 'Toot?'

'Sure, thanks.' I took a sharp inhale and felt the white sting my nostrils, the chemical taste drip down my throat. I thumbed out a smoke then passed the mirror to Eric, who took three quick sniffs then set it on the desk.

Julian leaned back in his chair and as his shirt rose I could see the tattoo of the Nio, the protectors of Buddhist temples, stretching the length of his torso. He looked at the ceiling for a long minute, maybe trying to articulate his plan or pausing for a quick meditation, all while fingering the blue lotus medallion that hung on the end of a leather strap. Story was, he picked the medallion up from a Buddhist monk after two weeks of travelling through Thailand, meeting with business partners, because the blue lotus symbolized wisdom, knowledge and the victory of spirit over the senses. Two days later he shook on a deal with his connect to import kilos straight from the motherland. He attributed it to the medallion. It sounded like a hokey explanation, but I thought believing in that was better than believing in nothing.

'Eric said you're not too keen on your promotion.'

'Did he explain why?'

'I want to hear it from you.'

'Can I have something to drink?'

'I have mango nectar or scotch.'

'Scotch is fine.' Julian had seen a time-lapse video of a tooth left in glass of Coke. It dissolved in a week. He hadn't touched it since. I wasn't sure if the irony was lost on him or he just didn't care.

'So?' he said.

'I appreciate your confidence, really, but I'm pretty happy at the shop.' I took a glass from Eric. 'I keep business moving smoothly for you and still have time to work on paintings.'

'And Mason works two floors below you.'

I chewed on the inside of my mouth.

'I'm not going to powder your ass for you, but you might want to reconsider your involvement with her.'

'We're not involved, J.'

'I know.' He set his feet on the desk. 'But I also know you.'

I took a long slug of the drink then blinked away the sting. 'What's the gig anyway?'

'We're expanding, and I need you out in the field.'

'Meaning?'

'We might get some pushback from Ted Green and those tweakers up in New Hampshire.' He set a silver gun beside my cigarettes.

'What the fuck is that? I'm not killing anyone.'

He pursed his lips and shot me a look that made me feel seven years old, like when my mother found the *Juggs* magazines I'd stolen from Christian's dad hidden in my closet.

'Why would you say that?' He took a sip from his glass tumbler and swished it around his mouth. 'I'd never put you out like that.'

'He didn't mean it like that, Jules,' Eric said. 'Just not sure yet.'

I was sure that even in this dim office they could see my face burning.

'You're good at assessing situations, Michael, and that's the role I want you in.' He steepled his fingers. 'I'm giving you this so no one else gets that idea.'

Eric said, 'They've got reach like we're trying to have reach.' He patted the breast pocket of his jacket, insinuating his own protection he now carried, as if that was supposed to make me feel better about the whole thing.

'The Dalai Lama says that sleep is the best meditation,' Julian said. 'You can't trust a man to act rationally if he hasn't slept in two weeks and his skin is made of bugs. Know what I mean?'

'That's why the gun,' I said.

'Yes. That's why the gun.' He swirled the scotch around his glass then sipped at it.

I stared at the gun then slid it back to him. 'I appreciate the nod, but I'm going to have to decline. That's not me, J.'

He set the gun back into the holster under his robe. 'I respect that, but understand that I could have asked anyone. And they would've said yes.'

As we stood, Julian clapped my shoulder then slipped a few bills into my shirt pocket and held the door open for us, told me not to worry, that everything was going to be okay and he believed in me. I did not skip on my way out of the office and considered that a small victory. Paul was the only one sitting in a chair. I gave Julian a hug and left with Eric, ignoring Paul as we passed.

'Wrist sore?' he said.

'Excuse me?'

'From jerking him off.' He snapped his gum with his teeth. 'Isn't that how you got the nod?'

'I was illustrating to him the proper method for anal sex as enacted on Mason in order to ensure your rectal comfort forthwith heretofore.'

'The fuck you say?' He stood close enough that I could feel his breath.

'Do you understand the concept of interrogative pronouns?' I said.

'What?'

'There you go.'

Eric nudged my arm.

'Paul,' Julian called from his desk. 'Get the fuck in here, you.'

He stared at me for a few blinks then turned toward Julian's office.

'Kind of tampons you use?' I said to him.

Paul turned, ready to jump as soon as I said go.

'See? I can use abbreviated English too.'

'You act damn smart, but it ain't nothing but a show.'

'I said get your ass in here, Paul,' Julian said, now standing by the door.

My fingertips tingling, I nodded at him. 'He's calling you.'

'If you don't have those college art words to make you seem like something special, everyone'll know you're just a scared little boy who'll never do nothing but nothing.'

I glanced behind me but only Eric stood there. No one else to hear.

Julian yanked Paul by his elbow into the office then slammed the door. Their voices were loud but made unintelligible by the thick door. I took long measured breaths.

'You're a dickhead,' Eric said.

'And he's a cocksucker.' I took the last drag of my cigarette and dropped the butt in a half-full Bud Light can sitting on the floor then stuck my hands in my pocket so Eric wouldn't see them tremble.

Paul lost his virginity to a snowblind Mason at some party she vaguely remembers and he was naive enough to believe he meant something. A few nights later, at another party, the mouthbreather hung on her, trying to find purchase in her heart with the rest of us. He'd been trying to make some philosophical point about Depeche Mode and "Personal Jesus" when he pronounced psalm with all the letters. Mason and her girlfriend laughed, I asked if he meant 'possum,' the holy rodent instead, and Paul has wanted to go all Captain Kurtz on me ever since. Really, the guy can't read without moving his lips. Expecting to end up with a girl like Mason had to be his own personal Hell.

But fuck him anyway.

'He is an asshole, but one day when he gets raging on that powder, he's going to break your jaw.'

I stopped Eric in the middle of the hall, all serious-like. The electro downstairs had turned to NWA, like God was smiling on me.

'Make him think I'ma kick his ass. When he drops his gat Mike's gonna blast.' Imagining this scene from above, I had to bite back a smile.

'What the holy hell are you talking about?' Eric said.

I pointed towards the music. 'Dude, NWA?'

'What?'

'MC Ren? From NWA. Who is playing downstairs right now.'

He shook his head and started down the steps. 'You need to get out more.'

Downstairs, the change in music hadn't done much to alter the scene in the living room. The two by the fire lay still, intertwined atop one another, like the heat had finally melted them. A group of China Girls kneeled around the glass table in the middle of the room, their mouths moving so fast they appeared slow. A dollar bill went from hand to nose to different hand to different nose.

Eric handed me a glass of something. 'Or would you rather have a forty of OE, gangsta gangsta?'

'You're so white, Eric.'

'Yeah. So are you.'

We stood like wildlife at a watering hole, surveying the room. I wasn't sure who were the lions and who were the sick antelope. Someone pushed the buttons on the stereo, swapping out Compton's finest for a Portishead record. I'd been into the song but had to admit that *Dummy* fit the scene much better.

'Christian coming back north for Christmas?' he said.

'Don't know. He left a message the other day but I haven't called him back. I haven't seen his mom in a couple weeks.'

'Lot of business down there. We could make a mint, I'd bet.'

'That's not our kind of town, Eric. Julian knows that.'

The two by the fire startled and shifted positions then passed out again.

'This is about more than business to him.' Eric sipped his drink and smiled at some girl kneeled by the table. 'You're an idiot if you don't jump.'

'I'm more Cezanne than *Little Caesar*.'

Eric had no reaction.

'Cezanne's a French Post-Impressionist painter. *Little Caesar* was the inspiration for *Scarface*.'

I tasted my drink. Rum and Coke, but I could barely taste the Coke.

'Don't be cute. Just think about it.'

I finished my glass without taking a breath. The room turned blurry for a few blinks. When it cleared, Eric was waving at the

China Girl he'd been looking at earlier, now lounging in a loveseat beside the fireplace and absentmindedly playing with her hair, the neckline of her shirt sloping so far to down that, even from across the room, I could see the lace pattern of her bra.

'I've got something to take care of.' He sharpened the crease of his collar, then patted my back and went to her.

I poured more rum in my glass and splashed in some soda then sat at the end of the couch, far enough from the girls to avoid being assaulted by their wild gesticulations or inane banter. Eric and the China Girl disappeared upstairs. I sipped at my glass and felt the alcohol's bite begin to diminish. The flames in the fireplace licked the air, smoke twisted from the tips of the fire. I wondered about sticking my hand in there. If it would burn to nothing before I would pull it out.

Chapter Four

Somewhere between glass three and four, some angelheaded hipster tripped on a China Girl's foot and landed beside me on the couch. Coke splashed over the edge of my glass, dotting my thigh.

'You just learn to how to walk?' I said. It sounded much more vicious in my head but the rum had made me sleepy.

'Brother, I can barely stand.' The guy held out his hand, the dusting of white on his beard seemingly shimmering in the light. 'I'm Dusty.'

'Mike,' I said.

He squinted and leaned back, as if trying to adjust his microscope and determine what type of virus he was examining. 'Yeah, I know you.'

'Cool.' I stood to refill my drink, though I knew I'd only slosh it around for something to do.

'You work in Thorne's, right? At the shoe store. What's it,' he said, snapping his fingers to jar his memory.

'Yes. That's me. I'm getting a drink. Nice to meet you.'

'You're the painter.'

I sat back down. 'How do you mean?'

'I've seen that triptych in Haymarket. That weirdo kid in there, the fat Robert Smith, he told me who you were.'

'Really.' I leaned back in the couch, swirling my drink around in my glass.

'You have any more of that?' He took a drink and a healthy amount spilled out the side, washing away some of the white.

'Not that small but I have some canvases in my closet and a couple others I'm working on.' I pulled a thin notebook from my back pocket and started flipping through the pages. He patted his hand on top, closing it.

'I own The Berkley Hunt pub. I do art shows. Come talk to me tomorrow morning when I'm not zapped. '

I nodded and shook his hand and wanted to slap myself in the face. Maybe he'd think it was just an artistic eccentricity.

'Is there anything you're looking for? Like themes or mediums or, I don't know, colors or something?'

Dusty started to say something but Paul's voice above me drowned it out. I slunk down in the couch and tried to hide my body between the leather cracks to avoid disrupting this conversation but his voice became even louder. I took a big gulp of the drink and his outline blocked my view of the fire. Dusty looked up at the mongoloid looming over us.

'You got more smart words for me?' Paul said. He was near to chewing his lips into fleshy strips. 'Can't hide behind Julian's ballsack down here.'

'This is Paul,' I said to Dusty. 'Grammar is Aramaic to him. He needs a Rosetta Stone to punctuate a complex sentence.'

'What?' they both said.

'It's a lang—'

'I know what it is,' Dusty said.

'What do you want, Paul? I'm having a conversation.'

'I want to shove my hand up your ass and make you my puppet.'

I looked at Dusty. 'Paul's about to go on a polysyllabic shooting spree. Beware.'

Dusty pointed at some vague point around the kitchen then stood up and walked out the front door.

'You fucking moron,' I said to him. 'What the everloving fuck is wrong with you, you mouthbreathing cretin?'

'You keep posing like that big brain's going to help you jump the line. I see you. I know that paint ain't just covering up your clothes. Once Julian realizes what a no-talent cocksucker you are—'

Eric's voice cut through the party, calling out Paul's name. Neither of us was willing to look away and give the other that satisfaction. In the reflection of a painting hanging over Julian's fireplace—bucolic Japan or Tibet or some Eastern countryside—I could see Eric's silhouette with his arms up, gesturing down the hallway, asking if Paul wanted Julian involved in this. I glanced up and Eric had his boxers on backwards and four throbbing scratches down his chest.

Paul looked down at me through squinted eyes. 'Your girlfriend's real sweet, watching over you like that.'

'He's a doll.'

He smacked the glass out of my hand, splashing some of the China Girls with soda. Thankfully for them, they had the reflexes to cover up their lines so it was only their backs that were covered in sugary liquid. Paul stomped out the front door, spitting at one of the lugs on the porch as he passed.

I watched the fire for a moment then poured another drink, slipped a smoke between my lips and went out back.

The stars winked at me in the blackness. I lay across one of the barca loungers on the back porch, smoke and breath mixing in the air. Being so far away from cities and their light, our night sky was a strange hue, a complete non-color. When Christian and I would camp out in his backyard, I would lie awake in my sleeping bag all night terrified that the sky would suck me into the blackness because nothing can be that unadulterated and that dark without having some massive malignant force behind it.

I held my breath when the door opened, thinking that if it was Paul coming back for more, maybe he wouldn't see the plumes of breath and would fuck off somewhere else to light cats on fire with gasoline or whatever it was he did for fun.

'Hey,' Mason said. She wavered in front of me like a mirage. 'I didn't know you were coming here.'

I took a drag because I didn't know how to answer that. Her words were covered in gel, too slippery for her mouth to handle.

'See, I can do it too.' She smiled, but her top lip stuck to a dry spot so it looked more like she was baring her teeth. Her nipples stuck out far enough to hold with my fingertips.

'Do what?' I suddenly wished I'd brought out my jacket so I could offer it to her, drape it across her shoulders and pull her close to me.

'Come on, Mike. It's me you're talking to. I know you wait in Haymarket pretending to drink coffee until I come out of the store.' She stepped toward me like she was on a tightrope.

'I'm just talking to him. I'm not doing that.' I wondered if I was now steaming in the frigid air.

She stretched her arms over her head and I wanted to bury myself in the hollow of her hipbones. 'What's his name?'

'Whose?'

'Exactly.'

'Oh the barista?' I said. 'Jimmy. He's Jimmy.'

'No, he's Jonathon.'

'Oh. Well, that's what he told me.' I tipped my glass and ice cubes hit my teeth.

She sat on the edge of the lounger and laid a hand on my thigh. 'I don't know what his name is but I knew you didn't either.'

'I'm just talking to him, hanging out.' I fumbled through my pockets, pulling out a small bag of white. I took two off the corner of my license and offered her some. She sniffed twice in each nostril, straight from the bag.

'I've seen the way you look at me.'

I had another snort. 'How do I look at you?'

She took the glass from between my legs and sipped at the melted ice. 'Like you're looking at a painting, trying to figure it out.'

When she leaned forward to the end table behind me her breasts brushed against my forearm and I was positive she could feel my erection and wondered what she thought of it. She sat back down with a coaster in her hand.

'I know you watch me.' She took the bag from my hand and

dumped a few thick lines on the coaster.

'I don't watch you. That's creepy.'

She set the coaster in my lap and bent down, hovering above it for a few long seconds until I almost called out, then sniffed long and hard, from the base of the line to the tip. She sniffed again, and rubbed the residue on her gums then on mine, letting her finger linger on my lips.

She grabbed my cock and I almost had a seizure. 'I think about it when I masturbate.'

I opened my mouth to say something, anything, and her tongue was on mine, slipping around my gums, the taste of chemicals and whiskey mixing with rum, her teeth biting my lips. I thought I spilled my drink on my lap until I realized it was her hand inside my boxers and I pulled her onto me, shoving my hand down the back of her pants to her warm ass. She let out a little yelp at the cold, then smiled and attacked me. I felt the stars winking down on me, light that had died thousands of years earlier coming to its final end over a frozen backyard in western Massachusetts.

She pushed her teeth against my ear and whispered, 'Fuck me.'

I pulled at the button of her jeans and she grabbed my hand.

'Not here, Michael,' and the way she said my name almost made me lose my erection but her pressing against me again kept it up. 'Upstairs, now. I want you inside me.'

Her back rose and fell so softly that I was vaguely worried she was suffocating in the pillow. I'd swum through her body like an oil slick for ten or fifteen minutes, making her come 1.5 times before she passed out and left to me take care of myself with some spit and an old pair of boxers I found on the floor. The fact that I hadn't limp-dicked her after all that white was a victory, though with skin and hips and breasts like hers it was a physiological impossibility to stay soft.

Every few minutes she'd cough and rustle, and I'd stroke her shoulders, run my palms over the curves of her torso and soothe her back into whatever abyss she was traversing. Thin white lines striated her skin, some of them logical while others seemed arbitrary. A few traced the soft curve of ribs into breast so carefully that it made me uncomfortably hard. Others ran at jagged angles and looked angry instead of seductive.

Mason and Alex had been together for two years. If there had been a prototypical union of the king and queen of cool, Alex and Mason would've laughed in their faces, saying they were trying too hard. Those two were so effortless in their hipness—like a Godard film come to life without all the self-reflexiveness—and it would've made the entire town throw up if they weren't both so damn nice. You'd feel guilty being jealous or snide about them because they just didn't deserve it.

Then Alex met Bianca. It could only happen with a girl called Bianca. Sometimes I wonder if that was even her Christian name or if she just adopted it because it fit so well.

Every group had a different story about Mason. Some said she chopped at her wrists the same way all our parents did the woodpile before the first big snow. Others said pills, sometimes chased with alcohol, sometimes with gasoline. In my perverse jerk-off fantasies, it was Turpenoid, just after we'd finished a transcendentally beautiful painting. I'd even heard she covered herself with blood and slept on the stone wall that marked her parents' property, waiting for the coyotes in the night. The pills theory explained why she only ever gave half a smile, that her mother's Vicodin had paralyzed part of her mouth, though I liked to think it was just wry, her perpetual, postmodern recreation of the Mona Lisa. Every variation of her suicide attempts only enhanced her allure. And all because of some Bianca who might not have even really been a Bianca.

I wanted to know what it felt like to be loved so severely.

Chapter Five

She burst upright in bed, chest heaving, trying to fill her lungs with air instead of the sleep that was trying to pull her under. I grabbed her and held her close to calm her. The morning sun cut fierce lines across the wall. I'd never slept.

She quivered against me, a baby bird that would not be soothed. I ran my hands over her head, down her hair, telling her that everything was okay, that she was safe.

With a tentative movement, she glanced up at me. 'Mike.'

It sounded more like a question than I wanted to admit.

'I'm here, Mason. We're at Julian's. It's okay.'

She looked down at her naked body and pulled the sheet up over herself before falling back to the pillows and pressing her palms against her eyes.

'Headache?' I started to tell her she could massage the space between her thumb and index finger because the nerve goes to the head but didn't want to hear her response so I just rubbed her side instead.

She said something and petted my hand before setting it aside.

I shifted in bed and caught a glimpse of her tuft of pubic hair. Pale blue veins branched under the skin of her hips, something I'd never noticed, though I don't know why I would have noticed it. It was dark last night and my only clear images of her naked body were composites of Parker Posey and fevered masturbation fantasies. 'You want to get breakfast or something?'

She let out a long breath, then sat up with her arm clamped tight against her chest. 'What time is it?'

I looked at my wrist though I hadn't worn a watch in years. 'Eight? Nine, maybe.'

'Shit.' She wrapped the sheet around her torso and shuffled across the floor, then scooped her blue lace underwear from the floor and worked it on beneath the sheet. 'I can't. I have to get to work.'

I slipped my boxers on under the sheets and leaned over to grab my jeans. 'I'll let you get dressed. You want coffee or anything?'

'Wait,' she said, reaching down to her purse, holding the edge of the sheet with her teeth. 'Can you turn around a minute?'

I heard the soft crumple of sheet landing on the floor and wanted to see her in the light of day with eyes not blurred by rum and memorize every inch of her. I felt a growing erection and grabbed my jeans before she noticed.

'Meant to give you this last night,' she said. I turned and she held a record in her hand. 'I had three at home. Thought you might like one.'

I had no idea what it was but tried to act flattered and unimpressed in equal turns.

'Some Japanese place sent us a couple when *Kid A* came out. They said it's not on the album but I don't know what the name of the song is.'

'I don't speak Japanese either.' Arms hanging to the side, I debated giving her a hug or kiss or some form of thank you, eventually landing on a *very cool of you*. I almost impressed myself.

'You should give this a spin, too.' She handed me a Patti Smith record and I heard that click again, the mental recorder turning on to capture everything I needed to make myself as cool as her. 'They occupy the same space in my head for some reason. Maybe because you go Radiohead, Sonic Youth—mid-Sonic Youth, though, like the late SST albums through *Washing Machine*, minus *Experimental Jet Set* of course—then Patti Smith. Like they make a sequence.'

I thanked her again then pulled on the rest of my clothes, left her in the room to finish dressing and headed down to the kitchen. The smell of a dead fire hung heavy in the living room. I had a flashback of reading Chandler novels in my English 101 class, with the exotic setting at Geiger's house turning rank and garish in the light. One of the China Girls slept in the fetal position on the couch, her bottom half covered in pillows-as-blankets and *skank* written across her cheek in feminine cursive.

The kitchen was empty but I found a French press with lukewarm coffee. I poured it into two tumblers. As I stepped back into the living room, Mason was opening the front door.

'Do you still want coffee?' My voice echoed against the high ceilings. I crossed the room so I wouldn't sound crystalline.

'I'll grab some on the way. I'm sorry, I'm really late.'

'Yeah, sure,' I said, walking to her. 'You know, Haymarket's got really good coffee.' I smiled as I said it, trying to make a joke.

She just nodded, though, stood in the doorway. 'Let me know what you think of the tracks.'

I leaned forward and gave her a gentleman's kiss on the cheek. She flinched slightly.

'I'll see you around.' She left.

Through the frosted window beside the door, I watched her walk down the street, hitting the panic button to find her car. When she pulled around the corner, I plopped down on the couch with my head on the China Girl's pillow. Her slow breathing gave the sensation of lying on a boat, cresting up and over waves. I started to drift off again until she lurched twice, then coughed and threw up into the seam of the couch.

I sat up and shrugged on my jacket, patted my keys in my pocket then left.

Chapter Six

The red light on my answering machine blinked at me as I walked through the door. Long, short, long, short. It was either broken or flashing some secret code I'd forgotten. I pressed the button then walked into the bathroom to throw cold water or bleach on my face.

'Hello, this is the Baltimore Police Department.'

Water dripped from my face as I rushed out of the bathroom, the faucet still running. *Oh God, Christian. What the hell did you do?*

'We're calling because of a found item registered to this residence. It appears to be a penis, though our lab has never seen one quite so tiny and with such a pronounced bend in the shaft, but still we can only assume it is in fact your penis. Our microscopes never lie, sir. We are the very best at penis—'

He tried to say more but couldn't hold back his laughs and hung up the phone. The second message started.

'Yo, bitch. I found yo dick, ninja. Shit be all crooked and my pet fleas were chewing on it—'

He didn't get nearly as far with the second one as the first. Message three started. I washed my face while he laughed at me on my answering machine for a good twenty seconds.

Christian was precisely the reason I'd suggested Paul find more words than fuck or fucker, because with friends like Christian, you needed a large arsenal of insults.

The phone rang. I picked it up.

'Baltimore Police Department can suck my cock and I made it easy because you've already got it, you stupid pigfuckers.'

'Michael,' Christian's mom said, 'you know we don't eat pork.'

Goddammit.

'I'm sorry.'

'Did he leave you a message saying the police found your

penis?'

'Were you in on this?'

'No, but he left me the same one. Only grey hair, not penis.'

I thumbed out a cigarette and lit it. 'He's a creative one.'

'Stunningly.' She paused for a second. 'I thought you quit smoking.'

I dropped it in the sink and ran water over it. 'I'm not smoking.'

'I was serious last week. I'll kick your ass and your friend's if you don't quit.' Her nodding was audible through the phone. 'Anyway, I thought I'd call early and see what your Christmas plans are. You talk to your folks yet?'

'Are there forks stuck into my eyes?' Pulling coffee from the cabinet, I shook some into the French press and started boiling water.

'I don't know if Christian can get home or not, so I wanted to make sure you knew you had an open invite.' Somewhere in the background I heard a crackling, though they didn't have a fireplace. More, it sounded like cellophane.

'I thought you were going to your sister's.'

'You have any extra forks?'

Fair point. 'Sure, then. I'll be over.'

'See you then, love.' There was a click on the other end of the line. 'And don't light a cigarette as soon as we hang up.'

'Love you, too.' I hung up and reached for my smokes, then stopped when the phone rang again. I swore she'd had my studio bugged. Reaching carefully like in a horror movie, I picked it up.

'Hello,' she said.

'Oh. Hi, Mom.'

Her breath coursed over the phone. I couldn't tell if she was out of shape or having a heart attack.

'Did you need something?' I reached for a smoke, figuring Christian's mom wouldn't be able to get me if I was already on the phone.

'You're coming to Christmas, right?'

'When is it?'

'On Christmas.'

I took a long inhale to center myself. 'At what time on Christmas will we be dining, Mother?'

'Oh,' she said. 'Seven or so, I think.'

'That's fine.'

'Great. Looking forward to it.'

'Should I bring a box of wine or will Dad have some?' I couldn't figure out who that guy was that I'd seen her with, but then again everyone around here knew each other somehow.

'Has he been drinking more?'

'How should I know? You're the one who lives with him.'

'Is he acting different?'

'Mom, I'm just asking if I need to bring booze.'

'Oh. Sure. That'd be nice.'

'Okay then. I will.'

'And if he tells you anything, you better tell me quick.'

I said, 'Sure, fine, whatever. I'll talk to you later.' I hung up and turned on the shower while the water boiled.

As soon as I'd stripped down, the phone rang again. *Jesus motherfuck.* Though the advantage of a studio apartment was never being more than five steps from anything, I was naked and stunk to high Hell. I hesitated to answer with another police call.

'Little Mikey,' Eric said.

'Don't call me that.'

'I saw you.'

'What?' The water in the kettle began to squeal.

'I saw you take her upstairs last night. Surprised you're not still in orbit.'

I held my hand in front of the steam until I couldn't, then poured it in the carafe. 'Whatever. No big deal.'

'My ass.' He laughed. 'You decide yet?'

'No. I have to go. I'll talk to you later.'

'Be smart, Little Mikey.'

'Don't call me that.' I said goodbye and hung up, then stepped into shower to wash away all the rum emanating from my pores before my meeting with Dusty. Yeah, sure, he owned a bar and invited me to talk after all the base had worn off. But that didn't mean I had to look derelict or perpetually shithoused to trick him into thinking I was an artist.

Chapter Seven

Inside the pub's front door lay a portal, apparently, because I'd found myself in London's East End. At least, what I imagined to be the East End from watching *Lock, Stock and Two Smoking Barrels* a dozen times. Scarves advocating soccer teams hung above the battered wooden bar. Beside bottles of booze stood trophies that I assumed were World Cups or English Cups or something, but looked like rec league leftovers enhanced with aluminum foil, spraypaint and varnish. Dusty waved from behind the bar. I was surprised he didn't call me guv'na.

My face must've been broadcasting awe because he shook my hand with a wry smile. 'Never been here, I take it.'

'It's impressive. Almost overwhelming.'

'I know where all the good stuff's kept, mate, ya ken?'

'You English? Or British or whatever it is.'

He tossed his head like his hair was blowing in the wind coming off the Irish Sea. 'Only in me heart.'

'Ah, right. Gotcha.' I pulled some Polaroids out of my pocket.

'I always planned on moving there. Then I couldn't. So I figured I'd bring it here.'

'Why couldn't you move?'

'Same story, different fiddle.'

'Met a girl so you didn't leave then bought a pub to stay occupied and found yourself with one pub and no girl?'

He stepped back. 'Actually, yeah.'

'Good guess.' I shrugged. 'And it's kind of like *Good Will Hunting*. But, you know, more British.'

He smiled and clapped my shoulder. 'Let me show you round.'

I nodded in the appropriate places, marveling at the black and white photo of some old soccer team, pursing my lips in appreciation at the carving of the bar's pillars. What he was expecting from me, I had no idea, but he needed to like me so I could score an exhibition.

'So,' he said. 'When can you hang?'

I gestured with the photos I'd been holding so long I'd almost forgotten about them. 'Don't you want to see my stuff?'

'You work for Julian and can't afford a real camera?' He laughed through his nose.

'Don't like them,' I said. 'You know in Africa, how they were afraid of missionaries' cameras because they thought the boxes would steal their souls?'

'Same thing, but digital?'

'More or less.'

He flipped through the pictures, making the same requisite noises I had with his Anglo accouterments but they sounded authentic as opposed to expected. He handed them back. 'I can't really see anything this small without my glasses but that triptych in the coffee shop was something special.'

'It was only a little painting.'

'Size is relative, Mike. Potential is absolute.'

I reached for my cigarettes for something to do, because I didn't know how to take such compliments, then shoved my hand back into my pocket, worried that smoking would seem gauche.

'It probably won't pay much now right now, but it'll get your work in front of a lot of people while you paint your ass off. Someone's going to come in and see it and you're going to need a deep backlist when they want you to do a solo New York show.'

I swallowed and stared at him. What expression my face held, I couldn't even imagine.

'Just make sure I'm on your guest list, mate, or I'll glass you.' His smile evaporated.

'Of course. Definitely.'

He slapped my shoulder again. 'Mike, I'm just taking the piss. Relax.'

'Oh, right.'

'Normally the split is sixty-forty—if it sells of course—but I'll do you seventy-thirty because I really want this exhibit here.'

'If it sells? You don't think it'll do well?'

'No, really, it's no reflection on you whatsoever. People will buy it en masse once they understand it.' He nodded to a concert broadside from the 60s. 'Like John Lennon said, though, times are tough for dreamers right now.'

'Yeah, I totally agree.' I'm pretty sure that's not at all what Lennon said.

He poured himself a pint from the tap. 'Fancy one? It's five in Blighty.'

'I'll pass.' I snapped the photos against my wrist. 'When do you want the paintings?'

'End of January.' He sipped at his drink, licking the foam from his top lip.

'I should be able to get some stuff together by then.'

'Let me know if that works. We can figure something out.'

'It's fine.' I could hear Eric's voice echoing in my head. 'I've got nothing but time.'

Later that night, I found my spot on the couch at Julian's again with some celebratory Jameson eighteen-year I picked up on the way over. No Bacardi or Tanqueray for me tonight. Only five or six derelicts milled about, but, it being just past eleven, our evening had barely begun. The moths might've still been en route to the fireplace.

I had the urge spend days drinking copious amounts of absinthe and laughing and dancing with Mason, which was my overall interpretation of the artist's life. Maybe throw in some bullfighting, though finding bulls during a New England winter might prove to be challenging. I stared through the flames and searched their rhythms for curvilinear patterns to form into shapes and figures, into internal landscapes comprised of staccato edges and chiaroscuro lighting. The bricks of the fireplace reformed, softened at the edges and bled over one another before differentiating themselves according to the depth of the plane and made me think I should look into cubism more. I saw hands extending upwards from boulders, the fingers pinched into an ostrich-like shape, with bloodshot eyeballs resting on the thumb pads.

Someone grasped my shoulder and the cubist hand-ostriches shattered. Fighting Paul would take too much energy and I wondered what would happen if I avoided injuring my hands and just sat there, what Julian would call passive resistance, and see if he'd still hit me if I didn't move. But Julian's face appeared next to mine, not Paul's.

'Even death is not to be feared by one who has lived wisely.' He held out his fist, and when he uncurled his fingers, out fell the blue lotus medallion. 'So I give my wisdom to you.'

I stared dumbly at the medallion, flipping it over in my palm. When I turned around to ask why he'd given it to me, he was already halfway up the steps. I wrapped the leather strap around my wrist, cupping the medallion in my palm. Chasing after him to gush about the exhibit crossed my mind but when I turned around I saw a black silhouette wavering in front of the fire. It moved with the rhythm of the flames. Elemental, almost. I blinked a few times. Mason threw her hips side to side as her boots devoured the floor beneath her, making her way to me. White rings hung to her nostrils, black wisps of eyeliner spreading from her eyes like swan wings.

'Fancy seeing you here.' Her smile was beatific but the words were comprised of all elbows and sharp angles.

'I was waiting for you.' I sounded so confident I almost surprised myself.

She held out a glass for me, whiskey and ice by the smell, and straddled my lap. 'I got this for you.'

'The drink or your vagina?'

Licking the rim of the glass, she raised an eyebrow then took a sip like a kitten from a bowl of milk. 'Want to find out?'

Her hipbones dug into my pelvis and when I bit her neck her sweat tasted of acrid chemicals. The damp silk sheets stuck to my back as I sat up. I threw her facedown on the bed and she let out a howl, digging her nails into my thighs and pulling me in farther, farther, harder and faster. A long reflection of moonlight down her spine, two throbbing shadows in the hollow dimples above her ass and the feeling of it squashing against my pelvis and stomach almost made me come until I saw a pair of stained underwear and frayed argyle sock with a condom sticking out of a hole in the toe lying on the bed.

'Dammit don't stop!'

She flexed inside and threw her ass back at me and I dropped the strangers' laundry on the floor as I came with a long grunt and shiver. I collapsed on her back, kissing her shoulders and speckling them with tiny bites. She lay with her face in the pillow but I could still hear her long sigh.

After a minute I rolled off her and threw away the condom. The room smelled like the inside of an aspirin bottle. A few snowflakes began to fall outside the window. I curled up next to her and though she didn't push me away, she didn't move either. Her chest rose and sank in a steady rhythm. I held my breath until we fell in sync.

'Hey,' she said.

'Yeah?'

'I'm going to masturbate, okay?'

'Oh, sure.' I lifted my hand from her stomach, let it hover between us, not sure where to put it. 'Do you want, like, help, or anything?'

She said, 'No, I'm fine,' but I wouldn't have been able to hear it if I wasn't lying next to her. The sheet above her crotch began to flick and twitch. She lifted her knees and I could hear the wet slap between her legs. Her teeth bit hard on her bottom lip. She whispered something.

'I didn't hear you.'

'Pinch my nipple.'

'One or both?'

Her breath quickened. 'I don't care just pinch it.'

I took one between my fingers and caressed the slope of her other with my palm. I felt myself start to grow, so I pressed it against her hip but she bucked her hips up in the air so hard I thought she'd break something until she gasped and shivered and clamped her hand between her legs. The sweat on her forehead twinkled like a tiara of broken glass.

'Thank you,' she said, then rolled over. Cold air filled the space between our sweaty bodies. We talked for a few minutes as I inched my way over to her and let my arm drift over her chest. She didn't pull away, but I couldn't tell from her breathing if she had finally passed out or not. As the snow floated through the air outside, I got closer to her until my chest pressed against her chilled back. I closed my eyes to sleep but it looked the same as outside, white slashes falling through a swathe of black.

She burst upright in bed, chest heaving, trying to fill her lungs with air instead of the sleep that was trying to pull her under. I grabbed her and held her close to calm her. The morning sun cut fierce lines across the wall. I thought I'd slept but couldn't remember.

It didn't take much to calm her this morning—she'd apparently been less sedated than the night before.

I lay on my side, watching her. Three bruises circled the back of her arm, another just above her hip. I kissed the ones I could reach and apologized.

'There's nothing so arousing as fear and submission and the threat of violence.' She looked at the ceiling while she spoke.

I couldn't remember if I'd given her those bruises.

'Come on, you're good at this game.' She glanced at me. 'It's from a book.'

'Never read it.'

She returned to the ceiling. 'I don't think you'd like it.'

We lay listening to our own breathing until it became too familiar.

'I have to get going,' she said, cinching the sheet around her chest as she slipped on her t-shirt.

'I thought I was buying you breakfast.' My voice held a hint of pleading and I wanted to slap myself. 'I mean, you said you wanted to go to Black Sheep in the morning.'

'I did?' She stood and picked up her jeans, shimmied them over her seashell hips.

'Last night, yeah. And then hang out.'

'Then obviously I was really fucked up because I'd never choose Black Sheep when Mama Iguana's has breakfast burritos that will make you see God.'

'Then let's go there instead. I'll treat. We can celebrate.'

'Celebrate?' The way she said it made my dick shrink.

'I landed an exhibition at a pub. It hangs in January.'

She stood still for a moment. 'Why didn't you tell me before?'

I nodded at her pelvis. 'Wasn't what I was thinking about.'

'That's fantastic, Mike.' Her mouth formed a smile but some hint of sadness hung at the edge of her voice. 'You should be really proud of yourself. Can I see the paintings sometime?'

'Of course.' Again, I managed not to jump in the air with the excitement of an 80s sitcom title sequence and internally congratulated myself. 'I'll show you a few after breakfast.'

She sighed and set her hand on my cheek. Her palm was warm with sweat but her fingertips were cold. 'Later, okay? I have to work and I really need a shower.'

'You work a lot. Why don't you just call out for a day?'

She stood with her jeans unbuttoned and stared at me. Her head hung heavy to the side, the dark circles beneath her eyes visible through the makeup. 'I would love to hang out and follow my every bohemian whim. That is one job I would be great at. But they're not hiring anymore.'

'I wasn't saying to be a wasteoid. Just—'

'You know what the difference between a vagrant and surf-bum is?' She pulled two yellow pills from her pocket and dry-swallowed them. 'A board.'

'Are those yellow jackets?'

She buttoned up and sat to pull on her boots. 'Nino will fire me if I do coke at work.'

I had no response so I folded her bra and handed it to her.

'If I could pay student loans with record-trades, I would. Not that it matters now, but. Besides, you can probably use the time to paint.' She held out her leg to tighten her laces and I felt immediately ashamed for being aroused. After the whole Bianca incident, she'd gone on indefinite hiatus from academia. The college didn't care about helping her out because they already had her hundred thousand dollars, and threw her out anyway. Knowing this much about her personal life from sideline observation triggered equal parts intimacy and unease. She pulled her hair into a sloppy ponytail, letting go a long breath. 'I'm sorry. Scotch gives me a headache.'

'You want to smoke something?'

'I got a call saying I'm about to default on my loans. They actually took the time to call my house.'

'Jesus.'

'My mom's the cosigner. We're fucked.' She exhaled hard again then sniffed quickly and pressed her palm against her eye. 'I was too zapped to remember to withdraw from my classes and now my mom's going to lose her house.'

I tried to offer consolation but only flapped my mouth like a fish trying to breathe air. And after I'd just bragged about the exhibition.

'Yeah, so, there's that.' She slid on her leather jacket and said she'd see me around.

I waited for her footsteps to disappear, then the front door close, before I rolled over and masturbated, picturing Mason in my apartment speckled with paint, Mason in her Queen of Vinyl clothes at The Berkeley Hunt for my art opening, Mason in a subdued but ravishing dress holding a cocktail at a proper gallery. But by the time her skirt rode halfway up her thigh as she threw her head back in laughter, the image slithered through my head of her shanghaied as a real-estate secretary in a boxy white blouse, of her and her mom walking home from the bus with plastic bags of soup cans digging into their fingers. I pulled until it hurt then fell back with my arms spread, panting and sweating and shivering.

That was a life for someone with sensibilities far more pedestrian than Mason. Someone comfortable in the mundane. A girl like her didn't deserve a fate like that. I could rescue her, take away that discontent and show I was worthy of her severe love.

No one had made coffee downstairs, though the hands on the clock had barely edged past eight. I boiled water and searched through Julian's cabinets.

Steps echoed in the living room. I peeked around the corner and saw Paul shrugging on his jacket, looking around like he was checking for anyone watching. He unlocked the door and eased it open, then closed it the same way Christian and I used to when sneaking out of his house.

'Double-check?' Eric said behind me. He had traces of lipstick on his stomach running down below his Burberry underwear. The bags beneath his eyes said he hadn't slept much, if at all.

'What's double-check?'

He smiled and slapped my shoulder. 'Don't be coy. It's unbecoming of you.'

'What the fuck are you talking about?' I scooped coffee into the carafe.

'For achieving nirvana twice in one week, you're surprisingly quiet.'

I scratched my chin and tried not to think of Mason's hips so I wouldn't get a boner in front of my friend. Not that it really seemed to bother him at the moment.

'It's complex.'

'Only if you actually care.' He grabbed a carton of milk from the refrigerator and took a couple long pulls, wiping the spills with the back of his hand. 'Can't sleep without a glass of milk before bed.'

I stared at the kettle.

'You realize what this means between you and Julian now?' Eric said.

'What?'

'It's not just economics.' He nodded at the medallion still tied round my wrist and gave his cocky-shit smile. 'It's complex.'

'You coming?' a female voice said. A hand with black fingernails snaked around Eric's chest and grabbed his crotch.

'Give me a minute.' He gave her a long kiss. She wore only his unbuttoned Fred Perry shirt and when she turned away I could see the profile of her breast.

'Cute friend,' I said. 'Same one?'

He looked to the side for a minute then shook his head. 'Why don't you go do something with her, something outside of this house? Go to a museum or park or something you two would like. Get some perspective on things so you can make a good choice. The right choice.'

'She has to work.' The kettle whistled. I poured water into the carafe and watched the steam rise.

'Enjoy yourself, Mike.' He cupped a hand on my shoulder. 'Don't get lost in your sketchbooks and find her gone.'

'I'm in, Eric.' I hadn't meant to say it, but as soon as the words left my mouth, I knew I meant it. 'I'll give my two weeks this afternoon.'

Eric gave a sleepy smile and shook his head. 'I had Davey

Shakes lined up a week ago to take your spot.'

'You knew I'd say yes?'

'There's no one else I'd rather be riding with than you.'

I stirred the coffee and poured myself a cup. It tasted of burnt dirt and water.

'To bigger and better things.' Eric held the carton of milk to me. 'Skål.'

I touched it with my mug. 'Yeah, cheers.'

Chapter Eight

'Yeah, this is T-Bone calling from the North Pole. Santa wanted to double check on your Christmas list. Says here you got three bumpy dick dildos on your list and two more double-ended ones. Santa says that's probably more than any one person should have but, hey, it's your butthole, buddy. Anyway, the problem is your Michael Jackson sex doll. You didn't specify whether you wanted a giver or receiver, so we'll probably send both to cover our bases. Don't like returns for Christmas, you know? It's just bad for business. Anyway sounds like you're the kind of pervert that could use both at the same time, so, you know, Merry Fucking Christmas, asshole.'

He'd actually made it through an entire message without laughing and I counted this as a win for him. I called him back but he didn't answer. I didn't have the energy to leave a detailed story and just asked if he was coming home for Christmas because it'd be nice to see him.

The clock read 9:30 AM. Eric said he'd call in a couple days. The biggest decision of the day stood before me in two stacks: *Star Wars* trilogy or *Godfather* 1 and 2. I decided to start in a galaxy far, far away and see what happened.

After Luke saved Han from the Sarlaac pit, I paused it and got take-away curry from down the street.

The galaxy was saved and the sun was still up, just barely. I rolled a joint and watched the snowflakes drift down on Northampton's rush hour. Three people honked their horns, though two were to let a pedestrian cross the street.

Night fell and *The Godfather*s played.

Fredo shouldn't have done it. He deserved what he got, though if I were in the same situation with my family, I probably would have gone Menendez on them a long time ago.

I ate the rest of the curry and smoked another joint and started *Goodfellas* because Sofia Coppola and *Godfather 3* can suck it. The phone didn't ring, no matter how hard I stared at it.

Sunlight threw itself against my eyelids, a small stream leaking through. I got up and stretched my arms over my head. My messages blinked. I hadn't even heard it ring.

'This is Southwest Airlines calling in reference to a passenger, one Christian Grady. He had a ticket booked from Baltimore to Hartford-Bradley but has tested positive for excessive amounts of dickhead, rendering him unable to fly. Our labs coded the virus and traced it back to you, sir. We recommend having yourself tested immediately, lest you spread dickhead throughout the population.'

The second message was Dusty, calling to say he had an idea for a themed show if I was looking for suggestions and please call him soon because he wanted to make sure we did this right, 'so we can put you on the map and get you the hell out of the Valley.' I stared at the blinking light while he left his number.

I rolled a joint and stacked up *Nightmare on Elm Street* 1-5 and *Scream* 1 and 2. I ate frozen waffles and Nutella and drank three cups of coffee. My sketchbook and paints called out for me but I couldn't articulate my limbs to move my body from the mattress.

It didn't matter. No one called.

Goddamned sunlight searing my skull in half.

The packing peanuts filling my head sloshed as I got up to piss and make breakfast. No messages this morning. I was pretty sure I'd called Christian back, but had a sneaking suspicion there was a long ramble attached to the message.

After the Kurt Russell extravaganza *Escape from New York/Escape from LA* double-feature ended, I called Eric. Mason's number sat in my mental Rolodex but I didn't think she'd actually given it to me, instead finding it through auxiliary methods, and I wasn't ready for that kind of conversation. The walls crept close and I'd start scratching away my skin if I didn't vacate the house.

'What's up?' His voice traveled a long way to his mouth.

'You sound like you're dying.'

'Long night.'

'Aren't they all?'

His breath rolled over the mouthpiece. 'You okay?'

'Yeah, fine. You doing anything today? I still haven't gotten over to Pleasant Street for the *Blade Runner/Metropolis* bill. Want to go?'

Murmuring on the other side of the line. I assumed it was female but couldn't be positive. 'It does sound cool but I've got a couple things to take care of today to get ready.'

'Well, if you get bored or whatever, you know.'

'What?' he said. 'Right, yeah. You're going to Julian's tonight, right?'

I muttered something approximating *I don't think so* though I knew I couldn't stay in the studio much longer.

'Cool. I'll see you over there.' He hung up before I could say goodbye.

The muscles behind my eyeballs ached and my retinas were cathode-ray sunburned. I couldn't bear watching another DVD so I lay on my bed staring at the ceiling, watching the shadows creep up my wall.

By four, I feared I'd have to make a suicide-pact with myself if I didn't see another person before nightfall.

The Drunken Gourd held only a smattering of daydrinkers, too late for lunch and too early for Happy Hour. Some rerun of *Friends* played on the TV behind the bar. Of all the shows to play, that seemed like the least likely. Two girls who likely went to Smith College sat beside me smoking Marlboro Reds, their heady mix of patchouli and militant-feminism overpowering the cloud of smoke I tried to lose myself in. One sported a buzzcut and the other looked like a linebacker who happened to play softball.

I butted out my smoke and waved for another Newcastle to celebrate not killing myself. Granted, I didn't feel like talking to anyone but a deal's a deal. This whole thing with Eric felt tenuous, but I told myself to stay optimistic. I'd get the lay of it from Julian tonight and make myself a comfy spot as consigliere, someone to work out logistics and forecast business, maybe put out feelers for new partners.

I would save her from ruin.

I left a few bills on the bar for the drink and opened my pack. Empty. Figured.

'Sorry, ladies.' I leaned over to the Smith girls. 'I just ran out. Can I bum a smoke from you?'

They regarded me with hooded eyes then said *no* and turned back to their conversation.

Happy Valley, my aching asshole.

'Isn't it extra points or something if a man asks for your help? You get a lesbian level-up, right?'

The buzz-cut one looked at me. 'Two levels up, actually.'

'So what's the problem then? You want a dollar for it?'

Softball leaned around her friend. 'Someone sees us give you a cigarette, everyone's going to want one. And there's only five left in the pack.'

I gestured around the bar. 'There's only three other people here.'

'Exactly,' said Buzzcut.

'And by the way,' Softball said, 'I'm not a dyke. I fucked your friend, Eric.'

I opened my mouth but the response was stillborn. The pint glass gave me something to do with my hands so I wouldn't look like a total fool, though I had a hard time seeing her and Eric. Any given day, I guessed. I finished the beer and stood to leave. Buzzcut grabbed my arm as I passed.

'For what it's worth, I am a lesbian.'

'Cool,' I said.

'No, because your buddy sliced up my girlfriend's palm.'

'Eric?'

'Julian,' she said. 'Lila kept quiet like she's supposed to and that cocksucker still cut up her beautiful, beautiful hands.'

Again, they'd caught me with nothing to say. I grunted and hurried out the door and headed toward my apartment. Slow thinking didn't bode well for this new career. At the same time, though, the girl shouldn't have gotten caught. Who the fuck passed in a bar we didn't control? People got stupid and got caught. That was their problem. Keeping your mouth shut was just keeping you above ground. That much should be a given.

But.

She got caught because she passed in the bar and someone saw her. Likely she passed in a sketchy way because everyone looked sketchy doing something they weren't supposed to. But if she looked normal, no one would think twice. Like, if she was passing a cigarette, which everyone always wanted in a bar, as Softball so explicitly pointed out. So if you passed product like cigarettes, no one would look at it sideways.

Holy shit.

A woman tisked at me. I hadn't realized I said it aloud.

Roll up the bags and put them behind the filter. Pass the cigarette and pass the product.

'Holy shit.'

I hurried to my car and drove straight to Julian's.

Julian wiped dust off the bottle of scotch and let me break the wax seal. Two packs of smokes and a dozen small plastic bags sat on the desk before Eric. He'd almost figured out how to do it, and it only took twenty minutes. That was why he was who he was, and I was where I was.

'This is going to change things.' Julian poured three fingers into a glass and set it next to the mirror. 'With this distribution, we'll need to increase our orders.'

'I'm bringing Mike to the meeting on Thursday.'

'Were you going to tell me?' I said.

'I just did.' He packaged up a cigarette, tamping down the tobacco flush with the tip before he handed it to me. 'A little lumpy, but god damn if that's not a beauty.'

'What'd I tell you, son?' Julian held out his glass to me. 'To the future.'

I clinked his glass and took a mouthful. It tasted like a marsh set on fire then put out with moonshine. The second gulp warmed my stomach and I didn't mind it. 'You sound like Noah Cross.'

'Mike,' he said, 'I don't even know who that is.'

'It doesn't matter.' I took two lines then held out my glass for another drink.

Instead of the scotch bottle, he slid me a shining silver gun.

'Really?'

Eric arched an eyebrow, as if it should be obvious.

'Guns aren't really my thing.'

'Ask him about Cezanne,' Eric said. He laughed at his own joke.

Julian leaned forward and patted my cheek, looked me right in my eyes and waited until I returned his stare to speak. 'Just listen to Eric and you'll be fine. You know,' he said, wagging a friendly finger at me, 'I always had a good feeling about you. Different from those lugs I hired. They're good muscle, but just muscle. You, son, you're something special. I'm proud of you.'

I took a long inhale and picked up the piece. The steel grip fogged with the heat of my hand, but it fit my palm much better than I'd wanted to admit. I extended my arm and aimed out the window, bringing the streetlamp across the street into my sightline, and laid my finger on the trigger. Despite the weight, the target didn't waver.

'Is it loaded?'

Julian breathed a laugh. 'What do you think?'

Paul was standing at the bottom of the stairwell. He never looked at me but continuously moved his body so I couldn't pass. Since Mason and I had recently spent two nights together, he'd somehow deemed me an appropriate target for all the repressed anger from her rejection. *Make yourself comfortable, fucko, because that's a long line.* But at least he'd dropped the Holden Caulfield shit and stopped looking for proof I was a phony.

Maybe that wasn't it, though. Maybe it was Julian, not Mason. He'd wanted in the game and saw me in his spot beneath Julian's wing. He had muscle, sure, but the cocksucker could never come up with something like the cigarettes, and I was pretty damn sure he knew it.

Hell, who knew. Maybe it was both, or neither, and he just couldn't stand me.

Whatever the reason, Julian's third scotch had bathed me in warmth and the white left my body tingling. I didn't feel like wasting the feeling on this ass-clown, so I stood on the step like I had nowhere to be, just sipping my scotch and looking around, and waited for him to adjust his position so I could slip by. He eventually relented, either from boredom or Julian's laugh echoing closer down the hallway.

I walked into the kitchen and saw a beautiful pair of legs supporting a lithe body bent over the counter with her face over a line.

I knew she'd come to me. All I had to do was show.

On Wednesday, our fourth morning together, she didn't tremble after she woke. Instead she lay back onto the bed, her arm draped over my chest, her leg over my waist. Her breathing came shallow as she snoozed on me. I thought it might mean she was falling for me.

Chapter Nine

Somewhere in the liquid moments between sex and sleep, Mason made a comment about Morrissey having the kind of profile that belonged over a mantel. I spent most of Thursday sketching out his portrait then lining it on the canvas, trying to keep my mind off the meeting Eric was taking me to. He'd said it was an easy in-and-out kind of thing, making some allusion to training wheels. I wasn't sure if it was supposed to ease my mind regarding the meeting or be a jab because I'd fallen a half-dozen times while drunkenly racing bikes around Julian's backyard two weeks before.

Five minutes before *The Simpsons* reruns came on, the phone rang. I picked it up with my pinkies, trying to keep the rest of my paint-covered fingers away from it.

'It's me,' Eric said. 'Plans changed. Be out front in five.'

'I thought you weren't coming until nine. I've got—'

'Be ready.'

He hung up before I could argue. I held the phone like it'd become self-aware.

Five minutes. I laid plastic wrap over my palette so the paint wouldn't dry out then scrubbed my hands raw. I'd just picked up the towel when the phone rang again.

'I said get the fuck out here.'

'Christ, I'm coming.'

'You're not. You're talking on the phone.'

'Because you just called me as I'm coming out. Let me hang up and I'll be out in a sec.'

'Get the fuck out here!' He hung up. I stuck the gun in my waistband and took a long pull of warm Newcastle, thinking it might do me good.

Eric wasn't smoking a cigarette so much as chewing it. Ash sprinkled over his black suit. I barely had the door closed when he took off.

'This isn't making me feel better, you know?'

'Mikey,' he said as he cut off a turning car, 'grow a fucking set.'

'Oh, fuck you. You two were the ones who roped me into this.'

'Then leave.' He shoved a Misfits CD into the stereo. His jaw pulsed under his skin. 'You're scared, you leave. You want to live this life, get money and girls or whatever the fuck it is you're after, you need to grow a set.'

'I'm not scared, dickhead. I just don't like having guns around.'

'Guns don't kill people. People kill people.'

'Thank you, Charlton fucking Heston.' I thumbed out a smoke and lit it, watching the countryside go by the interstate.

'At least he sacks up to what he is.' Eric snatched my pack and pulled one out with his teeth. He smoked half of it before looking over at me. 'Look, I'm sorry, all right? They changed the meeting place to somewhere in Vermont. I didn't even have time to get the right suit.'

'That one's nice.'

'It's a black Hugo Boss, Mike. It's too formal but the grey one is still—'

He swung around a tractor-trailer and narrowly missed clipping the corner of a Camry. They honked but he drove too fast for it to matter. 'It doesn't matter. I don't know what the place is like and I don't like being late. It's disrespectful and we need to tread lightly with these people. All those Northern Kingdom people are related. If Ted Green and them get word before we're up and running, it's going to be a logistical nightmare. So I'm a little stressed.'

Logistical nightmare, a nice euphemism.

I flicked my cigarette out the window and it arced through the blackness. The moon cast death-pall shadows over the fields interspersed with thickets of pine trees.

'Anything I should know before we get there?'

He took a few long breaths before answering. 'Just keep your eyes open and don't jump at a broken stick.'

We pulled up to a bar, as evinced by BAR painted on the piece of cardboard stuck in the window. It looked more like a truck stop outhouse, but this was a different scene from home. We parked between a red rusted pick-up and a Cadillac polished to a high-shine. I couldn't tell which one was our guy.

'You stay by the door. When I tell you, get the duffel bag from the trunk and drop it in the bed of that truck.'

'That's it?'

He lit another cigarette. 'Remember what I said about sticks.'

As he went inside, I pulled my hands inside my jacket sleeves. If I'd known we were going to be outside, I would've brought a barrel of brandy to go around my neck. A bearded man wearing a torn flannel stood beside me, presumably their version of me.

'Beautiful night, isn't it,' he said.

'My dick is frozen to my thigh.'

'That's too bad,' he said.

'I know.'

'Be better if it was your knee.'

Two red lights blinked across the sky, the plane passing in and out of clouds. I felt like there was steam coming from my head. I blew into my hands and rubbed them together.

The bearded guy let out a small laugh. 'You don't get up to the Northern Kingdom much, do you?'

'What the fuck is this Northern Kingdom thing?'

'You ever read a book, son?'

I spit on the ground in front of his boots. 'Once or twice. You know your letters yet?'

He gave me a nicotine smile. 'Only the ones I need to know.'

I stuck another cigarette between my lips, not because I wanted one but because I needed something to do.

'Mind if I get one of those?' the man said.

I couldn't help but laugh and give him a smoke.

Ten minutes of smoking and staring passed before Eric stepped from the shack. He nodded at the car and went back inside.

I popped the trunk and pulled out the duffel bag. It made a decent thunk when I dropped it in the truck bed, but not enough to be able to discern whether it was money or bricks. Though I wasn't positive I wanted to know, I couldn't stop myself from unzipping part of the bag to check. The man's grunt stopped me before I saw inside.

'Don't think that's for us to know, son.'

'Well, how will we know unless we find out?' I started to unzip it when the door to the house swung open. Eric took his time getting to the car but I could tell in the halting way he walked, like one knee just wouldn't bend, that this was not a good meeting. He pointed at the car and I opened the door.

'There are causes worth dying for, son,' the man said, 'but none worth killing for.'

I stood still, one foot on the dirt lot and the other in the car, the engine running.

'What's that supposed to mean?'

'It's from a book. Maybe not the one you read, though.' He smiled and I slammed the door. The gun dug into my back and I'd almost forgotten about it. Eric's car threw dust in the air and we drove into the darkness.

'Not a good meeting?' I handed him my smokes.

'No,' he said. 'Not a good meeting.'

Julian met us at a diner, which made me more anxious than the dead silence that filled the whole ride back. Eric had burned through the rest of my cigarettes and if I hadn't notched a few behind my ear I would've been chewing my lips off from nicotine deprivation.

He ordered three coffees and three fries, and a check right

now, please. I popped four quarters into the booth's jukebox to hear a little Stones and Four Tops and put a blanket over our conversation.

'Eric,' he said, kneading the tension from his palms out to his fingertips, 'in your reflection, do you think they're trying to get over on us?'

'There's something not right about the whole thing. Changing the meet, bringing in that guy we'd never talked to. Terms were met but not under the right conditions, you know?'

'A transaction such as this? We need to be sure.' He looked at me. 'Michael, what's your take?'

I sipped at my coffee. 'There are some causes worth dying for, but none worth killing for.'

'Camus?' He scratched his chin while looking into the air. 'Interesting, but ultimately irrelevant.'

'I'm just saying keep our eyes open.' I did my best *Godfather* hand gesture. 'I don't know what it is but something's up. I can just feel it.'

We sat and stared past each other, sipping coffee or lighting a cigarette or generally becoming unmoored inside our own skulls. I picked at my food, tracing the plate's cracked edge with a burnt fry. Besides the implication of Julian wanting to meet out in public, I was more disappointed than I wanted to admit that we weren't at his house. Now I'd have to seek out Mason if we were going to spend the night together, and the prospect of it not happening was more than I could take right then.

'Michael.' Julian said my name like it was the third time. 'The next meet will be in three nights. I want you to take the lead.'

'Me?' After stammering with the bearded sage and seeing Eric walk across the parking lot like that, to say that the prospect of leading the next meet with these guys made me uncomfortable was a Christ-fucking-a-donkey understatement. 'I don't know about that.'

'You know what you're doing,' Eric said. 'Our conversation

aside, you'll be fine.'

'No, I don't, Eric. And I certainly am not trying to get in with these guys if they got your panties in a twist like that.'

'You've been doing it for the last two years,' Julian said. 'We've been grooming you with the shoe shop. Then you brought me the cigarette distribution. You're ready.'

'Just move the decimal two points to the right,' Eric seconded. 'Actually, three.'

'You want me to handle a five-hundred-thousand-dollar deal?'

'Yes,' Julian said. 'I do.'

'But three nights is Christmas night.' I tried hard not to sound desperate, but the image of Morrissey above my TV playing Log TV, of Mason and I wrapped together like writhing snakes, of us smoking cigarettes and making stupid jokes, they kept flashing through my brain so fast it was hard to concentrate on Julian.

'I know it's Christmas. That's why we set it up.' Julian not celebrating Christian holidays wasn't an issue. More important was everyone else celebrating them. Even if there was a chance I'd miss Mason, it was good timing, especially if we were moving that kind of weight. And getting that kind of money.

Eric looked at me, held out his lighter for my smoke. 'You were made for this.'

I touched my cigarette to the flame. *You will save her from monotony.* 'What's my split?'

Julian just smiled.

Chapter Ten

I burst upright in bed with my chest heaving, then dragged my hand across my forehead. The phone rang again. The sheets beside me were cold, and I was unwilling to admit what I thought about that. I stumbled into the other room and picked up the phone as the answering machine kicked on.

'Who is it this time?'

'Can you do Christmas Eve instead of Christmas?' Her voice was already loose and I wondered if it was mimosas or breakfast wine.

'That's fine.' I searched through the napkins covered in thumbnail sketches on my kitchen table but couldn't find my smokes.

'Okay, good. Teddy has Christmas with his daughters and can't make it.'

'Is Teddy the guy you were hanging on downtown last week?

'Oh, Michael, you know Teddy.'

'No, Mom. I don't know any Teddy.'

'From my office?'

'It doesn't matter to me. What's Dad want to do?'

She actually laughed at the question. 'You know your father won't care as long as there's White Zin and ice cubes.'

'You mean he doesn't even know someone else is coming?'

'Michael, really.'

'Come on, Mom. Jesus.'

'You're always so dramatic. I'll talk to you when you've calmed down.'

I hung up before I said something vulgar that I couldn't take back.

On the counter sat a bottle of Jameson I picked up after the diner the night before. I stared at it for a long minute. Something about drinking at 9 AM felt pathetic and hereditary. Instead I rolled up a joint and put on the Patti Smith record then sat in the middle of palettes and canvases, picked up a brush and a daub of phthalo blue-green and let the bristles coast down Morrissey's jawline, launching off his chin and breaking through the wall around her heart.

The brush jumped when the phone rang, sending an errant splash of yellow into his hair. I tried to tease it out into a highlight, albeit a strange one, but the fucker just wouldn't blend. I dropped my brush onto the carpet and snatched the phone from its cradle.

'Hey.'

'Mason, hi.' Without thinking I cleaned my hands on my jeans, ruining another pair with long streaks across the thighs. I didn't know she had my number. 'What's happening?'

'Nothing,' she said. I could picture her on the other end of the phone, lying on the edge of her bed with her hair hanging down, her breasts surging forward, showing me enough to make my blood rush but not so much that I'd explode. 'Hadn't seen you in a couple days. Just calling to see if you were hanging out tonight.'

'Tonight?' I looked out the window and was surprised to find it dark, ten hours slipping between brushstrokes and into the ether. 'Let me get a shower and I'll meet you over there in a few.'

'I'll just come by your place,' came rushing out of her almost before I'd finished my sentence.

'Okay.' I told my voice to steady itself.

She said something that might've been *see you soon* but it was lost in the rustle on her mouthpiece. I scooped up the palettes and sketchpads and stacked them on the top shelf of my closet, then kicked a lump of clothes to the side and laid the painting against the wall. Multicolored fingerprints edged the doorframe and knob. I hid the gun behind some bowls in the cabinet. At the sink, I scrubbed my fingers with orange soap until my cuticles bled. The blue wouldn't leave my fingerprints so I crumpled a paper towel between my hands, drawing out as much as I could before pulling on clean jeans and rubbing a little deodorant near my neck in place of cologne.

I'd just pulled the needle off Patti Smith when she knocked on my door. A quick check over the place, shoving old boxers under the mattress with my foot, and I opened the door channeling Bogart hard as fuck.

'Hey,' I said.

'Hi.' She pecked me on the cheek as she entered. I followed the pattern of her fishnets from the top of her motorcycle boots to the bottom of her miniskirt.

'Can I get you something to drink?'

She spun on her heels and crushed her mouth against mine, her teeth biting my lip, tongue skirting in and out. I held tight to the back of her neck, trying to smash our bodies together until they were one. After eons she pulled back enough for us to breathe.

'Do you have any Coke?'

I kissed her mouth. 'Whiskey?'

She nodded coquettishly and slunk down onto my couch, taking her time crossing her legs.

There was only one clean glass in the cupboard. I glanced behind me and she was now standing before one of my paintings on the wall, so I emptied the orange juice from a glass in the sink and swirled some water around to clean out the pulp, then dried it on my shirt. She was still staring at the painting—a fish with hands swimming above a house that was only framed on one side—when I turned around.

'What does it mean?' she said.

'What do you think it means?'

'You're bored.'

'Could be.' I poured two fingers of Jameson into each glass and opened a can of ginger ale for hers. Two ice cubes cracked as I dropped them into the drinks.

'You're drowning,' she said. 'And your skin doesn't fit.'

I poured more in my glass and went to her. 'That could be it too.'

She turned away from the painting and looked at the glass in my hand, cocking her head.

'Sorry, it's ginger ale. I don't have any Coke.'

'Oh,' she said, and her tone drained the air from the room. She took a tentative sip from the glass and bit her bottom lip, the one I wanted to sink my teeth into. 'Sorry, I meant, um, cocaine.'

'I,' I said, showing her my glass for some reason, 'I don't have any.'

'Oh. That's fine.' She gave a tight smile and sipped from the drink like a baby bird. She examined the paintings some more, the stacks of records next to the closet that held her painting, smiling when she looked at the record on the turntable, glancing past the painted Japanese partitions concealing the mattress on which she would likely not be finding new uses for bungee cords in. The whole while I drank constantly from my glass.

'I got you a Christmas present.' My voice rose at the end of the sentence, trying to sound positive though it came out more as a question. 'It's not cocaine, though.'

She smiled again and continued to drink from the glass.

I let go a long breath. 'I can find some.'

'No!' She pulled herself back, embarrassed by her own enthusiasm. 'No, you don't have to.'

'It's no problem.' I swallowed the rest and dropped my glass in the sink, then grabbed my gun from cabinet without thinking. I didn't particularly care if she saw or not. When I turned to say goodbye, she was inches from me.

'Can I wait here?' She blinked a few times and for the first time I felt like she was really looking at me.

'Of course.'

She pressed her lips against mine, not bruising or biting like before, but caressing. She pulled back and looked at my eyes for seconds that stretched into eternities.

'You really don't have to. We can watch a movie, or something.'

'It's fine. Promise.'

'Are you sure?'

I nodded.

'I'll see you soon?'

'Soon,' I said. I closed the door and walked into the night.

Chapter Eleven

As I came to my car, parked two blocks from my apartment, a laugh rang out over the chatter of the street. If it wasn't already thirty degrees outside my skin would have puckered. I took a long inhale and slunk toward the bar on the corner, knowing already but needing some kind of visual confirmation. I stood at the edge of the sidewalk, lit a cigarette and looked around as if waiting for someone. In the reflection over my shoulder I could see my mother standing in front of some wine bar, smoking a cigarette—which she never did unless shitfaced—and yammering to some midlife-crisis in sparkle pumps.

I felt better that she was at least by herself, until the door opened and Teddy came out. He said something and she threw her head back, laughing as if nothing could ever have been so funny. She really was pretty when she laughed. I remembered my father chasing us around with his hand over his head, pretending to be Bruce, the shark from *Jaws*. We'd jump up on the couch and she'd try to be scared for me but just laugh instead because he was such a shitty shark, his fin crooked or his sounds *dub-dub* instead of *na-na*. Who knew? Maybe the years he'd spent in the basement with bargain-bin porn had eroded her sense of decency. Maybe she was actually happy, or maybe it didn't even matter.

I threw my cigarette into the gutter then walked back to my car.

Julian's house was surprisingly quiet for a Friday night. It was as if we were the planets of his mind-altering universe, orbiting around his sun and wherever his orbit took him, so we followed. Only a few miscreants skulked around the living room, with one guy unconscious on the lounger out back. Two girls sat on the couch, examining the molecular structure of the opposite wall, or incredibly fucking high.

'Julian? The man who lives here? Do you know where he is?' I pointed at the carpet and gestured around the whole room, as if it would make any difference to these to wastoids. 'Do you understand anything I'm saying?'

'Purple.' The one girl's smile spread into a giggle which devolved into a full-on fit. Her mouth stretched Steven Tyler-wide as she yelled, 'Your aura is purple.'

'That's from a fucking movie, you idiot.'

I asked another kid but he was just here with his friend.

In the kitchen, I took a beer from his fridge and dialed Eric's number. It rang five times before he answered.

'Where the fuck are you guys?'

'Now who's being a dickhead?' He laughed and breathed in, like he had a joint in his hand.

'It's been a long day. Where are you? I need to grab Julian for a minute.'

He pulled the phone away from his mouth and spoke to someone else for a minute. 'We're at a friend's house, figuring some stuff out.'

'What kind of friend?'

'Julian's kind of friend.'

I slugged down half the beer. 'Why didn't you call me for this?'

'You weren't too keen on coming into the fold. I thought this might've been above your pay grade.'

'You should've at least called.' Looking at myself from above, I had trouble recognizing this person on the phone.

'I should've. That's my fault.' He coughed into the mouthpiece. 'Go past Amherst, over 116. Take the second left and go to the end of the road. We're in the red house with cedar siding.'

'I'll be there in ten.'

Half of me wanted to call Mason and tell her I'd be a little late. The other half didn't want to risk her saying *nevermind*.

Red and black and brown all looked strikingly similar in the dark and I got lost twice trying to find the damn place, the whole time thinking *I should be painting, I should be getting ready for a show instead of driving around looking to score, but just think of how big her smile will be every morning for the rest of your lives and you can always get up early and paint*. I edged my wheels over the curb and walked toward the house. Groups of three or four people stood in the front yard smoking cigarettes. As I approached, I recognized a guy who was a weekly customer at Fast Feet for almost two years.

'Hey, man.' I shook his hand. I still didn't know his name.

'Mike, long time, no see.' He looked genuinely happy to see me. Something pinged inside my stomach. 'I keep expecting to see you at the store but never do.'

'Yeah, I got a promotion.' I looked over his shoulder for Julian or Eric.

'Congratulations! That's fantastic.' He pumped my hand like a politician.

'You seen Eric?'

'They're inside somewhere. Saw them floating around with that Buddha-dude.'

'I'll see you around.'

I stepped past him to go inside and felt a fist crack against my cheek. A collective gasp came from the crowd. I stumbled back and held myself upright with a lawn chair.

'What the fuck?'

Paul charged me again and I ducked away, stepping behind someone else. I could feel the breath rolling from his mouth. His eyes were primal, pupils surreal, chest heaving like a bull's.

'I told you not to touch her, you fucking loser. I told you I fucking told you.'

'You didn't tell me shit, you fucking lunatic.'

He grunted a few things I couldn't understand, yelling out *fucking fake* and *bullshit paint* before lunging at me again but he slipped on a patch of ice, cracking his chin open. Blood twisted down his neck but he didn't even notice.

'How are you supposed to take care of her? You're a fucking failure. She needs better than you.' He pulled at his hair, steam rising into the night. 'How she fall for all your art bullshit? You show her off to your slut mom and that wino?'

'My family's not your concern, you delusional Tony Montana motherfucker.'

He screamed, 'I told you,' and something in his tone brought flashbacks of my mother yelling at me down the hallway and father yelling at her for yelling at me then yelling at me for getting them into a fight and Mason rolling away from me and the disappointment when I handed her a fucking soda and the crowd gasped *what the fuck man, whoa man* and the glint struck my eye as it reflected off the sight of my gun, trained right at Paul.

'I told you to leave me the fuck alone.'

Paul's chest heaved, assessing the probability of me getting off a clean shot before he could tear me limb from limb.

I cocked the slide, pushing a bullet into the chamber. I tried not to smile.

Who was I?

I should be painting I should be painting I should be painting.

She will love you.

'You see me, you walk the other way. Next time you fuck with me, I'll shoot you in the throat.'

He tracked me as I backed inside, people parting before like I was a sociopathic Moses. I shoved the gun in my waistband and hurried around the house, searching for them.

I found Eric in the kitchen.

'What took you so long?' He popped a beer and handed it to me.

I shook my head. 'You holding right now?'

'Julian wants to see you.' He pointed to a wooden door with a Doors poster tacked to it. It was almost too much to take. 'Just knock, long, short, long, short.'

I started toward the door and he caught my arm.

'Are you dangerous, Mike?'

I didn't know how to answer that and pulled away.

A swollen redheaded man opened the door when I knocked.

'Julian?' I said.

'Let him in,' Julian called from somewhere inside. He patted a spot beside him on the Mexican blanket covering the sofa, telling me to sit. On the bookshelf behind him sat two sawed-off shotguns and something that looked like a bulletproof vest.

'Eric said you wanted to see me?'

When I came close, he leaned forward and clasped his hands. 'You feeling okay? You look upset.'

'Long day.' I nodded toward the other guy and Julian nodded. 'I need two grams.'

'You have business already?'

'Sort of.' I looked over my shoulder, maybe checking for Paul, maybe hoping for Mason. 'It's a personal favor.'

'If you have a habit, we need to talk.' He leaned back against the couch and crossed his arms. 'You know the terms.'

'It's nothing, just, a personal favor. Okay?' I sounded too eager for myself. 'I'm fine.'

He stared at me long enough that it made me uncomfortable, then nodded and said to get it from Eric.

When I turned he called my name.

'Those people Eric met with the other day, the ones you'll be dealing with.' A deep breath through his nostrils, exhaled through his mouth. 'I'm sending people with you.'

'Why do I need people? It's just talking, right?'

'It's half-a-million dollars,' he said. 'Tim and Brendan will ride in the back with you and Eric. Robbie here will have another car follow you with backup.' Despite every word he spoke, that vague beatific smile never left his face. Whether this was all a fun game to him or he'd finally achieved enlightenment, I didn't know, but it didn't faze me tonight like it had two weeks prior.

'Just give me what I need and tell me what to say. I'm your boy.'

I will save her.

He stood and gave me a hug. 'That's why you're you.'

I left the room and got two bags from Eric.

'You're okay with everything?' he said.

'Golden.'

The tachometer bobbed past the speed limit like a buoy on a stormy lake, trying to avoid getting pulled over with two grams in my pocket while still getting back to Mason. All the running around had cost me almost ninety minutes.

I pulled up and hopped out of the car, realizing as I got to my door that I hadn't locked my car. I chewed a mint before going inside.

A napkin sat facedown on my counter. Sketches framed her writing.

Have to work in the AM. See you. XO -M

I stood in the middle of my apartment, sweat cresting over my lip and into my mouth. The empty air throbbed around me. I dropped my jacket on the floor and poured both bags on the back of a sketch pad as I waited for *Casablanca* to load in the DVD player.

I inhaled until my skull swelled and skin ached and the sight of Ingrid Bergman broke me completely.

Chapter Twelve

I didn't sleep so much as slip between various levels of consciousness. Some were filled by shards of metal and broken boards speckled with nails. Others sloshed with amorphous gel that burned my skin as much as it left me weightless. Some just rang out with an ear-shattering silence, a white nothing that throbbed against my temples. The blue-black night sky held off daylight until it burst at the seams, spreading pink light through the abyss.

At eight in the morning I heard the first notes of Christmas music out in the street. Christmas Eve. Dinner with my parents.

There were two red slashes on the tip of my thumb and index finger, possibly from a knife.

I took two swigs of orange juice to put some sugar into my body so I wouldn't collapse facefirst on the sidewalk and pushed the button on my answering machine.

'Hey,' Christian's voice said. 'Call me when you get this. You don't sound well.'

'When did I call you?' I said to the machine.

'Mike, I'm worried about you. Call me, okay?' The message clicked. Another one started. Dusty this time, asking if I still wanted to show, since I hadn't confirmed and there was someone else interested, and he had better ways to waste his time than trying to coerce me into doing a show, and hey, it wasn't his life he was wasting.

I took a few more drinks of orange juice then left the apartment.

Three cars were beached in Julian's front yard. The front porch was empty, though I hadn't really expected his lugs here so early. I opened the door and went into the living room.

The two aura girls lay atop one another on the couch. All I could think of was the snowballs that rolled downhill in cartoons, but with trackmarked limbs sticking out in place of branches. I stood in the middle of the room and listened to silence thrumming through the house. A smattering of debris covered the kitchen: empty bottles, torn plastic bags and two spent whipped-cream cans, white foam sputtering from the tip.

I went upstairs and down the hallway. The lack of people wasn't as eerie as the lack of noise. There was always music or chatter in the house and for a few terrifying steps I had the idea that I was walking into a set-up. Cops or the Vermont contingent hidden behind the office door, Julian and Eric bound by wire with ball gags in their mouths.

I knocked lightly, as if I could ease into the trap, and when I got no response opened the door. A cold draft swept across the room, the curtains fluttering by the open window.

Sticking my head outside the window, I found Julian sitting on the gable on the far side, overlooking his frozen paradise. I hefted my leg over the ledge and shuffled the length of the roof. The sun hid behind the house and though the air felt at least ten degrees colder, it shocked my system into functioning order.

'Be careful you don't break a hip,' I said.

He gave a small smile. 'Sundowner's might be more of a problem, being in the twilight of my thirties and all.'

'That was my next guess.'

He watched me creep to the spot beside him, precariously lowering myself, then gave an appraising glance with his mouth screwed up. 'What's wrong with you?'

Where to start?

I curled my mouth and puffed out two smoke rings. 'I came over to apologize for yesterday.'

Turning his head back to the garden, he said, 'To me or Paul?'

I figured word would get around; what he'd heard had me curious, and maybe a bit worried. 'What are you talking about?'

'I'm not wearing a foam helmet.' He snatched the smoke from my mouth and took a long pull. 'Don't take me for a retard.'

'I wasn't insinuating—'

'I brought you in because you're smart and inventive and we can trust you. But yesterday? That bullshit was something else.'

'It's been a weird couple weeks.'

'You don't pull a gun unless you're already pulling the trigger. And you don't ever, ever pull a gun on someone within our group, or I will show you what it looks like.' He took a long inhale then flicked the butt down to the patio.

'I'm sorry, J.'

'We've got enough to worry about with these hillbilly tweakers getting improvisational on us, and I don't need you piling more on the plate for Eric and me. Especially when the reason I brought you into the fold was to help smooth things out.'

I stared out at the trees.

'So. I'll ask you again. What's wrong with you?'

In the mornings and evenings when my parents would stand on either side of me and scream until their faces were ready to burst from blood, throw remotes or pots or whatever projectile was handy, I felt myself leave my body. In the days before Christian left, as he, his mom and I packed up his belongings to send him away from us, I watched my hands move without any conscious thought. In the liquid moment when Mason took me between her legs, when our skin stuck and slipped and I tasted her in my mouth, I felt my body detach and evaporate.

Sitting on the gable of his roof while staring out over the frozen mountains in western New England on a bright Christmas Eve morning less than twelve hours after I smiled while pulling a gun on his friend, my mouth couldn't open wide enough as everything came pouring out in one long rush. My mom fucking Teddy and Mason wide-eyed fucking me and Christian's dad fucking off, leaving us all to fend for ourselves and every other fucking thing coming crashing down on my fucking head and my mouth kept moving even though I screamed at it to stop.

When the air around us finally fell silent and my mouth had

gone dry from talking, Julian sat quiet, staring at some point beyond us.

'In three words I can sum up everything I've learned about life,' he said. 'It goes on.'

I just looked at him.

He pointed to the east. 'Robert Frost. Used to live up the street in Amherst.'

'I thought it was the Buddha or something.'

'I never thanked you for that statue.' He pulled a cigarette from my pack and held out his hand for my lighter. 'I appreciate it.'

'I didn't think you'd noticed. You didn't say anything.'

He paused before lighting the cigarette, staring at me through the still flame. 'I've been a little preoccupied. But I notice more than you think.' He nodded at my hands. 'Like you don't have paint all over you like normal. That worries me.'

'Why?'

'Because you love it and you're good at it. Which makes me wonder if this promotion is breaking you.' He picked up an acorn and flicked it in a long arc. 'Your wheel was always spinning evenly when you were at the shop. You had a balance between art and business. It's what made you so vital to our operation. It's why I brought you in. But that wheel is now wobbling.'

'I've been considering some stuff, recently, I guess.'

Leaning close, he set a hand on my shoulder, patting it a few times. 'You have to be gentle first with yourself to be gentle with others.'

I lit a smoke for myself.

'That one's the Buddha. Or one of the Lamas, I can't remember.' He let a cloud of smoke drift from his mouth. 'My point is that you can only control what you can control. You have the power over you, over what you let affect you. Me? I have control over what affects me, which includes you.'

I stared at him for a minute, trying following his ouroboros logic.

'I'm sorry for all the shit that's going on with you. You're a good kid stuck in a bad streak and I don't think you deserve it. But I need to keep the things around me in order if I'm going to retain control of myself.'

The wind blew through the trees. My hand twitched. I tried to remember a line from my English class, something about miles to go before sleeping.

'So you're saying to chill out, or I'm out?'

He didn't nod or shake his head, just moved in some vague manner. 'All I'm saying is what I'm saying.'

After my cigarette burned down to the knuckle, I pushed myself to standing and leaned over to give him a hug. 'Merry Christmas, J.'

He hugged me for longer than I expected, and I blinked back a few tears. 'I'll see you tomorrow night before the meet.'

'I know. But that's not Christmas anymore,' I said. 'That's something else.'

Twinkling lights and wreaths adorned with pinecones and red bows hung on the lampposts along Main Street. A surprising number of people ambled up and down the sidewalk, though they didn't seem to be doing last-minute shopping so much as just enjoying the atmosphere. Kids chased each other through the parks and parents laughed and joked with each other. I wanted to punch each and every one of them in the throat and at the same time was dying to be in their photos.

Passing Mama Iguana's, I was struck with a severe need for a burrito. I felt pretty disgusting, considering it was barely eleven, but couldn't remember the last time I'd eaten, so I gave myself a pass on it. Film posters hung on the wall, the Mexican version of the old Hollywood star system I figured. The obligatory steer skull rested on the end of the bar, but had dirt and a clutch of cilantro growing out of it. Being Northampton and all, it was probably organic and heirloom. I got a table by the window and ordered a michelada. The waitress didn't say anything.

When she set the food before me, I dug in without ceremony, chunky salsa verde and rice falling out the end into my cupped hand. I sucked the food from my palm and imagined I looked torn from some nature documentary. As I wrapped my mouth around another huge chunk, I caught a glimpse of Mason through the window. Part of me wanted her to come in and the other wanted to beat the shit out of that first part. She walked past the restaurant and I couldn't decipher how that made me feel.

I took a long drink of the beer and concentrated on the hot sauce and salt burning my lips.

'I told you their burritos were good.' Her voice came from behind me and made me jump.

I mumbled into my food.

'Can I join you?' She held a small bag with green and red tissue paper sticking out of the top. In my head, I imagined her pulling out some rare Smiths live album signed by the band, Johnny Marr and Morrissey getting over their feud just so she could say sorry to me.

I pushed the empty chair out with my foot. She lowered herself and set the bag before me. 'Open it.'

Inside the bag sat two cans of Coke.

'Too soon?' She nibbled at a chip from my plate.

I took a bite so she wouldn't see me smile.

'I did have to get up early for work today.' She dipped the chip in salsa and a piece of tomato fell back into the bowl.

'Okay.'

'I just wanted you to know that.'

'Thanks.' I chewed my burrito until it liquefied in my mouth.

'You just took longer than I expected.'

Fighting to control my breathing, I took another bite so I

couldn't yell as the images of Julian's empty house, Paul swinging his fists, the shotgun sitting behind Julian crashed though my head.

'And I felt kind of, I don't know.' She looked around the restaurant aimlessly. 'Familiar?'

'Familiar?'

'I didn't know what to do, so I just left. I felt uncomfortable being there when you weren't.'

'You could've stayed. We have been.'

'At Julian's place, not yours.'

'You knew it would've been fine.'

She looked out the window. 'It's different.'

The waitress returned and asked if I wanted anything more. It was hard not to laugh. Mason took another chip from my plate and dipped it in salsa, offering it to me. I took it and didn't bite or kiss her fingers.

'I've got dinner with my parents tonight.' Even with food in my mouth and shrapnel in my head, I couldn't stop myself from talking. 'It's at six but you can come over later, if you want. I've got your present and all.'

She smiled into her hand, maybe trying to hide it because of guilt, or trying to be coy.

'That'd be nice,' she said.

'I was going to watch *Black Christmas*, if you want, and *A Christmas Story*.' I poked at my food. 'It's not really Christmas without *A Christmas Story*.'

'Was that fish painting for the show?'

'Not sure yet.'

She nodded and said that sounded great. I wanted to blurt out the plans for the future, that she soon would not have to worry about anything. That her mother and the house would be fine. She stood and gave me a kiss on the cheek before heading back to work. The cool print of her lips throbbed on my skin. I watched her walk past the window again, giving a slight crooked smile from the corner of her mouth then disappearing down the street.

I took another bite then leaned back in my seat, thinking about how to package the portrait, whether I should use twine as a bow or if the threads would get into the oil paint. The night seemed so far away yet throttling toward me, and the armed meeting with Julian's tweakers coming way too fast behind, and then it hit me like a brick in the face that the only thing standing between me and Christmas with Mason was dinner with my parents.

I waved to the waitress and ordered another michelada and a double tequila.

Chapter Thirteen

'So,' my father said, swallowing the dregs of his third glass of pink wine before we'd even finished eating, 'what's happening with Marlon?'

'Excuse me?' I said.

'Richard, leave him alone,' my mother said. She patted Teddy on the wrist, apologizing on behalf of her husband. Though I still hadn't figured out what I thought of Teddy sitting at our table, I had to admit she looked great. The black dress shimmered without being gaudy, and she'd reigned in her cleavage to go for demure, it being a holiday and all.

'Isn't that her name?'

'It's Mason, Dad. A marlin is a fish.'

'That's right. Mason.' He took a few slugs from the bottle sitting in the ice bucket then poured the remainder into his glass. 'You've been pining after her long enough, I was just hoping something came of it for you.'

'She's not a retirement fund. I don't put in then wait to get my money's worth.' I stuck more ham into my mouth and stared at my plate, not willing to acknowledge that was exactly what I was doing.

'Why not?'

'Richard! Honestly.'

'Nothing wrong with asking, Gina. You're a smart man, Mikey, working hard. Got the best of mine and your mother's genes.'

'Please don't call me that.'

'Richard, please,' she said.

'Don't be embarrassed, Gina, that's a good thing,' Dad said. 'You're a good woman and a damn sight smarter than this one here.' He pointed at his chest.

'You're not stupid, Dad. You're drunk.'

If she held her napkin over her chest in astonishment one

more time I would not be able to stop myself from screaming. It wasn't even as much being embarrassed that pissed me off, but that she expected anything else once Dad had a couple glasses in him. As I picked up my fork, the light reflected off the tines and I thought of my gun, pointing it at Paul, pointing it at the tweakers. I couldn't figure out why I thought that and so I set down the fork and drank my wine.

You will save her. You will save her.

'Come on. Let's be civil.' Teddy balled up his napkin and stuffed it beside his plate. 'It's Christmas.'

Dad tipped back his drink, ice cubes clinking against the crystal glasses that hadn't been used since Reagan was around. 'It ain't Christmas, Ted. It's Christmas Eve.'

'Jesus,' I said. 'Can't we just eat dinner in silence like a normal family?'

'Michael, please don't use that language at the table. It's not appropriate.' My mother apologized for me, now.

'So, Teddy,' I said, trying to change the subject, 'how's real estate? Has Mom gone *Glengarry Glen Regina* yet?'

Dad didn't care about my small talk with Teddy. 'He pays his bills, gets his business taken care of, he can do whatever he damn well pleases, Regina. Come on, now. You told your old man the same thing when we were following the Dead, remember? "I am woman, hear me roar" and whatnot.'

'Dad, come on. Just eat your dinner.'

Would the money come immediately, or would I have to wait? It's not like they could wire the money or write a check. I could stop by Mason's on the way home and give her the real present.

'You should've seen her, Mike. All flower-power and bra-burning. Damn, Gina, you were a pistol if you were anything.' He rested his chin on his fist, eyes loosening to focus on some vague point in the past. He gave a small laugh that came out as more of a sigh. 'Thirty years and still got no idea why you picked me from the crowd.'

I shoved a roll in my mouth.

What if someone got stupid? Would they have guns?

My stomach felt close to bursting. Between the burrito this afternoon and all the food I'd choked down just trying to stay quiet, I'd probably doubled the amount I'd eaten all week.

Would we still do the deal if they changed the location again? They could be setting up an ambush and I wouldn't be able to go by Mason's and give her our future.

I should've gone to Julian's and had pho with him instead.

What did a man's face look like when you put a muzzle on his cheek?

It doesn't matter.

You will have a gun and you will save her.

'Did you know, Richard,' my mother pointed her fork at my father—who was still awash in reverie—her tipsy hand wavering in the air, 'that your son no longer works at the shoe shop?'

'How do you know?' I said.

'Because Louis told me when I stopped by to see you.'

'What, when you were out with Teddy?' I will point guns at people to save a woman so she will love me. I will point that gun at anyone at this table to get them to shut up.

'We're colleagues!' she said.

'What are you trying to say about me?' Teddy said.

Dad had found his way back to our table, draining the rest of his glass. 'Well maybe he's got something better going on and doesn't need that crappy job anymore.'

'Okay, tell us then, Mikey,' Teddy said.

'Don't you call him that, Ted,' Dad said.

'What are you doing now?' Teddy said.

'I'm in the olive-oil exporting business.' Christ, all of you just shut up.

'See?' Dad said. 'He's an entrepreneur.'

Do you have any idea how obscene it is arguing about these trivial fucking things in the comfort of your warm home with cheap wine and dry ham? Do you know who would kill for this? I would kill to provide it.

'There is no olive oil out here,' my mother said.

'Because I exported all of it.'

'So you're unemployed,' Teddy said. 'Or what is it, "between jobs?"'

'No, asshole. I deal drugs and walk around with a gun. I'm buying a bunch of cocaine and heroin tomorrow night.' Shut up shut up shut up shut up shut up shut up.

'Honestly, Michael,' my mother said, swilling from her glass. 'Do you have to be so sarcastic all the time? It's exhausting.'

'Hey, at least it's something to fill the time,' Teddy said.

I slammed my silverware down and stood up so fast my chair fell over. My mother leaned back slightly though Dad just stared bleary-eyed at the space between her and Teddy, whose jaw tensed, probably trying to figure if I was going to make a move on him.

'Merry fucking Christmas. You all deserve each other.'

I swatted at my glass and it wobbled but didn't fall. Teddy snuffed out a laugh.

I spun away from the table and stormed down the hallway. I heard my father say, 'Now see what you did,' and my mother snap at him but I snatched my jacket and threw open the door and couldn't hear what she actually said. I slammed the front door and walked to my car.

No one came after me.

Chapter Fourteen

I almost crashed my car into a lamppost when I rounded the corner and saw Mason sitting on my steps, a Santa hat leaning cockeyed off the back of her head. She stood as I walked up the sidewalk and it was all I could do not to run to her. I hugged her for probably three seconds too long at the bottom on the steps, then mumbled something and led her inside.

I told her to make herself comfortable on the couch and I poured us two drinks. Whiskey after a couple glasses of wine would likely leave me with a headache in the morning, but I didn't much care at that moment.

When I turned around she averted her eyes from the dusting of powder on my table. I sipped from my drink and told her to help herself. She salvaged two thin lines and snorted one, leaving me the thicker one. My message light blinked furiously. Christian, probably. Maybe Dusty as well.

Handing her a drink, I said, 'I didn't get a chance to wrap your present. I hope that's okay.'

'Of course. I don't care about that.' She sucked air through her teeth after she took a sip. I thought it was just the streetlight making her skin look so pale, her cheeks so sunken. I turned on another light and she looked even more morose.

I opened the closet door. 'You should probably close your eyes so it's a surprise.' When she closed them, I pulled her painting from the closet and laid it on her lap. My fingers and arms tingled with excitement.

'Go ahead. Open them.'

When she did, her eyebrows scrunched together and lips pursed. She titled her head slightly, then rotated the canvas a little.

'Very cool.' She reached into her purse and got a cigarette. 'Homage to Picasso?'

'It's Morrissey.'

I drank more and tried not to bite off part of the glass.

'Oh, yeah.' She nodded her head repeatedly. 'Yeah, totally.'

'You said he had the kind of profile that should hang over a fireplace.'

'I did?' She still hadn't looked at me, her eyes probing the canvas.

'Last week.' I took the rest with a gulp and blinked away the burning tears. 'At Julian's, when we were talking.'

'You're very talented, Mike.' She sipped and smoked. 'But I don't have a fireplace for it.'

'That's not the point.' I snatched her glass to refill it and whiskey sloshed over the edge onto the carpet. At the counter, I pressed my palms against the sink, breathing deep a few times. I dumped the bottle into our glasses and had a long sip before turning to her.

'You really don't remember talking about that?'

'I'm sorry, I don't.' She took her glass.

'But we talked about the Smiths for, like, forty-five minutes. You remember nothing?'

She shrugged as if she was testing new muscles. 'I don't remember every conversation I have, Mike.'

I paced before her, drumming my fingers on my glass. I should've had fucking pho with Julian. I should've hid myself in Christian's trunk and left this whole fucking state behind me.

'Do you remember anything we've ever talked about?'

'Don't be stupid, okay?'

'Don't fucking call me stupid.'

'I'm not saying you're stupid.' She stood and set her glass on the windowsill. 'Just don't get so upset if I haven't committed every exchange to memory like you have.'

'I don't memorize dialogue but I'm present during our conversations. I remember what you say because I like talking to you. I remember little things because they're important.'

'We're not in a movie, Mike.' She shouted and I thought she

knew it.

'I'm not deluded. I understand what's real.'

'Do you?' She stepped toward me. 'Do you know what's reality and what's in your head?'

'Now who's being stupid?'

'You are.' She poked her finger in my chest. I wanted to smack it away. 'Whatever I am in your head, I can't be that person. Whoever you painted that thing for, it's not me. Because that person doesn't exist.'

'You're a horrible person.'

'I'm a real person, Mike. We're all horrible. The person you painted that for is just a collection of all the things you're missing. That person is a gigantic fucking hole. I can't fill that hole. I won't.'

Breath rushed from my nose. My eyes burned. My fingers twitched and curled.

'I was going to help you. You and your mom.'

'You what?'

'You said your loans were overdue and your mom had signed and,' my hands twitched in the air like epileptic birds, 'so Julian said he wanted to give me a bump up and I was going to help you.'

She stood in the middle of my apartment. I couldn't tell if the shiver was my eyes or her pallid skin.

'You were going to give me thousands of dollars. Just like that.'

'I just wanted to help.'

'Just like that,' her words, a leather strop sharpening the edge of her voice, 'you were going to give me thousands of dollars.'

'A hundred thirty-three and change, actually,' my voice dipping, falling.

'Do you know how fucking insane that sounds!'

I heard a click. No, a snap.

'Get the fuck out of my house.'

'Why would anyone ever do that?'

'I just wanted to help!' I screamed so hard the room blurred.

She turned on the heels of her boots and stomped to the door, then paused. 'I'm not the one you need to fix.' Then she walked out.

I ripped the phone from the wall and threw it at the fridge then kicked the door closed behind her. Before I could think, I went to the window, smacked myself across the face three times. 'You do not watch her. You do not watch her.'

Pacing the perimeter of my apartment, I passed the canvas and wanted to kick it. I passed the canvas and wanted to break it. I passed the canvas and wanted to chase her down the street with it.

I passed the canvas and hung it on a nail above my bed, letting whatever it meant watch over me as I tried my hardest to drown.

Chapter Fifteen

Krampus had exhumed himself from whatever dark recess he'd been buried and decided to concentrate all of his pent-up loathing and unholy terror on my head. I lay in bed trying to reassemble myself. My skull had been scraped to jagged contours by splintered boards and broken promises. My mouth had been used to clean the streets of all its salt and Christmas Eve revelry. I rolled over and caught a whiff of the empty Jameson and felt a fist of vomit climb up my throat. I wrapped my lips around the bottle and emptied my stomach. Tendrils crept into my nose and the smell made me lurch even harder.

Twenty minutes later, I dragged myself into the bathroom and stuck my head beneath the bathtub spigot. Hangover washed from me in streaks of yellow bile and cold water. I stood and the water streamed through the sweat on my back. Wrapping a towel around my head, I caught a glimpse of the phone I'd ripped from the wall, now sitting in a sink full of water. It was too much for me to handle, so I pulled clothes over my body, gargled with mouthwash and put an unopened bottle of wine in a paper bag.

When I sat down in my car to drive to Christian's mom's house, I felt my gun press against my spine. I didn't remember grabbing it.

Her voice echoed from somewhere inside, saying either *Come* or *Un-done*. Though she was a big John Donne fan, I figured it was the former and let myself in. Her house looked more like a time capsule than a domicile, preserving the two months after her father died in amber for all eternity, but it still held all the warmth I remembered from growing up over there. The space where the couch had been was still empty, but some debris had been tracked over the area, so at least she wasn't avoiding it altogether as she had been before.

I made my way to the kitchen and found her waving her hand

before her face. The air smelled of cigarette smoke. 'Sorry for the smell. I made banana muffins with chocolate chips for you and they burnt some.'

'It's okay.' The walls of my stomach lashed out at the thought of solid food.

I held up her wine and said *Merry Christmas* then kissed her cheek. She pulled me back, holding my shoulders and looking at me.

'Is everything okay?'

'Just drank too much last night.'

'At home, I mean. Your dad's called here four times looking for you.'

'Why?'

'I don't know. He said you didn't answer at your apartment.'

The phone floating in my sink.

'Can you give me a minute?' I picked up the phone hanging on the wall.

She nodded at the coffee in the pot, set a muffin on the table for me and went into the living room with her cup of coffee.

'Dad,' I said when the phone picked up.

'I've been calling you all morning.' His words came in swirls and rushes, out of breath and still drunk or drunk again.

'I've been having phone problems,' I said. 'Why'd you call?'

He took a long breath. 'Your mother's in the hospital.'

'What?' I spoke into my shoulder, fighting to keep my voice down and away from Ms. Grady. 'What happened?'

'They got into an accident.'

'Why aren't you there?'

'After you left last night, they kept drinking. Teddy couldn't drive so she took him home. Police called after midnight.' He exhaled into the phone, like he was fucking annoyed with me. 'I'll just be in the way, Mikey. What am I supposed to do?'

'Go see your wife.'

'Maybe I'll head over later after—'

I hung up the phone, harder than I meant, and pinched the bridge of my nose until an explosion of rainbow dots shot across the kitchen. I bit down on the back of my hand and hoped to taste blood. In the nose, out the mouth. In the nose, out the mouth.

'You okay, love?' she called from the living room.

I pinched the inside of my bicep as hard as I could, blinked to focus myself then went in.

'Yeah.' I sat in the armchair beside her. 'He wanted to know if I was coming over for dinner tonight.'

She arched an eyebrow. 'A little excessive calling four times for dinner, isn't it?'

I just shrugged. 'You know Dad.'

The grandfather clock ticked. She blew steam from her cup and took sips like a sparrow drinking from a puddle. I held a muffin in my hand I didn't remember picking up, setting small bits in my mouth to make her happy.

'Have you talked to my son recently?' She placed her cup on the table next to a small box wrapped in red paper, a green and silver bow atop it.

'He's been harassing me on my answering machine for the last two weeks.'

'Has he done the Chinese one?'

'Chinese?'

'He's calling to confirm my order of poo-poo platter and cream of some young guy?' She breathed a laugh and scratched her nose.

'Kind of inappropriate.'

'A bit. But, you know Christian.'

'I thought he was coming home for Christmas.' I chewed and chewed but the muffin never seemed to disappear.

'He was supposed to, but it didn't work out.' The clock chimed eleven. She picked up the box from the table and handed it to me. 'I got you a Christmas present.'

'Sorry. Yours isn't real fancy, but I thought you'd like the label.

It has moose on it. They're wearing sunglasses.' The bow glittered in the dim lighting.

'I'll be taking care of that tonight.'

'Should I open this now?'

'I'd like that.'

I pulled the end of the ribbon, letting the bow slip down and unfurl, then peeling back the paper inch-by-inch. I could feel her eyes on me and I felt like I should give her a show or something. The box was plain brown paper, with a single letter M stamped in silver ink. It was austere but elegant, fitting her usual nature. The top slipped off and inside sat a tarnished gold ring on a simple gold necklace.

'It's Dad's.' Her voice cracked when she spoke, tears cutting through her resolve. 'He and Mom saved for two years to buy their rings.'

I swallowed a hundred times to keep myself together. 'Shouldn't Christian have this?'

'I'm saving Mom's ring for whenever he meets someone I approve of.'

Her laugh shot through my façade and I watched the hands on the clock move until I could get myself together.

I moved over to the arm of her chair and half-hugged, half-collapsed on her. Her tears ran warm against my cheek. Her breath flowed over my skin, the spirit of her father becoming tactile in the room.

'I wanted you to have it, Michael. Just to know that it's possible.'

We sat like that until my back ached and I had to stand. 'You mind if I take a nap for a bit?'

'You know where it is.'

I gave her another long hug then went down the hallway, pictures of their family—his dad, even—hanging on the walls, and into Christian's old bedroom. It was the same as when we were seventeen, posters of *Evil Dead* and Nirvana thumbtacked to the walls and a small hole behind his dresser where we used to hide his bong. I lay in his bed and stared at the ceiling, spinning the ring around my necklace, the blue lotus clicking against it.

I woke with a shudder, gasping with my hand over my mouth. Darkness surrounded me. The sheets wrapped around my leg like tentacles pulling me down. It took a minute of spinning the ring around my necklace, slowing my breathing, to remember I was in Christian's old room, and another moment to realize this was the closest contact we'd had in over two months.

In the living room, Christian's mom had her legs draped over the chair's arm, a chunky afghan tucked beneath her thighs and back. The wrapping paper and her coffee sat in the same spots as when I'd gone to take a nap. The clock read six, though my body said four years had to have passed. I leaned down and gave her a kiss on the cheek. The faint smell of smoke clung to her mouth.

'Love you,' I said, pulling the blanket up over her shoulders. 'See you soon.'

I nudged the door closed then went to my car. I thumbed a cigarette out of the pack and lit it, lifted the gun from beneath my seat and started driving to Julian's for the meet, imagining what it would be like to hold half-a-million dollars, if even for a minute.

Chapter Sixteen

Cars scattered across Julian's lawn at random angles. People stood outside smoking cigarettes and something else full of acrid chemicals. Music blared from inside, Smashing Pumpkins it sounded like, and vibrated the air outside. Voices yelled and voices laughed. Walking up the sidewalk to Julian's backyard, I had the vertiginous feeling that he really was the center of a universe and that might make him a god. He'd corralled all of these lost souls on Christmas night, pulling them from whatever warm and loving family rooms they should've been in to indulge and numb them. Or maybe it was warmth he gave that brought them here, people who had a family they couldn't face, didn't want to face.

I pushed open the gate into the back and found a few people milling about. Eric paced the edge of the patio, trying to appear casual while hitting on some China Girl with long black hair, but I could see the tension in the way he pulled on his cigarette. When I got close, I shook his hand. The gun rubbed against my back, though it wasn't cold like I figured it should be.

'How're you feeling?'

I shrugged. 'Good as I can, I guess. You?'

'Ready.' He bared his teeth in an attempt at smiling. 'Willing and able.'

'Yeah, something like that.'

'Mike, this is Eliza.' He gestured toward me. 'Eliza, Mike.'

'Charmed, I'm sure.' I flicked my butt into the bucket and turned to go inside.

'Hey,' Eric said.

'Yeah?'

'You're ready, right?'

I nodded.

'I mean, ready, ready.'

I glanced around at the lost, milling about the backyard. 'I have it in my waistband if that's what you mean.'

'You ready with it?'

'You want me to pull it out and show you?'

He clapped his hand on my cheek like Michael Corleone.

'Don't do that unless you're planning on murdering me,' I said.

'This is birth, Mike, the beginning of a new day for us.' He sipped at his beer. 'It's anything but death.'

The bass hit so hard I felt my intestines shudder. Or maybe it wasn't the stereo. I navigated through the kitchen and into the living room. Standing next to the fireplace, twitching and gesticulating like every third frame of his film had gone missing, was Paul. I dipped my head and poured myself a drink, keeping my back to him the whole time. Every party, every night here slipped over one another, superimposing couple over couple and friends with lovers and enemies. Two guys with shoulders thick as steer tried to do handstands on a wooden chair. Why they ever thought a rickety-ass chair would support their weight was beyond me, but they did make a nice spectacle when the chair finally broke, the one falling and catching the other with his feet and creating a mass of overfed humanity.

I poured myself a drink and downed it, poured myself another and took the bottle with me.

A cold hand touched my arm. I took a deep breath before facing Mason, because I knew without looking that it would be Mason, because it couldn't be anyone but Mason.

'Hey,' she said.

I sipped my drink and stared at her.

'Your phone has been busy.'

'I tore it out of the wall and found it floating in my sink this morning.'

She bit her bottom lip to stifle a smile and I felt something inside myself rip. 'Why are we still doing this?'

'Doing what?'

'Pretending like we're something other than what we are.' She took my glass and drank from it. Someone behind us yelled. "Mayonaise" played on the stereo.

I pointed into the air. 'I love this song. I put it on every mixtape for years.'

'We're good at what we do. Don't let your brain destroy this.'

'Sweet angel, you have made me no longer afraid of death.'

'I hoped you'd like that record.' She sipped again, licking a bead of whiskey from the rim of the glass, and took my hand in hers. 'Does that mean I have you again?'

'It means whatever it means.' The yelling continued, my name coming out of the commotion. A glass broke. I turned like my entire body was encased in thawing ice.

'You so fucking tough now, fucker?' Paul stomped across the room like he could break through the floor with each step. The two steer scuttled away. 'You don't have a gun, you're not so tough, are you?'

'This is not the time, Paul. Not tonight.' The CD skipped and "Mayonaise" started again.

'You scared without your boyfriend next to you? The fuck I tell you about being around her?'

'Paul.' Eric had to shout to be heard above the music. 'Chill the fuck out.'

'This is me and him, not you.'

'This is all of us, you stupid fuck,' I said.

'I'm sick of this.' Eric pushed past me, leaving the girl near the steps. 'Julian's going to have your ass, cocksucker.'

'I told you to stay away from her,' Paul said.

'If she's your girl then why does she keep fucking me?' I turned to follow Eric upstairs and felt fingers digging into my arm. They spun me around, gin splashing from my glass.

'The fuck you say to me?' His eyes were primal, the white or crank or whatever had been shot into him disassembling his body cell by cell.

'She's no one's girl, you retard. You want her, take her. You don't, fuck off and leave me alone.'

I yanked my arm away and as I set foot on the step, white stars exploded across the room. Paul fell on top of me, the momentum of his follow-through throwing him off-balance. I reared back and sunk my elbow into him twice, then kicked out my foot to get free. When I stood I saw a piece of wood hurtling at me. It smacked against my elbow, the pain so bright it was visual, so strong I felt my body begin to untether from my brain, the reptilian portion seizing control.

I lunged forward, catching him off-guard, and sunk my fist into his cheek. He hit me with an elbow but I wrapped my arms around his waist and threw him to the ground, landing on his chest, pinning his arms down with my knees and pushing my fists into his face over and over, his face becoming my mother's and my father's and Teddy's and Christian's dad and Mason's and Julian's for putting me in this whole fucking mess. I felt my hands start to swell but threw punch after punch after punch, the medallion slapping his face, until he swung the piece of wood again and caught me across the nose. I fell back, cupping my face as he rocked himself to his knees. We stood facing each other, him wavering between above- and below-consciousness and me vibrating with rage.

I reached back and pulled the gun from my waistband, the metal now as cold as my skin. Blood poured and when he breathed it sputtered. He held the piece of chair, ready to drive the stake into my heart and end me forever and the small warm-blooded part of my brain said *please*.

I raised my gun and trained it on his throat. My hand should've been shaking but it wasn't. My blood should've been cold or racing but it wasn't. I should've been prepping for the meet or railing out Mason or home asleep in my apartment with *Casablanca* on repeat but here I stood with a gun pointed at Paul's throat and a tickle in my nose and not one bit of remorse or doubt.

'I'm being gentle to myself now.'

I started to squeeze the trigger and heard Mason screaming, 'No!' and I flew forward when she tackled me, my finger squeezing and my head exploding with the blast, the gunshot so loud I felt it in my eyes. My nose smashed into the carpet. I shoved Mason off me and pushed myself onto my knees.

Eric yelled and yanked me up. I saw Paul sheltered beneath one of the steer who broke the chair. 'What the fuck are you thinking?'

He had started to push me toward the door when an unholy wail tore through the room, the noise of a girl having her soul ripped from her through thousands of tiny cuts.

The girl with long black hair that Eric was talking to kneeled on the carpet like she was praying at church. A boy lay cradled in her arms. I stopped to look, to help, to say I'm sorry but Eric's hands kept me pushing forward, out the door.

The air stung the inside of my nose but passed over my skin as if it was water. Eric smacked the back of my head and pushed me again.

'Do you know who the fuck that was?'

'Fuck Paul. And fuck you, Eric.' My legs tingled and I thought I might pass out. 'That cocksucker has been after me forever and you've never done shit about it.'

Eric pushed me again and reared back his fist for a second before dropping it. Steam rose from his scalp.

'Because he's Julian's partner. Paul. The guy you just obliterated. That's Julian's partner.'

I just stood there.

He reached into his back pocket and pulled out his wallet. 'You have to disappear. Don't ever come back.'

'What?'

He paused, locking my eyes. 'You fucked up. You need to be

gone.'

'I'll go talk to Julian.'

'Are you listening?'

'We'll work it out. He loves me.'

'He said you're out if you lost it again. What do you think he'll do when he sees what you did? You going to call that love?' He shoved money in my hand. 'This is all I have. Go. Now.' He opened my car door.

'Please, Eric.'

'Do not tell anyone I helped you.'

'Eric, don't—'

He hurried back to the house. The music inside stopped. I heard Julian bellow inside, heard sirens echo in the distance, heard the girl scream and scream and scream and scream.

I slammed my door and started the car.

I drove.

PERFECT
EDGE
BOOKS

"There are many who dare not kill themselves for fear of what the neighbours will say," Cyril Connolly wrote, and we believe he was right.

Perfect Edge seeks books that take on the crippling fear of other people, the question of what's correct and normal, of how life works, of what art is.

Our authors disagree with each other; their styles vary as widely as their concerns. What matters is the will to create books that won't be easy to assimilate. We take risks, not for the sake of risk-taking, but for the things that might come out of it.